For Bernie —
Nice to meet you! I
hope you'll like the
book. All best,
Sheri
6-30-07

S T R A Y

a novel by Sheri Joseph

STRAY

a novel by Sheri Joseph

MacAdam/Cage

MacAdam/Cage
155 Sansome Street, Suite 550
San Francisco, CA 94104

Library of Congress Cataloging-in-Publication Data

Joseph, Sheri.
  Stray / by Sheri Joseph.
    p. cm.
  ISBN-13: 978-1-59692-201-3 (hardcover : alk. paper)
  ISBN-10: 1-59692-201-X (hardcover : alk. paper)
  1. Musicians–Fiction. 2. Triangles (Interpersonal relations)–Fiction.
I. Title.
  PS3610.O67S77 2007
  813'.6–dc22
                                                        2006019863

A portion of *Stray* previously appeared in *The Kenyon Review* in a different form.
ANGELS FROM MONTGOMERY
Words and Music by JOHN PRINE
© 1971 (Renewed) WALDEN MUSIC, INC. and SOUR GRAPES MUSIC
All Rights for WALDEN MUSIC, INC. Administered by WB MUSIC CORP.
All Rights Reserved Used by Permission

Manufactured in the United States of America
10 9 8 7 6 5 4 3 2 1

Book design by Dorothy Carico Smith.

CHAPTER ONE

I t was a compulsion: at every mile marker they passed on the drive
to Florida, he flicked his wedding band with a thumb nail. He kept
his eyes on the road. Paul's voice was a soft continuous mono-
logue from the passenger seat, remarking on the landscape, laughing,
luring him by slow degrees into *remember* and *we've always* and *us* and
our, and by the time they reached the gulf-side condo where they would
spend the weekend, the sound of that voice had curled up to purr in
Kent's ear, louder than the waves eight floors below their rooms. He
felt it as a vibration from within his own body rather than without, now
that Paul had gone out on the balcony to look down at the beach.

Standing in the dim interior of someone else's vacation home—a
living room with glass-topped tables and pastel furniture and framed
square prints of seashells on the walls—he gave the ring a twist. Outside,
Paul's blond head was crowned in a brilliance of late-day sun, his hands
braced on the wrought-iron rail, and the same chill wind that carried
through the open doorway the faint shouts of children and gulls ruffled
the shirt along Paul's shoulders and flattened it to the lean contours of his

torso. He was twenty-one. In three years, it seemed he had changed little, same downy stem of a neck and stuck-out ears flushed deep pink along the rims. If an inch taller now, broader in the shoulder, his body was still cut as much for Peter Pan as for Hamlet, the role he claimed to have played in a college production the year before. But he was not the pliable thing that had lived in Kent's imagination over the missing time, and it was good to have a minute to adjust to the reality of him—Paul, there, in his willful and difficult flesh.

Probably he was waiting to be coaxed back inside. One foot was hooked behind the other, his face canted toward the beach where there were only a few off-season tourists like themselves—couples strolling the winter sand, a family or two on blankets. Children, yearning for a chance to swim, dashed to test the surf with their toes again, and again, though it was January and they must have known the water would never be warm enough.

Kent tuned to the inner vibration that made his empty hands at his sides quiver. It sounded like *wrong, wrong, wrong*, timed to Paul's steps as he returned inside. To be here was to be already out of control. But he had a plan, insubstantial and fine as a wire. To indulge. To remain detached.

"You're married," Paul said. They were kissing, fumbling with buttons.

"I know that."

"Why?"

"Because I am. Don't talk about it." The contentious breath rose in Paul's chest, and Kent pressed a thumb under his collarbone. "What do you care about that? I'm here."

Paul considered, eyes level. "I don't care about that," he said, and his next kiss was assault, a bashing of lips on teeth.

He said it again when they were naked and cooling in a damp knot of sheets. Outside, the gulls quarreled in muted shrieks and the gulf shushed them, over and over. Paul raised himself on an elbow and said, "You're married"—as if the marriage and not his presence in this bed were the character flaw Kent should examine.

"And if I weren't, would you be interested in me now at all?"

Paul huffed. "What's that supposed to mean?"

"Nothing. Nothing. I don't want to fight," Kent said, though he couldn't help asking it, couldn't help wanting, partly, to know the answer. At one time, little had been so worthy of Paul's disdain as a played-out trick.

Paul settled back reluctantly against him, the high-strung mood still palpable in the taut muscles of his back. But here was an instrument Kent hadn't forgotten how to play, in long, slow strokes, smoothing the static from his skin until he eased and relented.

"Do you have any idea how much I've missed you?" Kent was glad to say it, though it needed to be revised. There wasn't room in the weekend to admit too much of the personal. "Missed this," he said.

Paul breathed under his hands. "When you're with her, do you think about me?"

There were three answers to that: no if he had any sense, yes to make Paul happy, and the truth. But the last two were the same—he couldn't revise memory to make it otherwise—and the second, from this place, was all he could find the strength to care about. So with a word, he opened the first door on his marriage.

☙

It was not about Maggie. Maggie's near-black eyes lit with humor, cherub cheeks, brows so aggressive and dark against her flour-white skin that "pretty" didn't fit. Just short enough to qualify for "cute," she claimed, but he found her beautiful in her strangeness. She was thirty, he was thirty-one. Together they were called a cute couple—he mainly for his eyes, a sleepier brown than hers, and his head of dark shaggy hair. He liked his mass beside hers, enough of him to fold her in—Maggie in pilled flannel pajamas like a child's, dreaming of legal briefs and the betterment of mankind.

Maggie in gray winter light at the kitchen window, wearing one of his sweaters, moth-bitten sleeves that flapped loose off her hands. "It's snowing, look," she said. Her face was serene, framed in wispy, every-which-way hair and tinged pink at the tip of her nose. When he held her from behind, the top of her head nestled his chin. Arms crossed around her, he breathed from her scalp, watched the wind drive across the side-yard a fine, dusty snow that began to catch and gather along the edges of green blades. The first snow of their marriage, and who knew if it would be a blizzard, unseen in the history of Atlanta, falling to bury the creaky house they had shared for little more than a year. What if the roof didn't hold? What if the furnace broke? He should have considered these things earlier.

"It won't stick," she said. And he believed her. For one, she was a Mennonite, consulted daily with God. But more, she was the sort of person who was instantly trustworthy about things she couldn't possibly know, like future weather.

It was at that moment he decided. Because he loved her, and not the reverse. Because he needed to keep them safe in this house, forever, or in the better house they would one day build. "I have to go away this weekend," he said. Knowing this part at least was the truth offered him no solace. He closed his eyes, cheek to her hair. "I have a web design conference. Down in Florida."

A small lie, to normalize the bigger truth. He liked to think that in this way he was open with her, always, if through a veil, that on some level she understood what he needed her to. The torment he'd passed through, the regret and longing that still plagued him—these things.

"That should be fun," she said. "Sun, sand, eighty-five degrees."

"I doubt it."

He'd told her before, in fact, everything that mattered about his last long-term relationship, though he'd said it was with a girl named Kristin: a girl who had been too young for him, nearly a decade younger; intensely passionate but also selfish, mercurial, incapable of fidelity; a tornado of a girl indifferent to the damage she caused, because Maggie would not have understood a boy. She would have worried it meant he was gay, which was not quite the case. She'd imagine enormous, serial trouble that in reality was more local and left of center. So Kristin was a truth with a different name.

He wanted to do the same about this weekend, to somehow bare his soul within the lie of it. To say something like, "There are things around us—we two together—that aren't us, that are bigger than us in some ways but also separate, that don't hurt us. They don't touch us." And Maggie, who knew more than he wished she did about the messiness of the world, who lived most of her life with it and apart from him, would have been quick to understand and agree.

He almost said, with fullest possible disclosure, "It's unfinished business, and I can't tell you about it. It's something I have to do, and then I'll come home." He hated himself for lacking that courage.

But it had nothing to do with her at all, or their marriage. It was Paul. It was that, no matter where his life had arrived, some ghostly piece of him haunted this small room of the past, though memory troubled him less and less frequently as time went on. But still, it might have been one of these fevered, half-conscious walking dreams that, at seven p.m. on a Sunday, on the fifth floor of a university library, brought them quite suddenly face to face. Paul at the opposite end of a row of shelves, both of them frozen in recognition. Seeing him there brought back in a rush every other instance over the past three years when he had imagined catching sight of him in just this way, in a hundred other public places. But Paul had said New York, Los Angeles, Paris, said it would be a city bigger than this one, and far. Atlanta was barely an hour's drive from where he'd started. Kent had simply never expected to see him again, except in the mind's tricks, those random, blind-side memorials.

And now. It seemed a private trouble had followed him from the last life into this, like bad credit, too sordid to bother his wife with. He had to go away for a few days, tend to something necessary. He wasn't sure what. But necessary.

Red royal shrimp. Or royal red shrimp. It was one of the two, no question, and they could not sit down to eat until they had found this delicacy—Paul marched them out of one, two, three restaurants that professed to have no idea what he was talking about. Later, past ten o'clock, they were in bed with a pizza: mushrooms and anchovies, one of the rare things they had ever managed to agree on.

"I can't believe those idiots." Paul's mouth was full as he spoke, tomato sauce dotting his chin. "This area is, like, famous for red royal shrimp. People used to think they were trash in the nets until someone figured out how to cook them. You flash-boil them, like lobster. Dip them in butter, god it's good. We've always had red royal shrimp here, every single time."

Kent grimaced faintly at the *we*, which did not include him. "How many times have you been here?"

Paul rolled his eyes and conceded. "Twice." Shirtless, he ate sprawled on his side, lifting the long wedge of pizza to dangle over his mouth. Kent had removed only his shoes, ate cross-legged with a spray of napkins over his knee.

"With him, I guess. What's-his-name."

"Bernard. He's not as awful as you think."

During the six-hour drive, Paul had spoken enough of his present life to reveal that Bernard, the owner of the condo, was well into his fifties, and Paul's college professor before he had moved Paul into a spare bedroom and began paying his way. As Paul explained it, Bernard was not a horny old man but simply a philanthropic soul with more money than he could use, a lonely, kind-hearted man who chose from time to time to sponsor a bright and talented member of the younger generation as the lad worked to achieve his full potential. "Potential in *what*?" Kent had to ask, since Paul was on his third major somewhere in his senior year, and seemed to waffle between his "acting" and his "writing," and—Kent would bet on it—spent more time in bars than engaged in either one.

But, he reminded himself, Paul's life was his own business. Remain uninvolved. All talk was small talk, mere conversation.

"And he knows you're down here this weekend. With me."

"Like I said, he's a decent guy. Generous. I don't exactly parade guys in front of him, but he's aware I'm not a monk."

"No, you're not."

Paul smiled, dropped a languid arm over Kent's thigh and rubbed denim with a knuckle. "How would you know? You don't know me at all anymore."

Kent considered that—Paul chewing dinner on the bed's disarray, his careless eyes cast toward the wall, the lamplight in the heavy gold of his lashes—and wondered again what he was doing here. *Call Maggie,* he reminded himself. He checked his watch, careful not to move his wrist in doing so because Paul had quick eyes, hair-trigger moods. It was ten-fifteen. He needed to be dialing within the next forty-five minutes.

Paul sat up and wiped his greasy hands on the sheets, a smirk of apology lodged in the corner of his mouth before Kent could voice an objection. "Relax, will you? We'll change rooms." He lolled his head along one shoulder to meet Kent's eyes. "Let's fuck in every room."

Words, voice, eyes, mouth—Kent never knew which one kicked the breath out of him, tilted him forward. Paul's power had always been this way, planetary, disquieting, inexplicable, effortless, while past his shoulder a thousand men waited like shades. But they were illusion. Kent knew this much. No matter how real they were somewhere, how real in Kent's mind, Paul had no thought of them. He didn't hear them whisper from dreams, past or future. If ten minutes after they parted ways on Sunday night Paul might be with someone else, that was not yet. Here, now, he was Kent's alone, eyes fixed on him, blue and absolute.

For a second, Kent made an effort to hold in mind what he needed to remember, and then abandoned the effort. Such ecstatic relief, to not think. He licked the tomato sauce from Paul's chin, and more from the pale, hairless hollow of his stomach, and they were out of their clothes, and the pizza box was on the floor, and it was eleven-thirty and too late to call.

⤙

Paul recited the things other men had bought him. "I was with this guy for a week," he said, fingering one of three bracelets, a complex chain of interlocking silver. "He was from India. His name was *impossible* to say."

Kent was surprised that none of the three was from the professor. "He bought me the leather jacket," Paul offered. "He likes to buy me clothes." They lay under the sheet, speaking softly as if they might wake someone. The room was dark except for the flickery gray-white light of the TV, the sound too low to hear. Beyond the heavy drapes, the sky would be pinking the water with first light any minute.

"You should buy me things," Paul teased.

"I don't have any money."

"No. You have a wife."

Kent closed his eyes briefly, until the words were gone. It was only the two of them alone in the bed. He touched the inside edge of Paul's middle finger that curled on the sheet between them, thinking how much he might have given on a bad night to have just this much of him.

"I don't love any of them," Paul said. "But you love her, don't you?"

"Stop."

"Sorry." He brooded, the skin of his forehead twitching.

It was a quandary for Kent, whether to enjoy this new helping of power. He was used to Paul having all of it, lording it over him. He didn't want to consider the likelihood that he had his marriage to thank for the pleasure. And then, what Paul ever showed was mostly shell, like those spiraled sea creatures polished to a dazzle and coiled to a point, testament in itself to what a raw and tender thing lay beneath. Any visible twinge of his distress was rare enough to make Kent flinch, to weaken him before he could enjoy it.

He nudged two fingers between three of Paul's, took the lightest hold, knuckle to knuckle. Their hands were back to back, as if to avoid too much connection, but the result seemed more intimate than holding hands. A week before, when Paul had suggested this trip, Kent had told himself it would be a fling, a balm for longing, a one-time indulgence in the peaceful life of his marriage. But here, now, he couldn't seem to imagine the end of it. His plan was so wire-thin there was almost nothing out here in the middle to see or hold on to.

"Don't sleep," Paul said. Kent had let his eyes close, and the next time, Paul was astride his chest, thumbs jammed into his eyebrows. "*Don't sleep.*"

The weight of him forced a chuckle from Kent's lungs. "Ever?"

"Not until I say."

They were making new rules, it seemed, so Kent took the opening to goose him in his hyper-ticklish ribs. Paul sprang clear but didn't flag the play, only set his jaw and came back for more until he was shrieking off the edge of the mattress.

He returned with treasure. "Look, this was under the bed." He rolled out a tube of lipstick, a cheap, stale red, gave Kent a narrow look. "Did you bring a girl?"

"That looks like it's been down there a while."

"One of Bernard's old fag hag theater buddies must have left it." Paul leapt up from the bed, flicked on the lamp beside the vanity mirror. He proceeded to smear the lipstick over his mouth.

Kent rose and stood over his shoulder, watching in the mirror as Paul drew the full circle, openmouthed, a single bold stroke. Greasy swaths reached far past his lips into the faint blond glisten of stubble. He puckered and pouted in the mirror, bared his lower teeth like a model mugging for the camera. Standing naked in the lamplight with his red mouth and fierce gaze, he looked less like a woman than a savage.

Kent was repulsed, and awed. He felt dizzy. "Look at you," was all he could say. Laughing, Paul turned and kissed him with deliberate roughness. Back in the mirror, his mouth was a faded mess, half printed away, but the red on Kent barely showed, as if somehow color had vanished between them. He leaned in and kissed Paul's neck, his ear, half hoping that Paul would paint him to match.

Undistracted, Paul glared into the mirror. He drew his mouth in fresh red. He shoved his bald chest forward and traced one nipple, filled it in. The lipstick wore down to a nub under the force he used. Around the other nipple he made a bull's-eye ring, a thick glob breaking off at the end of the circle. Kent took the tube from his hand, and Paul stood passively, with half a smile, while Kent drew a garish heart around the second circle.

Paul's turn. He smoothed a hand over the canvass of Kent's chest. "Too hairy," Kent said, but Paul drew anyway a line down the center, lightly; there was little left to waste. He set the spent tube on the dresser and leaned into Kent's arms. In the mirror, his body was an immaculate white curve, his face against Kent's shoulder stunned, used, whorish.

"Paul, god," Kent whispered, "angel," and turned him, propelled him backward to the bed. Another condom from the bedside box, and Paul took up fistfuls of the bedcovers, throat arched out, but his eyes were distant, almost disengaged, a faint smile playing in his painted lips as Kent moaned into each thrust like a lost soul, a wounded animal.

⫘

"I'm about to head out," he said to Maggie, nine-thirty a.m. "Yeah, I slept in a little, but I don't really have a session until ten that I can't miss."

Maggie had been at work for an hour, was on her third cup of coffee, and it was Saturday. "I thought this was your weekend to sleep," he said, though he'd never worry about waking her at this hour and hadn't tried her at home first.

"I've got to go down to the jail again," she said, sounding perky. "One more talk with Jamal and then I give up."

"Mags, you gave up on him last week."

"See, I need you around to remind me of these things."

"You're crazy, you know that."

"I'm persistent."

He'd stopped a year ago saying *relax*. It wasn't in her nature. But it bothered him immensely, the idea of sweaty, grunting criminals pushing her around—even if they were seated and chained—forcing her to work harder than she needed to. "You want me to come back there and smack him a little?"

"Oh, that's what I need. 'Don't mind my husband, officer, he's just here to rough up my clients who fail to contribute to their own defense.'"

He chuckled, receiver to his face, that little curve of space like a room they seemed to share, somewhere in the air between Florida and her cluttered, cheery Atlanta public defender's office. She would be in casual clothes today, something artfully mismatched from a vintage store, a boyish girl-woman without make-up. On the bulletin board beside her would be photos of her with her arms around the released murderers in whom she found so much pain and beauty; a blown-up line from Eleanor Roosevelt ("You must do the thing you think you cannot do"); a card he had given her after a tough case had gone sour, of a fifties-style comic-strip woman with a wind-up key in her back, saying, "I love my job! I love my job!"

He turned, and Paul was standing in the doorway, squinting against the living room's white sunlight. The room with Maggie dissolved. "I've got to go," he said, deadpan. "I'll call you later."

Paul was back in bed, the tight mound of him lumping the covers. Kent crawled back to the place where he had awakened, apart.

Covers rustled. "Was that her?"

"Yes."

More rustling. Kent closed his eyes, sheet to his chin. "What'd she say?"

"Not much," he mumbled. "Go back to sleep."

"What'd you tell her?"

"That I was fine, on my way out the door." He opened his eyes to the dormant wooden blades of the ceiling fan, an arm behind his neck, hearing Maggie's low voice speak through her morning again, intimate and without suspicion.

"To the conference?" Paul snickered, dragged a fingertip along Kent's bicep. He wanted so badly, Kent knew, for this to be a joke between them, but Kent couldn't indulge him. He rolled away, face to the pillow.

A few hours later, Kent awoke more rested, heard the shower running. He got up and cracked the drapes on a day that had turned gray, thick with clouds, the surf mounting and restless. Far out, there was a white sail, and he couldn't help checking the weather for her sake, gauging the distance to the bay. He guessed the boat a thirty-footer. If it was some novice hotshot who thought open water took no particular skill, he'd be in trouble pretty quick.

He turned to face the ravages of the room. For one clear moment, he saw himself standing there, bare-ass naked in the middle of the stupidest thing he had ever done to his life, and he was ready to pack. There was nothing rational in being here and nothing good about it for anyone involved—not even for Paul, who had breezed out of his life after two on-and-off years of being repressed and thwarted and misunderstood in every way Kent could think of to do it. Not that his efforts had ever left a dent.

He tried to locate a reason Paul would accept for leaving now. And then, how he might explain to Maggie his early return. Hand on the bathroom door, he ran the possibilities, while inside, the hiss and slap of the water reflected the shape of the body moving under it. He opened the door to a roomful of steam, slid back the shower curtain, stepped inside.

"What are we doing?" he asked, with something desperate in his voice. "Why are we here?" Paul smiled and went to his knees, which was and always had been, for better or worse, his best and most eloquent answer to everything.

The sun came out in fits, minutes, between a soot-bellied cover of clouds. The storm seemed to be holding off. They had an almost private expanse of white sand stretching out from either side of their blanket and back to where the dunes began, golden with sea oats. Behind the dunes rose their tall building, pink stucco tiered with multiple balconies. Another like it was visible at the farthest point before the next cove. Between were low bungalows, blue, tan, white, set on pillars against the tide. To the west, a pair of middle-aged men and their wives fished with rigged poles set into the sand. A group of college kids started a volleyball game. Periodically, others passed along the water, winter-tanned in twos and threes: old brown people, couples, buff joggers warmed enough to bare arms and legs to the chill breeze.

They were barefoot in jeans, long-sleeved flannel over t-shirts. Paul lay on his back, cloud-gazing through orange-tinted, silver-rimmed sunglasses, knees bent, arms outstretched and hands upturned as if he were staked out for some primitive torture but planning to enjoy it. Kent sat in the opposite corner, facing the water. They had brought a cooler full of cheap beer in cans and had killed the first six hardly moving from their spots.

"I get bored with my classes," Paul said to the sky. "All of them. They're too easy. I want to do something different, but I don't know what."

"You're writing plays, you said."

"A few." His nose wrinkled. "I don't know if they're any good. Bernard calls them 'Christ-haunted erotic journeys.' How do you like that?"

"Am I in them?" Already he wanted to withdraw the question. It wasn't even exactly what he wanted to know, though he was curious about his own role in whatever had been produced, or would be. He'd always suspected Paul of harboring the sort of untried brilliance that might suddenly burst forth into real art—though the medium remained, like Paul's concentration, loose. He was too much of a sensualist, too young to bother yet with lasting expression.

Paul crooked an arm under his head, looked up at Kent over the tops of his shades. "Maybe. Do you want to be?"

Kent cracked a new beer and looked out to the water's horizon. At every new topic, it seemed, he reached one of these walls, as if their conversation were forced to turn through a maze no bigger than their blanket. It was painful to know that to a stranger, to anyone else at all, he would mention that his wife ran a soup kitchen, that she was writing grants to fund halfway houses for her paroled prisoners, that she volunteered in a store founded on the mission of fair trade with third-world countries. Try volunteer work, he might have suggested, the solution to boredom if nothing else. And yet, to Paul, he could not even raise the subject. Paul's questions—*do you want to be?*—tapped seductively from the other side of one of those same walls, and Kent could do nothing but smile wanly and look away.

"I didn't think you would," Paul said. "Well, Bernard's all hot about producing one of them next fall, but I don't know. I might try to get away from the theater, do something different. I get tired of all the faggots, you know?" Kent laughed, incredulous. Paul laughed too. "I mean, for real. Like, Bernard—he's an old queer from a mile off, and everyone else I know lately is so fucking gay I want to puke." He upended his beer can over his mouth, and Kent sensed something not quite sincere in this, Paul fishing in an idle way for reaction.

"Are you being serious or what?" Kent handed him another beer from the cooler, opened, and Paul sucked the foamy top from the can.

"I've started hanging out at a frat house," he said after a minute. "How's that for serious?"

"What?"

"Don't think I can pass? You don't think I can funnel beer and scratch my balls and talk about snatch with the best of them?"

"What the hell are you talking about? And no, I don't think you can pass."

"I am an actor, you know. You've just never seen me act."

"Lately," Kent said, but considered Paul: reclined on his elbows, chin tipped toward the sky, supremely at ease in his body, even masculine. His voice seemed to have lost the stagy punctuation that used to flare when he was nervous or defensive. Now it was so smooth and soft that, over the gulf, Kent had to strain for the sound.

"You do seem a little different," Kent said.

"I would, I guess. To you. You seem different to me."

"How's that?"

Paul crossed his ankles, bare foot not quite brushing Kent's knee, and studied him with the angelic gaze that hadn't changed a bit. Kent had long ago ceased thinking of angels as sweet—those lofty, perfect creatures who had no patience with human weakness and no time for pity.

"Colder," Paul decided, mild but exacting. "More distant. Guarded. More afraid. If that's possible."

He slurped his beer and went on lightly. "These frat guys I've been hanging with—I really like them. They're kinda dumb, as you'd expect, but I don't care. Isn't that funny? I crave the company of straight guys. That's my curse, I guess. Comes from growing up in the sticks in Greene County with nothing but rednecks to lust after for miles. And, well, I don't have you anymore."

"Paul." Kent shook his head, knowing in advance the futility of warnings. "God, be careful."

Paul waved him off. "I'm fine."

"These guys think you're straight?"

"More than that." He grinned conspiratorially. "They might give me a bid. But what's the difference? A frat house is just one big cover for straight guys who want to jerk each other off in secret and call it brotherhood—am I wrong? They're gonna love me."

Kent bit his tongue—*remain uninvolved*. But it was hard when he knew this was Paul's real life, more than wordplay. Even at two or three

removes, Kent fought the urge to take a fist to everything that waited
to harm him.

"You scare the shit out of me," he muttered, and watched the waves
build and roll flat. Meanwhile the rational voice not yet banished
entirely from his head listed again, gentle reminder, the many reasons
they had broken up.

Paul smiled fondly at his fear. "Promise you'll never change. By
the way, if you moved two inches closer to me, who exactly out here do
you think would even notice?"

Kent met his eyes, settled into a long gaze without moving any
closer. There were so many things to leave unsaid, and the crucial one,
he knew, was love, or anything that sounded like it. The wind blew
over them, stinging their faces with a light spray of sand. Already their
hair was gritty with it. Though they would shower twice, it seemed certain a few grains would stick to their scalps, stow away in their crotches,
follow them home.

At dinner, no red royal shrimp, but Paul was too looped to care,
and they ordered martinis and a bottle of wine and an assortment of
unidentifiable seafood, fried. Later, back at the condo, Paul mixed more
martinis, and then they were out on the beach in the chill of the night,
clutching plastic cups full of gin.

"I just want to know if she's pretty!" he shouted, his voice ragged
in the windy dark. All decorum on this topic had worn away over
dinner, when he'd squeezed out of Kent—what could it hurt?—her
profession (lawyer), and where they had met (in a music store), and the
color of her hair and eyes (deep brown, both), and now Maggie was
with them. They had no more walls to keep her out and no memory of
the walls.

"Is she like your mother? You can tell me *that*. The dark hair and eyes. It's a mother thing, right? Do you look like brother and sister together?" Paul walked apart, staggering a bit along the water's edge, and in the weak light from the buildings his head was thrown back, his arms out away from his body as if he might spin a circle. "I bet they do," he said, a private chuckling aside to the sky.

"Paul." Kent's voice, and its hundredth calling of the name that night, didn't carry far against the wind. "Can we please drop it?"

"No." Paul circled back. "Stop telling me to shut up. Who says you get to say what we talk about. I'm just taking an interest in your life, which I'd say is being polite. So tell me."

"Tell you what?"

"If she's pretty."

"Paul—"

"Long hair or short. That's all!"

Kent gasped out a breath. "Short. Okay? Please stop." He palmed the back of Paul's head with his free hand and tried to steer him into a facing position. "You're drunk."

"So what?" Closer, Paul's voice softened almost to a whisper, but there was a strained note that ran through it like a whine. From some-where out of their prior years came a brief, disturbing body-memory, but it was Kent begging, as drunk as Paul was now, saying *please, one night, just stay…*

"Do you really think I would hurt you?" Paul said. "What are you afraid of?"

"Everything."

Paul stepped back, stung. "Afraid of me? You think I'd hurt you."

"No, no. That's not what I meant."

Paul walked away with slow, wandering steps, and Kent followed, aware that he needed to rein Paul in, calm him, and that he was too drunk himself to be very effective. Off to their right, they passed the volleyball players, now trying to build a fire back toward the wind-break of the dunes.

"Valentine's Day is coming up," Paul called back, his voice light. "Don't worry, I won't expect anything. I already got mine, didn't I?" He laughed. "But you, sir, you got a lot to make up for at home. That's flowers *and* a box of chocolates for her, I'm betting. Dinner, movie…anything else? Will you fuck her? Or do you two call it some-thing different? Or does she even *do* it—"

Kent grabbed his arm hard and jerked him around. "Enough."

Paul let out a teary gasp, hid his face behind a hand. "I'm sorry," he mumbled. "That was…I didn't mean that. I'll shut up now, I promise. But god, Kent, just talk to me. I'm not the enemy. I won't hurt you."

"I know you won't." Paul slumped against him, and Kent held him with one arm. "But my marriage, that's…it's separate from us."

Paul sighed, and his voice was calmer. "So there's an us?"

"Let's just enjoy the weekend."

Paul smiled a little. He took Kent's arm and led him along, ignoring Kent's suggestion, yet again, that they go inside. "Come on, it's a nice night. It's the beach. Gotta enjoy it while you're here."

The tide was in, and the waves forced them into softer, looser sand, until Paul gave up trying to walk through it and sat, dragging Kent down. Side by side, they faced the water. The sand was dry but so cool it felt damp beneath them.

"Are you glad you came?" Paul asked quietly, his arms around his knees.

"Glad? No. But if I hadn't come, I'd be at home miserable. Worse, probably."

Paul shook his head, watching the water. "Why did you get mar-ried?"

"Because I did. It's my life now. Stop asking."

"It doesn't make sense."

"Well, guess what. Your life has never made a bit of sense to me. So here we are."

They sat in silence for several minutes, the waves folding up onto the shore closer and closer to their feet. One more night. Paul slid over and took hold of Kent's collar. "If you're gonna torture yourself later anyway, better get your money's worth."

Kent almost laughed, that Paul had said aloud the hopelessly cynical thing he had been thinking—except that he kept pretending he could keep the two things separate: have only pleasure now, save all the pain for later. Paul was already digging for the buttons of his jeans, and Kent caught him back by the arms. "No way. Time to go back inside, for real."

"Come on. Don't pretend you can hold back now."

Kent kept a bracing grip on him, and Paul's voice climbed sharply in response, louder and louder. "Two weeks ago you were fucking me in a public toilet, for christsake! In the fucking *library*, ten minutes after you laid eyes on me!"

"Calm down. Let's just go inside. It's cold—"

"It's not *cold*." Paul jerked out of his grip and stood. "You're such a baby."

Kent pulled himself out of the sand. Paul stood a little ways off, facing the water where the night was transforming itself into splendor. "Look at that, will you?" Paul said. "Wow." The moon, nearly full, was engaged in a fitful struggle with the fast clouds, covered and clear and covered again, and then it tore loose, illuminating an operatic swell of water and moving sky.

"Better idea." Paul smiled over his shoulder, shrugged out of his jacket. "I'm going swimming."

"The fuck you are."

Paul laughed, and his humor vanished. His voice fell low with seductive urgency. "Come with me."

Kent stood staring. It was three simple words like these that had once led him into another night, blacker than this, the night he first met Paul, and was dating girls, and Paul was seventeen years old. Five years later, and here he was, still stumbling through that same unending night on the trail of Paul's voice.

Paul whipped off his flannel shirt and t-shirt, kicked off his shoes. "Live your life, Kent. Let someone else do the worrying for once." He opened his jeans, grinning. Kent turned about-face and walked away, long strides away from Paul and back to the condo, not looking back.

But with each struggling step through the loose sand, another part of him moved back to Paul, a ghost that was not afraid, that shed its clothes and slipped with him into the gulf water as if it were any summer night, as if there were no stingrays beneath the black surface or jellyfish or sharks, or sharp stones or rusted curls of metal, and most of all no wicked undertow to drag them together into the water's belly, beyond the farthest hope of return. He went with Paul, and together they dove deep and sprang back to the surface like seals, laughing in the cold, rolling chaos of water for no reason except that they were alive and it felt good.

⇌

In the condo, alone, Kent buzzed with a dim anger. Maybe Paul would drown and he'd be rid of him. But if he died, the cops would have to be called and Kent's life would be over that way. At least he felt himself sickening of the surfeit. By Monday, it would all be behind him.

Soon Paul was scratching at the door in his underwear, soaked, shivering out of his skin. "Jesus fuck, Paul. You want to kill yourself? You want to drown or just die of pneumonia?" Kent hauled him inside, wrapped him in a blanket where he convulsed, blue-lipped, trying but unable to speak.

He hadn't intended to remember tenderness, but here it was again. He drew Paul a hot bath. Sitting beside the tub while Paul relaxed by degrees and the shaking stopped, Kent felt mute with unwanted relief to have him back unharmed, and next caught himself half admiring what had once infuriated him: that foolish daredevil bravery with which Paul flung himself at the world, at any whim. He watched the bathwater slip and bead over the unbroken integrity of Paul's skin and tried to bring back his anger, as if he could choose what to feel.

"My bones are still frozen," Paul said with a sleepy grin, face resting on the tub's edge. "I don't think they'll ever get warm."

Kent frowned his disapproval. "Was it worth it?"

"It was amazing." His eyes were brim-full of the irony that said Kent couldn't fool him or pretend they were strangers. "What kind of question is that?"

Kent shook every grain of sand from his clothes before he packed them, bagged the ones in plastic he needed to wash, though he could tell Maggie he'd spent a free hour on the beach. As they tossed their things into the car, he inspected the floor mats and the bottom of the trunk for sand, for anything amiss, thinking about how, as they neared the Atlanta skyline, the sun would be setting behind them and Maggie would be unlocking the doors of the stone church on Baxter for the Mennonite congregation's small evening gathering. When he turned the key on their empty house, her alto voice would be joining the other singers', a cappella, beautiful as a single flower in a field but inseparable from the harmonious union of sound.

They were ready to leave, heading toward the door, but Paul stopped. He stood unmoving in the living room.

"What?"

"I'm not ready." He went and sat on the sofa. Kent stood in the door for a minute, before going to sit beside him.

"I don't want to go back yet." He said it like something reasonable, looking at his knees.

"Paul."

"You're already back there, aren't you? You're thinking about her. You're thinking about getting there, and what she'll cook you for dinner and what you'll…talk about or whatever." He gave Kent a level look. "Let's stay. Just another hour."

"We can't."

"You choose her over me," he said, simply, flatly, but emotion flared in his face. "You can't choose her. That's fucked."

Kent rolled his eyes. "Can we have this discussion in the car?" Before Paul could snap back, explode, Kent took hold of his shoulder. "Paul, you and me, we were lousy as a couple, you know that. We broke up because we don't work." He restrained himself from saying *you left me, remember?* Easier to think of it as the mutual thing it should have been in anyone's rational world. "We make each other nuts. We've got nothing together."

"It's not nothing."

"Fine. We have great sex."

That would end it, Kent knew, because Paul would be unable to think of anything that mattered more. He wouldn't see the lie at the back of it, wouldn't admit he even cared to hear there was more between them, still, than sex. If they stayed another hour, Kent might be deluged in all there was, overwhelmed, lost.

And if they left now, he told himself, it would fall away behind them, eventually, like the water and sand, turn peaceful and remote like memory.

Paul mocked him. "You have something more with her, I suppose?"

"Yes."

Their faces were inches apart, eyes locked, Paul breathing through his flared nose, but any fight was beneath his effort if he saw Kent would win. "Fuck it," he said. "Let's go."

In two months, he would be twenty-two years old. Kent followed him out the door, wishing he didn't know just as certainly that Paul would stiffen against touch, would tip his forehead to the passenger window and gaze in a listless, soulful way at the passing palmettos and cows, punishing him with silence until Alabama and he couldn't bear it anymore and would simply begin speaking again as if nothing had ever been wrong.

CHAPTER 2

At the courthouse in Plea and Arraignment, the conference table was nearly buried under scattered sections of the *Atlanta Journal-Constitution*. Six defense attorneys, most of whom had bought their suits from discount racks as Maggie had, traded comics for lawn and garden advertisements, offered opinions about pop videos, or chatted over cellphones while waiting to speak to the ADA at the end of the table, Spencer Griggs. Maggie had Spencer's ear, because she was small and female and willing to use a half-feigned, breezy, heedless charm to assert herself as first.

"Suspect stopped at roadblock," she read quickly from the DA's police report. It was her first case on the day's calendar—Rodney Goings, seventeen-year-old African-American male. She skimmed for a glimpse of who he would be and what he had been through. "Car reported stolen, suspect fled…Oh, listen to this. 'Suspect placed in restraint on ground. Suspect scraped his face on concrete.' How does that happen, do you suppose? He had an itch while he was down there?"

Spencer, who exuded a waxen perfection and was dressed as if he'd been cast as the hot new black lawyer in a stylish legal drama, gave her a perfunctory smile. He wasn't her usual ADA. They didn't have a rhythm down she could trust.

"Suspect bit the officer," she continued. "Well, that's not nice. Tried to swallow twenty-five hits of MDMA—what is that?"

"I have no idea," Spencer said, reading another file.

"Crystal meth? Ecstasy?" She asked around the table but no one knew.

"Here's what I figured out about an hour ago." He handed her another report. "This is your guy too, on an outstanding warrant from January. Used a different name at the time. And besides this, he's out on bond on a rape charge from November."

Maggie steeled herself. To refrain from judgment was nearly automatic, though she felt it still as an internal process, slight mechanical adjustments of the mind and body. Evasion of the law, assault. Rape. Behind the words was a story, and the task of making young Mr. Goings human for a judge or jury would begin with herself, her first and toughest audience. This was the work she felt God had given her on earth, and often she worried the job alone could crush her without this extra requirement, this impossible contortion of love.

"Well, I see he's staying out of trouble," she said cheerily. "Showing up for court like a model citizen. How about probation?"

The routine earned her another smile from Spencer, who within the next five minutes would weigh the facts before him and hand down a sentencing recommendation like one of those old carnival machines spitting out a man's fortune. Rodney Goings, here's your life.

Spencer's new report, which she skimmed, told her Rodney had shot another boy in the leg after an altercation over a female. "I know that song," she said. "Someone talked to my baby. I had to shoot him down." Meanwhile, she scrawled the details of the first charge and the current one on the inside of her file folder—no telling when she'd get her own copy. She was glad she had only the shooting and the stolen car/drug possession/officer-biting to deal with. Another attorney, no doubt court-appointed like herself, had already been through this dance on the rape.

They racked up the charges. Predictably, Spencer countered her "possession" with "possession with intent to sell" and her "resisting" with "assault on an officer"—words lobbed gently from one side of the scale to the other, waiting for a balance to declare itself. "How 'bout 2P?" she said, like a rapid bid at cards—two years probation. She would never have tried such a callow move with her regular ADA, but not knowing Spencer, she was wary of opening too high.

"Don't waste my time," he muttered.

Now she had to wait until he felt like acknowledging her again. Jonathan Alder—dangerously senile, precarious toupee—sidled up opposite and started nudging his case into Spencer's notice.

"Are you done, Maggie?" Anna Perkins asked, from the chair to her left.

"I'm waiting," Maggie told her, with the dreamy smile of an obedient, chastised daughter, "for an offer. Are you done with that Rich's flier?"

Anna passed it, and Maggie studied with ravenous attention the rows of gold and silver chains, diamond pendants, and heart-shaped earrings she had no earthly need for. Meanwhile, Spencer had opened the narrative on Toupee's case, and Maggie inserted sweetly, "Um, shall I just tell Mr. Goings that the DA is so hurt and offended by his actions that he disdains to make an offer?"

With a barely audible sigh, he slid the paperwork back into his reading range.

She went back to her sale flier. At work, in the quieter moments, she often felt her father over her shoulder—a sterner, more skeptical version of him. *Lawyer*, he would scoff, clucking over her poor, thin efforts. They had argued over this choice, just as he, a doctor, had argued with his own father, who had believed with his generation that farming was the only respectable Mennonite profession. Most days she felt certain her own chosen work was the Lord's work as well, that she could do as much here as her father could in his mountain charity clinic. Maybe more. It amused her, too, to imagine herself leading a covert Mennonite infiltration into the snarls of the American justice system— though there was nothing secretive about her faith, no hidden agenda. She was like anyone else.

And that's the problem, her father would say. *Among them it is too easy to forget, lose your way.* She sensed the truth of this on court days when her files stacked up, one upon the other, ceaseless and relentless. How could she accomplish even small good, let alone do battle against the world's deeper wrongs, when she barely kept her head above the petty caseload?

Her finger traced the serpentine glitter of a bracelet in the ad, and her father watched this too. *Magdalena, you are too much drawn to the world*, he scolded her, and she smiled at the thought. Sometimes her father and God spoke to her with one voice. She wondered whether she had merely given God her father's face. *I know*, she said, *I know. Come on, I'm only looking!*

"Two years prison," Spencer said.

Maggie blinked up at him, stood. She gathered her file and with a half-guilty swipe tucked the sale flier into it. "Okeydoke. I'll see what Mr. Goings has to say and get back to you."

⌒

The deputy on duty led Rodney Goings from the holding cell to a claustrophobia-inducing conference room, made entirely of bolted-down metal—walls, floor, tiny table with bolted-on seats—all of it painted the same flat cornflower blue. They took seats across from each other. Maggie was used to this now, facing violent men alone, though the clanging shut of the door as the deputy departed never failed to shudder through her bones.

Wrists cuffed before him, he was a powerfully built boy, older-looking than seventeen. He had large, long-lashed eyes, a thin mustache, overgrown fingernails, overgrown hair from which two or three loose braids jutted at random. Scratch-like scars marked his face. A tattoo on his forearm read "Zone 3." His expression was dull as a child's after four hours of cartoons, empty of hostility or fear or even specific interest. He nodded when she introduced herself and told him, "I've been assigned to represent you."

"Do you know how come they ain't give me no bond?" he asked, his voice soft, without inflection.

She told him she would get to that soon and reminded him how this worked—she would ask him about what happened, and then she would try to explain to him where he stood. "Okay," he said.

She told him about the roadblock, the car he was driving—a friend, he said, gave him the car. He agreed in syllables—"Yeah," "Uh-huh"—to nearly every question she pulled from the report, even the ones that didn't make sense, as if his answers had no relevance to him. "I just want to know why they won't give me no bond," he said.

"We'll talk about that. Can you tell me about how you got arrested? The two cops—what did they do?"

"They put the cuffs on me and put me in the police car."

"That's all? It was all pretty peaceful?"

"Yeah."

"Then what?"

"Then they drove me around and asked me questions."

"Nobody got hurt?"

"No."

The deputy came in with Rodney's lunch: a boloney sandwich in a plastic baggie, a packet each of mustard and mayo tucked in with it, and a paper carton of Hawaiian Punch—like something his mother might have packed. Rodney didn't look at it.

"Did they take you to Grady Hospital?"

"Yeah."

"Why'd they do that? Did they say?"

"They said I had to be medical cleared."

Once, with a client like this, she would have assumed these answers were intentional evasiveness, a long habit of offering whatever the authority figure seemed to want. She tried another line. "Where do you live, Rodney?"

"With my mom. Greenwood Terrace."

"You two get along okay?"

"Yeah."

"It says here your mother had a warrant out on you. Did something happen?"

"No."

She sighed. "Rodney, are you seeing a doctor at the jail?"

"No."

"Are you taking any kind of medicine for your nerves?"

"No."

"Is there anybody who comes to talk to you at the jail about how you feel?"

"There's a shrink there. She said I was a schizophrenic."

"Okay. Anyone else tell you that before?"

"My mom said I have two personalities. And I went to the psychiatric high school for two years."

What she found truly stunning, still, was that she would never be told by anyone else that this client, like maybe ten percent of the young men who stumbled across her door, had been diagnosed schizophrenic. Probably by several doctors. Rodney must have had miles of files in sundry schools and clinics around Atlanta, and yet there was no record that would follow him far enough to land by some automatic process in her hands. She would have to go dig each one up herself.

She had only a few more questions, important to Rodney's case but more important at the moment to her own peace of mind. "Rodney," she said, in the same gentle, disinterested tone, "do you hear voices in your head that tell you to do things?"

"No."

"Do you see anything unusual in the room, or anyone else over here"—she waved a hand through the air around her head—"besides me?"

"No," he said, and though it may or may not have been true, it made her feel better to hear it. Once a client had pointed to a little devil sitting on her shoulder, and another hiding in her hair. Another client told her that her whole body was fringed in flame.

"Can I get a bond today?" he asked. He was just a child still, in his man's body—she wanted to put her arms around him, tell him that it would all be okay. But there was nothing she could offer to change the fact that he would sleep in a cell tonight, a victim of forces that made no sense to him.

Even if she filed for him today, she explained, it would be two weeks minimum before his bond hearing. "But I can't file today anyway because your case is too complicated. We have to do some other things first. I'm going to send over someone to talk to you at the jail—his name is Mr. Harold. You'll like talking to him. He's a social worker, not a doctor. I'm going to write all this down for you so you'll know what we're doing and how long it will take. Can you make out my handwriting?" she asked, her careful test for literacy. "Do you need your glasses?"

He said his reading was fine, and she wrote down a makeshift time line on a clean sheet. "And this is my name up here, Maggie Schwartzentruber. It's a weird name, so you can just call me Miss Maggie. Is it okay with you if I represent you?"

"It's okay," he said. He took hold of the sandwich and brought it closer. "I want you to do everything."

A full day in court meant whatever she could scrounge for lunch— today it was a baggie of Oreos bummed from Brad Latham, the new guy in her firm. He was a year out of law school, trying his first murder case, and every night that week he had called her at home to freak out for an hour. She'd pinch the phone between her ear and shoulder and say soothing things while she sanded dresser tops or sorted laundry. "Go ahead, take them all," he told her, about the cookies she had ferreted from his briefcase. He was waiting for the judge to come back from chambers. "I'm going to throw up anyway."

Maggie would have liked to hang out and be supportive, but she had two more of her own cases to push through—one aggravated assault, one simple possession—and then it was back to her office at the Fulton County Justice Cooperative two blocks over for the real and ongoing work. Today that was the Jamal Cole case. She counted herself lucky to work in this firm of twelve, a nonprofit group with the distinction of being the only public defenders in the state's most urban county who were certified for death penalty cases.

She had been struggling with this case for close to a year: Jamal Cole, twenty-eight, child murderer. No way to delude herself or anyone else that the cops had nabbed the wrong guy as the murder had involved hostages and a two-day stand-off—a small white house surrounded by cop cars and S.W.A.T. team sharpshooters, every minute of it captured for posterity by aerial news crews. Inside the house, Jamal held two neighbors, his pregnant common-law wife, Patricia Hollis, and her five-year-old son, Josiah, at gunpoint. Before it was over, he had stabbed the boy, flayed him, and doused him in a toilet cleaner containing hydrochloric acid—"to make sure he was really dead," by all accounts. Shortly afterward, Jamal Cole surrendered.

It was the kind of case the media would not stop loving, the kind of case that made otherwise gentle people of few opinions start screaming for the death penalty. She understood the impulse. With plenty of gruesome cases behind her now, she could still feel reflexive disgust at a police report, the urge to drop the whole file to the floor like something contaminated. *Lock that one up. Nothing too severe.* Many capital cases, she had found, followed emotion in precisely this manner. One day, if she ever became cynical enough, she could offer this advice as a lawyer: beat your child to death with your fists, rape women in the missionary position, unload a handgun into someone's chest—just don't get creative. By all means don't break out the toilet cleaner or the public might perk up and notice you're depraved.

Harold Czarak, the social worker on Jamal's case, came into her office looking exhausted. "Maggie, I missed you! Where were you?" He dropped his long body into a chair, in a puppet-like skew of limbs. Harold was only a year younger than Maggie but she thought of him as a kid, maybe for his freckly, somewhat chinless face and his haphazard energy.

"Court all day, sweetie," she told him. "Got one for you to go talk to as soon as you have a chance. Another schizo teenager, looks like."

"Great, what'd he do?" Harold, who played basketball once a week with whatever boys among his files happened to be at the Rice Street Jail, asked this question with weary, good-humored patience, like a camp counselor inquiring after the behavior of a mischievous charge.

"Bit a cop, shot a kid, stole a car. Rape on an earlier charge. What's MDMA?"

He blinked up from a brief drowse in the chair. "Uh, that would be ecstasy."

"Holding twenty-five hits of that. Tried to swallow every last lick, which is how our cop got his hand in the way. Of course the kid remembers none of this. Very sweet, but nutty."

"Oh, god," Harold groaned, "don't say that unless you have candy. I'm about to pass out. I'd kill you for a mint."

"Sorry." She chuckled, rubbed her eyes. Open in front of her was the Jamal Cole file, and it seemed far less pressing than the grumbling emptiness of her own belly. She had so little time for any of them. It became easy to generalize, sum them all up and brush them aside—especially when they were hard to look at, as most of her clients were.

"Did you get anywhere with Jamal today?" she asked Harold.

"Yeah, got a few things. I'll tell you about it. Want to grab something to eat?" He looked at her wistfully. "Go down to the corner for a gyro, maybe?"

"I have to go home to my husband." This still felt like a strange thing to say, an excuse of some kind, though she and Kent had passed their first anniversary and she should have been used to married life by now. In the old days, her structureless life, she would have stayed at the office until nine p.m. without noticing the hour. Church business had always been useful for calling her away at various times—to attend Ten Thousand Villages board meetings, to work in the soup kitchen or the store. Now she sometimes thought she had acquired the husband mainly because having one seemed to compel her home for dinner.

"Lucky dog." Harold smiled a little, picking at the chair arm. His girlfriend, whom Maggie considered not nearly good enough for him in the first place—sullen, snotty, and not too bright—had dumped him about three months before, and he was just now starting to come up out of his misery enough to cast these envious looks around at other people and their lives.

He filled her in on his day's peregrinations—digging up old social services records, speaking to people from Jamal's childhood. As with most of their clients, their goal was to establish a source for his impulse that might enlist the sympathy of the jury, the judge, the DA, and, not unimportantly in all this, the victim's family. This generally meant dipping into the past, a place almost certain to be painful and chaotic, often willfully obscured. From Jamal himself, they'd gotten nothing but a flat-affect admission of guilt. He knew what he'd done was wrong, would say, "I deserve to be put to death." But he was not especially remorseful. From time to time he mentioned the boy was bad by nature. "I did what I had to do, and that's all I'm gonna say," Jamal said, and closed his mouth.

"The stepfather was bad news," Harold reported. "Looks like he was in the house off and on since Jamal was three, until about ten. Violent, abusive, mainly toward Jamal, I think. The grandmother implied molestation, but she's a bit dotty. Hard to keep her focused. She mentioned a half brother, four or five years younger than Jamal, the stepfather's kid. He's dead now, drive-by shooting. The mother is still alive but out of touch, somewhere in South Carolina."

Maggie nodded to all this, turning it over. "What's your gut say?"

He gazed toward the window, where the winter light was already falling toward night. "The usual. That he lived through hell."

"He reproduced the situation," she added. "He was surrogate father to another woman's son."

"He told the cops to shoot him," Harold said. Their voices were thin as gossamer, casting this delicate web of story across the room; they watched its slim attachments catch here and there. "He came out of the house screaming 'Shoot me.'"

"It was self-directed. He was killing himself."

They breathed in silence, letting their web sit untouched. It was far too fragile to bear the first step, to bear even much scrutiny. They would let it stay overnight, see what structure remained by morning or what had been caught.

"One more thing," he said. He unfolded himself from the chair and took out his wallet, selected from inside a small, bent photograph—the miniature sort made of children at school. At first Maggie thought it was Josiah, but it wasn't. It was Jamal. Though the photo was creased across its length, she recognized the cocoa skin, the broad forehead. There was something a little wild in the eyes, desperately eager, and his smile, more like a grimace, was a strained novice effort to approximate happiness. He appeared battered, both front teeth knocked out, until she realized he was only a normal first grader who had shed his baby teeth and was waiting for new ones to grow in.

She clipped the photo to the upper corner of his file and tried to smooth out the crease line with her thumb.

On her way home, she stopped by her sister's house to pick up a loaf of bread. Whenever new people visited the Mennonite church, it was tradition to pay them a visit within the week bearing loaves, and Maggie had somehow agreed to this week's mission. She had planned to bake that night, but Lila had insisted she was baking anyway. "Besides," she said, "your bread might run people off."

It was especially charitable of Lila to make church visitors her concern as she didn't belong to Maggie's church—belonged, in fact, to the only other Mennonite church in Atlanta. Both were small, and once they'd been one. Several years back, they'd suffered a disagreement over a plan to hire a woman pastor and had broken apart. For Mennonites, pacifism was more or less in the blood, like the ability to sing in perfect-pitch four-part harmony, and any little clash could send factions into extremes of retreat to avoid a confrontation. Everywhere it was the same story, Mennonite churches divided, divided again. Their father's joke: "Wherever two or more of you are gathered in His name, there shall be another split." But the two Atlanta churches remained friendly as sisters, like Lila and Maggie in their separate houses.

Lila had married John Yoder, the only marriable Mennonite man in the city—or so Maggie contended, having been, at various times during her single years, fixed up by Lila with the rest of them. Long before Maggie's arrival in Atlanta, Lila had also found the perfect house: a Victorian fixer-upper in a derelict in-town neighborhood called Edgewood, at the border of Inman Park, that seemed to take the Yoders' presence as a signal to awaken and renovate itself. A dozen years later, Maggie was lucky to live on Edgewood's more pinched and meager side, her house half the size at twice the price, and she tried not to begrudge her sister the blessing of her wrap-around porches and leafier shade and the now-beautiful old house where she busied herself with producing John Yoder's perfect children at the appropriate interval for geniuses, one every seven years.

In the kitchen, Lila handed her a loaf wrapped in foil and red ribbon, still warm, along with a second in plain foil. "That one's for you," she said, of the ribbonless package. "To take home to your poor starving husband."

Maggie set them on the counter. "Wow, check out the cut!" Two-handed, she reached over her sister's seven-months-pregnant belly to fluff her newly short hair. As children, their hair had grown long and straight, past their hips—they hadn't been allowed to cut it. Combing and braiding had been a daily chore. Now, as adults, they seemed to be dueling with shorter and shorter cuts. Maggie's dark hair kicked out in wisps along her neck. Lila's, lighter and russet-tinted with flecks of gray, was now capped close to her head and feathered back on one side.

"Don't copy it," Maggie's niece, Chloe, admonished her from the table where she was doing homework. "Yours is cute the way it is. Hers is too short, don't you think?"

She wasn't really asking. Ever since Chloe had hit puberty, she had put herself in charge of all family issues involving taste and propriety. She had also decided entirely on her own that Mennonite was cool. For the sake of family and tradition, she said, not *just* for beauty, she wore her honey-brown hair the way they had as girls. Today it swept loose over her shoulders and past the seat of her chair. To conceal her braces, she spoke almost always in a kind of terse, pointed mumble, but it was a vanity that she had managed to package into an unsmiling diva persona that worked beautifully for her—as if the world were just a little too vulgar to warrant her full emotional engagement.

"I don't copy her, I'll have you know," Maggie reminded Chloe. "She copies me."

"Oh, please!" Lila said. "Who got married first? Who moved to Atlanta first?" None of this sparring was exactly fair, since Lila was eight years older. She patted the mound of her belly. "You'll have one of these next."

Chloe snorted and said, "Yeah, you're falling *way* behind there," as if the one in progress were Lila's tenth and not her third.

Maggie sat at the table. The teapot whistled and Lila filled two mugs. The kitchen was already aromatic with the fresh-herbed pork roast in the oven. "I think I'm not having any," she said, kind of experimentally. "Of *those*, I mean."

"Good for you!" Chloe barked. "The world is overpopulated. But try telling some people that, who can't even be bothered to eat vegetarian."

"I have too much to do," Maggie said, a little insistent though Lila hadn't said a word. "There are so many messed up people in this city— I really think I have my hands full as it is without making more of them."

"Amen, sister," Chloe muttered, pencil scratching along her paper.

"You go, girl."

Lila considered her, mouth a straight line, and Maggie knew she was once again being assessed for damage. But Lila wouldn't open the door to past traumas with Chloe in the room, and she shrugged herself back into a lighter mood. "You don't mean that. You're just being out-landish, as usual. You're young!"

"Always younger than you. But not that young." She ran her hands back through her hair, which felt too long suddenly, unruly. "I'm serious, when am I going to change a diaper, huh? I don't really have a big interest in diapers, to be honest. I'd have to hire a nanny and that's no way to raise a kid."

"I'll be your nanny," Chloe said. "I need the money."

"It's just not me." She felt the need now to reassure her sister that she was fine. "The mom thing. I'm a lawyer. My house has"—she searched Lila's kitchen, her hand-sewn curtains and terra-cotta tile—"*dirt* in it. And very rarely any bread to speak of."

"Have you mentioned this to Kent?"

This took her off guard. "Kent? Why?"

Lila pursed her mouth primly. "Well, I think he might want kids."

She scoffed, and then looked at Lila harder. "Really?" But the idea was ridiculous. "Why, because he's a guy? This is your theory, that all men have some biological drive to reproduce?"

Lila sipped her tea. "When they get married? I'd say, usually. They're thinking it somewhere. Besides, he's got that whole dad vibe going on. You know, like at family picnics, that manly grill-guy-giving-piggy-back-rides-and-holding-the-baby thing."

"But we aren't that way," Maggie said, though it was hard to find the words for what she meant—especially without insulting the whole child-bearing endeavor. *We're complete in ourselves*, she wanted to say, of her fragile one-year union. "Not all marriages have to be like that. They can be about other things, can't they?"

"He would have some gorgeous kids," Chloe mused. Kent had been giving Chloe guitar lessons, and ever since, she had decided that Maggie had married a babe. And had no qualms about making the pronouncement before anyone, including the babe in question.

"Hey, you! Where's my support? Overpopulation and all that?"

Chloe shrugged. "The gene pool is good. Look at *her* kids. It's worth adding more of us to the world." She tapped her pencil thoughtfully against her chin. "But what about a last name? McKutcheon-Schwartzentruber would be a cruel thing to do to a kid."

Maggie squeezed her eyes shut, hands out like a crossing guard to stop both of them. "Okay, that's all on that topic." She stood up, casting a critical eye on Lila's belly—really, there was something horrifying about the whole concept. Though she knew it was a perverse feeling, she was nearly nauseated by the sight of her sister in this state, with another person—a complete stranger—pushing out the front of her denim jumper. It was a boy, they knew, already named Luke, and he would join Chloe and seven-year-old Seth and probably be every bit as perfect as they were. He would poop cotton candy and never cry.

"Thanks for the bread," she said. Lila and her daughter exchanged dry, quizzical glances, and Lila rose to attend to the next stage of her family's dinner. Maggie took her bread and went.

She would have liked to think she'd arrived at her life by accident. In truth, there had been a turning point, in her second year of law school, when anger, if not God, had twisted her path. It wasn't the rape that happened to her but the anger it had left her with, of a sort she'd not realized possible in herself or others. Her sense of humanity darkened with it, altered to accommodate an ever-present, visceral awareness of the anger in the world. At times she was certain it was the greatest of human problems, more terrible than hunger, greed, or disease; other times it was no more than the problem she'd been given. She'd resolved to do battle in the Mennonite way, with work.

It was almost a relief, to be so clearly called. Years before, she'd chosen a law school with a social justice emphasis, planning vaguely to help the homeless, as her whole life she had felt committed to "helping"—in whatever way she might—the vast, hazy crowds of the less fortunate. Her second year delivered a mission. The discovery that she herself was capable of wishing a man's death, of sanctioning it at the hands of the state, gradually led her into activism against the death penalty. As with social justice law, she found it a cause already lousy with Mennonites. She fit right in. From there, it was no great leap to see that her own anger, the anger in violent offenders, and her intense fear of them, at least in the abstract, amounted to a sign that she should devote her legal work to violent offenders.

The hardest part, she soon found, was the urban life her work required. Her first jobs—internships in cities far from family—forced her to live alone in studio apartments where she jolted awake at any noise and called her family too often and too late at night. The job offer in Atlanta came as a gift, and not only because it would allow her to advance to death penalty work more quickly than she'd expected. In Atlanta, she would have Lila.

When she looked back now on her first two years in Atlanta, it hardly seemed she'd had her own apartment. Two or three nights a week she'd eaten dinner at Lila's house, she babysat on weekends, spent countless evenings in the kitchen playing Dutch Blitz—Chloe at ten and eleven often beat the grown-ups at the Mennonite card game they'd been playing all their lives—and sometimes lingered late enough that she slept over in the spare room. Without consciously envying Lila's life, Maggie spent enough time in her lovely rambling home with its honey-toned hardwood floors and hydrangea bushes and authentic wainscoting that it mapped itself onto her life as a kind of goal, a future in waiting. She could picture herself in similar surroundings.

She'd never been one of those girls who dreamed of marriage. Work was enough. Her work included the church, which extended into Lila's family too, since so much of Yoder family life was woven through with service. Quilting for a relief sale or planting shrubs at the county halfway house was their version of family fun and a social life—just as such work had served in John Yoder's family when he was a child and in their own when they were girls. If Maggie could have chosen any life, she might have, in fact, moved into the back bedroom of Lila's house like some overgrown adopted daughter.

Then Kent came along, a surprise, a man who was ready and knew what he wanted and nudged her down the aisle before she noticed it happening. An *infidel*, of course, as Lila with tongue-in-cheek scorn called Maggie's many non-Mennonite attractions over the years. "Maggie likes the lost causes," she would say. "Can't pass a stray without stopping the car." Someone "of the world," her father would say, more serious, a phrase he applied to anyone not sealed inside the circle of the church. "Magdalena, girl, why must you always fall for these clumsy, stumbling men of the world?"

When she first saw him, he was seated cross-legged on a low, carpeted platform in her favorite music store, a twelve-string acoustic guitar across his thighs. From her angle he was all broad shoulders and wavy mess of hair, the edge of his cheek sometimes visible as he bent over the guitar to pluck out an artful bluegrass melody in a minor key. Usually guys who performed in music stores annoyed her, but this one seemed unaware of listeners, played the way other people engaged in polite small talk, because the presence of the guitar itself seemed to compel it. After a while he strummed into John Prine's "Angel From Montgomery" and began to sing in a clear tenor voice about being an old woman, without a hint of irony. Something in the combination of his warm, appealing voice, his skilled fingers, and his manner of delivery, the seeming insistence that there was nothing silly in the lyrics, made her decide she liked him, this utter stranger.

Two minutes later, when she brought her sheet music to the register, the store manager, a hefty biker-looking guy in a denim vest with twin braids of beard falling from his chin, introduced them. The manager's name was Derek, and she knew him only from casual conversations in the store about service work and music.

"Kent's looking to do some volunteer work," Derek told her with a wink she couldn't quite read.

Kent looked baffled. "No, I'm not."

"Sure you are. We were talking about this. You want to stop being a hedonist and do something useful in the world."

"Oh. Right. Yeah, I guess I wouldn't mind some of that." He looked her over with guarded interest as if he were being introduced to a drug dealer. At first she mistook the sleepy abstraction in his eyes for the residue of actual drugs, which would make her next on the list in his search for feel-good self-actualization. She almost laughed, except that she knew the type, knew he fancied himself serious in this quest—another latter-day hippie who would beg to work the soup line every day rather than once a week, then become bored and vanish before the month was half over.

"Sure," she said. "If that's what you want, I can hook you up."

"She's a Mennonite," Derek said.

Kent opened his mouth and shut it again, gave her an embarrassed, blinking smile.

"Don't worry," Derek said. "That doesn't mean Bible-thumping freak. It means she's got a hand in half the charity work in the city. And you should hear her sing too. Sing circles around you, boy."

She rounded her eyes at Derek. "And when have you heard me sing?"

He crossed his arms and gave her a sphinx look. "Your reputation is known to me."

Almost from his first day at the soup kitchen, Kent was attached to her side like the stray dog Lila would accuse him of being. Still it was weeks before she began to take his interest in her as something more than discipleship. He followed her to a few short-term church projects, took her to coffee and lunch to talk about the city's various and appalling needs, about all the good without end waiting to be done. Because of her long-standing involvement and special skills, her own hours for service were devoted mostly to management, to head work; she was a member of many nonprofit boards. He wanted hands-on, sweaty *work*, hammers and shovels and heavy lifting. She suggested charities where she had little or no involvement, and he went happily, as if on assignment for her, coming back with enthusiastic frontline reports over dinner.

As they began seeing more of each other, then officially dating, Kent was undergoing an awakening he seemed determined to invent for himself. In long, late-night conversations he told her that he'd been unhappy for a long time and that he now understood it came from living selfishly, without any goal but to pay his rent and feed himself. He had given himself over to pleasures while contributing nothing of value to the world, until he found he'd become a thirty-year-old kid, stalled in a life of temp work and garage bands.

But Maggie knew by now he was no kid. Under those frivolous bachelor habits, he was a serious man, almost alarmingly introspective—not self-absorbed as he put it, but, in a positive way, concerned with himself. In this he was much more like a Mennonite than like other men of the world she had known. Without a God to take himself to, he examined and judged and adjusted himself with the same rigor. Like a Mennonite, he didn't just talk about doing good in the world; he did it.

It was close enough. Close enough at least to sleep with him and dismiss him, because this was what she had been doing in recent years—ever since May of her second year of law school. Between that time and this, she'd had sex only twice, and she had liked both men until they put themselves inside her and changed everything. Afterward, her limbs went cold and rigid at their smallest touch and she sent them away without another chance, changed her phone number, hurled herself back into work. Kent, she thought, would be dispensed with in the same way, and this is what she hadn't confessed to Lila while being fixed up with all those unworthy Mennonites: that it wouldn't have mattered if they were perfect, that their fates would have all been the same.

She slept with Kent and waited. The reaction didn't come. Until that moment, when she understood she wanted him, she hadn't known the weight of her own fear or guessed that, beneath it, she harbored such an intense desire to be comfortably naked with a naked man, to feel pleasure that way and look forward to more of the same. To be normal. She had not believed the man to grant her such ease existed, and here he was. In an ecstasy of relief, she'd had sex with him nearly every night for three weeks. He caught her enthusiasm like a contact high, added it to his own zeal for his newfound sense of himself, and they were very soon engaged, very soon married.

Sometimes now she worried this had all happened too quickly. When he slept beside her, she lay awake watching him, vigilant in her startled, grateful love, and she prayed that they had not aligned themselves askew, left a crack. In the dark, she was aware of a fault line in her own life, at least, one she had spackled over, sanded down, hoping to pass herself off as someone fit for marriage like other people. But she would never feel like other people. When he touched her, his fingers knew this, handled her as if the wrong pressure might cause her to collapse into dust, even though in the light she was stronger than him, stronger than anyone.

She wondered if he sensed her deception, if that's what it was, and so kept his eyes always a little averted, not wanting to know. He seemed to need to believe in her perfection. In their bathroom he might playfully bump her shoulder at the sink while brushing his teeth, but would leave the room when she used the toilet, as if he couldn't bear to think of her having those sorts of needs. Always, there was a hint of deference in his manner around her. But maybe it wasn't so wrong—or even unusual—if under the ordinary surface of their marriage she played the saint for him while he kept her safe in the dark.

At the McKutcheon-Schwartzentruber house, a somewhat shabby blue-and-white craftsman's cottage, a ladder traced a silver diagonal gleam in the dark from the sideyard bushes to the roof. Maggie passed the jonquils popping up along the walk, hopeful things in the still-frigid air, and she noted the three-legged chair leaning on the porch rail and the unfinished iron bird, a rusty stork-like notion of Kent's in construction since November, awaiting his discovery of the proper material for legs. These unabandoned projects were the essence of Kent.

The bird had cone-shaped coils for eyes and a latent jaunty expression. It was both art and adorable, or would be, a potential for adorability waiting to emerge that Maggie could see clearly and would herself have welded into fruition in a night's effort. Yet every day the bird leaned against the wicker settee at the same angle, in the same phase of stalled development. The problem, she thought, was not a deficit of meaningful attention, but that Kent devoted himself in full earnestness to too many things. He pleaded the case for his projects— he had a table on the more secluded back porch that grew small forests of miswired, damp-rusted appliances and broken clay pots and various remakeable doodads—with an eloquence that made her feel hardhearted. Nothing was ever abandoned, he assured her, offering for each one, down to the saddest example, such elaborate and cherished plans for completion or restoration that she believed him and granted indefinite extensions on grace. Nothing in the house was ever broken that couldn't be fixed, nothing ever so far gone that the trash would be mercy. She loved him for this, even as she grumbled past the unmoving mess.

Kent was seated on the rug before the fireplace and bent over his guitar, face lowered in rapt attention. He was wearing his green flannel robe, as if the guitar's siren call had caught him out of the shower before he could dress, and a twist of damp hair straggled over his forehead, but otherwise he was the picture of the first time she had seen him. It was this very guitar, even—the Martin D-28 she had bought him for his birthday, after they were engaged.

"There's a ladder on our house," she said.

"Oh, yeah." He seemed puzzled by this. "I was going to, well, I started to look at those gutters, you know. I think I can unbend that sagging spot and just repaint over the rust. They need cleaning too, but I just did that one section so far."

She nodded. Truthfully, she would have been happy to call someone to come and replace all the gutters with the expensive ones that never needed cleaning—do it and be done. But Kent had ideas, many of which involved a ladder and multiple trips to Home Depot, and she was determined to suppress her conviction that there was a simpler, better way to do everything, along with her itching need to check tasks off the list of her life. She wanted to let him have his ideas.

She sat on the sofa near him, plunked down her briefcase, kicked off her shoes. "Look." She lofted the silver package. "Lila made us bread. Hi, you." She leaned to kiss him, taking the robe's lapel between her fingers.

"I should get dressed, huh?"

"Well, eventually. I mean, there's the ladder."

"I'll finish that tomorrow." Reading something in her face, he said, "I promise. I mean, I'll do what I can on it."

She tried to keep the dismay from her voice. "But the ladder shouldn't be up at night. Someone could take it, or—I don't know, crawl up on our roof."

"Who's going to crawl up on our roof?"

"Elves. Leprechauns." He laughed, and she said, "Seriously. Serial killers with chain saws. Little children, fragile children whose parents have expensive lawyers, will climb up there in droves."

"You're hilarious."

"But you'll take it down, right? Tonight?"

Because she'd had savings and he had not, they had made the down payment on the house and virtually every mortgage payment with her money. Because she had conceived of a house in Edgewood before she had met the husband to go in it and because it was her money, she had led the march into the whole house idea, pushing for quick decisions on matters she herself had weighed far in advance. Of course Kent wanted the house, had chosen it with her, but the uneasy sense remained that it was more hers than his. She now knew that under Kent's drives toward change lurked deep tendencies for inertia and complacent contentment. If it had been up to him, she often thought, the idea of owning a home might only now be occurring to him, might not see reality for another ten years. Along with a broad effort not to nag, she tried very hard not to make sounds more home-ownerish than his.

"I'll get dressed." He smiled, raked a hand back through his damp hair. "I made chicken picatta."

"Oh, good. Yay."

Instead of standing, he resettled his fingers on a chord and strummed, then another chord. A song began to form.

She listened awhile. "Do you remember what you were playing when we met?"

"I was playing a lot of things," he said, glancing up with a smile, but his fingers bent whatever song he had started into the chords of "Angel From Montgomery."

She sighed, settled into the sofa. "I was thinking about that today. About you sitting there in the store, this good-looking guy, singing that song. 'I'm an old woman, named after my mother.'" But his sense of humor didn't tend to register this sort of observation, so she said, "It was freakishly cute."

He started singing as he had in the store, and this time she joined him on the chorus, harmonizing the alto line. Once, he had coerced her into singing with his band—pulled her up on stage for an unrehearsed duet of "Break the Chain," and she had blushed with breathless pleasure for the next two hours over how good everyone said they were, but later she had made him promise never to do that to her again. It was fine for him, but she felt silly and vain singing rock.

He stopped after the chorus, set the guitar aside. "You want to change or something? How was your day?"

"Oh, the usual. Grueling and sisyphean." She trailed him into the bedroom and flopped on the bed while he went into the closet to find his own clothes. "It's a weird song, isn't it?" she said, while he slid khakis up over boxers, the curve of his upper back lit by the closet bulb. "'Make me an angel that flies from Montgomery.' It's like that Zen hotdog joke, 'Make me one with everything.'"

He came out buttoning a shirt over a chest muscled from pumping weights and lightly furred. The hair tapered to a narrow spout down the center of his belly, where he kept a roll of extra flesh he was always trying to lose though she sort of liked it. "What are you talking about?" He sat at the end of the bed, lifted her nylon-stockinged feet into his lap and began to rub them.

"You know"—this seemed important suddenly—"like, make me an angel. Are you talking about yourself, or are you placing an order?

Does this old woman want some angel to come flying out of Montgomery to rescue her, or does she want to *be* an angel?"

His thumbs rasped along her insteps. "I think you're overthinking it."

"Probably." She sat up to watch him work. "That feels good. Will you change clothes for me too? I don't want to move."

He set her feet aside and crawled up beside her, leaning on one elbow. She took hold of his cuff and buttoned it. She could smell the chicken steaming in the kitchen—it seemed to her he'd been cooking a lot lately. The house was freshly vacuumed, the bed made, the recycling at the curb—all these things he did and she failed to give him credit for. Their faces were close in the shadows, the only light from the closet, and he leaned to kiss her, his hand sliding down over the rough tweed of her suit. For some reason, she was overly aware of this, scrutinizing their gestures with each other as if through someone else's eyes. Lila's, maybe. Or that devil her client had seen on her shoulder. The sensation disturbed her enough that she stopped the kiss.

"Do we have a good marriage?"

Silent for too long, he studied her. "Why do you ask that?"

She put a hand on his hair, which was cool with dampness. "Just wondering. Don't—" She shook her head, sat up. "It's just the Yoder house. Gets me all freaked out. Maybe it's that I work so much—do you think I work too much?"

"No." He looked blank, at the edge of worry.

She waved a hand through the air to erase it all. "It's fine. We're fine. I mean, but...should I have taken your name? And the separate checking accounts. Lila says feminism's all fine and dandy, but if you want a marriage to work, two people shouldn't try to be equals. Even though I happen to know that *she* makes all the decisions over there. That 'man of the house' crap is just a story she likes to tell—"

"Is this about me?"

"No." She stopped, tried to track where his mind had gone. He could be self-conscious about his lack of a real job in the face of hers. He cobbled together freelance work, brought in decent money. But she always left in the mornings before him and, unless he had band practice or a soccer game in the park, he always beat her home.

"No, I promise." She sighed into a smile, took his hand. He was watching her intently. "Look, just forget I said anything. There's nothing wrong."

"Okay."

"You know, I really was planning to think about the name thing. I just never got around to it."

"I don't care what your name is." His voice was firm, almost tight in his throat. He kissed her cheek and got up to check on dinner.

After they ate, she had just started to wash the dishes when Brad Latham called. She scrubbed while Brad told her how badly he had screwed his case today, how Judge O'Brien was an asshole who had it in for him and maybe he should just quit the entire profession and bag groceries for a living, a career that would perhaps allow him to make it through a day without going catatonic in the restroom from nausea and fear. "I think I'm getting an ulcer," he said, "if I'm lucky. Otherwise it's stomach cancer."

An hour after they had gone to bed that night, something roused her. But her dream had turned the bed to another angle, placed it in her apartment from law school, so she woke caught in that old life, alone with the sound—a faint groaning and popping, like wood under stress in a far room. Her body flooded with instant heat, a train roar in her ears. Through the steady in-and-out of her breathing she slowly climbed back into waking sense and her present life.

Kent's place was empty beside her. The sound was only him. She

got up and followed it into the back room, a kind of study and all-pur-
pose room crowded with books, computers, storage boxes, his weight
bench and her exercise bike. He was pawing through boxes.

"Honey? It's one o'clock in the morning. What are you doing?"

"I couldn't sleep. I'm sorry." On his knees, he shoved aside a box,
looked distractedly at the pile of old junk amassed on the floor before
him. "I came in here to look at that wall." He pointed to the spot he'd
cleared the boxes from. "I want it gone. I want to take down that
wall"—he held his hands palms out to the back of the house, as if to
frame his vision—"and add a sunroom from here maybe, all glass,
looking out on the yard. And a deck off to the side, wrap it around.
Then, see, we can fit stairs here and bump up into the attic, put in a real
master bedroom with a bath. What do you think?"

"Great," she said. "Wonderful. You're taking the wall down tonight?"

He smiled with weary sadness. "I was just going to look at it, I think.
But then I got sidetracked. All these boxes of my old crap. They're just
sitting in here, this big stupid mess. I want to pitch them all out. I should
have done it a long time ago."

Of all Kent's mess, she was truthfully a little fond of the boxes. She
had tried more than once to connect to this part of his life—to get him
to call up old friends from before her time, for instance, let her meet
them. But he didn't seem to keep in touch with anyone. If not for the
evidence of these boxes, she might have imagined he'd come into being
at the moment she met him. He seemed stuck now in some kind of
despair over the project, so she sat on the floor beside him. "Look," he
said. "These are, like, my college notebooks or something!"

She stroked his arm. "Let's go to bed. Leave the boxes. Leave the
wall standing, for tonight at least."

"Okay, you're right. Let me just—" He reached to gather the
things he'd removed into a pitiful stack. "Are you sure you married the
right person? Because, you know, Brad, or Harold...neither one of

them would have brought all this crap into your house. They'd have probably built you a whole new house by now."

She laughed, assured him she didn't need a whole new house or a different mess. But she wondered what had drawn him out of bed at this hour to ponder changes. Was it the silly question she had raised before dinner? Or was he in here making mental blueprints with half a thought to babies, somehow imagining she must want them? Looking at him with the clutter of his old life gathered around him, it struck her how little they knew each other still. She'd had this sense before, as if marriage had not joined them but had only drawn their two lives into a parallel course. They lived in one house and said they loved each other—they did love each other—and they remained strangers.

When they went back to the bedroom, he ducked into his closet, came out with a flattish box the size of his hand. "I know it's not Valentine's Day yet. But I'm not sure about this, so open it now."

He placed the box in her hand, unwrapped, velvet, and her mind began racing past it, leaping ahead to Valentine's Day four days away on the calendar in its allotted place in their lives, and she froze. In the air around her head was barely perceptible crackling, like the ghost flames of her client's vision, and she was afraid to open the box. But she did. It snapped wide on hinges and inside was a silver chain with a very simple diamond pendant that said none of the wonderful things it should have but instead *something is very wrong here* and then *he's having an affair* and she snapped it shut again. "Oh, Kent." She pressed a hand to her mouth. "Why are you giving me this?"

He grinned nervously. "Do you like it? Is it too fancy? You love to look at them so much, I just thought…But I didn't know if you'd really wear it, if something like that would go too much against the Mennonite grain."

Now she was so confused her eyes were welling up, because obviously this man did know her after all, knew her down to the minutiae of her ambivalent longing for the very thing that he had given her. Maybe she did work too much. She was tired, she spent all day around criminals. But this gift was too much, too extravagant, more than he could afford.

"If it's wrong," he said, "I just want to know, so I can fix it before...Oh, hell, I should have just waited. I don't know why I had to bring it out now."

"You hate it," he said—she was openly crying. "And...you hate me." He held her gently by the shoulders, as if reading her mind through this connection. "You, let's see, you can't believe you married the moron who would get you something this vulgar and worldly and expect you to wear it..."

"I love it," she finally managed to say. "It's perfect."

CHAPTER 3

T he knit-cotton jersey, cream and gray, was a size too small, with a faded look reminiscent of boyhood—the sort of thing a twelve-year-old might throw on day after day without a thought—and for this reason Paul selected it from among the others. Trashy, Bernard would say. Look at all the nice shirts you have, the fine material. But he wouldn't stay to hear the professor's opinion. In the mirror, he drew the jersey down over his chest, snug along the slim stretch of his torso. He checked over his shoulder for a tight posterior curve, then went about disarranging his hair to match the model in the Abercrombie and Fitch catalogue folded open beside him. It was over-grown on top (*What's up with this?* Kent had said, lifting a wisp from his eye), and Paul liked the playful, careless way it fell over his forehead, the paler blond of it. He wet his lips in the mirror, looked down and up again with a shy smile. Maybe not twelve, but in the right light he was seventeen. And a virgin.

Professor Falk sat moony and cross in the next room, getting him-self soused on good wine, Chet Baker on the stereo. *God save me*, Paul thought. He was late, and he had a plan, which was to announce his leaving and slip through the door as quick as he could. "I'm going out," he called. But he was stopped in spite of himself by the sight of the man's feet in charcoal-gray mules. The bare, blue-veined, nearly hairless tops of his old-man feet.

"I don't doubt it." The professor was absolutely still on the sofa, drill-bit eyes boring into Paul. His robe with its silk lapels was the same black-red as the wine in his glass, as if matched with care. From the silk cuffs of his pajama legs, his white feet protruded, propped on the ottoman.

Stalled halfway between the sofa and the condo's front door, Paul fidgeted. One hand stole up behind his right ear to pinch a hank of hair like a subway strap. Behind him, he felt the exposure of the wall of glass, the night skyline of Atlanta looming over his shoulder. "Do you want anything?" he asked. "Before I go?"

"No, my dear. Run along." Bernard lifted the glass in toast to his passing. "The boys are waiting."

His smile, a bleary stretch of closed lips, told Paul he'd had enough of the wine already to spend the evening despising him, and Paul couldn't bear to be despised. He'd have to pause to adjust that. Besides, he was mesmerized by the feet. The skin there, waxy, transparent, shockingly loose, appeared little more than a slip-cover for the bone beneath. They seemed to hold a coded message of the man's vulnerability, his looming death.

The rest of him could still convey a hushing authority. Those hawk-browed eyes, goatee the color of gunmetal, razored to a point. What on other men might have seemed flaws—the faint bubbling of ancient scars along his jowls, a head half-bald—looked on him purposeful, the manifestations of greater wisdom and experience than the common man was ever granted. His spine bowed slightly at the top, as if he were too tall to live among men, as if at any moment he might unfold himself and spread great leather wings tipped in claw. But that strength was only a memory now, like Paul's desire, lingering in his atmosphere like a smell. Once Paul had twitched at the man's every blink, measured his own breath by the precise click of his boot heels against the stage floor. Once he had idled through acting exercises, waiting his turn, with fantasies of putting his mouth on that dome of skull-taut skin. "Dr. Falk," he would say, testing the pliant f, the low roll of the l, "um, excuse me, but…Dr. Falk?" Any silly question, for a chance to let his mouth shape the name.

He moved to sit, close enough for his knee to graze the robe-draped thigh. Watching the feet, he could pretend not to be pinned by the glower of indignation Bernard had long turned on the world at large—which had never taken due note of his genius nor treated him as he deserved—and had lately been reserving for Paul. He settled a hand lightly over the top of the nearest foot. It was dry and cool.

"To what do I owe the pleasure?" Bernard's voice was slow and precise, deep and hollow as an enormous bell. If lifted above this lowest decibel, it would fill an auditorium. Paul stroked a thumb over the flaccid blue vein that crossed his ankle, and Bernard swayed forward, as if any small kindness were no more than a door to push through.

"Don't," Paul said. He studied the vein.

The hand lifted toward him stopped and drew back. "Don't what?"

"Talk to me that way, like I'm hurting you." He dropped back to rest his cheek on the cushion beside Bernard's shoulder and blinked up at him, doleful and wounded—the Innocent unfairly accused. *What's your objective in this scene? How do you achieve it? Choose a verb.* Bernard's gaze softened in return, because at least Paul was quiet and sitting close, surrendered to his sphere for the moment. And that quick, Paul was forgiven, adored again.

"Have a little wine before you go."

"How can I? You drank it all." Knowing this would prompt an offer to uncork the next bottle, Paul reached over him and snatched up the glass, tossed back what remained in two gulps. "There," he said, laughing. Bernard looked pained. He caught the dribble of wine from Paul's mouth, brought his dampened fingertips to his tongue.

Paul ignored this sort of thing when he could, but it was getting worse. When he'd first moved in back in the fall, Bernard had been on hormone suppression, and Paul could have danced naked on the dinner table without eliciting more than a moan of concern for the Ethan Allen. Now Bernard had switched to a light course of chemo and the old longings had returned. They stewed visibly in his eyes and emerged in his temper, his reproaches, the way he kept spiteful score of Paul's aloofness and neglect of him—of all his failures of affection. They prompted frequent references to his *health*, that card he'd kept tucked away for so long out of pride.

"My prince," he said. "Remember it?"—and this was another tactic of late, this maudlin reminiscing about Hamlet.

"Don't start with that again. I mean it."

"Why? Why do you hate it? We were beautiful together." The rapture in his face darkened at Paul's silence. "One day, I think you will come to appreciate what I did for you."

Paul ground his teeth. "I did. I do. Just—"

"I mean, truly, appreciate. It will come upon you," he whispered, portentous, mid-scene on his own stage. "It will knock you over."

A part of Paul always listened to this man, and tried now to locate a better attitude. Hamlet, after all, had been the brightest moment of his life, the best thing he'd ever done. And to be chosen by Bernard Falk, who had waited his teaching career for a worthy lead, was probably— he knew this—a higher honor than he could deserve. But Bernard spoiled it somehow by speaking of it. *My prince*—he meant it mainly as reminder of all the nights they had stayed late to fornicate on the stage and in the costume room and the orchestra pit. That, too, had been an honor, Bernard's esteem and his lust two halves of the same rigorous aesthetic. For a student, it was a rare thing to be endorsed by both. But now, unable to lay his finger on the crime, Paul felt vaguely misused. Maybe he only despised his naïve self and how awed he had been, starved for any little indication of the master's approval. Or he wanted to keep what was good about the past to himself, not have it twisted into another whip to reproach him with.

"Fine," Bernard said at Paul's silence, mouth tight—and now he was the wounded one. Slick. It seemed he had little better to do these days than calculate such moves, one more black mark on his scoreboard against Paul. His long-fingered hand passed in a lingering way over Paul's shoulder, critiquing the texture of the shirt. "Not hoping to impress anyone, I guess."

Paul smiled faintly. "Why wear a good shirt I'm just going to peel off and pitch in a corner?" He locked his eyes on Bernard's with a little sexual heat that kept Bernard looking back, made him swallow his anger at the words and lean in for more.

"You're becoming a little cruel, you know." But with Paul so close, allowing the touch to continue, the words would not sharpen; they sounded almost like admiration. *That's right*, Paul thought. *Your turn to lick my boots.* But he felt more sadness than pleasure in the power.

They had been close once. In the fall, it had seemed they could talk for hours—it was nearly friendship—and there was a lot, still, that Paul would have learned from him. Now all he wanted most days was to get out the door with minimal harassment. But he didn't see much use in apologizing for his contempt when Bernard was too lust-addled with simple proximity to notice it anymore.

As if on cue, Chet started in on "My Funny Valentine." Smiling drunkenly, Bernard said, "Get that good shiraz from the rack, why don't you? You can try a glass."

"I can't. I'm picking up Eric and Sylvie. And I'm late." He fetched the bottle and the corkscrew, set them on the table. "Save me some and I'll have it later."

Bernard resumed his pout. "I'm afraid that might be out of the question."

"Don't sit here and drink all night, okay? It's not good for you."

"Let me worry about that." Bernard's jaw rippled as if contending with a sour taste, and his eyes dropped. "I don't think you need reminding that I'm a grown man, with rather few pleasures left. Now run along to your good time."

Paul let out a breath. For half a second, he considered staying. This was the servitude the man had reduced him to in recent days, by starting to allow cancer into the room with them, invoking the near future with *Perhaps it's time to travel* or *Soon I may need...* How could he leave a dying man? But Bernard had heard the bitterness in his own words, and he added more lightly, "Be careful, will you? And lock the door."

"Okay." Paul lifted a set of keys from the hook and rattled them. Dr. Falk disdained to turn his head. "I'm taking the Benz."

"Fine, do as you like."

Leaving him should have been pure joy—his friends aboard, the lit city reeling past the windows of a silver Mercedes with glove-leather interior. It wasn't Paul's fault the accolades had passed Bernard by, left him nailed to the cross of academia, parroting Stanislavski to the bored and talentless youth of Georgia until he became old and died, unloved and unappreciated.

Not *died*. Will die. Willdiewilldiewilldie.

"Honey, don't let him get to you." Sylvie's fingertips fussed around the edges of her perfect make-up in the visor mirror. With lemon yellow hair pasted in cake-frosting curls along the sides of her round face, she was the kind of adorable that would be called chubby if she gained five more pounds.

Eric leaned up between them from the back seat. "How'd you get stuck nurse-maiding that geezer anyway? I don't get it."

"Duh, what's to get?" Sylvie retorted. "Where's *your* Mercedes?"

"But really, so what?" Eric reached to tilt the rearview mirror so he could touch his already arranged and frozen hair, then admire his cheekbones and heavy-lidded gaze. "There's such a thing as your own life. You shouldn't have to dwell on death at age twenty-one, I say. Or money."

"Aw, isn't he noble?" Sylvie pinched Eric's chin and planted three tiny smooches on the side of his mouth. He dove over the seat in response and kissed the exposed swell of her cleavage, which made her shriek and shove him off. Last time Paul had checked, Eric was gay, but ever since those two had moved in together they'd been awfully kissy with each other. It was annoying in a way he couldn't quite define.

Sylvie rubbed his arm. "You're so quiet! This is really bothering you."

He fought off a quick blur like the threat of tears, and with it an impulse to stop the car and eject them both onto Peachtree Street so he could have some peace. They were headed to Crush, a huge, noisy, crowded club, and he was in the wrong mood. "I need something," he told Sylvie. "What've you got?"

"What, like an Advil?" She unclasped her purse, and then gave him a closer, sidelong inspection. "I have some X…"

"Maybe," he said, then shook his head, though he'd meant something like that. A shift, a bump, a change.

"Hey, hey!" Eric whooped. "Girl's holding out on me!"

She smacked his hand away. "I've only got one, and you owe me already. Paul"—she dangled a tiny ziplock with a white pill inside—

"it's yours if you want it."

"He doesn't want it, he doesn't do X. Split it with me! Girlfriend, please!"

"Okay, fine. But you're buying them next, cause know what? *I* ain't your sugar daddy."

"Sugar mama." He poked at her until she grinned. She bit the tablet in two and handed him half.

It was the end of February, the weather mild with a foretaste of spring, and they had the windows rolled down a few inches. Madonna's *Ray of Light* played cool and soft and somehow maternal from the CD player. The Fox Theater was in golden spangles, headlights sliding toward them like whispers and promises and they were so much a part of it all in their own fine lights that he should have felt better than this.

"What am I supposed to do, seriously?" He turned left down Ponce. "The man's a vacuum for attention. It's like, I have to ration it."

"Don't give him anything," Sylvie said. "What does he expect? You live there. That's what he wanted, right? That's the deal."

"Yeah." She was right. He was only supposed to share the condo like a roommate. At most, he stood nearby at public appearances and smiled benignly while Bernard petted him and called him his protégé in leering, suggestive tones. The whole charade had been necessitated by the hormone suppression, that brief season when Bernard's missing libido had left him feeling he had something to prove.

"It's like this," Paul said. "He wants me, I hold him off. It's like the natural order. If I stayed home, he'd flip. He wouldn't know what to do but put his hands on me, and we don't need to have *that* scene."

"Girl," Eric said, switching into his comic queeny-mode, "hell, I say fuck nobility. If he's putting *me* in the will, he can put his hands any damn where he likes!"

Paul stifled a laugh. "There's no will. I'm not in the will!"

"Of course there's a will! And what makes you think you're not?

Who else is he leaving all that to?"

Paul squirmed. "I don't know, but not me. He's got nieces, and he's involved in all kinds of charity stuff. Foundations and...Trust me, he wouldn't give it to me. He's got more sense." They fell into silence, in which they all watched this prospect of inheritance settle down upon Paul like a robe, like magic. The amount and source of the assets were largely mysterious to Paul, and uninteresting, but he knew some portion had come by way of a former lover who had died—"years before you were *born*," Bernard liked to say with snide hyperbole—an artist whose paintings adorned every wall and whose gifts and possessions about the condo Bernard would nod toward with dewy-eyed fondness.

"He's not rich," Paul said. "He just believes in nice things. It's part of his, whatever, ethic. Philosophy."

"Well, that ain't no poor man's philosophy, you know what I'm saying?"

"I don't want his money!" Paul cried out, alarmed. "I want—" But he couldn't finish the sentence.

"That's good," Sylvie chimed in, nodding like a shrink. "What *do* you want?"

The answer was almost there before him, hazy, his father in it somewhere like a nonsensical appearance in a dream, and the house in remote Greene County that he hardly ever visited anymore. But home was the last thing he wanted, that place where he didn't fit right and never had.

"He's not dying, anyway," Paul said. "He's fine. He's probably healthier than me."

"Why, what's wrong with you?"

"Nothing's wrong with me. I mean, he's in remission. So, like, he's probably going to live another twenty years, and by then I'll be far too old to interest him." The truth of the prospect struck Paul like a slap, along with a brief, queasy image—himself somewhere past forty, abandoned, unattractive to anyone. "Oh, god, how depressing is that?"

"Work it, baby!" Eric shouted out the car window at a group of college-age guys on the sidewalk headed toward the club.

"I want Kent," Paul said, so softly that Sylvie made him repeat it. "I said I want Kent. I want my damn boyfriend."

"Who, the married one?" Eric and Sylvie exchanged a glance. Eric patted Paul's head and chuckled. "You sure know how to pick 'em, you know that? Old men with cancer, married men. For real, Paul, it's not like you don't have options. I see who you hook up with—like, say, that guy last week, who was plenty hot, and young, and maybe even semi-available—"

Paul whipped the steering wheel toward a side street and hit the gas, so that Eric grabbed both headrests. "Whoa, girl, where we going?"

The new road before them was deserted and hilly, lined with warehouses. They flew over a set of train tracks, and Sylvie and Eric braced themselves in their seats, openmouthed. "We got time, right? This is my new way. Crush by way of the Edgewood detour." He felt a wicked thrill at the power of the engine, the reckless speed like floating, danger and direction and passengers all subject to his whim. A Benz, he figured, had the right to its own traffic laws.

No one spoke during the trip. Paul slowed a little, turning left here and right there, half by instinct, on roads he didn't know though he drove as if he knew them. Several minutes later, he parked at a curb. The street was narrow, lined with close-set, one-story wooden houses that had been shabby ten years ago but were now loved again, restored in colors like sage, pink, white, lavender, turquoise. With its rocking-chair porches and arty wind chimes and flags, the neighborhood exuded an air of determined cheer, a hint of self-congratulation. Kent's gray sedan was at the opposite curb directly in front of their house. Cars were parked along both sides of the road; Paul didn't know which one was hers.

The front yard was tight to the sidewalk, planted with a hodge-podge of bushes instead of grass and enclosed in a low, peeling white-picket fence. A flagstone path led from the gate to the porch, five steps up. The front door was armored in the kind of wrought-iron security gate meant to look like decoration. Matching bars, tipped in a series of ornate spikes, crossed the lower half of both front windows. Hers, Paul thought. She would have insisted on such pretty precaution.

"Now what?" Eric, faintly snide, broke the long silence that had come over the car. "You could go ring the bell. Ask him if he wants to come out and play with us."

"Shut up, Eric," Sylvie murmured. He slumped back in the seat.

Paul closed them out, stared at the house, one hand set against his mouth. Along the two front windows, heavy-looking white curtains were drawn shut. Behind the left one was a light.

"There's nothing to see!" Eric insisted, as if to a child.

It might have been the TV room and they were in it together, just behind the curtain, sharing the sofa. Or they were getting ready for bed, engaged in the routine of every night that required no thought and ended in the slow, warm inevitability of their bodies coming together beneath familiar sheets. Perhaps he moved toward her tonight, slipped a hand beneath her nightgown. But Paul thought not. In drifting off to sleep, he might roll against her back, almost accidentally, slide his arm around her waist, bend his knee into the crook of hers, without fully waking or stirring a thought of sex. They shared a bed, Paul was sure, with the cozy, desireless intimacy of siblings. It was that kind of mar-riage—though Kent wouldn't say so, wouldn't tell him anything about it, and Paul had never seen them together. He'd seen her only once, a glimpse from behind.

"She's not that pretty," he said, nibbling the nail of his index finger.

Sylvie lit a cigarette. She blew smoke through the gap in her window and leaned over to rub his thigh. "Aw, sweetie."

It was the fact that he slept. Paul couldn't stand it. Once, it had been otherwise, back when Kent had lain awake beside her thinking of him, trying not to think, trying to relax and not fidget, then trying not to wake her as he rose to shut himself in the bathroom. This much he had told Paul, knowing he would like it. But now he felt the sleep in the house. And knew with bitter burning conviction that this sleep was also because of him, because Kent had given in to him and called him twice or three times a week, in the late morning or afternoon. He said *now*, and they met somewhere sleazy and fucked.

Sylvie passed him her cigarette, cupping his hand to steady it. After a lungful of smoke, he felt calmer.

Eric, who couldn't bear silence, entertained himself by making random chocking sounds with his tongue. "You should get rid of the wife," he suggested, his tone sincere and helpful. He leaned up close to Paul's shoulder. "Hire a hit man. Or, you know, there's always the phone. Call her up one day and tell her how hubby likes cock. Bet that would shake things up."

Paul frowned at the lit window. "He doesn't like cock. He just likes me."

"Well," Eric laughed, "you got a cock or not?"

Depends on how you look at it, Paul thought. Sylvie cut in— "Eric!"—waved him off like a gnat. "Paul, honey, don't start listening to that kind of shit, okay? Things like that can get in your head. But if there's anything I've figured out in this world, it's that the married ones stay married. No matter what they say, or who they fuck. Or how great *you* are."

Sylvie's touchstone for this and most of life was a tortured affair with her father's tennis partner when she was sixteen—an experience she related mainly in dark allusions as if her friends were all too familiar with the epic poem of the thing, recorded somewhere in her own teenage blood and spanning several diaries. But she had emerged a "stronger person," or so the story went, as well as a self-professed authority on straight men and married men and basically all men. As far as Paul knew, she didn't date, didn't go out anywhere with anyone except to the gay bars with them—and it wasn't to dance with women, either. He and Eric had nudged her to try the lesbian thing, half teasing, without luck. She was content to let her male friends have all the sex and to remain their advisor as needed.

"You don't know him," he told her firmly. "Believe me. He's not some closet case out for a thrill. We were together for two years before she came along."

He liked the sound of this as he spoke it, even if the accuracy wobbled a bit. It had the ring of a higher truth. Yet Eric and Sylvie mulishly refused to grasp the significance of history until Paul wanted to beat them both with a switch. "We go deeper than marriage, that's all," he said. "You can't possibly understand."

Silence again, and Paul sank further into his seat. He didn't know what he wanted here, maybe just to see the light go off. But it didn't, and he began to feel the pointlessness of lingering. Whatever he was doing, he didn't need Eric and Sylvie along in the first place. He flicked on the headlights. "Okay, boys and girls, that concludes our tour of heteroworld for this evening."

"Thank god," said Eric. "I so prefer to make an exit before the cops show up."

Paul eased from the curb and they were on the road. He was surprised to feel only relief in leaving, to shake loose of whatever hook had drawn him here and free himself again to the night and the open city.

Before Kent's return, Paul hadn't spent much time thinking of the past. "What next?" was a more interesting question, or better, "Who next?" He'd be caught up in infatuated romps for a week or two, a month at most, before his sight-hound attention was on to new quarry.

There was only Kent.

He still didn't know why, what it was about this one man. Something in the puzzle of his sexuality, perhaps, had kept Paul interested at first. Kent was his own creature: not closeted, nor bisexual, exactly; if a label fit at all, he was simply, senselessly, straight. For a time, Paul had made a campaign of this nonsense—casting aspersions, pushing politics and pop psychology, swatting him with slogans over the breakfast table. Kent yawned, lifted mildly amused brows. He didn't have a "sexuality question," he insisted. "I'm just very into you right now. It doesn't matter to me that you're a boy." (To which Paul, vexed, had responded, "It doesn't matter a little?") Back then, Kent's greatest concern in life had been the garage band he played in with Paul's stepbrother. The four guys in the band could make an evening of a case of beer, slumped around for hours in someone's shithole apartment, watching a game or talking about bands—what to name theirs, whose last CD had been far superior to whatever the hell until Paul wanted to kill himself. They were a bunch of straight guys. No way around it. The only thing about Kent that didn't fit was his being unbothered by the gender of the person he had lately decided to share a bed with.

And he was amazingly good in bed. Which was baffling, to the point that Paul asked him repeatedly how it could be so different with him, so much more intense. "Well, you're emotionally involved," Kent suggested once. "Maybe you should try it more."

It was true—they were in love, the experience as novel for Paul as it was for Kent. Seducing one of his stepbrother's crowd after a few beers had been an appealing challenge, no real shock. But when his homophobic jerk of a brother's best bud started calling him baby and doing his laundry and asking what he wanted for dinner, that was a different script altogether. He had not been fortified against the change.

One night became another, three, four, a year, and they were established. Their home was together. He had a boyfriend.

The crush of love propelled him through weeks, months, when he
had no real interest in other men. Through morning classes, he
dreamed of his boyfriend. Together they were one soul, curled into
each other and sealed inviolable somewhere above the gritty world
where Paul wandered in the in-between times for tricks.

He refused to lie about this, to obfuscate or apologize. "You work
all day," he argued, "you have your band, you go off and do things
without me. What's the difference? It doesn't affect *us*, what I do with
other people."

They were so happy at times it was easy to forget how miserable
they were, all the yelling, throwing things, the countless break-ups.
The quiet days. The boredom. Worse, the fear of boredom to come,
which was killing for Paul. Over time, Kent had coaxed him to slow
down his guerilla-style assaults and linger over his lover's body, to
postpone the climax, to wind out pleasure like a kite string. But Paul
never fully escaped his youthful conviction that in a moment's stillness,
an eyeblink, his lover might look away, then rise and leave him. So he
kept moving.

The violence of jealousy was satisfying, in a way. It verified love.
No matter what broke between their hands, their union remained separate, untouchable—Paul felt this as truth, so that even when he was the
one storming off on *never again,* meaning it too, he knew they were forever and without end.

He was eighteen, turned nineteen.

"Then I grew up," was how he put it sometimes with dry scorn,
though he rarely found reason to tell this story. Why dwell on the past?
It had been surprisingly easy to leave for good—building for a long
time, yet it seemed to him now a day's whim, a sophomore-year
transfer and a simple walking into a fresh new life. In Atlanta, he never

found time or reason for missing Kent. With so many new people, new places to explore, he reveled in the weightless freedom of having no one at home to report to and make him feel like crap for wanting to live a little.

He kept memory in a shoebox in the attic of his new life, until the day Kent appeared in the flesh. Slow at first, then a tumble, a whirl. He'd been unprepared for the effect of sudden meeting and staggered with it, felt as if time and space peeled apart around them and all the air was sucked from the room along with the books and shelves and librarians and sleepy students all *whoosh* gone out the windows, leaving only the two of them, eye to eye. And he remembered then what his gut had never forgotten: the uncracked sphere of them where nothing ended.

But there was the need to breathe again, to locate speech and pass off some normal-sounding words. Small talk between the library shelves, as if they were two people. Kent looked good—clean-shaven now, a few more pounds. Paul closed in, read the yes in his eyes, unmistakable, though he was busy mumbling something vapid about his job. In one locked gaze and less than half a minute, they were in the library men's room.

When telling the story to Eric and Sylvie, according to the genre requirements of the sexual exploit, he'd highlighted the sandpaper irony of what followed: "So there we are. Not a word, mind you, no debate. He shoves me against the inside of a stall door, fucks me standing, and my-hand-to-God he moans in my ear, 'I always wanted you this way.'"

"You mean standing?" Sylvie had asked.

He rolled his eyes at Eric. "No, girl. Keep up now. He meant in a bathroom stall, if you can believe that one. I swear, I could have whipped around right there and knocked the shit out of him too, after all he put me through on the topic of me being a skank."

But he had not reacted, there in the stall, and he never told the rest of the story—how he'd been too caught up reveling in the still-familiar smell and the feel of this body, stunned with Kent's presence, knowing it would end in mere minutes and they would tug up their jeans awkwardly and say very little before they left in their separate directions and never saw each other again, because what else could happen? Only, maybe, that Kent would never come and they could stay trapped forever in some kind of glorious loop, in the act that seemed to have transported them instantly back into the ecstatic and fragile happiness of certain rare late hours in bed. Kent was saying his name, in a voice that told Paul he must have felt, too, the illusion of a vanished time that itself would vanish in seconds; Paul moaned in response, and then, in the last remains of thrusting and grunting, his eyes fell on Kent's hand pressed up against the wall, and there was a gold band around his finger.

And time stopped after all. He felt that ring drop into the center of him, and rings upon rings rippled out from it like water. It sank down and took the place of the sphere that was them, and now, six weeks later, there it sat. It would not be moved.

The Crush parking lot was full, so Paul drove around until he found a spot down the block and back on a side street. It was another neighborhood of close-set houses, but these were two-story, more affluent, with tall shade trees that gave an intimate feel to the dark. In the nearest house, a light back in the kitchen revealed with absolute clarity a hanging basket of onions and, below it, the edge of a table, a little piece of someone else's life lit richly like a painting.

"Look, we're in the suburbs," Eric said. "How charming. Let's all get married and move here."

"Oh, don't even say that." Paul reached over the seat to cuff Eric's head with rough affection, seized hold of Sylvie's hand. "Listen, you guys. You're like my best friends, really. I mean that, even though we've only known each other six months."

Sylvie patted his cheek and simpered, "We love you too, puddin'."

"So that means if you ever hear me start talking about buying a house or settling down or calling some man my husband, or any kind of idiotic shit like that, you have to promise to get a gun and shoot me on the spot. Can you do that? In fact, just to be safe, shoot me when I turn thirty. We should make a pact."

"Done, honey," Eric said, distracted by his X kicking in. "Let's move, I gotta move."

Inside Crush, they dispersed—Eric for the dance floor, Sylvie for the bar, Paul for his fishing pier on the landing of the stairs. Overlooking one of the vast dance floors, the railed platform was halfway between up and down, an uncertain pause that nestled to one wall, where Paul—uncertain boy, his role of the moment—could set his back.

Later the straight suburbanite tourists would arrive and hammer themselves into every chink until it would count as anyone's feat of courage to cross the room. But at this hour, the club was merely full, the floor below undulant with bodies and washed in red. Mostly men. Madonna again, like an evening companion, from the eighties now, played from the DJ's booth, and the dancers waved their arms in exultation, ripples over the crowd surface.

"Hi, there. Need a guide?" Close-cropped hair, savvy eyes, younger than his usual catch from this spot. Tight shirt, tight beneath. Two cherries bobbed in the dark drink in his hand. Paul had been gazing up into the constellations of tiny white lights that glittered far in the blackness of the ceiling, as if he had never seen such wonder, and the guy leaned close and pointed into them. "That's Ursa major. Orion's belt."

Paul blinked. "You know stars."

"I'm Tyler. Available for any sort of tour you might need." He insinuated cool fingers into Paul's hand. "Lemme guess. Emory, freshman, majoring in...Undecided."

Paul grinned, looked down. "Uh, sure. Paul. Freshman. In college."

Tyler flung his head back in mock horror. "High school? Oh, lordy-lord. You eighteen, at least?"

"Of course," Paul said, eyes round. "At least."

"Ever been to a gay bar before?"

"Oh, yeah. Sure. Is this a gay bar?"

"Now you're playing with me." He bent close to finger a seam that ran along Paul's shoulder as if he were making a necessary or helpful adjustment. "You want to see my apartment?"

"Is that on the tour?"

"It's close. Bet I have something there for you—help you decide."

Tyler was thirty or so, and in Paul's categorical system he was tabbed instantly as a diversion, drama-free. By the time Sylvie had circled back to find him, Tyler's hands were parked almost chastely, politely, on Paul's hips, while his tongue nudged toward Paul's tonsils.

"I see you found a friend."

He might have introduced her, except that names were hardly the point, unworthy of a pause, and he couldn't bear to break the kiss. He was already falling in love with it.

"No one ever kisses me!" She lolled her head along his shoulder.

He hooked an arm around her and parted from Tyler to give her a damp, lingering smooch at the hairline. "Kiss Sylvie," he commanded, and Tyler obliged at the opposite cheek. Told her she was cute, too, before Paul leaned in again to halt the chit chat. With one hand he turned Sylvie by the shoulder and sent her on her way.

Outside, the night sky was hazy brown, the stars invisible. Tyler's place was close enough that they could dash down a street, around a corner, up a rickety exterior flight of stairs, and arrive before feeling they'd truly left the club. Paul felt as if he'd teleported to this room over someone's garage, in a giddy absence of decision.

"It's, like, this family downstairs." Tyler gasped—they had run all the way. "The house, I mean. It's totally separate. Mom and Dad and little kids. Nice folks."

"You rent from them?"

"Yeah." They were in each other's arms again, Tyler slipping the shirt up from Paul's waistband as he danced him backward around the room. "This is the kitchen"—a counter with a sink, a hot plate, a toaster oven—"the bathroom"—he indicated a door—"living room, *solarium*"—he nodded to the window, a low shelf of books—"the library. And the bedroom." The bed—a mattress and box spring on the floor—sat rumpled in a corner of the only room there was.

"Cozy," Paul said. On one wall, a mantle with no fireplace held framed photographs of smiling strangers. Several featured Tyler and a beautiful brown-haired girl, the two of them wind-tossed and cheek-to-cheek like a honeymoon.

"It's all I need." Tyler grinned contentedly. "We could sit"—they veered toward a sofa, which was buried in piles of clothes—"but, well, it's laundry day. Oh, here's a spot." They tumbled onto the bed, Paul flat on his back, giggling breathlessly.

"You're more like twenty, aren't you?" Tyler said.

"I'm whatever you want."

"Okay. How 'bout you—what do you want? Looking for a daddy? Want me to take care of you?" Tyler was sliding into a role of his own, one he was too young and slim to pull off with much conviction, and Paul tried to conceal his displeasure. Still in their clothes, and the first sour taste of boredom already upon them.

"You wanna be my little boy?"

"No," Paul said, almost sharply, the bright bubble of his desire scooting from reach—he might have heaved up off the bed and left.

But he knew the moment would pass, and it did, as he softened his voice with kisses along Tyler's neck. "No. I just want you to get naked."

⤙

"You ever feel like you're becoming an expert on Atlanta real estate?"

Paul was shooting rattlesnakes at the bar, feeling philosophical, but Eric was not the best of conversationalists when twirling on G, which he was probably still imbibing from his squirt bottle of blue Gatorade, on top of the X and anyone's guess what else.

"Oh my god, last night"—he'd told this story earlier—"I was in some *double-wide* in Alpharetta. Tackiest furniture you ever saw."

"And you got tied to the tacky headboard and spanked?"

"How did you know?" Eric shoved him away roughly, then grabbed him back in both arms, his mouth to Paul's cheek. "Dance with me, sailor." He humped Paul's hip.

"Dance with yourself, freak. And get that off of me."

But he followed Eric to the dance floor anyway, to escape the man who was ordering the rattlesnakes—George Babbish, with his short-man's military bearing and his eyes that looked forever on the verge of weeping. Part-owner of the club, and other "spaces" as he called them, he was nearly always a sentinel over the scene from his corner of the bar. It was hard to talk to him he was so shy, but whenever he saw Paul, at any distance, he stared with the sort of unabashed helpless lust that tended to draw Paul, against his best efforts, into its orbit. It was the way pedophiles looked at beautiful children, the way Bernard looked at him in unguarded moments, the way men in the cars of his youth had stared, never moving their eyes until they let him back out on the side of the road. Most of them were middle-aged, unattractive. Half of them married or closeted. They were too easy. But the desire of such men,

Paul knew, was the only pure thing in the world—unmixed with self-regard or the smallest suspicion, even postcoital, that the blond vision before them might be human and flawed. It was worship, nothing less. And worship was a bad drug for Paul, the one he had the most trouble resisting.

In darkness, men moved without going anywhere, languid and sinuous, frantic or spaced out, packed close against each other in a breathless humidity of cologne and sweat. Swift blades of light, timed to the pulses of circuit house music, sliced through the crowd to illuminate bare arms and shoulders and the eyes that passed over him, over others, everyone sampling everyone. George's eyes were on him—Paul couldn't help checking.

"Uncut, you know," Eric said in his ear. "About eight inches, mmm-hmmm."

"No shit! And you know this how?"

"Oh, honey, please. You can have all the elderly, okay?" He took a long swallow from his bottle. "Goes to my gym. Believe it or not, he can benchpress, like, one-eighty. Not bad for an old fart who's otherwise kinda pathetic."

"He's only forty-something," Paul protested, before he could stop himself—he had no business with any thoughts that involved George Babbish naked. George had once sent him anonymous roses backstage, had yet to so much as kiss him on the cheek. He didn't do one-nighters.

Paul danced at Eric's shoulder, scanning the opposite horizon for a better object for his thoughts, then forgot about it, eyes closed, the music moving in his body. He revolved, the crowd spinning to streaks of red light around him and, across the room, there was Kent. Or for a few seconds he thought it was Kent, really him, as if desire might be powerful enough to draw him up from the marriage bed and straight to this room, as if finding Paul would require nothing so mundane and earthbound as knowing where to look. But the man turned his head, became a stranger, and Paul's throat dried, feet stopped at the center of the room.

He needed water, that was all. George had his next rattlesnake ready, even better, like a shot of chocolate milk, and he steadied himself with a forearm on the bar, smoothing the sweat back from his forehead. "Are all your clubs this noisy?" he shouted to George after a minute.

Facing the crowd, George should have set a balancing hand on Paul's back as he leaned toward his ear, but now as always he held back from touch. "We just opened a new piano bar on Tenth. A nice little space. I'd like it if you came by some night."

"Maybe I will."

He wasn't sure if there was anything to want from this man. But he felt an urge toward some brand of contact beyond mere conquest. Here was a man, however strange, who kept Paul's name close, might have whispered it before sleep like a spell. A tight turn aligned him crotch to hip with George, who looked down into his drink.

When George met his eyes again, with silent plea, Paul said, "You know I can't be your boyfriend."

His face hardened. "That old man doesn't deserve you. I get so angry thinking about him with you."

Over some weeks, in the abbreviated exchanges permitted by club noise, Paul had given the impression that he was kept, and he saw no reason to correct it. It was all bar talk, the language of attraction over shot glasses, and Paul had let him believe further, because he had wanted to believe, that Paul was vaguely unhappy, that Bernard mistreated him in murky, inexpressible ways. The quick flare of response in George's eyes had reminded him of Kent, just a little—those lightning protective impulses. It had driven Paul crazy back then, that Kent refused to believe he could take care of himself, but now the memory could sneak up on him and leave him gasping with remorse, wondering why he'd put up such a fight. To have someone worry whether he was safe suddenly seemed a rare, sweet thing.

"I might leave him," he said.

These were just words, he'd thought, more fodder for his character: doe-eyed waif in thrall to what might be a monster. Audrey in *Little Shop of Horrors*. But his heart pounded in his throat, and George set a hand on his shoulder. As if the words might be true, Paul swallowed and blinked—imagined running through rain-drenched streets, escaping in secret. Taking up with George, little flashes of bed and bar life.

And the fiction had compelled George to break his rule—the hand on Paul's shoulder, comforting. It was an offer to save him.

"Do you want to go somewhere and talk?"

"No, no," he said, trying to smile it off, but he wanted to cry. The honest concern in George's eyes made him hate himself, bow his head so he wouldn't have to see it. But he wanted so much to be saved. He swayed closer, until George's thumb was an almost imperceptible touch under his ear. "I'm sorry," he mumbled. "I have to go home."

It was still full night, five a.m., when he dropped off his friends and returned home alone. *Home*—an odd word for Bernard's tower of glass. After six months, he still had to remind himself he lived there. The sky seemed darker now, but still no stars. Light pollution, it was called, the way city lights came between him and the whole galaxy above.

When he had lived in Greene County, on nights he made it back home from his teenage explorations with time to spare before curfew, he would lie back in the grass and find the Big Dipper, the Little Dipper, Orion's belt, all of it so bright and alive in the depth of black, all seeming so close. Since long before he could name the constellations, they had been his, at one with his notion of God—Jesus living in his heart, a lesser residence. His God of the night sky was a beautiful man with streaming hair and a gnarled and knotted body made of stars, poised over him with a stern, possessive gaze, and more than man, a disembodied sensation of everything—the air, the world, his life—that brushed his skin like warm breath. Praying as a child had been the same as thinking, and even as a teenager flopped drunkenly on the spinning grass, he continued to feel that presence among the constellations, though he'd been exiled from God's house and had forgotten how to pray.

If he were back home now, his father would be rising to start his day, would take his coffee out onto the porch of the old house, and even in the gray light of dawn his stars would be more visible than these. Or perhaps his father had lost the habit, altered his morning routine. Paul wouldn't know. They didn't talk much anymore.

Upstairs, he dropped his jacket on a chair, hung the car keys beside the door. The second bottle was empty on the table. Bernard was passed out on the sofa with the lights on, his mouth open against a cushion to emit soft, whuffling snores. "Bernard," Paul said. He leaned close. "Bernie?"

The blanket over his legs had slumped to one side, leaving his feet exposed, and Paul adjusted it to cover them. The act made him feel unbearably tender and deprived, flickered forward into some future after the man's death. Paul wanted to talk to him. He half wanted to kiss him. What he really wanted to do, more than anything, was curl up and sleep in his arms, though if Bernard had been awake Paul would have gone straight back to his own bed without ever forming the notion. But he was asleep, so Paul clicked off the lamp and lay down beside him, settled his head on the meatless bone of the man's thigh. Bernard snored on, undisturbed. Paul closed his eyes and tried to sleep.

CHAPTER 4

By the determined dip and rise from her side of the mattress, he knew when she was up—usually before the alarm went off, and at the same moment, he imagined, as she woke. Awake and rise, like a beatitude, the consummation telegraphed through a seam in his dream, and next the post-shower snicky padding of her bare feet on the hardwood and the flowery water-smell of her hair, as if the shower had taken no time. Through the soft chiming of hangers, the sliding on of clothes, he dozed, and when his eyes finally opened of their own accord, there was no more trace of her in the room than the indentation of her pillow. As if it were a shrine, he admired the shape of the hollow place and didn't touch it, feeling thankful for this proof of her, the invariable heaviness of her head.

Most days by the time he reached the kitchen, she would be gone to work, the ticking coffee pot half-full, crumbs and a wadded napkin on the table, and he would stall there, muss-haired in his robe, forgetful of what might draw him into the day without her. *Today I have a wife*, he would tell himself, *and she has left these adorable crumbs*, for he glimpsed in every small detail the ghost of a future without her.

Today she was there herself, along with her crumbs, a coffee cup and plate beside her, papers spread. Her presence banished fear, as did the unregarded bagel tilting from her fingers, the reading glasses perched on her nose with their dark, bold rims like something a child would draw—frumpy-chic, she called them, sassy glasses. Slutty librarian glasses, he called them, though she would not have made the casting call for that porn flick, not even for his private viewing. Such fantasies went dark before they started—his own hand, if not hers, over the projector's lens.

"Hi, you," she said, her morning voice gravelly. Her hair was still damp, folded in curls around her ears, and she gave him a playful, crooked smile. "Did you know you talk in your sleep?"

"What?" He ruffled his hair. "What did I say?"

"It was a whole speech or something. It was very strange."

"You're kidding." He turned away for coffee, heart pounding. "So, go on. Was I profound or what?"

"It was just mumbling, whispering. I couldn't make it out." Her look was especially keen, knife points in her black eyes, and for a breath he felt like a cornered witness on her stand. But she bit her bagel, moved on to everyday things—she had a church meeting that night, remember, and don't forget to get bananas from the store, and oh, did she mention that she was being interviewed on CNN next Tuesday? Because with Maggie the everyday was often packed this easily into the same bag with the remarkable.

⸚

Three years before, when the pillow he woke beside was bent to the contours of Paul's face, he reached for it automatically, flipped a corner, punched it back to buoyancy, and stroked the creases free.

Often, he washed the sheets and made the bed, restoring it to a bodiless state. Erasure pleased him, so deeply that it might have been his own four-square life being cleansed and remade, or simply, on a lazy morning, shaken back into smoothness—like Paul's pillow, waiting for nothing but the certainty of being marked by him, again, and soon.

Kent kept a cubicle in each of the two office suites where he was currently on contract, indefinite freelance jobs where he designed websites and solved the problems that arose. Neither job was permanent. Most of the people in these cool green and beige places without real walls didn't know his name and he didn't know theirs. He wasn't entirely sure what these companies did, though one had to do with online investment and the other with credit—helping potential lenders decide who was worth the risk.

Often, there was little for him to do. Because of the nature of his contract, he could have gone home—could have, in fact, done most of what work there was from his home computer, but he felt the need to put in an appearance. To be at work, like the sort of husband his father's life had prepared him to be.

Lately, he spent hours playing Minesweeper. Practice taught the patterns revealed in the numbered blocks, so that he could flag a mine, open the surrounding blocks, flag another mine in rapid mouse clicks without pausing for thought. He could now whip through the expert level, ninety-nine hidden bombs, in a little over two minutes. An exploded mine ended the game, and the presiding smiley face frowned, eyes ex-ed.

It was a stupid, pointless, mind-numbing game. It made his back stiff, made his eyes water and cross. But he couldn't stop. At the end of each game, he had only to click the yellow face, and it smiled again, blank and innocent as before. The game returned to its clean, covered grid, the mines waiting beneath in their random patterns ready to be mapped, and he couldn't resist. He began again.

The first of February, and Kent stood before the impenetrable burnished bolted door of Paul's building. It seemed like months since their beach trip, though it had been only two weeks, and to continue now was beyond possibility. There had been one slip, but it didn't count—a meeting of less than thirty minutes in a shabby room Paul had picked. Kent barely remembered getting there, had been so distracted by the intensity of his guilt that the sex was mechanical, joyless, incomplete, so unquestionably bad that he had ended up apologizing in monotone, "For everything. For today. For calling you in the first place. For letting this happen at all. It won't happen again, I promise."

Five long days, and he was dialing the phone, now mashing the buzzer at Paul's building. Paul eventually pushed out and stood before him, arms crossed.

"You hung up on me."

"I thought I was doing you a favor," Paul said. His hair stuck up a little on one side, and his eyes were squinty with recent sleep, though it was noon and a weekday.

"Don't just hang up on me. I wouldn't call you if I didn't need to see you."

"Need. Go home to your wife. Tell her what you need."

"Can we go inside?"

"Where, my house?" Paul laughed. "Fuck, no. I live with someone."

"In the car then."

It shouldn't have surprised him that Paul proceeded to stand there and make him beg for what he didn't want, or that beg was exactly what he did.

⇗

Maggie worked too much, too hard. It was who she was, the Mennonite in her. And her job was no mere self-fulfillment or paycheck but the business of righting wrongs, saving men from death, as if, Kent thought, he were married to Batgirl. It baffled him to think of such a small, quirky, humorous person carrying around the weight of so many lives. Even when she was cracking jokes about her files, he imagined them as stones on her back. When she moved lightly through the house, in their bed, murmuring in the voice she used on no one in the world other than him, he imagined these men with her still, like invisible balloons attached to her limbs that urged her away and elsewhere. Making love to her was not, thankfully, like performing in the midst of this company—she did not allow them into bed—but knowing the value of her slender time, he couldn't help feeling a certain pressure to be worthy of it, and succinct.

And he couldn't help remembering, in moments, that one of them had once touched her. Not one of her clients, precisely, but it might as well have been. It had happened long ago, before this job and well before he knew her—the rape. She'd been in law school. An intruder entered her off-campus apartment while she slept. "And what?" he'd asked her, when she dropped this piece of information without ceremony into a dinner conversation after they were engaged—he'd been unable to think of one word further to make the question more specific. They were in his apartment, seated before plates of trout and creamed spinach. "I got raped," she said, eyes averted, a shrug rolling through one shoulder. Her tone conveyed no drama and no self-pity. She said it as if the news were both serious and mundane, a misfortune unworthy of special notice, and as if there were no more to tell.

"Are you okay?" he'd asked her.

"Oh, you know. Okay enough. I try not to think about it."

He had wanted to know, and not to know, exactly what had happened, who the man was, how it had been for her. "Did they catch him?" he asked lamely—every other question that came to him threatened to hurt her somehow.

"No." As if to keep the bareness of the answer from calling forth another question, she added, "Most of them are never caught."

Once, after they were married, she'd yelled at the local TV news. "You're shocked by that? Oh, please! *Shocking*—what a fucking stupid word!" Kent, who had managed not to erase but to bracket the word *rape* in her life story, had to rewind his mental tape to hear the newscaster again: "a shocking rape in a quiet suburban neighborhood."

"Women are raped every day, every minute, you moron! It's not shocking. *Most* women are raped. It's life. There, it just happened again, while you were busy thinking of that sanctimonious word." The rigid knot of her body on the sofa, knees drawn up to her chest, made him wary of touch, mute and uneasy. "Sorry, honey," she said, and patted his knee as if he were a dog she had startled, her concentration back on the news.

"How can you do what you do?" he'd finally asked her, when she had brought her third rapist client figuratively home to the dinner table, laying out for Kent over mouthfuls of pasta as much of the case's nastiness as confidentiality allowed, how tricky it would be for her to get clemency. Her quizzical look goaded him, and he forged on. "I mean, you chose this profession—*this* one—chose to defend these men. I understand the whole philosophy of redemption and social justice and changing the world into a kinder, gentler place, really I do, and I don't mean to…but how can *you* do it? Doesn't it—?" Again, he couldn't finish, couldn't say "hurt" without feeling like a perpetrator.

"I think that's why I do it," she said, with a smile to let him know it was okay. "I had all this anger and I had to deal with it. You can't go to the Lord in anger. He says, 'Be first reconciled with your brother.' But I never knew who this guy was, so I guess this is the way I address it."

He felt his own anger simmer. "Like the pacifist thing? Turn the other cheek?"

"In a way. Yes. I know, it's easier to understand when it's about war, or police brutality. And if I actually had to turn the other cheek to this, I don't know that I could. All I know is that mentally, emotionally, this is what I've been given. Do you see? My first duty is getting myself right before God. But I can't just say, okay, I won't be angry anymore. It's too strong for that. So this is my work in the world."

He understood it now, in a one-sided way. He understood her work, her religion, these things she talked about. He saw the intricate web her intentions made, how it connected her to all other people, the living and dead, past and present, cause and effect, one harmonious whole. Because she worked literally to change the world, she was in balance with herself. She was the only person he'd ever met who was content in her own skin, not continually yearning after something she couldn't name. Without being in the least complacent, she was at peace. Walking through the rooms of their house or reading a book, she radiated a peace he could feel like a warmth on his own skin, and he understood that this was a rare and now essential element of his own life.

What he didn't understand was what she wouldn't talk about—that event that had knocked her off balance. It lived in her somewhere, but she would not show him where, or what sort of face it wore, and he was not sure he wanted to know. When he touched her—the sweet parting between her legs, her breasts with their small pink tips and soft, rounded underbellies that made him think of the curve of the Earth— it was always in part a prayer for forgiveness and a promise of reverent care. In truth he lived in awe of her body, of what he touched and of the hidden, terrible, bracketed part of it that he could not. It came to him in flashes, his fingertips on her breast, a glimpse of violence like a memory lifted from her that could tighten him to a stop even as she lay loose-limbed beneath him, a madonna smile playing in her lips. Mostly he was afraid, and he tried, with uneven success, to forget the reason.

What he remembered: sweetness. Paul in a docile phase, their first summer together and marooned on the island of the bed, speaking a new world into being. Their clothes were lost in the sea off the mattress edge, the bedstand awash in take-out and tequila remains. They slept deeply and tangled, breathing together, waking into sex, speaking each other's words, and dropping back into sleep, in effortless rhythm.

He had never been so in love, so together with another person.

"Because I'm a boy."

"No. Maybe." He didn't know the answer. "Because you hold nothing back. You don't hide parts of yourself."

Once he woke to Paul sucking him, but oddly—his head stone-heavy on Kent's belly and only his tongue and throat pulsing in slow rhythm, like a child nursing and half-asleep.

He remembered how long it had taken to get to this stillness, and what a miracle to feel Paul trust him. They talked about his other men, men programmed to lie as Paul lied, so that "love" was just part of the turn-on, a word from a script. "It's not like a betrayal," Paul said. "It's exciting, but deep down you always know it's a game, like all the other stuff you say during sex. It's just what you say."

It was a year before Kent could say it in repose, without wincing or thinking about it—"I love you"—and after he felt the gravity of Paul's reaction, he said it all the time.

"I don't think you're lying to me," Paul said. "I don't really know what to do with that."

Paul would say it too, in effusion—that he'd never felt this way before, never would again. Later, in anger, Kent convinced himself it had never been real. No matter how sincere at the time, Paul remained a child who had never learned the difference between a lie and truth, who hid many things, who was good for little more than a first-class fuck and a lot of jagged drama, and for a long time Kent had made himself forget the island where they had been together, where the truth lived in his bones and he didn't have to think.

⟿

The strange thing: he was falling in love with his wife. The sight of her filled him with anxious longing—not lust precisely but bodily need, a desire to have her skin-close and under his protection. It was, incredibly, as if there were another man, poised to seduce her and steal her away. All he could do was place himself near her in the house, hope that some gesture or word of his would convince her to stay with him, that he was the more worthy of the two.

He had this vision of the future: himself, divorced. He trailed after Maggie, pleading in silence. It was a likely enough future that it had almost become his story already, one he pictured repeating for the young unwary in later years. Take care with what you have, young man, do not lose it all as I have done.

Holding the buzzing receiver, he clocked each second in which he could choose, now, to turn aside, put down the phone. He dialed Paul's number, ten digits pressed to the keypad with emphatic intention.

It was that Paul made sex so easy. He originated every move, yet somehow, subtly, led Kent with a ballroom dancer's kinetic telepathy through each step and turn, so that Kent felt himself to be the active force. The dream was hard to resist, his own athletic prowess, his supremely able body. In Paul's orbit, he rarely took a false step or doubted his partner was in thrall to him, gone from the world and reason. And though Kent had any number of boundaries in bed, Paul had none, savored all of Kent, every inch of him holy and equal like the body of God.

"This is the last time," he said in the car, dropping Paul off. "It has to be. We have to say goodbye."

"You mean what we just did—that was the last? I don't think so."

"Why not?"

"Didn't feel like it. But if you say so." Paul smiled. "Goodbye."

He was right, of course. Kent couldn't get beyond a forced recitation of the words, as if "The End" itself held the power and could change things. But if this were really goodbye, his body would mount its own desperate counterplan right there at the curb. And there was no outcry. They kissed and Paul got out of the car, a sleepy glance back over his shoulder as he pushed open the door of his building.

～

When he needed to clear his head, he went to work on the purple house in Cabbagetown. Recently purchased by Maggie's church, it was slated for renovation in hopes that it could one day serve as a temporary lodging for Maggie's indigent clients fresh from lockup. Lately, though, a new movement was afoot to accommodate instead refugees of foreign wars—or perhaps as well, in addition to, for this was the sort of thing that could gently trouble the Mennonite gatherings for weeks on end. Not which group was more deserving or would create fewer hassles, and not the bare question of whether a congregation of twenty souls could afford to buy a whole house for anyone's care. It was how to identify the greatest need. It was how to ensure that no room of this house ever sat empty while someone, of whatever rough origin, lacked a bed.

Or a roof, Kent thought, as he dragged sheets of mildewed linoleum down the steps to the dumpster parked in the yard. The porch steps bowed as he descended. Inside, the pipes wept rustily at their joinings, exposed in one interior wall where someone had beaten a hole in the plaster. The hall floor tilted so drunkenly that the doors were out of frame; the bathtub slumped toward the foundation. Rats lived in the walls and left their urine smell and sticky droppings on the multiple levels of garbage. But the roof was good. Which meant, at any minute, one of the church members was likely to show up towing some nervous-eyed family, newly washed on the shores of Atlanta, with no English and nowhere else to go.

. He began with the garbage, then the reeking turquoise carpet, which came up to expose good hardwood beneath. Pulling out the bathroom linoleum, though, yielded a floor so water-rotted that he made immediate plans to rip it out, down to the foundation. Soon he was up to his waist in the house, his feet on the earth beneath. Then down on all fours in the crawl space, praying he wouldn't have to brain a rat with his flashlight, where he discovered cracked floor joists and at least two points where the foundation needed to be jacked up.

Random Mennonites appeared from time to time, donned surgical masks and pitched in. "Gosh, you're here a lot," they told him. And, "We really want to thank you for all the work you've done," because even though he was Maggie's husband, they knew he was not one of them, did not pretend to be.

On the day the city truck came to pick up the dumpster, he heard a peeping cry from the broken cinder block under one corner of the steel bin, a comical two-tone: part bird and part whispery silence. He called to it and it emerged—skinny kitten, dingy and matted. It was one of those mongrels born an accidental beauty, would clean up long-haired and white and probably pass for some kind of purebred if set indoors and fed a little. It appeared almost too young to be on its own. Trotting toward him, in a stride that broke its pitiful bleat-whisper into dashes of sound, it seemed certain of who he was. Kent scooped the cat up, and from his first touch the elastic wedge of its sternum roared with purring.

"You almost got crushed, kitty," he said, and wondered what he was meant to do with it. Maggie would see it in such light, as purposeful, a manifestation of a larger plan. "You hungry? Want a bath?" At each word he spoke, the roaring radiated through his hand louder and faster, the cat more still.

≈

"This has to be the last," he said to himself before he dialed the phone, and later, to Paul, in the storage building full of the last decade's forgotten office equipment that he had a key to. As far as he knew, he and Paul were the only people who ever came here. "You have to help me," he pleaded.

From the green leather sofa, musty and cracked, he watched in a limb-locked fog as Paul skinned out of his clothes and stood before him, carved of pallid marble, eyes in shadow. "I can't help you with that."

If you care about me at all, Kent wanted to say, and stopped himself. He couldn't afford to wager anything on that claim. *If you loved me* echoed back at him from their past life together, all the times he had tried to corner Paul with a syllogism, so repeated and shrill with frustration that soon Kent was the one who sounded childish. He and Paul slipped often enough, in the tangled time of Kent's mind, into their old apartment and the sheets of their bed beneath the blue neon glow of the alley window, and the last thing Kent needed to do was to take Paul's hand, in the rational light of afternoon, and lead him there.

Paul knelt on the cushion beside him, tore a condom wrapper with his teeth. "Lean back," he said, gripping Kent's cock like a rudder. "Slouch down."

"Like this?"

"No, wait, new plan. Stay put." A knee passed over Kent's thighs with quick grace, and Paul was backward across his lap, bending back in a taut curve to slip his tongue into Kent's mouth.

There was a nearly decipherable language in these positions Paul chose—lately the ones that required little of Kent, including his opinion. He puzzled over it, fingertips tracing clues along the sinews of Paul's back, which fell into spells of meditative torpor followed by upward surges, excruciatingly slow. The unventilated heat of the room dampened Kent's thighs, stuck his back to the stiff leather beneath him. They didn't speak. In a kiss, achieved only at Paul's whim, Kent floundered in a rush of love, and in the next kiss bristled at the unmistakable coldness, the calculation.

It made him furious, ready to seize Paul by the throat and scream *Look at yourself. You're not human. Do you feel anything? Can you care about anything?* But the mood passed quickly and he sank further, nearly passive, under Paul's power. He shut down his mind, diverted all energy to nerve endings, and wanted nothing beyond what he should have wanted, if *should* retained any meaning: Paul's body, his own, these couplings.

Paul was in ascendancy, and as he rose, he closed himself off. It was a role, Kent was certain, a familiar one for sure but granted heft and authority by the recent acting experience: Paul as siren, pure sex. He donned the cloak with indifferent ease. It was the siren who had no other interests, no other self, glowed with animal heat and buried the rest. The siren certainly had no feelings other than lust, and Kent knew the phase they had entered by the fact that they argued less, hardly at all.

"Just ignore me," Paul said, from time to time, if a blue mood crept near—tears once, or close to it, over nothing. He covered his face, turned aside. "Ignore me." And Kent, mid-act, was happy for the excuse to do just that. It seemed not like authentic sadness, only the by-product of the rigorous control Paul imposed on himself, escaping randomly like steam. The next minute he would be rearranging their positions in clipped commands or goading Kent on with the raunchy phrases and moans of a porn-flick whore.

Dressing, he barely looked at Kent. He didn't cling or beg more time, ask when the next meeting would be. Instead, he stretched languorously in the dusty sunlight from the warehouse window, scratched himself, dropped casual blame on the night before—a night without Kent—for his yawning or stiff neck. He dressed as he would with any trick, cordial, without connection. He leaned in for a last deep kiss— "Mmmm"—as if Kent were a dollop of buttercream icing left after the cake had been eaten, and Paul might have been that alone in the room with his own pleasure.

⌒

Once or twice a week, Kent went to Derek Tompkins's place to play music. He and three other guys, sometimes four, brought their instruments and sat around Derek's living room with a few beers, playing generally whatever came into their heads. Sometimes they started sounding so good to themselves that they went public—played a party or wedding, usually for one of their friends or relatives. Every man in the band was married. Most had children, including Derek, whose little girls had learned from infancy to sleep undisturbed through an evening's worth of hootenanny improv, feedback screeches, and laughing from the living room.

Derek's wife, Joanne—whose stout frame neatly matched her husband's in smaller version—cleared bottles, brought more, freshened the chips, and made wry, caustic comments on the limits of their talent.

Sometimes another wife would come along, another child or two would be added to the mix, and there would be an impromptu party—kids shrieking around sofas, leaping over power cords, dancing to their daddies' rockabilly and rhythm and blues. But mostly it was just the guys, who between sets talked about their mortgages and their wives and their kids.

These were men, Kent thought, who were faithful—though he wanted desperately to ask them, as a group or individually, "Have you ever cheated? Been tempted? What would you do if you were?" He invented hypotheticals to slip into the conversation, but stopped himself every time, fearing it would give him away. Seeing his depravity, they would withdraw, confide their suspicions to their wives, and all married people would unite in league against him. At times, when the talk turned to extramarital fantasies, he thought he could read the same furtive impulse in another man's eyes, the suppressed, serious question. *Have you ever? Would you? Should I?*

Maggie did not attend practices, though she had met these people at parties, been in audience for a half-assed gig or two. He knew they all liked her, their wives liked her. While she was no man's idea of hot, she was one of those women who became exponentially more attractive in the knowing, and he knew most people came away from a conversation with her considering him lucky in the match.

"You're cheating on *Maggie?*" they would say, in disbelief—he could almost hear it. "Is there some problem between you guys? What's wrong?"

⌁

The kitten, round-eyed, newly bathed, skittered from behind the sofa. It appeared disturbed by the texture of the floor beneath its paws, afraid to step with too much weight. At random, it leapt straight into the air as if bitten, then shook itself and calmed.

Kent had given up trying to determine a sex. Who would have imagined sexing a cat would take more than a glance? But each time he went to look, it took offence and twisted away before he could puzzle out the pattern of ambiguous bumps and openings. He'd used the vegetable brush to tease the mats loose, a process the cat had tolerated with whole minutes of patience, and now its long coat glowed with an ethereal white softness that begged for touch. There was something a little disturbing about it—too much beauty let loose in the house, calling all that attention to itself.

"Don't worry," he told Maggie, "he's just visiting. I didn't want to leave him there to get run over. I think he must be someone's pet."

"Pretty kitty." She lifted and set it on the kitchen counter. "Oh, wow, it's so soft! And clean."

He wanted her to stop looking at it, didn't want to admit the day's labor he'd spent on it. In spite of this, he asked, "Can you tell the difference between boys and girls?"

She lifted the feathery tail, causing the cat to collapse on its hip, roll around to slap at her hand. "I used to know how to tell," she said, laughing, searching while he tried to pin it into stillness for her. "It's pretty young, but maybe it's neutered already." She blew fluffy hair aside, while the cat mewed and squirmed. "I give up."

Released, it leapt down from the counter, bolted under a table, and Kent was glad for its rapid exodus. "How was your day?" he asked, pulling her into his arms. He smoothed the flip of dark hair from her forehead and kissed her mouth. "Did you save the world?"

"There's only so much I can do." Her upper body was tipped back against his arm, her gaze turned down to where their pelvises met. It was enough like a dance position that he took one of her hands and began to waltz her around the kitchen, thinking that she would laugh, but she only watched his face as they danced with a crooked smile.

"What are you looking at?"

"Nothing." Still the smile, the piercing eyes. More and more, she was watching him this way, as if he were going senile and she were monitoring the signs.

"Do I behave strangely?" He knew that he should have been worried, but his question was only playful. He was happy, dancing with his wife, didn't know how to feel guilt when he was thinking only of her.

"Little bit," she said.

⁂

Maggie was out: at the church, or working in the store, or meeting a client after hours, or attending a meeting of one of the three charitable boards of which she was a member. They arranged dates for dinner and she flashed off again, lips pressed to his cheek.

It wasn't that he felt neglected—he needed nothing more from her. It was only that he had this time alone to tie his brain up in knots with the effort to undo, to go back and set everything right. To set Paul right, and it was this he kept coming back to—that dry, amused look in Paul's eyes while Kent's gut twisted in agony. He could whirl into Kent's careful life and off to the next conquest without pausing to make a distinction.

It was, ultimately, that Maggie was coming home. Later that night, she would lie beside him, and nothing yet threatened the certainty of where she would be and when. It was that Paul, for all the availability of his body, never lay beside him, would tonight lie down somewhere in the void.

⁂

Paul sat on the steps halfway up a concrete walk that led to a house Kent had never seen before, an address Paul had given him. "Did you move?" Kent asked him.

"No." Paul lifted his eyebrows, daring another question, made Kent drag out of him word by word that the house belonged to a "friend," some person named George—Paul's aloofness letting him know that a sexual relationship with this man was both probable and not up for discussion.

And apparently, Kent had been summoned here for no reason other than it pleased Paul to have this information forced out of him. The man didn't even seem to be home. Kent scanned the porch windows as Paul opened the cardboard box, lifted out the cat. Laughing, he held it before his face, draped limp over one hand.

"Wow, you went all out, didn't you? No, seriously. You got me a cat?"

"It seemed like something you could use in your life."

He plopped it down beside him, where it crouched to sniff at the grass. "I hear these are expensive. You must have paid, what?"

"If you don't want it, I'll take it back."

Paul's eyes flashed up at him with something between anger and amusement. "A cat. God, Kent. All right." He shrugged. "That's supposed to mean what?"

"It means nothing. It means I thought you'd like it." The kitten was moving away with gingery steps through the grass, and Paul didn't give a glance in its direction. Kent suppressed an urge to grab him by the hair and shout. "Maybe it would be good for you," he said, with careful calm, "to have a connection to something. You know, something living. Something real."

Paul's gaze, baleful in the overcast daylight, settled on him, and Kent began to sense for the first time the lameness of this gesture, the absolute wrongness of a gift on which he indeed had spent nothing and Paul would spend everything, a gift meant to change Paul's life and seal Kent firmly in his emotional orbit for at least the lifespan of the animal, even while the animal slowly took Kent's place, allowing him to widen the distance as he pleased. But it was too late to truly take it back, and Paul heaved a sigh, glanced down to its snowy coat.

"Sit," Paul said, leaning back on his hands. Kent sat on the narrow step beside him.

"You remembered my birthday."

"Of course."

"That's kind of sweet." They were close, not touching. Paul looked tired. "I'm twenty-two, you know."

"You're a baby."

He cracked half a smile at the concrete between them. "Not in gay years." The kitten pushed its head into Paul's arm and he picked it up, held its narrow body against his face somberly, like a pillow. "You know, you're the only man in the world who thinks I'm *too* young. What's crazy is ten, fifteen years from now, you might still be thinking that." With a faraway smile, the cat in his arms, he rose and walked up the porch steps.

That night, Maggie asked him what had happened with the kitten. He told her he'd given it away to someone at work.

"Honey," she sighed. "Why'd you do that? We could have kept it."

He'd been unprepared for her disappointment. "Oh, I don't know. A cat? Us? We've never talked about a pet, have we? I thought you weren't a cat person."

"I know," she said, conceding. "But I kind of liked that cat."

⌒

Derek's place, a party two years before. Derek's burly arm across the shoulders of his pregnant wife. "*She* is great," he said, nodding toward Maggie, who was laughing with some other people across the room. Meaning, she's the one. Grab that one and marry her.

Kent was already aware Maggie was different from other women he had come across in the past year and thought about dating. In the four months they had known each other, they had become friends, to the point that he couldn't think of anything he'd rather do with a Saturday than follow her around yard sales while she tried on hats. This is what they had done earlier that same day, and when she had come across an electric razor still in its box, they had driven down to the penitentiary and left it for one of her clients, who was having a problem with ingrown facial hair. He knew that all her energy and light was rubbing off on him, making him a better person. He felt, beyond mood, *good* around her. He was certain he wanted to be with her tomorrow and felt a little jealous of the group that was in her company at this moment— two taller guys bent smiling toward the low thrill of her voice. Marrying her, though, had not yet entered his thoughts. The concept seemed almost bizarre at first—Maggie, wife—though what more should he want?

He refilled his cup at the keg, wandered into eavesdropping range. She and one of the guys were talking about a service project they had both coincidentally worked on, trading names of people they knew. "Oh," she said with enthusiasm, "what about…" her hand on the guy's arm for emphasis. Maggie knew everyone, or could find a connection within a minute. Wherever they went, stores and restaurants and out on the street, people ran up calling her name like groupies and long-lost friends: DAs and fellow volunteers and the mothers of her clients. "This is Kent," she always said, the words weighted as if she were offering them a gift, but he knew the gift was his. She connected him to this vast world of people who did things that mattered. And yet in a brisk winter wind, she shrank and burrowed under his arm, letting him shield her, and it seemed to him amazing that she chose him of all these people to lean against.

And this guy she was standing with now. Kent knew him slightly—

single, another musician, tall and wiry and confident of his charm. And he'd volunteered with Maggie, shared her passion in it—how long would it take him to notice what Derek had, snatch her up for himself? She was the one. He went to her, put his arm around her and kissed her hair, and her smile grew warmer. "Scott, this is Kent."

Here, what he was supposed to want. He'd spent a year haunted by the one he had not wanted to begin with, the one he might have been glad to be rid of if he could have believed him gone. Paul stormed off angry, cooled, and came back—always came back. For months on end—four? five?—Kent had lived in twilight, barely leaving his apartment, not depressed precisely but stalled in a sort of limbo of anticipation, unable to imagine a not coming back. Even when he moved to Atlanta, then prodded himself into noticing girls—never boys, which relieved him—he continued to float in a provisional present, the future in wait for Paul's return, not by choice or desire but simply because Paul had so warped him that he was now shaped this way.

But, his arm around this woman, he saw how he'd been deluded. He could choose, desire anew, change his life. He made his choice, and nothing had ever felt better.

It was going on eleven o'clock, a Thursday night. No one responded to the buzzer at the condo, and at the house where he'd last seen Paul, where Paul might not even have spent a single night for all he knew, the porch light burned before darkened windows. Four messages on Paul's voicemail, and Kent was now full-on losing his mind, cruising bars where men loitered along the street and in parking lots, sometimes engaged with each other, sometimes standing alone or in threes and fours, peering into his car from their staked positions in a cool, continuous broadcast of potential. He had never in his life come alone to

places like these, had in fact entered a gay bar only twice, Paul dragging
him by the arm. Even in the old days, when Paul's idea of a social life
was their nightly battle, he had never been reduced to this extreme.

At a dive called Rico's, a name he'd heard Paul drop enough in the
offhanded disdain accorded anyone who didn't know these things, he
parked and went inside. A hustler bar, Paul had called it, which seemed
to mark it in Paul's universe as sleazy enough for midweek action. Still
in the doorway, Kent smelled leather, felt eyes on him from the red-
tinted dark. A low continuous boom of techno music came from somewhere in the back. A bar stretched the length of the room, the stools
mostly occupied and by men who looked his own age and older—grimy,
rough-looking men, though it was too dark to tell much of anything. He
spotted a pair of shirtless kids younger than Paul, so meatlessly thin they
must have been junkies. He'd clearly fallen into some uncharted circle
of hell, and no Paul in sight, but the throb of music led him to a back
doorway that opened on a throng of dancing bodies.

He was ready to plunge through this second door and sort through
the few dozen dancers whose faces were periodically lit with the roving
light when his cellphone rang. He cupped it to his face with relief.
"Where are you?"

"I'm at the library. Where are you?" Kent told him. Paul said,
"You're kidding."

He wasn't, he promised, and Paul's light voice switched to emer-
gency management. "Stay right there. I'll be there in three minutes."

Kent waited outside, picturing Paul undefiled in the library, bent
over an open book. Maybe he had a study carrel. Of course the carrel
would be near the restroom, and he'd seen for himself what use Paul
had for that. He paced, checking the street, ignoring the men who
passed in and out of the club or settled into the shadows nearby.

Paul appeared on foot, from around a corner—his car parked
down there, maybe, but there was also another dive club in that direc-

tion, close enough to walk from. Half an hour before, Kent had idled in its lot, pondering. He stepped out on the asphalt to meet Paul, who wore a t-shirt and jeans, no detectable cologne or alien smells in the air around him; even the pale bangs flopping over his forehead looked clean of the goo he often arranged them with. But then, this was Paul's new look—that guileless white-bread purity of youth, as if he had nothing to do with sex or bars and had perhaps just looked up blinking from his algebra homework at some insinuation to the contrary.

"The library, huh?" Kent's voice clenched with anger he hadn't expected. He felt deceived in general, tricked somehow into coming to this pit.

In the midst of forming other words, Paul halted several feet off and crossed his arms. "Not that it's any of your business."

"So you can tell me anything, I guess. You play these games. How I am supposed to know whether you're out screwing around or home studying or what, when you drop all these hints—"

"What hints?" Paul looked stung. "What are you talking about?"

"And maybe there's nothing—nothing going on at all." Kent stalled out, deflated, seeing this was a truth as likely as any other. All hints, Kent knew well enough, were by design, Paul's way of saying *see how little power you have.* "How am I supposed to know?"

"You're not," Paul said quietly. "Anything else?"

"Okay. Okay." He dropped his head back, eyes closed for a moment, began pacing a loose, restless circle. "God, will you *look* at me? Will you look at what I've come to?" He was talking to himself mostly, but he gestured with a sharp wave at the club's neon sign and the shadowy men who stood watching and whom he only then really noticed: a small, half-bored-already audience that he and Paul had drawn like some pair of married queens squabbling in the street.

Paul shook his head, muttered, "I knew it, as soon as you said you were here. You are flipping out." His gaze followed Kent's to the watchers and he smirked. His hands went to his hips, voice raised. "Maybe when you leave your *wife*, we can talk about what I do with my time."

"Nice." Kent took him by the arm and pulled him away, steered him into the alley at the back of the club where his car was parked. "Look," he said, turning him loose. "Just answer your damn phone when I call. Can you do that much?"

"I had it turned off." He studied Kent's face with a steely, pained concentration. "But here I am. So tell me what you want."

Kent's shoulders dropped. "God, you know, I don't know anymore. I really don't." He laughed. "I came here looking for you. Doesn't that mean something? I'm out here risking everything for you, and *you*—" Again, though he knew Paul to be at fault, he couldn't locate the reason for his anger. He could accuse Paul only of not being in the place he'd come to drag him from. Feeling exposed still, he drew Paul back into the shadows, against the bricks where the club noise thumped palpably like a heart.

"Just spit it out, Kent. Whenever you're finished soul-searching, that is. Try giving it a name." The tired look was back in his eyes, that look he had no right to at his age. "You want me to blow you or what?"

"Shut up." Hands at Paul's hipbones, Kent pressed him flat to the wall, a rush of comfort in the grip and proximity. His hands slid upward, hooking Paul's shirt in the crook of his thumbs, and his fingers locked into Paul's armpits tight enough that Paul whimpered, went slack against the wall in reflexive surrender.

This submission was the quarry he'd been chasing down, and he felt a wind shift in his desire. It might now be within his power to crush Paul between his hands, obliterate him. He held that possibility for a minute, then put his mouth on Paul's chest, on the nipple flush to the hard, clean flatness of his torso. Riveted and spare, none of Maggie's buoyancy, her generosity and fullness. But he needed this too. He needed both.

"You're gonna spend the night with me?" Paul said, at the top of his ear. "Run away with me? Don't kid yourself. You're going home to your wife."

Kent pulled back. In the shadows Paul's face was perilously soft, stripped and vulnerable—finally, he'd been touched by something, though Kent almost wished for the shell back, didn't know how to answer for the drive that had pushed him to this.

"What do you want, Kent?"

"Just get in the car."

Paul complied, flopping pettishly into the passenger seat beside him. He rolled his window down, adjusted the seat extravagantly, reclined on his arm in the window frame. "So where we going now?" he drawled. "Another sleazy motel?"

The gate to the warehouse was chained at night, but for twenty dollars they got a room with a bed by the hour. He would be home by midnight, probably before Maggie, who had been called in by the firm for a late-night counsel on a death penalty case. It was the same room, as it turned out, that they had used once before, but in daytime, before he had discovered the warehouse, and now Paul stood in the window and looked out at the anonymous, empty street with its pawn shops and Quickcash stores, their signs darkened under the yellow streetlights. His earlier mood had mellowed away, forgotten, and he nearly glowed with a private happiness. Headlights crossed the far wall, passed over the chair where Paul's clothes lay, illuminating multiple long white hairs caught in the fibers of his shirt.

"So this is our new place." He crawled up onto the bed and knelt over Kent, his face serene in the dim light from the window. "Our new apartment. I think we should register for new curtains, new sheets for sure. Do you think I should wear white?"

Kent said, "Stop talking crazy."

CHAPTER 5

In the last year of his life, on a Tuesday, at the age of fifty-seven, Bernard Falk woke to the realization that he needed love. No, not the frivolous thing he had always pursued under its name that was really some combination of sex and regard, but love embodied, someone who would exist out of love for him. The understanding shaped itself as he lay motionless on his back and the window's boxed sunlight crawled by clock-measured increments over the floor, up onto the bed, squaring finally over his pelvis beneath the white duvet. It might have been light from an X-ray, the technician beside him guiding the panels toward revelation. Beneath the duvet, an unaccustomed bodily quiet. Though wobbly with hangover, he was otherwise free of pain, and the corporeal voices that generally growled, whispered, or whined their afflictions, reported minute-to-minute on their states of being and then, like an asylum, proceeded to howl and bang for analysis, this morning were calm.

He lay waiting, until the sun altered the room by another degree. Lights up. Enter, a boy. He smiles bravely with love, despite evident worry. He carries the man's breakfast on a tray. *Did you sleep? Are you feeling well?*

But. He could lie here all day and on into the evening, and no one would come through that door. And if he were unable to rise, what then?

Paul was meant to be that boy, as good as pre-cast in the role. Before Bernard knew his name, he had spotted the necessary quality in his eyes: a sweetness combined with a wide-open, all-or-nothing hunger for knowledge. He was one in a class of twenty arrayed on the stage for Acting I, a raw beginner and already tipped over the border that divided earnest student from devotee seeking a master. Bernard saw eyes like those rarely—*suckling eyes*, he called them—but enough to know they would stay on him through class, would trail him from the room, would seek him after hours; that eventually such a boy would live to please him. And for a time he had.

Bernard swung his feet to the floor, edged them into slippers. Outside his bedroom, the condo was sunny and silent, the scattered treetops below the bank of windows opening new leaves that would soon all but obscure the park view, and he couldn't help recalling that at leaf-bud time last year he'd been the man who could draw a boy's gaze, virile, in his prime, a leading man who passed for forty. Even on a good day, there was this: illness had launched him twenty years into the future, body and spirit.

From the front door, a trail of clothing led across the living room—jacket, then t-shirt, jeans—the last deposited in the hallway that led to Paul's door. Bernard stooped for each with increasing annoyance, feeling his knees creak. He put his ear to the door. No sound from beyond, no item of clothing draped over his arm that didn't belong to Paul, but that didn't guarantee the boy hadn't snuck someone in there with him, in defiance of unwritten rules never yet defied, at least to Bernard's knowledge. He inhaled hesitantly from the t-shirt, smelled only the acrid smoke of whatever club.

Normally he wouldn't disturb that door, not for any reason and certainly not at the ludicrous hour of eight a.m. when Paul wouldn't begin to stir until noon. But this morning he felt impelled by some justification and opened the door quietly.

Paul slept on his belly, one bare shoulder and arm above the sheet, alone but for the kitten that lay across his neck like a white fur boa. The two of them appeared comatose, too deep to twitch at Bernard's slight noises. Where sunlight striped Paul's sheeted form in narrow bands, Bernard's eye was caught, diverted as in an Escher drawing, invited beneath. He stood snared. Then, instead of dumping his armload as planned, he moved about the room and gathered up the other soiled members of a rather expensive wardrobe, cast into corners and over the desk chair, though he could launder and fold every stitch the boy owned and still not be guaranteed enough of his time for a thank you.

In the afternoon Paul emerged to propagate his mess again beyond the bedroom. Bernard collected and stacked the plates—"Honestly, the *plates*"—with their pizza crusts and fruit rinds from Paul's vicinity, mid-sofa, his usual spot for whatever rare minutes of the day he elected to breathe Bernard's air. Rock still, eyes lit from the TV. "How many meals do you eat a day? We can't count proper dinner, of course, since you're never home for that."

It was infuriating when Paul went deaf to him, as now. Yet part of Bernard was pleased not to disturb the fixity of those eyes, the absorption that produced a giggle from time to time at his brainless cartoons—an insouciance like a kind of nakedness in the living room. It granted access, and Bernard hovered, collecting, his gaze unnoticed.

From the coffee table he plucked an open playscript, held it before him like a dirty rag. "Do not tell me you accepted that awful awful part. That Cyrus or Slinky or—"

Meeting his eyes for once, Paul snatched back the script. "Silas.

What's so awful about it?"

"Where shall I begin? You've played Hamlet. Do you grasp the difference? That lowbrow excuse for—"

"No, actually, forget it. I don't want to hear." He flipped to music videos.

"Mark Westlake is not a playwright, Paul. That much should be clear even to you. He's a poseur. And the part is not right for you."

"What do you know? You haven't even read it."

What did he know? Bernard turned on his heel for the kitchen. A year ago, Paul never would have dreamed of speaking to him in such a way. A year ago, the question would have been sincere, and Paul kneeling at his feet for an answer.

He had once thought it pleasant to have this little whiff of sex about the house, this piece of scenery. It was like having a view to a field of shining horses he never rode. But lately the proximity was more than he could bear. Sometimes he felt he was dying of love, like some teenager, had to remind himself that the object was less than worthy. He was a select piece of Georgia white trash in prince's clothing, every item of it provided by Bernard himself. He'd done his best to polish the boy, educate him in at least the appearance of class if not the reality, but lately Paul seemed to be reverting to his vulgar ways out of some mysterious and unjustified spite, which Bernard had to endure quietly along with the rest.

There had been scoffing when Bernard had cast him, this cracker kid with his shy eyes and softly elongated vowels, a shade too small and slight for the Dane. But Bernard trusted his own eye. Under his guidance, Paul had grown into the part, acquired a manly grace, then a tethered violence that on stage broke loose in alarming ways, to terrorize Ophelia, force his mother to the bed. He had become in that slip of a body something other than himself.

When Bernard returned from the kitchen, thudding techno pop

played from the set and Paul was using the sofa's back as a ballet barre, folding himself onto one raised leg, the t-shirt riding up from his frayed army pants. Not to startle him from his agile display, Bernard spoke quietly, hoping he might listen to reason. "Have you considered the reputation of the man you are working with? You might think of, well, your career, if nothing else."

Paul snorted. "What career? Why do you care?" He bent his body left and right with languorous, meditative ease. "Oh, I get it. You think he wants to fuck me."

Bernard remained beyond the threshold, tugged by the murmur of pleasure in Paul's voice—could he call it playful?—yet blocked somehow from entering his own living room. "That is not at all what I'm—"

"Here's something I never learned from you. Everything is not about sex."

Just the bare word in Paul's mouth, the near-acknowledgment of their history together, made Bernard's blood thrum. An intentional tease, perhaps, Paul tricking out little threads of their past, as he seemed to do more and more lately until Bernard was forced to live a piece of each day in these memories.

The first remained his favorite and the most easily called up: the costume room. Hamlet needed a costume, and it was more than legitimate to bring Paul, newly cast in his first leading role and shining, all but bursting, with a visible will to please, untouched outside of a few lingering adjustments to his posture in Acting II. His Hamlet, Bernard had decided, would wear something never before seen on stage. Anachronistic, shocking, extreme. They were alone after the first read-through, most of the building in darkness, and Paul leapt into the project with gusto. *Like this?* Silver neoprene pants. A vest of green fur. A military cape of Napoleonic vintage. Laughing, breathless changeling, Paul rollicked through the costume room, dove into musty racks, stripped off one thing, added another. *This? No, this.* A fedora. Scarlet kimono. Spike-heeled boots. And emerged from the drapery of racks utterly, gloriously naked, in a black feather boa. He spread his arms back slowly while one nervous toe dug at the floor. *This.*

If Silas was nobody's Hamlet, the fact became irrelevant with the boy in the costume room before his mind's eye. "I could help you, if you like, with the part," he said, helpless. In his vision, the other Paul remained close enough to touch and nearly trembled for approval. "We might make something of it, I suppose."

"Really?" Chin at his ankle, Paul gave him one of those cow-eyed, once-bitten looks that Bernard found more insulting than sarcasm.

"Yes, *really*. Let me read it. We'll talk it through. That is, if you still think my opinion is worth anything."

"It's not that, Bernard." Straightening, he let out a gasp and shook his head. "I could use your help, if you mean it. If you want to waste your time on what you think is garbage, when there's nothing in it for you." He leveled a cool, doubled-barreled blue gaze.

"Ah, but the pleasure of your company. Let's not forget that."

⌒

Paul had not been the first. Bernard was well aware that he had made a career of obsession with boys at precisely this stage, college students with a little bit of mental acuity who were beginning to awaken to themselves, to feel their own legs beneath them and sense their own power. A select few had dazzled him with their excitement in discovery, and he was happy to let them blather on about Baudelaire and Wittgenstein, to pretend their every observation was both brilliant and original to the world, simply to watch the play of light in their eyes.

But after teaching for twenty-odd years, he was almost past deluding himself that any of these boys was truly a wonder. Any notion to the contrary was likely only his moribund teacher's soul straining after a sense of purpose in the wasteland, not to mention an excuse to be near certain boys, to demand their time after class. To experience their gratitude, in whatever form that took.

And was Paul a wonder? His Hamlet had impressed others, at least, and Bernard remembered the performances with a painful nostalgia, for it was the last time the theater had moved him. Paul might have been that protégé he'd always dreamed of, might have gone on to a true career if Bernard had been able to stick close as guide. But when one's mortality began to write its own script, he'd found, it was hard to be bothered with play-acted drama. Now it could do little more than pain him vaguely from time to time, amid the chorus of other pains, that however close he lived Paul must be left to his own scattershot devices and the clutches of imbeciles who would ruin him.

The previous summer, his costume designer friend Jodi had given him a Santeria candle called Radiant Health. She'd bought it in a head shop as a joke, a serious joke, offered as remedy for a case of the flu. But it was his first illness after his diagnosis, and combined with the disturbing effects of his various medications he had managed to convince himself he was dying. Alone, miserable. She brought him some soup, did a load of laundry, told him, half joking still, "You ought to find some hot boy to move in here." Maybe so, he thought. He'd forgotten the candle, then came upon it in a closet some months later. Lit it— what the hell. Seven days later, his doctor's appointment had yielded his best PSA numbers to date.

It had been on his calendar for a while now: his next blood draw, and this task along with it. He needed another candle. He was not a religious man, and this he often regretted. The comfort of a loving God was enough, almost, to make him jealous of those dull-witted enough to believe in such a thing. He would have liked to think that a church, whatever church he might have belonged to, was out there praying for him.

He would have appreciated, say, a Catholic mother about now, sending out continual prayers to the Virgin. But even for the sake of superstition, or simple comfort, he couldn't make himself enter a church.

The head shop, though—this sort of magic contained its own irony, and the idea pleased him. He scanned the dusty shelves at the back of the store, where rows of candles in tall glass jars were grouped by color, painted with their powers in English and Spanish. Court Case, Job, Reversible. "I'm looking for Radiant Health," he said to the frizzy-haired woman at his elbow, who was half his height. He felt timid and ridiculous. "A candle."

"This is the only one," she said, and handed him from a low shelf a candle labeled Healing. He would have to settle, apparently, for a process, something less than health, less than radiant. But even his disappointment seemed absurd, and he tucked the candle into his arm. One more scan of the shelf, and his hand was called to a blue one labeled Come To Me in glaring white paint. That was the one, his compensation. He held the two jars, one in each hand, and something told him to pick one, focus the mojo. He returned the lesser Healing to the shelf.

Now he burned the blue candle, Come To Me, on his dresser. He wrote Paul's name on little slips of paper and fed them daily to the flame. Crescents of black ash gathered in the surface of the wax.

⌒

Paul called the cat Baby. He carried it everywhere, flopped over his forearm or shoulder like a rag sweater. He slung it on its back into the crook of his arm and covered its face in kisses. Bernard—who didn't recall granting permission for a pet—felt his allergies hovering in the wings, though failing to achieve an undeniable presence, whenever the thing was near.

The cat never imposed itself on him, perhaps sensing he might accidentally boot it across the room, and yet it irritated him past all reason, more than any of Paul's other slovenly habits. It struck him, somehow, as a sign, like an ashtray or wineglass that could only have been left by a hidden lover. Bernard felt this person lurking heatedly about their borders, meeting the boy in hotels or entering at night through his bedroom window. It hardly mattered that they were eleven floors into the sky or that the windows didn't open. Or that he had no expectation of the boy's being faithful in the first place—faithful to what?

"Come and go as you please," he'd said, "sleep with whomever you like," and truly, if Paul ordered his sexual partners by the dozen, this caused Bernard little more concern than to envy the opportunities of youth. But one man—the thought was nearly intolerable.

The most obvious sign: flowers, two identical vases of red roses that Paul signed for with the same grimace of distaste and rushed to his room, stonewalling Bernard's questions: "No one." "Just this crazy guy." Mark Westlake, perhaps—almost his style, though Mark was more likely to expect lavish flattery than to give it. A third batch arrived a week later while Paul was out, and Bernard, in his own home, felt entitled to pitch the envelope and leave the open card pinned amidst the leaves, the vase set on the coffee table like their newest decoration: "Are you angry? Remember I'm always here for you. —G."

Recently, too, there had been strange calls. Or perhaps only a single call, for the others had been nothing but breathing and long silences. Once, a male voice had spoken. "*I could kill you*," it said, so deep it sounded fake. It brought to mind the rancid acting of his students, any one of them, or maybe younger kids horsing around, but could have easily been a grown man. Vernon Dodd, his archenemy from the condo tenants' association, had made similar calls in the past. But not him, because after a long pause the voice blurted, "*You stay away from him*," a guttural roar before the line went dead.

Stay away from Paul, he supposed, though he didn't know how much farther away he could get. A wrong number, possibly. But he clung to the hope that Paul had told someone they were lovers. Never mind whom, for the moment—to say it, he'd have to be able to imagine it, and imagination for Bernard had become kissing cousin to reality.

March, the month of the early rehearsals for Mark's play, had brought the first flowers, then the cat, more flowers, the calls in there somewhere, and by month's end Paul's sofa appearances began to grow more frequent, more horizontal, the cat on his chest. They lay together unaccountably idle at midday, looking clubbed, bedraggled. His usual Paul was little more than a flash of color, like a bright forest bird shooting from room to door, or dipping in for a meal and a little cash and Bernard's keys.

"Don't you have class?" Bernard asked him, the third afternoon in a row.

"I can skip it. I don't feel like going." The bend in his knees revealed the broad rip in his jeans just south of the ass—*that* pair. Today's too-small t-shirt, black, onto which the cat released numerous long white hairs, read "Got lube?"

"Oh, that's disgusting."

Reaching under the cat, Paul peeled up the shirt, popped it off over his face. "Better?" He tied it kerchief-style over the cat's head, and it submitted with barely a blink of its slitted eyes. "Now Baby's the cheap little tramp. Yes you are."

"You shouldn't handle that poor thing so much, you know. You'll make it sick. It doesn't look at all well as it is."

Paul resettled the cat on his chest, the new bareness of which had kick-started some subconscious motor of Bernard's brain toward routes to touching. "How's the play coming? Shall we work on that role?"

"Not now, okay?" Perspiration glistened along his hairline. Bernard was half-convinced the cat was sweating as well.

"It's not in the least warm in here." He reached for Paul's forehead, and Paul, instead of squirming away, gazed up at him with limpid worry.

"Something's wrong. I feel dizzy. And light and hot and... I don't feel like doing anything."

Bernard stroked the hair back from Paul's forehead and laid the backs of his fingers to his temple, marveling that he allowed it. It was as much as he'd touched Paul in months, and he couldn't help eroticizing the moment, trying as many of his own skin surfaces as he thought could pass for nurse-like.

"I think my heart's beating too fast—feel it." But his own palm pressed hard to his chest, and with the cat snugged up close beside there was no room.

"You were dizzy a few days ago. In the kitchen."

Paul groaned and turned away, drew up his knees around the cat. As slow as he could manage it, Bernard moved a hand down the length of his back. In a fervor, he wished for true illness, the feeling so sudden and strong it was like anger. He willed heat from every new patch of skin, that Paul might remain this passive, under his care. If sick beyond fever, sick unto death, he might relent, come back to share what life remained.

But his skin was everywhere cool, and Bernard knew this would prove no illness in any real sense. AIDS—Paul was too careful. Whatever his specious symptoms, he remained young and strong and untouched by his own mortality, untouched by Bernard's, the cruel despot of a realm Bernard could only crawl about the edges of, begging and afraid.

"You loved me once," he said softly, not meaning to.

Paul hauled himself laboriously upright. "Love is bullshit." A jagged edge in his voice made it sound more despairing than cynical. He squeezed his eyes shut, bent over his lap with thumbs pressed into his eye sockets. "Wouldn't it be funny if I actually died? Who would even care?"

"*I* would care."

Paul went rigid. "You're just saying that!" He nearly yelled it, cheeks flushed, and he blinked as if startled by his own reaction. His face hardened. "You don't mean anything you say. You never have."

"Darling—" Bernard stood, shocked, as Paul scooped up the cat and headed for his room, slammed the door. He sank to the sofa again. "Well." Odd. Nothing he had done or said in recent memory had provoked such a storm in the boy, or even seemed to affect him.

Over the next several days, Paul's symptoms thickened and thinned, multiplied and grew strange. He went to the internet, came back with tintinitis, vertigo, eczema, and a host of attendant conditions Bernard had never heard of. Though most of them sounded hysterical, even fabricated, the insides of Paul's wrists flamed with a scaly rash that was undeniable. "Stop scratching," Bernard said. "You probably caused it that way."

But Paul didn't insist either. He mentioned his new symptoms in uncommitted ways, as if testing their exotic sounds on his own ear, and sometimes Bernard caught him in a reverie, fingertips at his lymph nodes or pulse points, looking for all the world as if he were falling in love with his own inchoate disease. Sacked out on the sofa, he almost always answered with a mournful sigh, when asked, that he was "fine." *Lazy*, Bernard thought, *is what you are. Malingering from school and lost in your own pretty head, while I am truly ill. And do you ask how I am, ever?*

There were moments that affected him, when he was struck by Paul's lethargy, his lack of appetite, and the lavender marks that had appeared under his eyes overnight. The cat seemed to mimic him, hunched turtle-like on the kitchen tile with its eyes half-closed. It crept about in a drugged slow-motion, began to appear greasy and thin. Together they snubbed the food Bernard prepared to tempt them, stared glassy-eyed at the TV. An hour later, it would all seem his imagination—Paul eating a bowl of cereal, scooting out the door. Recovered enough to be gone for hours, whereabouts unknown.

If he had wanted to, Bernard might have guessed, even tortured himself imagining the man: handsome and cruel enough to knock Paul into this stupor and then rouse him from it. He hadn't meant to eavesdrop on one of Paul's desolate calls to his girlfriend Sylvie, his monotone from deep in his sofa pit so meaningless that Bernard was lulled into listening ("I don't know. I just feel it. I used to. But now it's—I don't know. It's slipping. I can feel it tilt. I can't anymore. I know") and then couldn't stop himself before meaning began to coalesce: "He says he's ending it. I know, he never does, but it's—I feel it coming now. This is it. It's slow-motion." And the unbelievable selfish gall: "I feel like I'm going to die."

It's only heartbreak, you twit, Bernard thought, before erasing the whole notion. There was no man. He was off at rehearsal, nothing more.

When Paul was out, Bernard fretted, set his fingertips to the pulse at his groin. He could hear his doctor's voice from his last examination—"You're not dead yet"—news she had delivered without a hint of sarcasm, as if she read it directly from the lab results. The numbers were not good this time, not what they had hoped for (he cursed the candle he hadn't found). But his heart was still a fine machine, his lungs clear, his male equipment, praise god, in functioning order and, with a little pharmaceutical assistance, downright reliable. Removal of the prostate from the first would have been the preferred treatment—they had urged him to do it and be done—but here he was, a whole man still, and a love life not out of the question.

Perhaps it was his doctor's stalwart habit of privileging the positive that made Bernard hear his last hours ring in every word. *Carpe diem, old man*—she might have said—*because, well, you're dead tomorrow. Let me rephrase. Tomorrow you'll be dying, probably slowly and without grace, incontinent, bedridden, unable to warm your own broth or wipe your own ass for a good many months on end, and by the way, do you have someone willing to handle these matters for you? Because I'd suggest you line someone up pronto.*

His friends—kind, intelligent theater people of sufficiently long acquaintance, like Jodi, like Tristan and Daniel—had their own partners, their own busy lives. And he couldn't bear the thought of hired help, some efficient, disinterested nurse tapping her nails until the last breath released her.

Paul had been a case of bad timing. Had the diagnosis come during that narrow span of the boy's enthrallment, Bernard had no doubt that he would have dropped out of school and pledged twenty-four-hour service at his bedside. But something ineffable had clicked, like a light switch, and before *Hamlet* had closed, Bernard's power over him vanished abruptly and forever.

He needed that again—if not Paul, then another Paul, the way he had been—someone who would love him unconditionally. On sabbatical now, his access to the one or two luminaries the campus might cough up was limited, and no magic candle was going to make a new boy appear at his door. He sat at his computer, logged onto the internet. There were a few chatrooms he frequented with good luck for cybersex, and often he found one or two correspondents who wanted to meet in Real Life. Maybe tonight he would get up the nerve to invite one over. Maybe one of those lonely souls would be the one to love him, to stay. But as he began typing in m-e-n, "Meniere's disease" popped up in the browser bar, startling him like a sudden message from beyond.

Paul had been using his computer.

He had his own, but he preferred Bernard's larger screen and more comfortable chair for less private use. Bernard clicked the browser bar. There were the last fifteen websites Paul had been to, a free-associative collection of the generalist and the arcane, but most of them were clearly medical pages. The fodder for a growing hypochondriac. He couldn't help smiling.

Then one arrested his attention, there in the center of the list, four down: the Prostate Cancer Survivors Project.

He opened a bottle of wine, waited at the granite kitchen island for Paul's return. He wasn't sure how to feel in this new light, but he was too excited to sit. Somewhere, the boy had become lost—he began to trace this now, how it must have started during the play. Toward the end of the run, all the attention of minor stardom had gone to Paul's head a little. He would fall into annoying thirty-second trances of deafness. In performance, he would make spontaneous changes in the blocking, the delivery of a line, as if daring Bernard to stop him. That they were artful, adept changes, so much the worse, for the seed of his pride was a bad one. Bernard saw how it might have easily grown to disdain, branched into imaginary grudges. But clearly, the boy still cared for him. And perhaps he didn't even realize the depth of his feeling, since this recent illness looked sympathetic in nature. As Paul's mind urged him away from Bernard, so his body drew him back. It was perfect, after all. He had never really wanted a new boy, only this one returned as he had been.

By the time Paul arrived, Bernard was on his third glass of bordeaux, which aided enormously in his effort to shed his lingering resentment. In fact, he had begun to feel touched by the boy's predicament, his stumbling efforts to cross the divide and return to love. The idea had brought him once or twice near tears, so that when Paul's key scratched the lock and he appeared at the door, wan as ever, Bernard went to him instantly with open arms. "Oh, my dear boy. I am sorry."

He hadn't meant to go so far—he had nothing to be sorry for—but the depth of sadness in Paul's eyes compelled it. And the line seemed the right one, for Paul accepted the embrace, his cheek to Bernard's chest. "How did you know?"

He stroked Paul's hair and thought of the candle, Come To Me, those burnt curls of paper that had brought about this end, and it occurred to him that in the old stories, desires achieved through the dark arts rarely arrived in the form intended. Paul leaned against him without fight, and the residue of the world outside clung to him unmistakably. His trouble, Bernard sensed, was something that happened out there, not in here. Another man was nearly a smell left on his clothes. And for some reason, perhaps because he had the boy in his arms, he felt a shift of sympathy. It almost resolved into a wish, that he could help Paul toward whatever happiness he'd been chasing.

"Know what?" he asked.

Paul wiped his face, now wet with tears. The cat, he said. He'd taken the cat to a vet. The cat had leukemia.

"Oh." Bernard drew him to the sofa, filled the waiting glass with dark wine. "Here, drink a little."

Paul tipped the glass to his lips and swallowed. He told Bernard about the blood drawn, the tests run, the prognosis. "They kept him there, in the hospital. They put an IV in his little leg. I went back to see him and he was lying in a cage with this big cone thing around his head. He looked awful."

"I'm sure he'll be fine. You did the right thing." On any other night, even something as simple and pleasurable as a sip of wine, if Bernard suggested it, would have been met with resistance. But the cat crisis had drained Paul's reserve of spite down to nothing, so that he sat slumped and unguarded, the wine in his glass already half gone.

"I worry that he's alone. All those dogs barking. I think he's scared." He clamped his mouth shut, with a sidelong, guilty glance at Bernard.

Bernard's heart stuttered as he guessed Paul's thoughts. "What? Tell me." He modulated his words with authority. "Say it, Paul. You need to."

"I think he's going to die."

"There. Now look at me."

Paul stared at his knees, the stubborn pride tight in his jaw. But Bernard didn't need to repeat the command, and he felt a warm dawning of triumph when Paul obeyed. "That's right." With careful restraint, he drew the edge of a finger along the damp skin of Paul's face, a touch that brought more sadness to Paul's eyes, and Bernard felt lush and bountiful with generous spirit. "It's okay. I understand you've been afraid. You don't want to be too close to me. But I'm not dying. I have a condition, through which I may survive for many more years."

Paul nodded a little, looking down. "It's just a cat," he said. It was as much as he had ever acknowledged Bernard's illness, revealed his own fears, and Bernard waited in silence for more, a hand settled on Paul's bent neck.

"Scraggly old stray," he said, but in the effort of denial, the cat must have risen again to the surface of his emotional stew, and he blinked earnestly. "I'm supposed to be impressed he can pick up a cat off the street. You know, the vet said most cats that run loose around here have leukemia. And you can't cure it either. He gave me a sick fucking cat."

"Who gave you?"

The man, there he was. The outraged misery in Paul's eyes dulled abruptly. "No one."

"I'll get you a new cat."

First word emphasized ever so faintly—Bernard regretted it before it was out of his mouth, for it was too soon. But Paul only sighed, slumped further into the couch. "I don't care. I don't want another one."

He took a few swallows of the wine, and Bernard watched him closely, observed his posture and the set of his mouth, as he had during the boy's performances. This was his clay still, the medium of his art— the lithe young body, the mind that moved it. "You remember, don't you, our weekends at the beach last fall? How fine the weather was and how happy we were, sharing a bed?"

Paul nodded, and to Bernard's astonishment his eyes were unguarded, hopeful—he looked, in fact, too emotional to speak. It was the sweetest sight he'd been granted in a long time, Paul gazing at him as he had during *Hamlet*, waiting for the grace of knowledge.

He assumed his director's voice. "That's where we should be now. From now on. We can go back and be happy again."

"To the beach?"

"To bed, Paul. It's best. Trust me, you'll see." They had never, it occurred to him now, been in bed together except on those beach trips. They'd had sex in the theater, in his office, in a supply closet, in a stair-well, in the bathroom at a friend's party, but never once in a bed. And at the beach, they had slept only—and talked, cuddled, because Bernard had been on hormone suppression and incapable of a sexual thought.

"To sleep?" Paul looked sleepy as he said it. "Just lie together?"

"And more."

Paul smirked, eyes at half-mast. "To sleep, perchance to dream.

And by a sleep to say we end the heartache, and the thousand natural shocks that flesh is heir to. 'Tis a consummation"—he blinked—"wait, I'll get it. 'Tis a…" His lips moved rapidly, almost soundlessly.

"'A consummation devoutly to be wished.'" Bernard eased the glass from his hand and set it down, took Paul's face—his Prince—and kissed him.

Awakened, Paul pulled back. "Don't."

Bernard gripped him by the arm with sudden force, panicked as well as angry to feel him retreat. "Your teasing—it's a shameful way to treat a sick man."

Paul wrenched loose and was on his feet. "You're not *sick*. Not sick enough, anyway. You're a damn drunk, Bernard. If you'd lay off the booze, you'd be halfway healthy."

Somewhere between his fury at the ice-hearted curse, *not sick enough*, and the accusation that followed, Bernard lost his grip on reason. He staggered up from the sofa with something like an intent to kill, but Paul was waiting with lit eyes and they fell to a kind of shoving match, slapping, pinching, ripping. He was taller than Paul, should have been stronger but his body felt logy—*drunk*, he knew. They were physically fighting. He couldn't believe this was happening, and Paul was caught in the madness with him, his face in one flashed glimpse so rage-contorted it was unrecognizable.

Paul broke away first, scrambled back to put the coffee table between them. Bernard struggled to catch his breath, unsure if they had finished. Where Paul's knuckle had caught his mouth, he tasted blood.

"I'm sorry," Paul said. But his voice was harsh, and he held a restless crouch in his stance, as if he might lunge again at the first impulse. The wildness had not left his eyes, and Bernard saw in them what had become of his hopes.

"Why are you so angry with me?" he cried.

Paul opened his mouth as if to fire back a retort. Nothing came but his panting breath. "I don't know."

"You hate me, I think. Sometimes. You don't know how it pains me."

"I don't hate you." He swallowed and looked at the floor.

"You treat me like a criminal, when I truly feel I've given you things, Paul, great gifts. As a teacher. A mentor. And you don't seem to remember, any of it. What we were to each other." He sat on the sofa, rubbed his eyes. That paradise—he knew it had been real, for both of them, however brief, that they had each drawn immeasurable benefits from the other. And here was Paul even now, saying, "I know, you're right," but in a way that changed nothing.

"Was I really any good?" Paul said.

Bernard was almost too tired to look up. "What do you mean?"

"As an actor. Was I good?" Paul stood over him, hair disheveled, the lamplight at his back. Bernard had a box-full of still photos of his performance that were simply stunning, brimming with energy and emotion and light—whether due to the talent of the photographer or to Paul's immersion in the character, he couldn't have said.

"You were the best student I ever taught," he said, grudging and perfunctory. "You know that very well, I think. Didn't I tell you enough?"

Paul looked away in thought. "I guess you did. You said I was beautiful."

"Yes. You were beautiful. To me. You were like a dream."

"You told me I was perfect. Brilliant. Everything I did. You didn't even have to think about it." Paul stepped closer, presented his upturned wrists as if they were manacled. "Remember I had these same rashes? The whole time, during *Hamlet*. I couldn't stop scratching, till they bled."

"I don't recall—"

"You had to put make-up on them," he said sharply, "before I could go on stage. God, Bernard." He laughed and covered his mouth. "I had a stomach ulcer. You didn't know that, did you? I don't think I understood then, why it was so hard to do that show. I thought it was me. One minute I thought I was a genius and the next I was a complete fraud with no talent, everything was wrong."

Bernard remembered well enough Paul's bout of insecurity during the show, his hothouse delicacy—couldn't eat, couldn't sleep—his timid questions and quick scowls and silences. Between performances, he seemed to exist in an almost constant state of terror, but stepping on stage he would close his eyes once, breathe it out, become the Prince. "I told you over and over that you were perfect. You just wouldn't believe me."

"No," Paul said coldly, "I guess I didn't."

"My life's work, and you couldn't trust me to know the stage?"

"I wanted you to like me. I guess that's my fault. I liked it that you liked me. But you know, you'd look at and critique every other jackass on the stage, but never me, no matter what I did. Like you couldn't see me."

"That's ridiculous. I must have neglected everyone *but* you." But he found with some consternation that he could not recall correcting in his Hamlet a single misstep. There had been no misstep, only night after night of flawless performance, and that, he knew, wasn't possible. Worse, he was haunted by the way Paul's every gesture and pose on the stage could lead him into daydream, to the naked body soon to be under his hands and in the throes of an act that might occur on the same stage but had nothing to do with the play.

He cleared his throat. "My dear, what do you want from me? Did *I* give you rashes, or…? I don't understand."

Paul pressed his hands over his eyes and sighed. He sat beside Bernard, carelessly enough that their thighs touched. "Never mind. You're right, you gave me many things, better things. Really, I'm grateful." He scratched his wrist in an absent way. "Like in the fall, when we used to talk?"

"Stop that, for god's sake." Bernard took gentle hold of his hand, and Paul didn't flinch or pull away. The scaly patch inside his wrist was as defined as the map of some country. Bernard drew a thumb lightly over it, wondering if, half hoping still, he could be the cause. But he knew he was not.

"Who gave you this?"

Paul shrugged. "No one. It's just eczema. It's caused by stress." His expression was both distant and intimate, and his body beside Bernard's had become very still. The other man was with them now, an absence that curled around Paul where the cat had been.

"Who is he?"

Paul seemed not to hear the question. Then he made a thoughtful sound that was almost a laugh. "He's married. Does that make you happy?"

It did, a little. He rallied for a show of disappointment. "Paul. You know you can only hurt yourself, obsessing over such a person."

"I know." Paul turned to him, grave and weary, something wiser in his eyes than he'd ever observed in the raw student of a year ago. This struck him for the first time—he was not the same. They were more like equals now, Paul in the act of passing him, moving like a comet out into the world Bernard was leaving. Having him now would quite likely be a richer thing, more complex and satisfying, like well-aged wine.

"I can give you things," he tried, hands pressed between his knees. "A man like that is obviously not capable of…providing what you need."

"What's that?"

His gaze still rested on Bernard's face as it had in the old days, waiting for an answer. But all Bernard could think of that might tempt the boy faded into wordless oblivion against his own terrible lack.

Paul smiled briefly at his indecision, sucked a finger into his mouth and, to his surprise, touched it to Bernard's lower lip. "Sorry," he said, the wet finger stroking at what was probably only a spot of blood—the cut was inside—but Paul worked with gentle care and then, as if by accident of leaning too close, kissed him softly on the mouth. Bernard didn't move. Paul kissed his cheek and paused to rest there, skin to skin. "I'm so tired," he said. Bernard felt fever-flushed, too weak to react, and his heart raced until he feared he might be dying this very moment. But he went on living, as Paul left him on the sofa, disappeared behind his own door.

CHAPTER SIX

The sky was overcast yet bright with an oppressive metallic whiteness, as if the invisible sun had been spread thinly to every corner. Paul spread white butter on toast. It was a struggle to keep his eyes open in the glare, to force his languid hand through the gestures that led toward food. Across from him at their patio table, George shoveled eggs into his mouth and stared. He had acquired a hard gaze of late, like Bernard's, not lustful anymore but vigilant, as if searching continuously for any crack in Paul's nature that he could pull apart and crawl inside of. It pinned Paul to his seat, and he didn't have the energy to pull loose. *I know you*, it said. *I know what's best, so sit back and do what I say, young man.*

"I wonder if you take me seriously." George had grown a beard in recent weeks, inspired by some offhand comment of Paul's, and as he spoke there was a piece of egg trapped on his chin. Paul's eyes locked there helplessly. "I wonder if you understand how serious this is, or could be, between us."

Meanwhile the sky rested at the top of Paul's head like something he balanced there, a collapsing circus tent. Stress was making him sick—he knew this, knew it would pass and that he wasn't dying from some obscure incurable disease, though he harbored a candle-flame of hope that his own future might lie in a hospital where a somber doctor would announce a diagnosis. A single, simple answer to everything—he found something so sweet and comforting in the idea of this fate that he knew it was not his.

"Do you hear me?" George asked, and Paul had trouble hearing much beyond the nasal quality of his voice, the gratingly fey edge of it. "You are someone I could love, Paul."

Here he was, on his twelfth-or-so date with a kind man he could no longer stand to be near, somehow having descended by degrees far enough into a relationship that it was necessary to find a way out of it. To say George made him ill would be unfair. But he felt so often leaden and queasy in the man's presence that George came to feel like the cause. From the beginning he'd been insufferably patient with Paul's distraction. He'd sent flowers—a little disturbing, since Paul had never told him where he lived—and escorted him to a few sumptuous, barely-touched dinners, until he gave up and started bringing him instead to sit in a chair here on the patio of his own restaurant, to watch while George ate.

The ridiculous part was that they had not yet had sex, at least not that Paul counted. They kissed rather a lot—or Paul endured being kissed: rigid, wet, bristly, unpracticed things he eventually guided away from his mouth. Once out of boredom, he'd rummaged his way into George's pants to jerk him off, much to George's embarrassed gratitude. And once, when George finally seemed ready to cross a threshold, Paul had lain face down and naked while his body was kissed and tasted inch by inch, a process that tickled at first and then continued so adoringly long that he'd fallen asleep. The lack of consummation had been more relief than disappointment, since he'd let these few way-

ward events happen only out of guilt—a guilt that arose entirely from
his own automatic mechanisms, since George seemed to want them not
much more than he did.

Now George was taking a month's worth of public appearances in
each other's company and a few failed, awkward attempts in private
and calling it love. Watching him eat, he experienced a pure, cleansing
contempt for George, the egg on his chin and the slack, half-camou-
flaged flesh along his jaw and this proprietary brunch with the patio full
of waiters—George's employees—eyeing each other meaningfully
over his head as if they knew everything about who he was. He could
have laughed. He wanted to roll his eyes and argue but he couldn't
bring anything through the heavy drape of his surface. The most he
could do was force a bite of toast.

The week before, Kent had ordered burgers and fries at a drive-
thru, though Paul had said he wasn't hungry. "You need to eat. You're
losing weight." He seemed almost angry about this, as if it mattered to
him, kept demanding to know why he wouldn't eat until Paul said,
"You know."

Kent didn't look at him. "Maybe I want to hear it."

Paul felt cornered between the food and an answer, as if to keep
quiet would mean he'd have to eat, an idea that brought him to the edge
of panic. "Fine. You're making me crazy. Are you happy? You're all I
think about. I just want to be with you."

Kent nodded, with a grim lack of surprise, as if these months had
been little more to him than waiting for those words. "You're too late."

"Paul?" George said.

"I heard you." He had too many things on his mind, and he refused
to let George and his feelings be tossed into the fray. Yet he was aware
of blocking the scorn from his voice, letting his lethargy infuse it
instead with a kind of mopey depression that George would have to
pity and forgive—Paul had Big Problems Elsewhere, the theme of

their relationship. Even on the verge of casting the man aside, he tended almost subconsciously this garden of a context in which he could continue to be loved, from afar and forever if possible. The cellphone vibrated on the table next to his hand. He tried to ignore it.

"I want to help you, and you won't let me. I don't think you're capable of seeing the way he controls you. The way you let him."

Who? he wondered for a moment, of all hims picturing the soft-coated and whiskered one—his cat controlled him. This felt more accurate than George's obsession with Bernard, as if Bernard were the sole reason Paul fell short of soulmate perfection. Any blemish he revealed compelled George to spring again upon this source.

"No one controls me," Paul said.

"Then why don't you leave him?"

"I just can't, I told you. Not now."

"He's abusive, and you know he'll only get worse."

Paul regretted not making up a better story for the scratch on his forehead and the pale hint of a bruise beside it, souvenirs of their scuffle so minor that no one but George had spotted them. "He's really not," Paul said softly. "It was just one time. An accident."

The sadness was back in George's eyes, that blinking earnest confusion. It broke Paul's heart when middle-aged men looked that way, and filled him with the urge to run—men who were good-hearted and strong and accustomed to easy progress in the world, suddenly baffled by the failure of their best effort.

"My dad came to town last year, from out in Greene County," Paul said. "We had lunch right here on this patio. I think it was this table."

George warmed. "I didn't know you had a dad nearby. Does he come to town often?"

Paul shook his head, poked his eggs with the fork. "He doesn't know what to do with me."

"Because you're gay?"

"We avoid the topic. He tries. But I guess it's easier on him if he doesn't have to see me too much."

George responded with an embarrassment of sympathy and useless comfort that Paul tuned out. He took hold of the phone, held it tightly in his closed hand. "I need to check this," he mumbled, though he didn't right away, only held the phone. Then he cradled it against his ear and played the message—the vet himself, not an assistant—aware of the building pressure from across the table, the subsonic rumblings of George's displeasure.

"I have to go. Sorry."

"What is it? Paul?" George trailed him between tables and down the steps and the sidewalk, calling *Paul, Paul* the whole way like a forlorn crow until Paul had to hide his face in his hand. He was glad he'd parked out of sight of the patio, since George caught up to him as he fumbled for his keys, turned him by the arm. "You're going to run off in the middle of breakfast, just because he says jump? He knows about us—is that it? You can't go. You have to tell me what's happening."

"It's not him. And there's no us, George. I told you, it's not that way."

"That's because you're not thinking clearly."

"Look." Paul jerked away. "This isn't working. Just believe me. You don't know anything about me or what I'm dealing with right now. I don't know why you think you do. But you can't fix it. You can't do anything—" To his dismay, his voice crested and broke, flooded with tears. "Fuck, damn it." He stamped the pavement, pressed one eye with the heel of his hand. This man was no one to him, had no right to see him this way. "Go finish your eggs," he growled.

He drove through tears and sobs, without memory of how George had looked, abandoned there on the curb. He wasn't sure how he had let it go so far, except that Kent had spun him into a crisis of uncertainty and there was George, handing out free awe and protectiveness and solicitude and that kicker, a nearly platonic, paternal love.

At the animal hospital, another man waited to corner him with demands, accuse him of his failings. How much did they think he could take? *They*, men, the world, the universe. God. He was being punished. He couldn't go back far enough to trace all that lay unforgiven on his soul like years of blackened gum on a sidewalk because he was too stubborn, too angry to pray.

"God," he said, aloud in the car. But it sounded like an expletive, even over sniffles, and Jesus did too when he tried that name. "I can't. I'm sorry."

By the time he had his hands on the kitten, which lay on a towel in its steel cage breathing through its mouth, his tears had dried and he was blank and calm. And this time, when Dr. Carey insisted that they couldn't keep prolonging it, that it was painful for everyone and pointless to continue, Paul said fine. Just like that. He stroked the cat, which still glowed unearthly white even after the serum filled the catheter and its eyes dulled and its jaw stopped gaping, and he didn't cry like some little bitch even though the doctor stood there watching him and waiting for it.

⇗

"I know what you're looking for. A man who's a little reckless. Dangerous." He seized a fistful of the girl's hair, a coarse mess of brown curls, and she whimpered. Her mouth was close, her breath hot and cinnamon-smelling. She stared into his face in mute shock—he tried not to notice how her jaw moved like the cat's. "You think I'm dangerous?"

He was out of his head, his focus zinging around somewhere up in the rafters, and he stepped back, held up a hand. But Mark said keep going, so he took a breath, eyes back on the girl. Slice, he thought, sever. Penetrate. Slower, he gathered her hair like a handle at the back of her head, something to fling her by, stared at her parted lips until he was ready to bite into them like fruit. He was dangerous. "You've never had a man before," he said, his mouth curling toward a smile.

"If Devon knew I was here—" she cried, soprano and shrill.

"Shut up." He kissed her hard, felt their teeth click, and through it, a surge of anger that made him want not to hurt her, exactly, but to plunge deeper into her mouth, into her body. He actually felt his dick stir.

It was good, and Leah gasped as they broke apart, smiling faintly. "Fantastic," Mark said, and Paul stepped back unsmiling, turned away, shook it off.

"Paul, don't ad lib."

He blinked. He had no memory of the lines he'd spoken. "What?"

"'Shut up' is not a line. But keep that kiss, that was the stuff."

Paul nodded, cracked his neck, hopped on the balls of his feet. He was both empty and buzzing with a jangling energy he couldn't vent. It didn't help that Kent was watching, back in the blackest shadows of the empty theater near the door. He'd watched three rehearsals in the last two weeks, so stealthily the others never seemed to notice him, and always he slipped out before it was over. Paul never saw him enter or leave. He locked eyes with him now. "Can we take a break?" he asked Mark.

"Yeah, you're done for the night. Good work. But Paul." Mark stepped closer, massaged his shoulder. "A little uneven."

"I know. I'm just—I'll do better."

"Relax. Focus."

"I know."

"And tell your boyfriend over there to wait for opening night."

Kent was waiting for him in the hallway outside, as if it were perfectly natural for him to be there, as if they had planned it. It seemed a bad sign that he leaned casually against a wall and met Paul's eyes without apparent guilt or evasion.

"You're right," he said. "You can act."

"No, I suck. Tonight, at least." Paul checked over his shoulder. "The *play* sucks. As you've watched enough to know. Is this your new perversion?"

They stood close, leaning together against the wall with a foot of space between their bodies. "I like watching you," Kent said, his voice too mild to mean more than that. "From a distance, when you're not paying attention. It helps with perspective."

"Helps you feel in control, maybe?"

"I've been having trouble. With that, I guess. And—" He stopped, glanced around as if for help. "I just like watching you."

Paul looked at his shoes. "I'm glad you do." He didn't want to think about how much he had hoped for Kent to be here. His insides were a void, a spinning, growing weakness. Maybe it was only that he hadn't eaten, but he'd felt all day since the vet clinic as if he were going to fly apart, and he had to stop himself from explaining this, that he needed Kent's hands on him, now, just to hold him together. That Kent was the only one who could do it. He crossed his arms, gripped his own elbows. "I'm glad you're here."

"I wasn't going to stay." Kent looked off through the window toward the night-lit parking lot. "But I've been kind of in awe of what you're doing up there. I thought I should tell you that, I guess."

Something broke in Paul, melted, and his cheeks burned. It was more than a compliment. In Kent's eyes and voice, the words themselves, his entire being, was the assurance that this was simple honesty, offered in generosity, without ulterior motive. It nudged at Paul's bleakest and most buried truth—that standing before him was possibly the only good man he would ever know, the only one he could ever fully trust.

And yet, he was leaving. Over and over, Kent said they were finished, but he wouldn't leave for good by saying so. Perhaps those nights of watching rehearsals had shaped his resolve. There seemed little doubt that this critique, a kind of blessing for the life ahead, was code for goodbye.

"Don't," Paul said. "We can go somewhere."

"I can't."

He braced against the slide, as if the land were slowly buckling beneath his feet. He couldn't slip, not now. In the last month, he had steadily achieved control over his senses, his drives, become so rarefied that he might have been breathing ether, adrift and untouchable above the world. It was the angel that had power over Kent. Paul saw himself this way, winged and robed, bringing grace at his own whim or not, making demands that were arbitrary or senseless but never driven by longing. Bring me a single red plum, he might say, or cut off your hand. But he could never say *stay*. He could never say *just this once*, or *please*. He swallowed it back word by word and the void went on spinning.

"I want to talk to you about something," he said. "An idea."

Kent shook his head, eyes dim with purposeful inattention. He was already gone, already home with her. The car last week, the nauseating smell of fast food. Maybe in that moment, admitting he wanted something, Paul had lost him.

The instant before Kent moved toward the door, Paul stepped out alongside, then into the lead. He opened the door, and they were walking together toward Kent's car. "I have a friend who owns these clubs around town," he said, calm, spinning, "and sometimes he's looking for musicians. You know, a band, or maybe just you by yourself—you could play guitar and sing."

Kent stopped, looked at him quizzically. Paul moved up close beside him, against the car. "They're cool clubs. There's one—it's not gay or anything. Sort of a piano bar." This was true, could be true, all of it, if he could make himself stomach George a little longer, and talk George into it.

"I really have to go."

"Kent." His vision purpled, returned. He reached out carefully to steady himself, pinched the button placket of Kent's shirt to stop his fingers shaking. "Please. When do I ever ask you—" Kent's hand was on his shoulder, maybe to push him away, but for now it was contact, and he surrendered to it like falling. "I need...I want to make love."

Kent closed his eyes as if the words were painful, took the hand away. "God, you're so manipulative. You'll say anything."

Paul caught his breath, stricken, uncomprehending. The words, maybe. He never said *make love*, it felt too forced, too foreign in his mouth, too silly. But this time he hadn't even noticed—it had just come out that way.

"This is better for both of us," Kent said, his voice not harsh but not gentle either. Paul was shaking, gathering himself into his folded arms as Kent stepped away. "Go home. Go back to your life."

"What life?"

Kent sighed. "Go play with your cat."

It was not delivered as the slap Paul felt, but it was all he needed to recover. Spine straight, breath stilled, feet firm against the earth. "Oh, that? I gave it away."

He was impressed with the drawl of boredom in his own voice, and the skin along Kent's eyes registered a wince. "What?"

"It was kind of a pain. And Bernard didn't like it, so." He sighed. "What do you want from me?"

Kent's eyes went cold. "I have no idea." He turned, got into his car, while Paul unfolded himself and stood rigid, hands at his sides, counting his breaths. Before the car was gone, he turned away.

☙

His name was Silas Kingsbury, and he had served four years in prison. Fresh out in the free world, he was horny to the roots of his teeth, rampant as an animal, jonesing for pussy—any pussy. He was dangerous. He had been hurt—raped, Paul thought—in prison, and he hated men but he hated women more, even as part of him searched for one who would shield and suckle him. Because it was ultimately his mother who had failed to protect him, he could never stop wanting her, never stop blaming her.

"It's all about the mother," Bernard had once told Paul. "The prison of pussy."

The toughness was an act, Paul decided, in his slow, loving layering of this man, as if he were building him from papier-mâché. All bluff and self-protection. His small stature would be his greatest liability, so he learned to fight young, made the gym his church and skipped rope until his chest ached, endured grueling reps on the weight machines, tearing and building while the sweat ran. He enjoyed the sense that others in the gym observed his self-imposed torture but would never approach him, that the conventions of the space offered him a bubble of perfect solitude in which to create himself out of sweat.

Meditating upon Silas, Paul had been going to the gym, enough that he imagined his own shoulders expanding, new definition in his biceps and abdomen. In the mirror, he examined Silas emerging from within his own skin like some *Twilight Zone* transformation, and it thrilled him and made him nervous. At the end of his disastrous day, he could go to his room, ignoring Bernard's chirping questions as he passed, shed his clothes before the mirror, shed Kent, shed need, shed himself. Become Silas. However shallow and poorly drawn on the page, however weak his lines, Silas was more substantial than Paul and his problems, more important.

Silas wanted to be a good man. He believed he might actually be one, and he had ordinary dreams for a normal life: wife, a house, kids.

He was certain, in the way that only an unreflective, deluded, narcissistic man could be, that no matter how damaged he had been he could be a good father, better than his own. His success would be his revenge against his parents. It would make them cry, one day, to see how beautiful his life was in spite of them. He was the worst kind of white trash, and yet in his hopeless yearning there was something Paul pitied and adored.

Here, Paul knew, he was divided. The lust he felt was for Silas himself, who drew so much of his energy from the rednecks of Paul's youth—the ones who had been the most brutal and luggish and stupid, whose beatings had always felt testosterone-driven enough to amount to a sexual act. His stepbrother in particular—Paul shivered before the mirror. And though he could never have those rough boys, he had Silas here with him, in a way, his fantasy man contained and pliable.

But the lust Silas felt was for women. The verb, to fuck—simple as that. How to wrap his mind around that? How, as Silas, to feel it? Pussy. He practiced saying it, watched his lips form the word.

He had tried this before, come close, with Hamlet. But Hamlet's drives were far more complex, even convoluted, his heterosexuality present but submerged. The goal was to trap, to evade. Hamlet was the fox, and so was Paul—it was almost easier.

When he had first started running the lines with Leah, his partner, it had occurred to him to enter the character through Kent. To see her as he might. It hadn't helped with the task at hand—his stepbrother was the touchstone he needed—but Kent was the one on his mind and where his desire lay. Somehow, it seemed to him that if he could make himself look at this girl with lust in his heart, he would draw closer to that part of Kent's life that had always been so mysterious and disturbing.

He told Leah much of this—she seemed safe, a near stranger and fellow actor with soft brown eyes—and asked her for extra practice kissing. A few nights after rehearsal they had made out in the shadows of the darkened stage in secret, the wetness of her mouth pleasant, supple, and undemanding. She was tricking herself into a little crush, he thought, the way she welcomed him, and as he critiqued their perform-ance—they were pretty convincing—he glimpsed how he could trick himself as easily. How a kiss was an act, love was a word he could say; how he could marry such a girl, become a different person. All he had to do was stay in character, forever. He and Kent could live out their lives as friends, like other men, free of strain, meeting from time to time to sip beers over the grill while their children played in the grass. On his wedding day, his father would embrace him, all effort rinsed from his love, and he would watch as his life became easy and normal and sweet.

It all came down to an acting problem, he thought. Did he merely act, or did he become? He feared he didn't have the talent, on the stage any more than in life, to be other than himself. Some nights, like tonight, he watched in a state of numbed panic as Silas melted from his body, from the shadowy crevices that cupped muscle and bone, the illu-sion of taut, tethered power pouring away until only his own insubstan-tial form remained, nearly translucent, weak as a breath.

⚊

He opened his eyes to the walls of Bernard's bedroom in morning light, unable to feel surprise. Whenever he had turned in the night the cool slip of silk sheets had reminded him where he had come to, the depths of his degradation. Bernard was not in the bed now. So he had awakened to Paul beside him and done nothing.

He would have wished to forget the whole previous night, but there it was, how he had entered the darkened room like a child driven by unreasoning need. "Can I sleep here?" Bernard had squinted from beneath his raised eyeshield, maybe only struggling to complete his transition from sleep, but his response was stalled to the point Paul couldn't bear the tension, the chance that out of bitterness or pride he would say no. "I'll do whatever you want," he said. "I just don't want to sleep alone."

Bernard's expression, a sort of befuddled sternness, didn't change, and he didn't speak, only turned the covers back. Paul slid in gratefully, close enough to smell the mouthwash on the man's breath. He waited for a signal, instruction. Bernard draped an arm around him. After a minute, Paul turned, nestled his back to Bernard's chest. They were both clothed. He felt Bernard nuzzle his hair, and that was all. Later he wondered if Bernard had completely woken up, so quickly was he breathing evenly, then snoring in Paul's ear.

In sleep they had shifted to different sides of the bed, but he remembered sensing at some point in the night that Bernard was also awake, by his rigidity, his silence. That he was puzzling over this— wondering why Paul was there, what to do with him. Even then, faking sleep, Paul had sensed how this night's weakness would cost him, no matter that the bed provided little of the comfort he had craved.

For the gift of his solitude this morning, he would probably also pay. Not today perhaps, but soon. The silken pillow-topped mattress, the clean daylight—nothing could have been more luxurious or felt more like a trap. It galled him, as if somehow Bernard had engineered every trauma of the day before that had led him to this.

Time to move out. He could go back to the dorms, he thought, though it was well past midterm—they most likely would not let him in until summer session. He could find a friend, maybe stay on Eric and Sylvie's couch. There was George. The possibilities were few, and each one seemed fraught with increasing trouble. He had no money saved.

He rose and crept over to his own side of the condo, without running into Bernard. He took a shower, dressed for the library, where he was determined to spend the day getting caught up on his neglected coursework. Kent, gone—though Paul wasn't ready to acknowledge the reality or make a place for it among his other problems. In the momentum of the day, something would happen to bring the reins back to his hands, or he'd make it happen. He was no one's bitch. He rolled his sleeves before the mirror, curled his lip and snarled at his reflection. *Pussy.*

From the dresser where his watch and jewelry lay he picked up— it was lying there—the cat's red leather, silver-studded collar. It stopped his breath. Not that he had truly forgotten, but it brought him back into the moment—the life seeping through his hands, and he couldn't hold it back. He had not consented. Never. He saw then with sudden clarity that Kent and the cat were the same loss. That the cat was exactly as much as Kent had ever intended to give him: a diversion, a bit of comforting fluff, too feeble from the outset to last long.

Something began to burn in his chest, a cold fire. He stood breathing through it, felt its light grow and candle his skin. He buckled the collar onto his wrist. It fit perfectly.

Late afternoon, Paul stood in the quaint commercial district of Virginia Highlands, before a store that sold tribal knickknacks. Ten Thousand Villages, the sign read, over a window display of stone carvings and beaded bags and one long, bright machete amid a scattering of polished stones. Clutches of weekend shoppers brushed past him. The doorbell tinkled as a shopper exited the store, and through the window he watched as the woman inside went back behind the counter, to the fat books that lay open there.

He went inside, announced by the bell. Every hair on his arms and legs stood erect, as if a thin current ran from the floor to the top of his head. As she began lifting her eyes to acknowledge him, already smiling, he turned his back to her, moved toward some shelves. He felt the solid connection of each step with the floor, as if he were heavy, powerful. Dangerous. At the back of the store were a few other idle shoppers, hidden by partitions, nearly out of earshot. They were not a factor.

She had not yet seen his face, but he had seen hers, knew it well. He circled around to an angle behind her, shielding himself with a display, fingering tchotchkes while she studied the books. She was shorter than him, smaller, but broader in design. Round cheeks, round face—or was it heart-shaped? Breasts. Ass. Beneath her jeans and her gray oxford-cloth shirt, there was a thoroughly camouflaged allure of flesh. More and more, it disturbed him that she was not beautiful.

One hand—dry-looking and pale with quick-short, unpainted nails—rose to tuck the hair back behind her ear. The gesture seared him, and he didn't know why. She moved and it hurt him. He picked up a chunky wooden frog, trying to lash himself back under control. *I am the angel*, he told himself. No one had the power to touch him. Least of all her.

"Aren't those interesting?" With a turn, a few casual steps, she was suddenly at the edge of his space. "They're from Vietnam."

Her voice was a surprise, lower than he'd expected, soft and wry with a murmur of gritty texture. Here she was, speaking to him as if he were anyone. He opened his mouth on silence. But his scalp tingled, brimming with possibilities. He removed the wooden rod speared through the frog's gut, stroked it over the ridges of its back. It was a sort of jungle noisemaker, the rattle reverberating from the gap in the carved mouth.

"That's the mating call," Maggie said. "Go the opposite way." He did, tail to head, produced a more hollow, yawping sound. "That's the distress call."

He continued stroking, until he imagined the rainforest, the drip of water from leaves, and the frog calling over and over for help.

"You own this place?" His words had a velvety, warm sound, not like a challenge. He felt the power of his greater height, the crackling potential of the narrowed space between them.

"No one owns it. It's a nonprofit." She went on, explaining that it was run by the Mennonites for the benefit of craftsmakers in the third world, those many villages of the store's name. That she was only a volunteer, like everyone else who worked there. Paul stared at her mouth—her lips thin, like his own—barely hearing. He needed to move away from her, before his building tension made him giggle, or howl. Or reach out with one slow finger to poke her in the cheek. A smile began to twitch in his mouth, and he covered it.

"Are you a Mennonite?" he asked, the stupidest-sounding question he could think of. This was all he really wanted, he thought—to play with her a little, to lounge in this forbidden space.

She straightened a row of tiny elephants on a nearby shelf. "Well, not everyone here is. But I am."

"A Mennonite?" His mouth dropped open, and he leaned toward her, caught so off guard that he forgot they were strangers. "You're a Mennonite."

She laughed, said yes.

"You're a Mennonite." He couldn't stop saying it. His mind whirled with buggies and women in bonnets, men with jaw-fringe beards. "What does that *mean*?"

She hesitated, seemed to be looking for an answer, and he realized that the question was a misstep. It wasn't seeking a definition but asking *what does that mean for you?*, even *what does that do to my sense of you?* It assumed familiarity, and in it, he felt how she was already more than the cardboard nemesis he had intended her to be.

He stepped away from her, rattled a shelf. Something was wrong. A tickle at his nostrils, and his fingertips came away wet with blood.

The room, packed with the multicolored crafts of the world, tumbled, and he gripped the shelf's edge with one hand, pressed his nose with the other. "Are you okay?" she asked him.

"Fine," he said. Her question hadn't sounded too alarmed, and he thought his own voice calm. "Just—" *Dizzy*, he was going to say, *a little dizzy, it's nothing*, and he tried to say it, to make it true, remaining fiercely upright. She was asking him questions he couldn't hear, and he thought *I'm having a stroke. I'm bleeding into my brain, right here in the store.* This struck him as a little funny, though he couldn't remember why, and he was frightened, but oddly quieted by Maggie's presence. Her hand was on his arm now. She would know what to do.

⫸

He slept, knew he slept, for nearly an hour, deeply, and when he woke, she was making tea. He lay on his side on a wicker love seat, under a quilt that she had spread over him, and he felt weightless, as if pillowed on air—like a child again, napping under one of his grandmother's homemade quilts. His grandmother had been the closest thing he'd had to a mother, and when she wasn't visiting to fuss over him, he'd dreamed himself a real mother who drew up the blanket and soothed him to sleep, never leaving his side. Under that spell, he'd always resisted waking up, because when he did she'd be gone—and it was that feeling that came to him now, the wish to stay sleeping a little longer when he knew the waking world was not the dream he had made it, and this woman's care could not be the safe thing he had allowed it to seem.

He was in the back room of the store. Maggie sat at a desk nearby making notations in a ledger. She smiled at him. "Feel better?"

He nodded, sat up, pulling his knees up to his chin and the quilt around him. The smell of steeping tea made his stomach rumble.

"Thanks for not calling an ambulance," he said, a little ironic. It had only been a nosebleed, a little light-headedness. He had more or less regained his senses before she asked him if he wanted to lie down in the back.

"You're welcome, Paul."

Her words registered through the sleepy haze of his comfort. Had he told her his name? She brought two cups of tea, sat beside him. He held the steaming cup in both hands and breathed in, the earl grey steam dampening his nose. "Sorry," he said, feeling shy beside her, "about all that."

He wanted to say something more—this didn't sound like enough. Shifting his face away, he touched a tentative fingertip beneath his nose. The blood had mortified him, though it hadn't seemed to bother her in the least—she'd coaxed him into a chair, told him to tip his head back, while he mashed both hands against his nose in wild hope that he could turn the blood back, reverse the flow. "Sorry," he kept saying, "oh, god, I'm sorry, I'm sorry," wanting to crawl through a hole in the floor. It felt like some defilement escaping, uncontrolled, into the mapped space between them. She brought him paper towels, patted his shoulder and said don't worry about it.

It hadn't been much blood after all. At least he hadn't fainted.

"Thanks for the tea," he said. "And the nap. I think I needed that."

"Glad to help."

"I just—" He searched, struggling with his need to tell her something, or impress something upon her. "I haven't been sleeping much, I guess. I don't eat. My life is kind of a mess."

She nodded in sympathy, and it fascinated him that she could follow this, both knowing and not knowing what he was talking about. He didn't want to like her eyes, to change his mind now and decide she was pretty in her way, but he couldn't help it. The nosebleed and the nap had ushered him into this partial, willful surrender to her, while part of him remained separate.

Where he held his cup propped on one knee, his wrist bore the red collar, poised between them. He turned it in his fingers. "My cat just died," he said, watching her eyes for recognition, but saw only a melting of more sympathy. "So that's one thing."

"I'm sorry about that."

"Oh, it's okay, I'm over it."

Over the top of her cup, her eyes were soft but direct. Just below her left cheek, on the hand that held the cup, her small diamond glinted. It was set deep into a slim gold band, with a second band—plain—over the top.

"You're married," he said. It came out soft and hollow like new pain, plain enough for her to hear.

"Yes."

His two words had shifted the context, just for a moment—as if, but for the ring, he might have next asked her on a date. In her answer he imagined something like apology, regret. His cheeks flushed warm, and he glanced down at his cup. His next question, which should have been about Kent, refused to form.

"Kids?"

She shook her head, smiling. Again something shifted, as she tilted her head. She wasn't going to ask him the same questions. It was in her eyes—that she took him for a kid himself, too young to have his own, too young for her even if she weren't married. Maybe she had already pegged him as gay, but for some reason this didn't seem to change anything in the softly charged space between them, the otherworld possibility it held. He couldn't shake the bizarre notion that they were about to kiss.

"This is really weird," he said, half in whisper.

She couldn't have known what he meant, or all of it, but she laughed a little, then he laughed. And it felt right somehow. Maybe blood loss had rendered him loopy. He had entered the store with a kind of unspecific vandalism in his heart and ended up owning something. He couldn't be sure yet what it was, but this room, this blanket, the tea warming his throat—he was happy, as if he had gotten a present he'd never thought to ask for. It was forming still, slender and tentative, but he knew it was more than new leverage. It might be something Kent couldn't take from him, couldn't get near.

"So, you're a volunteer here," he said, looking around. The room was stacked to the ceiling with more hand-carved and woven merchandise the store didn't seem to have room for. "You need any more of those?"

She smiled. "Sure."

CHAPTER SEVEN

Flesh, she thought, studying the damp gloss on her husband's closed eyelid. The pale mole on his cheek. She couldn't imagine that she herself slept so beautifully, and yet he seemed lumpish in this inanimate state—carcass-like. This, her husband, her span of flesh, like a plot she owned. The maleness of him, like other males, harboring drives more powerful than reason, than decency, than love. The eyelid didn't move, but she wondered where he was in there, drifting in what limbo after what dreams, and where he had been, and with whom.

A shift of his body enclosed her in his arms—he was awake after all, breathing into the hair along her temple. His hard flesh against her thigh. With small kisses, he traced the edge of her face as if mapping something precious, once lost and now found. Had she been lost? Maybe, she thought—but if so, never dangerously, only enough to clarify his love. She could feel the subtle change between them.

"Morning," he murmured. "Sunday. Church?" He was locating this day's reason she would leave him. "I thought the Methodists were making you meet in the evenings?"

"They switched us again. But I can lie abed a little while."

"Lie abed?" he teased, his lips brushing her throat, spreading warmth through her body.

"My father's notion of a sin. Of the small-scale variety." She assumed a version of his gruff, humorous voice. "Will you children lie abed while the good Lord's sun is in the grass?"

"Meaning you should be up and doing good in the world?"

"Meaning, I guess"—she smiled sleepily against his bare shoulder—"we shouldn't waste the blessing of a sunny day."

"He's right. We won't waste it."

"What a good Mennonite you'd be." She grinned as he worked the buttons on the front of her pajama top. "I suppose I could skip church this once."

"No. Go. I want you to go." His breathing grew coarse as if the idea of her going to church were somehow erotic. "I've been thinking. Maybe I should go with you."

This startled her. "Really? What's that about?"

"I don't know. I just think it might be good for me. For us."

She didn't like that *us*, which sounded like something damaged he meant to fix.

"Don't do it for us," she said, unable to keep the disapproval from her voice. "It's not important."

"For me then. You don't want me to go?"

"It's not that. I just think it's weird." She said it smiling, hoping he wouldn't intuit her worry. Here in bed, easing toward lovemaking, she felt his earnest honeymoon presence, as if he had recently married her again without her knowledge. If she was haunted by the sense of the *someone else* she'd been chosen over, that was only an idea, a ghost she thought she could banish now.

She lay with him afterward until he seemed to doze, then she eased herself up. He'd been to church with her before. *But why now?* she wondered, as she ran water for her shower, stepped into the tub. She would have been happy to see it as a simple urge to draw closer to her in the wake of whatever he had passed through, if he had. But Kent was not so simple. If it were guilt, even—but she knew he would contend with his own conscience and find his own peace, not seek it from religion. She sensed, in fact, that he had done this, righted the world so thoroughly to his own satisfaction that he saw no need to disturb her with a confession, and for this she found herself thankful, if uncomfortably so. For now, at least, she preferred to believe herself in the wrong, overly sensitive and suspicious, rather than to risk breaking the new contentment he had spun around them.

What a good Mennonite you are, said that father-voice in her head. *A good Mennonite wife,* though she had never thought of marriage, her own especially, in quite these terms. Pacifism was not only an ideal of her faith; it was in her nature. From early childhood, there had been no quarrels with Lila or other children, none between her cousins or their parents or her own, only effortless harmony. She remembered, in fact, her shock of awakening when she'd understood, around age twelve, that other families fought, that they even seemed inclined toward strife rather than away. But leaning away broke the church apart at every turn, and she began to wonder now with a new measure of disquiet about her happy parents and all those happy Mennonite marriages she had grown up with. What underground restraints had kept them from splitting as the church did at every whiff of conflict?

Drying herself, she noticed the sun gone, the sky clouded over. Back in the bedroom, Kent's body remained under the covers, his breathing slow with sleep.

Stay sleeping, she thought. She dressed as quietly as she could, hoping the comfort of bed would hold him. For if church proved stronger, it could only be that he felt in their life together some intangible lack, something he was still missing and looking for.

The Friday before, midafternoon, she had felt her eyes go unfocused over the Jamal Cole file. Three hours minimum remained to her day, her backside gone numb in the chair, and the elements of narrative lay dormant and scattered through the pages, refusing to cohere. She couldn't make herself look at it anymore, and her attention wandered to the random collage of cartoons, cards, and news clippings mounted beside her desk. One, a sticker slogan, read, "I never seem to finish anyth." Beside it was tacked an interview she had done the year before with *Atlanta* magazine, one quote blown up in bold beside her picture: "All of these men have little, beautiful things about them that will never be told because their lives will be judged through this one senseless act." She tried to feel connected to the words. It didn't help that Harold did his job so well, bringing her more and more complications on Jamal that had to be folded in somehow but seemed instead poised to topple all she had hoped to say.

Harold peeked around her door frame. "Ask me why I'm back so quick." He'd spent half a day in the field, tracking down a retired social worker from Jamal's late teens.

"Do I want to know?"

"He's got a record. Sealed. Juvenile."

She took a deep breath, but couldn't stop herself from asking. "What is it?"

"Assault, apparently. He beat up a younger kid in the home pretty badly, said he stole his walkman or something. Only, sounds like people stole from him a lot. He was constantly getting into fights. Had a bad temper."

She sank into her chair, hands over her eyes. She had wanted to argue that Jamal was a gentle man who would never harm anyone, that he had lashed out only in a confused psychosis against his own child self. Maybe, she thought, she could argue that other violent episodes had the same source, but her theory was stretched thin already. It occurred to her suddenly that her calling in life was quixotic at best; at worst a dangerous lie.

"Assault. Okay. Thanks."

"You don't want to know more?" He approached her desk, his look curious.

"Just type it up, will you?"

He turned with a shrug, but before he could duck back out the door, she said, "Harold, maybe we've done enough digging on this one."

He pursed his lips into a frown.

"I mean—" She stood, began pacing behind her desk. "You keep bringing me these things, these pieces of the truth, and once we know the truth then we're responsible to it."

"Maggie, this is what we always do. This is how we make our case."

"I know. But it gets so complicated and messy and ugly, doesn't it? Maybe it's better if we know less.

"Less." He mulled this over.

"The jury needs something easy to digest," she argued, weakly she knew, but feeling the urgency of this insight. It seemed odd this simple thing hadn't occurred to her before. "Wasn't our first idea so much nicer? And more in control, without all these new pieces to fit somewhere? We're the defense attorneys! Maybe, you know, it's not really in our best interest to look so closely."

He shook his head as if to adjust the reception. "Um, okay. Are you having a breakdown or what?"

⁂

It seemed silly, her urge to discourage Kent, and yet when she arrived at the church alone to join her familiars, she was grateful for her usual privacy here. They gathered on the second floor of the Methodist church, in a classroom reminiscent of public grade school—white linoleum floors streaked with green, bulletin boards covered in children's creations cut from felt. There was little to signal the room was a church at all except for the slate cross mounted on the podium, the low table full of candles in front. Around the makeshift altar they'd arranged a circle of plastic chairs, and here Maggie took her seat and traded greetings with the members and visitors—about eighteen of them today, black, white, and brown faces, Americans and internationals, those who had been raised in the faith and a smaller number who had converted in their adulthood, since the Mennonites didn't tend to advertise. Most of those present were her people in the ethnic sense as well as in faith, people with hoary Germanic surnames like Kropf and Nafziger, who were raised on farms playing Dutch Blitz, who emerged from the womb singing.

Never yet had she seen a cape dress in this room, but there were plenty of Birkenstocks, and almost everyone had chosen a job that in itself was the most prominent outward sign of faith—nonprofits, social workers, caregivers, activists. Like Maggie, most had achieved a level of ease in the world far beyond that of their parents, and yet they could never fully escape awareness of their oddness there, their ardent views half a beat off. This room was like coming home. No one here smiled at Maggie with dismissive indulgence or thought her quirky, or impractical, for approaching the world as something that might be changed through action.

A marker board announced the day's scripture and the order of the service: Welcome, Call to Worship, Bringing in the Light, Hymns, Joys and Concerns, Prayer, Words of Wisdom, Response Hymn, Benediction. Beyond this, the structure was rather open, with members suggesting hymns or leading the prayer at will. After they had split from Lila's church, they had formed a lay leadership, and now about a dozen of them, Maggie included, took turns delivering the sermon based on preselected scripture. This morning, a young graduate student in social work was giving a talk on the economics of single motherhood in the inner city—the sort of thing that passed easily for a sermon among them. She handed out photocopied graphs and statistics, managing without too much trouble to tie her thesis to the day's scripture, Micah 6:8: *He hath shown thee, oh Man, what is good; and what doth the Lord require of thee but to do justly, and to love mercy, and to walk humbly with thy God?*

As they sang the response, Maggie felt her spirit buoyed on the group's harmonies, and she wondered if it was selfish to keep this room to herself. Kent had been here a few times, just to see what it was like— to test, she was sure, the strangeness of her faith—and he had found it like other churches, only simpler, gentler, with better music. If anything had drawn him before, it had been the hymns—unpracticed, a capella four-part harmonies, which served as the Mennonite sacrament and converted into sound the ideals behind a good many of the sermons: let go of your selfish concerns, become part of a larger whole.

After the benediction, *Go in peace to love and serve the Lord*, they rose and chatted in groups, taking their leave. Rondell, clipboard on her broad forearm, reminded Maggie that she was up for the sermon in two weeks.

"Am I? Oh, right." She checked Rondell's list for her assigned scripture, sure that it would be something uncannily appropriate to her current crisis, as it often was. "Maybe I'll be less scatterbrained by then."

"You're sure to bring us something joyful." Rondell's plump face squeezed into a smile. "Out of the worst kinds of trouble, you always find the blessings."

"Do I?" This surprised her—with so little time to prepare, she often fell back on anecdotes from her case files. Though scrambled a bit, muted and cleaned up, they were still of questionable content for church, and she was left with a sense of her sermons as disturbing things, emphasizing the dark side of human nature.

"Your clients are so lucky to have you there to see the good in them. I feel like I know so much about the work you do!"

She smiled uncomfortably, her mind still caught in Jamal's case from the past week and, somewhere deep in the background, her morning with Kent. Maybe this was what her life came to—stories for church. She made fictions out of depravity, tortured the truth until her audiences felt uplifted enough to believe again in the power of good.

But she didn't have time to worry about this now. She had only enough time to finish her goodbyes and pick up a sandwich before she had to be at the store to open. Normally she didn't work at Ten Thousand Villages more than once every few months, but Lila, who nearly ran the place, was ready to give birth at any minute. Maggie now had her sister's Sundays, for the next three months at least.

And she had Paul, her new volunteer, who was waiting outside the door. "Hey, there, early bird," she said.

His smile brightened at her approach—lean body propped against the window glass, hands in his front pockets. She couldn't get over the doting way this kid looked at her. Saved from a nosebleed, he'd pledged himself in service to the store and to her. This was his second week. She was used to volunteers who were customers first, who had wandered in and become smitten with the place, but they were mostly older women with idle days. Few young men had ever arrived this way. Never a college student. And Paul's interest seemed, sadly, too hot, the sort sprung from some personal crisis or need. Such boys turned up often around projects for the homeless, always deeply sweet and intelligent and well-meaning but with an impulse to help that was almost a cry for help in itself, a way of denying their own hidden damage. She always liked these boys immensely and was sorry when they vanished, as they usually did, before the first month was out.

"I was hoping you'd be working," he said.

"You knew I was."

He blushed, grinning at the ground. "I wasn't *sure*."

She was just as glad to see him. It was nice having someone younger around the store, and Paul was a talker under that veneer of shyness. The last week they had gotten themselves into giggle fits while arranging displays, so distracted that Nettie, the dour old Sunday regular, had been forced to *ahem* at Maggie two or three different times for her attention to some store matter.

She fit her key into the lock, Paul bouncing a little beside her like a puppy that couldn't wait to get through a door, though there was something jittery about it too, jack-rabbity, his glance careening back over his shoulder as he entered ahead of her. She turned off the alarm, went to the back to unlock the safe and count the register bins. Paul waited beside her, rubbing his crossed arms. She asked him how he liked the job so far.

"I like it. It's funny, I like it more than I thought I would." The blush still colored his face, which was fine-boned under flaxen hair, his eyes lit with intellect. His skin was poreless and unmarked, like something just made. She'd noticed herself staring at him before: he was pleasant-looking in a way that seemed familiar, as if he were some distant cousin, or someone she had known long ago.

Four unopened shipping crates waited, stacked by the desk. "Why don't you see what's in there," she said. Paul grinned like it was Christmas. "It should be from Bangladesh, I hope. Watch out for spiders."

"Oh, you're funny."

"I'll be up at the register until Nettie comes."

She carried the drawer up to the register and turned the open sign on the door. A few customers came in, and she greeted them, asked a question or two.

Next in the door was Lila, in a denim jumper and sneakers, braced back into a waddle against the weight of her belly. "Oh my God, am I tired of this kid!" was her greeting. "I thought I'd come in and do a little work—maybe some exertion will get him moving."

"Does that mean I get to go home?"

"No, it does not. Who'll lock the store when my water breaks? I'm not going to stay long anyway. Chloe and I are doing stuff." Lila glanced back toward the street. "She's down shopping for dresses at Outrageously Expensive."

"That doesn't sound like Chloe."

"She's shopping for ideas. Then we're going to the fabric store. But I told her we'd come help for a few hours first, so I'll feel less guilty."

Paul appeared beside her with a question about his unpacking, and she introduced him to Lila. "My big sister," she told Paul, "and my nephew, due any minute."

"Today?" He peered from behind Maggie's shoulder as if she offered a bit of protection. In a stage-aside to her, he murmured with contained delight, "Are we going to deliver a baby in the store?"

"You'd like that, wouldn't you? Back to your boxes, before you tempt fate."

She got caught up talking to Lila about baby matters, both of them taking breaks to help customers. Nettie arrived, and Maggie sent her to prepare display space for the new items from Bangladesh. Every few minutes, Paul popped up beside her with another question, lingered over answers with more questions, then slipped away again.

"Isn't he cute?" she said to Lila.

"He's something," Lila said darkly.

"What's that supposed to mean? He's adorable."

"That's the flattery talking, I think. He's in love with you."

Maggie gasped in shock, though the idea pleased her. "Hardly.

He's gay."

"Who's gay?" chirped Chloe, the doorbell jangling from her entrance.

Arms crossed, Lila fixed her shrewd look on Maggie. "The cute new boy who's in love with your aunt."

"New boy where?" Chloe craned her neck around the store, and Lila nodded toward the back room. "I'm going to look. Back in a minute." Chloe dashed off, braids flying, before Maggie could restrain her.

She sighed, faced her sister. "You're nuts."

"I'm a genius mastermind."

"Your hormones have cooked your brain." Maggie's tongue played meditatively over her front teeth. "He's really not. He's just another stray. I think he needs something from me."

"What's that?"

She glanced toward the back. "Can't tell yet."

Chloe returned after a minute as promised. Regal and aloof, she leaned on the counter to toy with the end of a braid. "Now he's in love with me."

"Oh ho ho," Lila chortled. "Listen to Miss Thing."

"What makes you think that?" Maggie asked, deeply curious.

"That's for me to know. Just be glad I fixed your problem. You being married and all." Chloe mused on her hair tips.

"Well, I thank you, dear. But he's still gay."

Chloe's eyebrows lifted, unconcerned. "We'll see."

"And twenty-something."

She let out a gasp of disappointment. "He looks younger!"

"Not fourteen, he doesn't," Lila said.

Chloe moped. "I don't need fourteen. I prefer an older man."

When the Yoders had departed, the rain that had been threatening all morning began to fall, darkening the day and sending most of the shoppers home. Maggie let Nettie take over the register. In the back room, Paul sat cross-legged amid half-unpacked carvings of wood and soapstone, printing rows of tags on the pricing gun from the list in the catalogue. "Lonely back here?" she asked.

His face lifted and brightened. "Yes, and bored. Come help me."

She plopped down beside him. "Some of these things have me worried," he said, hefting vaguely phallic examples. "They look obscene. I mean, what do you do with *this*?"

"We sell sex toys. Didn't you know?"

She enjoyed the way she talked to him. Dropping the barriers she'd have to maintain if he were straight granted all kinds of permission, including permission to be silly, a pleasure she found almost nowhere else in her life. She could sit close, and little flashes of warmth and light between them could look like love. It was nice, a man other than her husband she could be close to without danger. She wondered mischievously what Kent was doing today and what he would think of her new friend.

"Do you pray?" Paul asked—taking up his religious inquiry from the previous week.

"Yes."

"Do you think God listens?"

She ignored the crisp edge of his voice, the faintest note of frivolity or contempt. "I think so."

He turned a carving around and around in his fingers, a knot of luminous ivory stone that appeared to be two or three separate arches but was carved all of one piece. "I used to pray. But then God pissed me off, I guess. Do Mennonites think if you're gay you're going to hell?"

"I guess some of them do. But I don't. My church doesn't. Paul, every denomination in the country right now is divided on that issue. But in this city you can be a gay Catholic, a gay Baptist, whatever, and there's a church to welcome you."

He squirmed with impatience. "That pisses me off too. That means you just believe whatever you want and make a church for it. What's the point? When I was little, God was something real to me. The church had power." He trailed off into brooding thought. Something hard crossed his face, vanished again, and he turned back to her. "Do you think God protects you? I mean *you*, personally. Because you pray."

She felt herself flinch, knew his quick eyes had caught it. "In some ways. Depends what you mean." This probing, she felt sure, was as personal as it was spiritual, seeking access to her life for some reason of his own, but he seemed already to know more about her than he could. His understanding—of her, of God—and his throttled resentment flashed alternately in his eyes. "I was raped," she said.

"Oh." He blinked but didn't look ready to run from the room.

"It was a long time ago." She took a breath, blurted out, "Talk about pissed off at God. Or at his creation, I guess. I was always more angry at man than at God."

"That makes sense." He leaned an elbow on the sofa behind him. "I think it's best not to trust anything with a penis." She laughed, and he said, "I'm serious. I don't. Men are scary."

"Not all of them. My husband, for example. You should meet him."

Paul was silent, his head propped languorously on his hand, his eyes half-closed. "What's he like?"

"Very gentle. Very sweet and shy—but in a good way. Strong."

"Sounds perfect." He put a little extra length on the word that might have been sarcasm, or just a good-humored show of envy. "Sexy, I assume?"

She grinned, slapped his knee, and he said, "Oh, come on. Is he good in bed? Mennonites have sex, right?"

"That's none of your business."

His smile faded, as if he'd been struck with a sudden thought. "What did he, you know, do? When you were raped."

"It was before I met him."

"Oh, right."

She drew her knees up. "It bothers him, I think. That it happened. Worries him. He doesn't like to think about it. Men, you know—most of them can't really understand that kind of violation." The familiar rage welled up to strain her voice, and she closed her eyes, talked it back down. "It's tricky territory."

"Yeah, I know what you mean, kind of. Maybe not about rape so much." As an afterthought to this, he added, "I was raped once." He gave her a bitter little smile. "I mean, it's not the same thing."

"Oh—" She put a hand over her mouth, quieting herself. "Why isn't it?"

"Lots of reasons." He looked as if he weren't going to say more, but then he sat up and leaned forward to meet her eyes. "It was in a car, this guy. I was going to say yes. I mean, that's what I was there for, but. Well, I guess he wasn't interested in yes."

She took hold of his hand, though he seemed okay. "He hurt you?"

Mouth parted, Paul gazed at their joined hands, silent for a long time. When he spoke, he sounded only distracted, as if he had forgotten it was his turn. "Not too bad, but—I think he was going to kill me. You could tell." A hand went to his throat, squeezing in a speculative way. "It just got real violent, real fast. I mean, I was a kid, I knew nothing. I was a virgin. But as soon as he got out of me, I kicked him off and got the door open and I ran. Got the hell out of there." He grinned as if amused.

"You didn't report it."

"God, no. And it didn't stop me from getting into another guy's car a week later, so. It must not have been that awful." He chuckled, eyes unfocused and elsewhere. "I guess I forgot about it. Never told anyone. Weird. I still don't get what I did wrong. I just wanted to do what he wanted, but he wouldn't give me a chance."

She squeezed his hand. "I know. There was nothing you could do."

He nodded, then shivered and seemed to come back to himself. His eyes widened facetiously. "See, men *are* scary. Kill you just for being nice." He extracted his hand from hers. After a minute he said, "Did you know the guy?"

She shook her head. "Mine came through a window. First warm night of spring, and I had the windows open to catch a little breeze." Her own easy, wistful voice surprised her. "I used to love sleeping that way, with night sounds coming in. I almost never open the windows at all anymore."

"You could. You have that husband to protect you." He handed her a figurine. She peeled off a price tag and affixed it to the bottom. He was right, and she felt grateful for this, a little rush of love for her life and its possibility of open windows.

"Thanks," she said, thinking he knew what she meant. She watched him more closely as they returned to their pricing, and he responded to the attention with sideways glances of mock anxiety, but she didn't smile.

"Why are you here?" she asked him.

He twitched, drew a knotted carving up to his chest like a shield. But his eyes were full of a longing she could almost read, like hunger—voracious, unspecific—and she remembered the waifish, eager way he'd accepted the tea she made, their first meeting. Somebody wasn't feeding this boy. Food, she knew, was not literally what he was seeking, but it seemed to her a perfect answer for the moment.

"Do you want to come to my house for dinner?"

His eyes went round, and she couldn't tell if it was terror or joy.

"It won't be fancy," she told him. "Probably chili and bread. My husband likes to make a big pot on Sundays. There will be loads extra."

"You mean today." He whispered it. "Now?"

"When we're done here, silly. We close at six."

She could see him shaking in a fidgety way, and she drew a breath to tell him calming things—they could take her car, he could meet her husband; Kent wouldn't mind a sudden guest. But before she could speak, he said, "Okay."

⟶

When the phone rang, Kent thought *Paul*. His body tightened, though Paul had never called his home, and he assured himself the response was dread and not something else reawakening, rainy Sunday and Maggie gone. A weird light sheened stacks of rainclouds, his view of them squared by panes of the kitchen window. With a thumbnail grown long as a guitar pick he dug at the lumpy paint clotted on the wooden frame, down to the splinters beneath. The whole window needed to be replaced. All the windows. Through a hole in the clouds, deep up inside, the heavens were boiling apart, and the phone rang its third ring, and he picked it up. But it was only Maggie, bringing home a dinner guest.

Last week, Paul had called him at work. Not on his cellphone but the phone on his desk. "Just checking in," he'd said in a pleasant way, as if nothing had ended between them, and actually, nothing had been said in the way of ending. But it was understood. In the ten days since parting ways in the theater lot, they had not seen each other or spoken.

"You doing okay?" Paul said, no smugness detectable in his tone. Paul who, as far as Kent was aware, didn't know where he worked. So maybe he's been in my wallet, Kent thought, or he's following me.

"Fine," Kent said.

"That's good. You know where I am." *If you want me*, he didn't say.

"Yes." *But*, he didn't say. Needed to say. *You and I are finished. I won't see you anymore.* Nothing could have led him in that moment to suggest a meeting. He felt, for the first time, free, Paul's voice inducing no more than a nervous discomfort at his failure to vanish altogether.

"I just wanted to see if you're mad at me," Paul said, fragile and tentative, absent of threat. "I don't want you to be mad." *To go away mad*, he didn't say. Kent heard it in the gaps and hesitations.

"I'm not mad," he said softly. He wished there could be some middle ground, some way to stay—what? Friends? He wanted, more than anything, not to see Paul again nor to send him away forever but to freeze him in time, transform him into something like a vase or a cup that he could set on a high shelf, out of his own reach or anyone else's. *Take care of yourself* was the closest thing he could think of to say, but even that sounded too final. "Look, I have to go—"

Six days since then, of silence. Paul might be just at the edge of his life, watching for his next chance, or he might be long gone, so fully distracted by other pleasures that Kent was a distant memory, if remembered at all. Kent could only hope that Paul would stay diverted, that his own current serenity would not prove a phase.

He heard them when they entered the house. Heard Paul say distinctly from the living room, "I like that. Is that from the store?" and Maggie's answer, their voices bright and breathy amid a rustle of jackets. They might have come in from a walk in the park together. For a disoriented moment, he felt this as truth, as if his obsessive efforts to keep them separate had been only an elaborate fantasy, and they had all along been living together, the three of them in this house.

But it can't be. The phrase repeated meaninglessly in his head, finding no purchase, because he knew that voice.

Standing in their bedroom, Kent had forgotten what he had come in for, and now Maggie was speaking his name as they passed by the doorway, musing on where he might be. He stayed behind the wall, in shadow, in shock. "You want a beer? I've even got limes, I think." They were in the kitchen, Paul's assent audible, and then it was mostly Maggie talking, all perky and friendly. He could barely hear what she was saying through the buzzing in his head, but he managed to grasp from a few words and her earlier phone call that Paul had been volunteering in the store. They had been together all day. And Maggie knew nothing.

"There he is!" Maggie said, for Kent stood in the doorway of the kitchen, before he'd decided to move there or thought of a plan. He felt a catapult of momentum from his hips up his spine to his fists, as if his body had decided without him to fly straight to Paul and kill him on the spot—grab him up by the throat and shake him dead and hurl him from the house. But under the normalcy of the kitchen lights, all the white tile and appliances, the violent instinct fell away. This was a stage. He felt it instantly—spotlight on him, and he had a role, if he could find it, in Paul's play.

Maggie leaned against the stove, a Corona in her hand, looking relaxed and happy. "*This* is Kent. Kent, this is my new friend Paul."

Paul sat at the formica table against the near wall, head cocked, smiling up at him. His plain olive-colored t-shirt was one Kent recognized: from the beach, so crystalline in memory he thought he smelled salt. Paul's fingertips played over the slick neck of his bottle. "Hi," he said, and his gaze was dead-on direct, glittering with pleasure. But nothing was betrayed in that surface that couldn't be accounted for by this event, his introduction to Maggie's husband, a man he'd heard about.

Kent knew he was looking too long—struck dumb, astounded, swallowing against his need to slap that smile. "Hi," he said, moving past to the refrigerator. He opened it and stared inside at the beer, trying to think.

"Hey!" Maggie's accusatory voice right behind him made him jump. "Where's mine, huh?" Confused, he looked at the beer in her hand, while she leaned on tiptoes closer to his face. Flustered, he gave her a peck, missed her mouth. She frowned. He got himself a beer, and she was still there, waiting for reparation, so he slid an arm around her back and kissed her slowly and turned to face Paul, snugging her close up against his side.

"So." Paul blinked up at him with perverse innocence. "Maggie says you're *not* a Mennonite. Is that true?" At Kent's silence, he chewed his smile, flicked those eyes to Maggie, his partner in crime apparently, for she returned the knowing look. They had secrets.

"I'm just playing with you," Paul said. "You'd know that, I guess, if you knew me better."

"Kent has his own ways," Maggie put in.

"Maggie knows how I am, right?" Paul cast his gaze at her fondly, and Kent felt sick with rage. Just her name in his mouth. And that look, as if he had some piece of her Kent had never seen tucked away in his back pocket. "It's just that I'm fascinated by the whole Mennonite thing. I mean, who knew?"

"We're freaky beings. Living amongst you." His unwitting wife, aiding and abetting.

"It's darn near enough to make me want to become one myself." Paul directed this roundly at Kent. "Just for the novelty of it. But you were never snared?"

Kent felt the strain in his own smile. He looked down at Maggie beside him, stroked the hair behind her ear. "I'm close enough," he heard himself say, to her. Then he looked at Paul, feeling more grounded. "My wife has enough faith for both of us."

Paul gave him a softer smile, something appreciative in the look, and so intimate Kent wondered how Maggie couldn't see it.

"You didn't lie," Paul said after a pause. Kent's breath stopped, until he understood that this was directed to Maggie. More secrets. She erupted in giggles, patting Kent's chest in a placating way.

"Here, honey." She took the unopened beer from his hand, turned away to open it for him and squeeze a lime wedge inside. Kent took the chance to glare at Paul, as if the heat of his eyes alone could drive him from the house. Paul's expression didn't change but seemed to absorb everything Kent gave him, heat and all.

"Maggie, Maggie, Maggie," Paul said in a musing way—a taunt, his eyes on Kent. He didn't look at her until the instant she turned to face him. "Is it short for Margaret?"

"Magdalena, actually." Paul looked startled at this, and she said, "Yes. The whore. That's me."

"Interesting. But—" He leaned toward her, troubled, and Kent felt himself slip mercifully off Paul's radar for the moment. "Your parents, aren't they very religious? Why would they do that to you?"

"My dad's a little twisted. You met Lila today—Delilah is her full name. He said if he had to pick biblical names for us, we weren't going to be named after some goody-goody girls who were slaves to their husbands." She glanced meaningfully at Kent, so deadpan that it rattled him for a second. She smiled and sipped her beer. "He wanted powerful daughters."

"Magdalena." Paul shaped the name slowly, with less pleasure. Something in it distracted him.

"Delilah was worse, actually," Maggie went on. "Mary Magdalene started out a whore, but she's the one who washed the feet of Christ with her hair." She shrugged. "You name a kid Magdalena, it can just be a way of accepting that we're all sinners."

"I guess that's true, isn't it?" Paul said, with a glance at Kent. "And we can all be forgiven. Even whores. Adulterers."

"Murderers," Kent said.

Maggie excused herself to the bathroom, leaving him suddenly alone with Paul. Paul's eyes widened in mock alarm. "Murderers. Good one."

Kent heaved toward him and Paul was instantly on his feet, a hand raised to halt him. "Careful. You get blood on her floor and she'll want to know why."

Get out, he wanted to scream, but he turned away and gripped the counter.

"God, you really suck at this," Paul hissed over his shoulder. He went to the doorway, checking toward the bathroom. "Listen. You need to not get angry. It shows in your face."

Kent blinked, trying to see what game he was running now with this semblance of assistance. "It's okay," Paul said, earnest, almost a whisper, "we're fine, I promise," and Kent closed his eyes, surrendered to the soothing of his voice. "She doesn't know anything. She won't, unless you blow it, okay? So just stay calm."

"I'm going to kill you, Paul, I swear to god." His voice cracked, a weak threat crumbling with despair. His love for Maggie in this moment was white-hot, his renewed feeling over the past two weeks attenuated to the verge of torture—he had never loved her so much. Or maybe it was only that he had never felt pain in the love, which was something he'd felt before only for Paul.

"Kill me later. Right now, I'm some guy you just met." Paul stepped closer—Kent could feel it, though his eyes were closed. "Relax. I told you I wouldn't hurt you. I'm not going to."

"Why are you here? What do you want?"

He opened his eyes, and Paul's face was close, the hard malice of his pleasure softened to a kind of tenderness. If he were in his own home, he couldn't have looked more peaceful. "I wanted to see what it's like, I guess. Being married to you. Is that okay, if I look and don't touch?"

When Maggie returned, Paul was back in his chair. Kent went to the bathroom, ran water in the sink, and stared at his reflection for a long time. He splashed his face and dried it slowly.

Giggling from the kitchen. A clinking of silver, sliding of drawers. He stood in the darkened room just beyond the door and didn't worry about being caught—they weren't thinking of him. They were setting the table, ladling chili from the pot. "No, *you're* the one." "Don't look at me!" "That is so crude." On and on about nothing discernable, like adolescents at a slumber party, and it chilled him that once or twice he had to concentrate to tell their voices apart.

"You think he's cute," Maggie said, a teasing accusation.

"Who?"

"Don't give me that. I think you were flirting a little."

"No, I wasn't!"

"I'm not blind. I caught a spark."

Silence, and Maggie's laughter. Paul murmured playfully, "What about from him, huh? You think I got a chance there?"

It was too much, the pure child-like fun in Maggie's laugh, and Kent couldn't bear what they were doing to her. He returned to the kitchen, if only to shut Paul up, and now dinner was on the table, the table moved to the center of the room. He took his place before his bowl and bowed his head—the three of them bowed their heads together—while Maggie said grace.

CHAPTER EIGHT

M aggie nudged his leg with the toe of her shoe. "Kent, tell him about when we were down there. About you and the cow."

South Georgia, her cousin's peach farm, with its tiny, self-sufficient collection of pigs and milk cows and chickens. The preserves on the table had opened the topic and now Maggie was trying to draw him into her limping dinner conversation with Paul. She sat at the small table's head, Kent facing Paul on the long end, though Kent had planted himself in the center, bull-like at the trough, feet on either side of his chair, while Paul edged his plate up closer to Maggie as if for protection.

Kent smiled at her as warmly as he could. "You tell it. You do it better than I do."

Something had shifted, in the still moments when Maggie said grace for them: Paul had lowered his head and become subdued. Over a spoonful of chili or glancing down to butter his bread, his eyes went misty, blinked clear. His voice was muted at the edge. His small compliments and questions, all for Maggie, were subtly strained with effort.

Once Kent would have suspected this was some imitation of remorse, an end-game bid for sympathy, but now he knew it was unintentional. Paul assumed roles so artful and intricate and full of deception that they drained him, left him depressed. Tonight he'd simply worn himself out too quickly.

The familiar quiet in Paul and the soothing clink of spoons on bowls, the commonplace talk now safely clear of him and his marriage, made Kent almost forget his anger and his fear, even nudged him toward a surreal sense that everything was under control—as if there were nothing novel in their gathering and nothing to conceal. Paul glanced his way from time to time, taking him in but not bothering to address him, as if he had lost interest.

Maggie, rolling her eyes back to Paul, launched into the cow story. Later she would be a little hurt. She would ask him why he didn't like her new friend. He'd have to answer her carefully. Maybe he shouldn't deny his dislike—he needed to tell her something, after all, that would make her abandon this friendship. Paul would scare only so far, and barring a gate would be as good as paying him to find a back entrance. Nothing short of murder—Kent stopped the thought midsentence, and the word came to rest in his head.

If he were capable of taking a life, Paul's might have been it. Kent knew this precipice, at least. This desperation. In their old life, though the violence had been contained, he had often felt how close it lay alongside sex, just as his love had been crossed with hate. But always before, thoughts involving murder had come from the same raging, reasonless heat he'd felt on finding Paul in his kitchen, the hyperbolic *I'm going to kill you* that might warn of violence but was finally less than sincere. He'd never before come to the thought coldly, as he did now, or begun to seek a means.

He shuddered, shook it away. Paul was to blame, making him think such things. He'd married Maggie partly to rise above those drives, and he knew her nature had shaped his love into such a different class of feeling that it could never turn to hate, never, no matter what she did. As a Mennonite, she was nonviolent—a pacifist—and this occurred to him in the beauty of new insight as something he might aspire to. He should be like her, or at least try to ignore the situation, let Paul burn himself out.

But Paul was in his house. He couldn't allow it, Paul touching all he had worked for, making him sit and speak, making him conspire to deceive his wife. Even the perfect story to prod her into forgetting the friendship, if he could find such a story, would be a lie, coerced from him by Paul.

"You okay, honey?" Maggie had halted her tale, which Kent had heard none of. She was staring at him with concern, and he realized he'd been staring at Paul.

He shook his head. "Fine," he said, "I'm sorry, I was just"—and it came to him, what to say—what, if not why. He settled his gaze immovably on Paul. "I was noticing how familiar you look."

Paul went blank, blinking toward the edge of the table as if counting game pieces, looking for the one he'd dropped. Kent leaned closer in curious study. "Don't we know each other? I'm sure we do. You just look so familiar." He felt a thrill of power, Paul's mouth open and speechless. "It was somewhere...some time ago. In Athens, I think. Yeah, that was it. You don't remember me?"

"I can't quite..." Paul's brow bunched. He shook his head.

"I know you remember. I was in that band with your brother. Or was he your stepbrother?"

"Stepbrother," Paul said flatly, swallowing a grimace. He sighed into a smile. "Oh, right."

"You two knew each other!" Maggie exclaimed. "That's amazing!"

"Oh, it was barely, not really." This, Kent thought, was the truth in some real way. At least this one thing he would not be made to lie about. "You were always hanging around, as I recall. Of course you were much younger. We weren't ever really friends exactly."

Paul nodded appraisingly, a sort of concession. "Yeah, you were the singer. I remember you." His fingers made a frame in the air for Kent's face. "You looked different then. Had some facial hair thing happening, maybe?"

Kent grinned—he nearly laughed, for just at that moment there was something disturbingly like pleasure in the privacy of their exchange. It was almost erotic. "Yeah. Got rid of that."

"This is so weird." Maggie gripped Paul's wrist in excitement. "So you were like a groupie, or what?"

Paul had to bite his lip to keep from laughing. "Oh, gosh, groupie. I don't know if that's what I was." He shot Kent a look both puzzled and threatening.

Kent smiled. "No, not that. He had his own separate world. Didn't you?" He knew that a thin film of innuendo coated his voice, and he didn't care.

Paul watched him. "I always thought you were talented."

"Me? Not as talented as some, I'm sure."

Maggie looked back and forth between them, interested but silenced by the palpable edge of things not said, the slight strain in their pleasantness. *Enough*, Kent thought. He scraped the last spoonful from his bowl. "Long time ago. I'm glad we had the sense to quit. The band, I mean. We were never really any good."

They finished eating in silence, but Kent could feel the stewing from Paul's side.

"God, it's crazy, what you remember," Paul mused, to Maggie, his volume back as well as the stagy tone he'd used before dinner. "It really wasn't that long ago. But I was such a different person back then. I was wild in my youth. I probably hurt people I didn't mean to."

Kent rose at that, gathered his dishes and Maggie's, let them clatter

into the sink under a jet of water. Paul went on, the innuendo in his
voice almost a match for Kent's. "It'd be nice if some of those people I
knew then could see me now. All grown up and mature. Maybe even
ready to settle down! They'd be shocked."

"Are you done?" Kent's hand was poised for Paul's bowl.

"Yeah, I guess so." He wiped his mouth, gave Kent a smile he
would have sworn was shy in any other circumstance. "Thanks. It was
delicious."

⌒

Their bathroom, pale salmon tile, a cream-colored rug. One bathroom, and Paul could feel how their bodies must share it, Maggie
maybe in a nightshirt and Kent with a towel around his waist, maneu-
vering around each other at the single sink. One tube of toothpaste, one
jar of Q-tips, one bar of oatmeal soap in the tub. Jasmine bubble bath,
hers. In the medicine cabinet, he touched each item like a totem, moved
it slightly: aspirin bottle and antiseptic cream, Kent's drugstore after-
shave—the same brand he'd always used—a dial pack of birth control
pills, where he lingered, tracing the bubbles. Two worn toothbrushes in
a wall holder. Creamy towels on the rack and one hung on the back of
the door, damp—his. He touched everything, a calming process, then
flushed the toilet, ran water in the sink, and walked out.

Maggie was in the kitchen, brewing coffee, slicing apple torte. He
paused at the open door of their bedroom. It lay in darkness, except
for the faint gold of a streetlight slanting in from the window to touch
the complex pattern in the bed quilt—blue and green and white, it
looked like from the doorway. A hairbrush on Kent's dresser, a
handful of loose change. A cut-glass box, heart-shaped, on hers. He
couldn't chance more than a ruminative pause, an accident of wandering and barely long enough for a breath, but the tangle of aroma

reached him anyway, lilac and cardamom, vanilla, Kent's sweet after-shave and the warm smell of their bodies caught somewhere deep in the bed.

It made him wobble but he braced his knees, moved forward through the living room, heel to toe. What if he fainted here? Kent had excused himself—things to do, he'd said, pressing e-mail to return, and vanished into the unseen back of the house. A computer back there, but what else? The not knowing, not seeing, pricked him. He would compliment the architecture and ask Maggie for a tour. It had been a surprise to be invited, but once she asked him, it was obvious. Of course. And here he was where he belonged, inside Kent's life.

In the living room, so little like the place he'd imagined, he memorized. There was needlepoint—needlepoint!—framed on the walls, Maggie's family tree. A hanging quilt depicting some Amish-looking old man. Maggie had told him that Mennonites and Amish were related sects, the Mennonites less conservative, more adaptive to the outside world, and that her own family had been Amish several generations back. The sofas were modern, neutral fabric, the rug a tribal batik, the floors dark, weathered hardwood. Blue-green leaves in a handmade blue vase. A small piano against one wall, music open to "O Perfect Love." He leaned to read: "O perfect love, all human thought transcending, lowly we kneel in prayer before thy throne."

God again—so the piano was hers, the music hers. Her faith entranced him and galled him, that she could believe with so little trouble, that she seemed to walk bathed in rays of love from heaven like a favored daughter, while he, degenerate stepchild, lurked in shadows unsure of grace. Something about this quality of hers must have attracted Kent. Her blessedness. He tried to imagine how, when she sang this song, it was true for her. He turned the page: "That theirs may be the love that knows no ending, whom thou forever more dost join in one."

A marriage song. He shuddered and dropped the sheet. Maggie

stood in the doorway with two plates. "Do you play?" he asked her easily, casually.

"Not well." She handed him a plate.

He wanted to ask if she could play this song, and if she had played it recently and why. If she would play it now. He pictured, for some reason, sitting on the bench to sing it with her while she played, though he didn't know the tune, their two voices rising together loud enough to call Kent out from the back of the house. He sunk the edge of his fork into the torte, across a rubbery wedge of apple.

"Let's sit," she said, leading him to the sofa. "I'll bring the coffee, and then you have to tell me everything you know about my husband."

He couldn't wait to call Sylvie, report the evening word for word. He held the creamy, tart bite on his tongue while he scanned the coffee table—a stack of mail, the phone bill on top: his name, their address. And there just beyond it, a wedding photo in a silver frame. Maggie with her hair longer, curling toward her shoulders, mouth open in laughter. Kent, looking off a little, an arm around her waist, hand flat on her white satin belly, his happiness quieter but no less genuine—an unposed moment that was wrenchingly, inexplicably, natural. Kent had never looked better in his life, never would again. They were outdoors, in an afternoon light that glowed along the edge of Kent's face. He was stunning. And he was hers, the evidence framed here in his hand. Paul had never seen him in a tux. Minutes later, the frame in his fingers, his tongue held a dissolution of torte and he couldn't make himself swallow. He needed to stop time, stop himself here in this house because there was too much of it. He didn't know what to want.

Maggie returned, set a cup and saucer before him. "I like your dress," he managed to say, because he had to say something. He set the photo back on the table, where it wobbled and smacked down onto its face.

He knew he had broken it, that Kent would call him a liar, that he had heard the sound in the back room and knew what it was. Maggie reached to set it upright—unbroken after all—and touched his arm. "No harm, see."

It was a few seconds before he could remove his pressed fingers from his eyes. "Yeah, okay." He was calm now, but frayed, recalled the anxiety that had threatened to break out into tears over the supper table. Easier with only Maggie to contend with. He felt Bernard's touch, briefly at his jawbone, a palm against his abdomen. *Find your center. Focus.*

"I can't believe Kent got married," he said, without emotion, fully removed from himself now. He spoke for the persona Kent had created for him, somebody's kid brother who used to hang around. He could only guess what that boy would become later in Kent's story, when he had Maggie alone and could twist him at will, probably back into the thing his stepbrother had reviled. Not faggot—he wouldn't say that to her. But whore, slut. At least that was the rumor, he'd say, to make it true, to remove it from himself. And Magdalena, how could she hate him for that? He'd told her as much that afternoon. He imagined her coming to his defense, shaming her husband for his judgmental, callous heart.

"Why?" She wiggled with pleasure into the sofa cushion, cut herself a large bite. "He wasn't the marrying type?"

"Oh, I wouldn't know."

"You must know something. Did he have girls all over him? Did they throw panties on the stage? What?"

He laughed in spite of himself, more at her alert delight in the excavation than at the image she raised. "He was quiet for a rock star. From what I could see. Sure, girls went for him. But I always had the idea he didn't care too much about that sort of thing. He was, I don't know, above it."

She smiled madonna-like at her plate, content to let that idea sit as they chewed dessert. Clearly it pleased her to hear it, this truth she must already know on her own terms—it wasn't just coy wordplay. Suddenly he wanted to tell her more, really talk to her. He had no one in his life now who knew Kent, who could offer other insight on that troubled soul, his maddening privacies. Sylvie listened, but she wasn't good for much more than half-distracted uh-huhs and dismissive advice.

"Above marriage," Maggie said, before he could think of a safe angle. "Is that what you mean?"

It surprised him, seeming at once to suggest a suspicion and to contradict his own wayward thinking. What could be above marriage? "Well," he stalled, "it was the kind of band where guys ended up married to groupie chicks, I guess. So he was above that. He always seemed different to me, from the others."

"You *did* have a crush on him," she teased.

He smiled, eyes downcast. "Not really. He was interesting."

"What about his girlfriend—did you know her? Kristin?"

"Kristin." Pronouncing it became a little seizure of memory—the name in Kent's mouth, after they'd lived together a year and Paul had one night tried drag on a lark, for a party. Gorgeous, svelte Kristin in garter-belted stockings and five-inch heels and small, elegant breasts made of dried lentils, real to the touch. Kristin in a chin-length, metallic-red bob, a micro-mini, tucked and taped into panties, tall and rocket-tight and legs to her ears like a runway model. He'd hidden in the bathroom for an hour, staring at himself in terror and excitement— he knew without question how Kent would respond. He wasn't sure he could bear to see Kent in the grip of that version of lust, and he knew, too, that he could not deny himself the chance to see it. "Close your eyes," he said through the door, and when he said open, Kent couldn't speak for minutes. "You can laugh," Paul said, but Kent could barely smile, reaching for a razored edge of red hair, then cupping a breast, reverent. (*I want to kiss you. You'll mess up my lipstick. I don't really care. You're gonna have to wait.*) With his downy skin and elfin features, he was real enough that Kent took him out to dinner that way, blitzed on the thrill of it, ushering him through doors with a hand on the small of his back and into chairs with playful grabs and little kisses on his neck and calling him Kristin, the name Kent admitted only then to giving his parents when they asked about his love life.

"Yes," he said. "I knew her."

"Listen to me," Maggie scolded herself. "Can you believe I'm asking you such things? It's ancient history, right?"

Of course, he should have said, but he swallowed against his dry mouth. It didn't matter that he couldn't answer. It wasn't a question. She was that sure, even looking him in the face. She wasn't stupid. It was simply beyond her capacity to imagine.

"He was crazy about her," Paul said instead, softly as if distracted by memory. "But you shouldn't let that bother you. I mean, you're the one he married, right?"

He hoped it would cut her just a tiny bit, a paper cut, enough to dwell on later. But she seemed not much concerned as she forked the last edge of cream from her crust. "Well. I don't know that I would have had the chance if she hadn't dumped him."

Paul stared, transfixed. "Is that what happened? I never knew."

"Apparently, she broke his heart."

"Well." He didn't know what to do with this, this thing Kent must have told her, straight out and simple that way, so it must be true. His fork rattle-tapped at the edge of his plate, and he clamped it down flat. He needed to get out of there, now. "This was really good," he said, smiling broadly, almost falling into a laugh, "everything. Everything was great. I really ought to get going."

Maggie smiled with disappointment. "You don't want to stay for Dutch Blitz? We can get Kent to play."

This stopped him—he'd forgotten about the Mennonite card game she'd told him about on the drive over. He had loved the idea of the three of them playing cards. "Can we do it some other time?" he said.

"I really do want to. It's just, well, I told you about the guy I live with, Bernard?"

"With cancer."

"Yeah, he's not doing so well, these past few days. I need to check on him." This was not even a lie. Bernard had been suffering from stomach pains and depression, and though Paul didn't feel homebound on his account, checking on him was truly in order.

"I completely understand. We'll do it some other time." They stood together, and she took the plate from his hand. "Oh, I need to drive you back to your car."

They moved into the kitchen and she called Kent's name, told him she was running out to drop Paul off. He'd forgotten to ask to see the back of the house, but it didn't matter to him now, and he'd be happy to escape without seeing Kent, who was surely back there on broil.

Kent appeared in the doorway. "I'll take him. I'm going out anyway, over to Derek's."

"Oh, all right," Maggie said cheerily. "Paul? Is that okay?"

He met the unreadable shell of Kent's eyes, and a cool, watery trepidation spread through his belly. "That's fine."

It was such a casual leaving, saying goodbye to Maggie, following Kent past piano and fireplace and dried grasses in a tall ceramic floor vase by the door. He plucked one out as he passed—they were plentiful enough—went through the wrought-iron door that rang shut against the frame behind him. In the cool indigo evening, he saw for the first time that Kent's porch had a corner of city skyline view, including his favorite, the tall bank building with its tapered peak lit in diffuse gold like a candle. Of course he'd never stood here before, looking out.

Blackly inscrutable, Kent stood on the walkway, waiting. Paul brought the soft seeded tip of the stolen frond to his face. "Nice view from here," he said, hoping his voice would slow Kent's thoughts, calm them. Kent said nothing, and Paul trailed him down the steps, dropping the grass beside the path.

They got into Kent's car. As soon as the doors shut them in darkness, Paul braced, but Kent only started the engine with his usual gentle motions. The car crawled out from the curb.

"Listen," Paul said, before he had anything prepared for Kent to listen to. What could he say? Sorry? "I know that was a little risky, but"—he flinched as Kent shifted in his seat—"we're okay." He needed this to be true, and as he watched the dark neighborhood slide by he knew he was talking to himself, trying to stave off a fear, unborn until now, that he'd done something irreparable. Kent's profile was impassive. So many times in the past two months they had driven just this way in this car, strapped in beside each other in silent anticipation.

He decided on a laugh, soft and amiable. "You managed to play along pretty well, there. A few tense moments, but you got it together. And that stuff about Athens. Kind of surprised me." Kent still didn't speak, but every minute the silence seemed easier and more normal, and Paul thought it could only help to go on talking. "Nothing actually happened, you know. Back there. The boundaries are all intact. She just had a friend over for dinner."

This sounded okay when he said it, but in the long silence that followed, it began to ring hollow and ominous. Kent pulled into a gravel parking lot and stopped the car. Hands on the wheel, he faced forward. They were in the Edgewood warehouse district where there were no streetlights, no people on the street, no nearby windows behind which people lived. When Kent spoke, his soft, strangled words were hard to make out. "I can't believe you did this to me. That you're doing this."

The pain in his voice made Paul nervous, sad. "I'm not doing anything."

"You came into my house."

"I was already in your house."

Kent turned to him, his face rigid in dashboard light. "What?"

"You said so. Remember? You were thinking about me. I didn't show up out of the blue to wreck a perfect marriage, so don't start telling yourself that story."

Kent lunged, and the edge of a hand clouted Paul across the windpipe. Choking, he backed into the corner, and Kent leaned after him until he found a solid grip, thumb pressed into Paul's trachea for a few tense seconds, a few clicks of difficult air in which Paul returned to the scene of his first car with a man, tears pressed into the corners of his eyes and a rising reflexive need to kick and claw. He clutched the seat with both hands, closed his eyes, and Kent stopped.

He transferred the grip to a handful of hair behind Paul's left ear, brought him forward. "Do you know I have a tire iron in the trunk? I want you to know that. That's what you made me do tonight. You made me picture that tire iron and what I could do with it."

He turned Paul loose, sat back in his seat, stared into the dash. Paul's breathing was audible and snagged with a residue of adrenaline fear. "You wouldn't kill me," he said as soon as he could speak. Now it was possible to feel Kent's violence as what it had so often been in the past, as much an indication of deep love and worry for his safety as it was anger. "You wouldn't do that."

Kent spread a hand in the air between them, made a fist, but gazed at nothing. He seemed sunk in wordless grief, as if the murder had been committed.

"You're making too much of this." Paul reached for his arm, but Kent shrank away. Paul sat back in his seat rubbing his throat. "You're angry, that's all. I get that. I guess I knew you would be, but I swear, I didn't do this to hurt you. Or her. I really like her."

He wasn't sure Kent was hearing him, the way he stared into the dash, head shaking a little as if in resistance to private thoughts. "This isn't a crisis. It's an adjustment," Paul said, relaxing a few more degrees, falling into the long habit of creating Kent's truth for him by speaking it. Kent had never known what to think, in anything involving him, or what to do until Paul spoke this way, the words steady as a rail to balance on. "It's really okay. We're going to be fine, all of us."

"I don't want you anymore." Kent's voice barely broke a whisper.

"Yes, you do. And I won't make you choose. We can all have what we want." He leaned closer. "You can believe this. I honestly like her. I wouldn't hurt her, any more than I'd hurt you. I want her to be happy." This seemed to him entirely true as he said it, though once he'd spoken he wasn't sure.

He reached for Kent's face, slowly. "I want you to be happy. That's all." The backs of his fingers brushed the rough edge of Kent's jaw, and it astounded him that he was allowed this, not slapped away, that his hand was only taken and set aside as Kent put the car in gear.

They drove on in silence. There was no one else on the road, and it seemed remarkable that Kent slowed for yellow lights and stopped at eerily empty intersections where no other cars waited or crossed, obedient to the law in a world that seemed to have abandoned them together. Paul's stomach floated, but the silence was calm at least. And something in the car's compulsory arrangement of their bodies, forward facing and together, seemed hopeful of a future that included them both. But Paul knew he hadn't been punished yet.

They stopped at the curb across the street from Paul's building. "My car's at the store," he said. He simply hadn't thought about where they were headed, and his correction sounded even to him like a non sequitur, as if Kent were indeed a kind stranger doing him the favor of a ride.

"You can get it later."

Paul heard the decisive edge, the grit of mockery delivered through a tense jaw. Kent killed the engine, looked at him. When Paul reached tentatively to open his door, Kent opened his own.

Kent crossed the street beside him and still, Paul had the idea that he was preparing some final speech, perhaps to be delivered on the steps. He loomed so close in the overhang at the door that Paul stood openmouthed, confused. Then he understood. Kent waved him toward the keypad, breathing on him as Paul turned and punched in the code. "Good boy," Kent said.

They stood strangely close in the elevator, facing ahead, but Paul set his shoulder into the cup of Kent's, shivering a little. It was a pleasant dread, the pleasure in Kent's returned strength. What was coming was bad, but it thrilled him a little, always, to have Kent take control. That was love, perhaps more than kisses, more than screaming, and it was something Kent arrived at only rarely. "Tell me what to do," Paul used to beg him. "Tell me what you want. Make me do it." But unless really pushed, Kent didn't understand the role, in bed games or in their tangled life, couldn't even fake it.

Bernard was on the sofa with a magazine. He lifted his reading glasses as Paul came in the door, and now Kent's arm was draped languidly over his shoulder from behind, his hand flat to Paul's chest, rubbing it, this precise gesture one he had possibly never made in their lives. "Um, sorry," Paul said to Bernard. "I didn't—I thought—" He made vague motions toward his room, endeavoring to lead Kent along.

"Hi, there." Kent planted his feet and waved. "You must be Bernard. The professor, right? I've heard all about you." He maneuvered Paul in front of him, kissed his temple with a squelching noise and then spoke with his mouth pressed alongside Paul's face, while Paul squirmed in this embrace and tried to stay still. "You've heard about me as well, I'm sure."

Bernard stood slowly and blinked at them, dumbstruck. The last few days he'd looked this way, shriveled and weak, enough to cause

Paul some worry. *Say something*, he begged silently, feeling as sick himself. The old Bernard would have given them a withering look and cut Kent to pieces in three remarks or less.

"Well, well." Kent laughed privately in Paul's ear. "You're not keeping me a secret, are you? I'm Kent." His tone was purely genial. "You know, the one he took down to your place in Florida. The one he's been spending all his time with." He toyed with the hair above Paul's ear. This acting foray was unusual for Kent, and more convincing than Paul would have expected but still a blatant hack job— surely, Bernard of all people would notice. "I thought it was about time I saw his bedroom, you know what I mean?"

"Of course," Bernard said, his voice soft and flat, nearly unrecognizable. He cleared his throat. "You'd be the married one, then?"

"Ah, you have told him! I was worried. Well, I don't think my marriage is going to last much longer. I mean, how could it, when I've got this sweet thing to tend to all my needs?"

Paul clamped his lips together. "All right. Come on." He dragged at Kent's arm, and Kent popped his eyebrows at Bernard as he was pulled away, down the hall and into Paul's room.

Kent stood inside the doorway, unsmiling. "Still a slob, I see." He touched a few dusty items on the bureau and made a face at the rest— bed unmade, books and magazines and clothes strewn about. He took off his jacket and pitched it onto the floor.

"Yeah, well, no one ever comes here," Paul said. "That was mean."

"I'm sure you can smooth it over. Just lie your ass off as usual." Kent jerked a desk drawer open, rattling the junk inside. "So where do you keep your toys?"

"My what?"

Kent gave him a sarcastic look. "I know you have them. Which drawer? C'mon Paul, pull them out and put them on the bed. All of them."

Paul did as he said, unloading his collection from the hiding places they shared with his porn magazines until the wad of bedclothes supported an impressive array, including several he'd forgotten he owned. Kent chuckled as each one came out. "Still a freak."

Despite the knowing tone, Paul was sure Kent had no idea what half of them were for, had used only one of them in his life. But he crossed his arms and held his tongue, as Kent picked up and hefted or dangled each one with a disgusted sneer, waved a flesh-toned phallic replica like a sword—"Self-explanatory, I guess." He finger-hooked the handcuffs out from the pile, spun them almost gleefully. "All right. Strip."

"Fine. Just—" He headed to shut the door, but Kent body-blocked him.

"Uh-uh. Let's leave it open."

"Kent."

"Yeah?" Eyebrows raised, he stood ready to listen with interest and even a kind of sympathy to any objection Paul might manage to form—the objection being part of the lesson. Paul knew this, but he also knew that Kent didn't have all the information. His renderings of Bernard, while never lies, had involved just enough detail to keep Kent wondering and jealous. Kent knew Bernard had feelings for Paul, harbored hopes, had arranged their lives in a sham of a marriage. But he didn't know of Bernard's precarious health or how his remaining life had slowly narrowed to include little beyond Paul and the obsessive intensity of those feelings. If he'd understood the cruelty of what they were doing, he would have at least let him shut the door. But Paul apprehended it only vaguely himself, and there was nothing he could say now that would make it clear or begin to sound convincing.

So he swallowed back even the beseeching look and piled his clothes on the floor, went to the bed as Kent directed. "On your back. Hands through the headboard." He set a knee into Paul's solar plexus as he fastened the cuffs, then rose and laid the key on the desk. Fully clothed, he stared down at Paul for some time under the full lights, as if considering this helplessness and its possibilities.

In the past, they had used the handcuffs now and then in serious play, when Paul's vaunted liberty became too much for Kent to bear. It had been Paul's idea, his offering. But now Kent's dark look, not unfamiliar either, that lurking potential, made Paul nervous again. Even angry, Kent could be trusted to take more care of him than necessary, but no telling what the night had wrought. Neither one of them, Paul thought, knew what they were doing now, but somewhere it had gone wrong, escaped their control, was no longer a private transaction in a closed room.

"Are you going to hurt me?"

"No," Kent said, with a slight softening in his face and his voice that Paul wanted to believe was the reassurance of love. He knelt on the bed, a palm firm on Paul's bent knee, the remaining toys scattered around them. "But you're going to be very loud. Understand me? You scream my name."

He nodded, yes, anything. He was calmer now. This was reconciliation. Though shaking and twitchy with desire—a touch made him groan—though he was hard and sure Kent was too beneath his clothes, he didn't beg for Kent's body. He didn't deserve it. But he'd take the simulation, quite close enough to real as it turned out, with Kent in charge of the implements, Kent in his own voice moaning as loud as he ever had. Twenty minutes in, amid their paired noises—Paul half forgot he was acting—there was an inarticulate outcry from the living room, and moments later the bedroom door was slammed shut from the outside.

That was enough—recompense made, slates cleaned. Kent leaned to touch his hair, kiss him on the ridge of a cheek. And Paul would take that too, grateful even if what was kissed was not him exactly, but some memory of him from years ago that his submission, and the cuffs, had called forth.

Kent stood and fished his jacket from the floor. It took Paul off guard, that he wasn't done yet. That all that had come before was only the prelude to his real punishment. "No, Kent. Enough." Kent gave him a look of dry pity from the door. "Wait, bring me some water," he cried, stalling with the only thing he could think of. "I'm thirsty."

"Yell for Bernard. I'm sure he'll bring you some."

"No, Kent, not funny. Don't. You've done enough." Not even the thumb in his windpipe in the car had triggered this level of mindless fear, and he strained against the cuffs, threw himself in one fierce jerk over to his knees and into an awkward hunch against the headboard. Though his voice was muted out of allegiance to Kent, it rose to a frantic pitch, and his face flooded with sudden tears. "You want him to rape me?"

This halted Kent, maybe the only thing that could have. He fixed Paul with a long, shadowed look of indecision, glanced out the doorway, back at Paul. "Would he do that?"

"I don't know."

Kent already saw through the lie. He came to the bed where Paul cowered and took rough hold of his chin, pulled it up to face him. "Would he?"

Paul swallowed. "I don't think so. But—" Kent rose. Paul's sobless tears streamed on unchecked. "Please, Kent. He's sick. Didn't you see him? He's got cancer, he's dying. You've hurt him enough." He pressed his eyes against his twisted arms. "Please, you've got to stop. You'll kill him."

Kent regarded him, mouth stretched in something like a smile. "Well, listen to you." He leaned to speak slowly at Paul's ear. "Is that you thinking about someone besides yourself?"

The voice tickling his ear canal shook a part of Paul awake in their old bed, in the darkest morass of their old life, and he remembered leaving it, and why he had left. Kent's punishments, however provoked, always arrived at the same end: to show that Paul was trash and his soul was dead. *You feel nothing*, like a box that Kent dropped him into for detention, and Paul lay inside it feeling the opposite—too easily wounded, one stripped nerve, nothing but feeling. But in the box, it was hard to disbelieve the one who knew him better than anyone.

"Of course, you're just playing your best card," Kent went on. "It doesn't require any real concern on your part. You're so damn good at this, sometimes I wonder if you even know you're faking."

All his performance, this day alone—the last of his energy had been spent in it. Paul tipped his face to the headboard, whispered, "You're right. I wouldn't know."

"And that argument has a hole or two. I'm not so sure it wouldn't be a nice boost for the old guy—to come in here and help you out of this. The key's right on the desk. Dry those tears for you. He might find that pleasant, after tonight, sort of a compensation. *You'd* hate it, though."

Paul's body rocked with nodding. "Yeah, okay, you're right. Just go."

But Kent brought the key and opened the cuffs, not speaking. He left, and Paul lay puddled on the bed, kissing his raw wrists, wondering if it was love to be released, and if Kent would ever come back to him now, and then wondering if Kent was right and he should lock himself back up and let Bernard find him.

CHAPTER NINE

Paul lived in a condo made of glass, something Kent had never fully appreciated from the street. The building had always appeared brilliantly armored, like bluish metal hurling back reflections of clouds and blinding sun. When he'd entered that evening and stood for the first time in the living room—high-ceilinged, track-lit, open to a kitchen gleaming with steel—the place had felt solidly walled, like a normal apartment. But now, as he passed through to the door, the lights were out and darkness rendered a profound change, the walls so transparent that the skyline was not a view but a presence and the city itself seemed to penetrate and flow through from every side, unobstructed like water.

Thank god the old guy had left, or gone to his own room—Kent could not have mustered the will to look him in the face. His anger spent, he could hardly remember what he'd been thinking to come here and torment this man, this complete stranger. He wanted to spit the bitterness from his mouth.

He wanted to be home. Being there, he thought, would be enough to return him to himself, make him a good man again or at least someone he recognized. But in the car, halfway there, he remembered that he was supposed to be at Derek's, and he drove past his turn and on toward Brownwood Park instead. It was ten-thirty, going on two hours since he'd left his house, and Derek wasn't expecting him tonight. Parked at the curb on his friend's quiet street, trying to decide whether to knock and with what cover story, it came to him that he had seriously fucked up. He wasn't thinking.

Or he was thinking too much about Paul. Over dinner, he'd made rash statements he now had to live with, and maybe it would be his own admission of knowing Paul from before that would sooner or later lead Maggie to the truth. Of course it might be just as likely to protect him, since that part of the truth could later come to light in a dozen ways. But he had been compelled to say it not for Maggie's sake but for Paul's—because in that moment, Paul had stepped to the fore, their struggle expanding enough to overshadow his marriage, to block it entirely from light. He had stumbled into duplicity, this alien state, and he had no aptitude. The understanding left him limp in the car, unable to make a plan.

Finally, he dragged himself through the deep tree-shadows of the screened porch to Derek's door. Derek answered his knock with Joanne quick at his shoulder, ushering him inside.

"We're just watching a movie, dude." Derek scratched his beard. "You're welcome to hang out."

"Did Maggie call?"

He knew she had, before they said yes. He could see it in their faces—Joanne's keenly curious, Derek's overly casual and averted—and intuit their suspicion from their lack of questions. He could almost guess how minutes before, they had been discussing his whereabouts, had even voiced the speculative word "cheating" loud enough that he could feel the echo of it in the walls.

He explained that he'd been planning to stop by, but he'd had to pick up something from work, had gotten a little sidetracked. Not believing himself, he added small details that sounded less and less credible, but they nodded anyway. They didn't seem interested to know why he'd been coming over.

Joanne said, "Maggie's at the hospital."

"*What?*"

"Don't worry. She's fine." There was a little smirk in Joanne's smile, something he hoped was merry and not sarcastic.

Derek broke in with decisive neutrality, as if to step his wife and her assumptions aside. "Her sister's having the baby. She said she thought you'd be over here, but not like she was worried or anything. She said tell you where she was, and she'd be home late."

"She didn't want me to go there?"

"Oh, no. Dude, you don't want to see that."

He drove home, feeling hounded. More than that, he felt guilty of heartless crime—let the hounds come, he deserved to be torn apart. His house would be empty, and knowing this made him certain of what he should do and what he most wanted, the only thing that would save him. He wanted Maggie to be home. He wanted to go straight to his wife and lie down beside her and tell her everything. He would prostrate himself and apologize and hope that she would have mercy and faith enough to let him start over and do better. He knew he could do better.

But, of course, she wasn't home. He checked the machine and found a message from her, a cheerful report of where she was, and Lila dilated at three centimeters, and maybe hours yet, morning, before she made it home. She didn't ask him to call.

Jittery with his own meanness, he rooted out a bottle of Maker's Mark from a kitchen cabinet, where it had sat untouched for six months, poured himself a shot into a highball glass, downed it and poured three fingers more over ice. Another mistake, if Maggie smelled it on him or he forgot to wash the glass, since drinking alone was one of the habits from his old life he had not carried into this one.

He turned on the TV, turned it off, picked up a magazine. He settled on the sofa with his drink, looking at words that didn't cohere for more than a sentence at a time. The bourbon's spicy heat on his tongue brought the thought of Paul where he'd left him, wrecked and insensible and probably lying there this minute, no matter that Bernard might find him that way. He picked up the phone from the end table, dialed half the number and stopped himself. He wanted only to hear his voice, hold the open line between them for a minute. Maybe then he could sleep.

Bernard might be with him now. Kent's fingers flexed on his glass, a burning in his chest strangely like envy that Bernard should have this chance to offer comfort, to touch him at all. No matter how disdained, how ill, the man could enter Paul's room and choose mercy, while Kent now had no choice left to him.

Paul was the one who should have been feeling guilty, the one who had crossed the line, and not he, who had been more merciful than Paul deserved. Yet he knew it was hardly the first time he'd justified himself with the same argument. As familiar as the drink in his glass, his remorse conjured their former life, a different sofa, and Paul a little younger but that same tail between his legs, crawling up into the empty spot between Kent's body and the sofa's back. *I know, you can't help it*, Kent might have whispered on any one of those nights, *and I didn't mean it, and I'm sorry*. But he was pretty sure he never had.

Paul lay as Kent imagined him at that moment, on his bed under full lights, having fallen into a catatonic reverie amid the litter of toys.

No sound from Bernard, though the door remained open and he couldn't make himself rise to close it. Even picking the tiny key from the cuffs that lay beside him required great effort, but he needed for some reason to put the key in his mouth, where his tongue turned it over, slipped it into a pouch of cheek. The metal was cool, slick, comforting. He wanted to swallow but he spit it back out. His face was prickly with salt, the pillow still wet.

His disconnection from the dampness reminded him of another time, a spell of dreams he'd all but forgotten. He'd been living with Kent then, nothing in particular wrong between them that he could remember—it might have even been one of those blissful times when they were in bed in daylight and home every night—when he'd suddenly begun to suffer from dreams that made him weep. He would begin in the dream, crying, and eventually wake up, and if he couldn't make himself stop he would go into the next room and turn on the TV. The sound he made was free of hysteria and nearly silent, so that often Kent didn't wake up at all, even for Paul getting up and then returning a half an hour later, calmed by a late-night talk show or an old sitcom.

Sometimes Kent woke first and had to wake Paul, ease him into his arms if he wasn't already folded there from their sleep. "What is it? Another dream?" Paul didn't answer. He never spoke on these occasions, consumed with the crying itself, a heavy, sleepborn thing that muffled his brain and swathed his body like a blanket. It was like waking in the midst of a gentle seizure, with no capacity to fight or think about fighting. Once or twice, he let Kent hold him until it ran itself out, but usually he pulled loose when he became awake enough to feel embarrassed, took his fit into the next room.

Twice, Paul didn't cry at all but shoved hard against Kent in his sleep, forced him to the edge of the mattress and nearly off before Kent managed to wake him and make him stop.

"You won't tell me what it is," Kent said, in bed the second week of it, when Paul was too tired to get up and no longer needed to, since the crying now stopped as soon as he was awake. But he didn't want to go back to sleep either. "It's just a dream," Kent said. "I won't get upset. Is it about something that happened to you? With someone else?"

"No. It's me and you."

"Where are we?"

"Here, in bed."

Paul knew better than to say more, though now Kent pressed him harder. *Am I dying or something? Injured? Is it you? What could happen in bed to make you cry like that? You know I'd never hurt you, right?*

And he did know this, though it was exactly what Kent said in the dream. *I'd never hurt you.* And then, *This won't hurt. You know it has to be done, right? You know it's only because I love you.* "I know," Paul answered in the dream, a little shaky every time as Kent soothed him, a razor blade pinched between his fingertips, and they both leaned forward to watch as Kent very cleanly and carefully sliced away Paul's genitals. It never hurt. It didn't really scare him either, and he trusted that Kent was right about this, that it had to be done. But it made him nervous to know what was coming, and then as he resigned to it, it made him sad, made him cry and he couldn't stop.

"Please tell me what's wrong," Kent said, stroking his wet face. "I'll fix it, I promise."

"You can't."

Paul woke to darkness, pressure, strange keening sounds, a pillow over his head. He'd dozed off on his side with one arm curled up before his face, enough of an air pocket there, now, in the hollow of his elbow that he didn't panic, and he thought he must be dreaming. He'd been worried he'd have his old dream again, after so many years, and part of

him almost hoped he would, if only for the God-like serenity and kindness he recalled in Kent's dreamed face. But his dreams had taken him
elsewhere then dumped him back here, at the site of that old nightmare
and others: his bed, under assault.

Near his ribcage he could feel the emphatic depression of the mattress under someone's knees, the taut fabric across his ear stretched
between fists, and little spasms of effort. His air pocket grew close and
hot. Sudden light then and cool air, the pillow gone, Bernard crimson
and gasping, checking him for life.

Almost instantly, because Paul simply looked up at him, Bernard
was in tears, showering him with filthy names, saying he deserved to
die. "You're right," Paul said. "I'm sorry. I'm scum." He meant it, but
he was enervated and sounded insincere even to himself. He almost
yawned. Though the pillow under his head remained damp, he felt so
dry that Bernard's crying annoyed him as dramatic excess. He was also
somewhat annoyed to find it was Bernard and not Kent killing him. He
heaved a sigh, sat up. "I'm really sorry, okay? That wasn't exactly my
idea."

"No? No?" Bernard smacked him sharply with the pillow twice,
then, unsatisfied with this attack, aimed it again two-fisted for Paul's
face. Paul caught it and forced it down; it felt a little like arm-wrestling
a child. Bernard hunched over the pillow in his lap, moaning, alcohol
dense in his breath and threatening to slur his words. "How could you?
I loved you." He pounded his own chest with the heel of a hand. "*I*
loved *you*."

Paul got out of the bed, embarrassed for both of them. He went to
the bureau and fumbled through junk for the cigarette and match he
knew he must have somewhere. Under a pair of jeans, he found an old
hardpack with three left.

"Oh. Now you're smoking!"

Paul released a stream of smoke. "Kill me in my sleep and then tell me I can't smoke. Honestly, I love that."

"You don't smoke. And you certainly won't do it in here."

Paul could see Bernard trying to scrape together a little dignity, straighten to a more casual sitting position. Maybe, Paul thought, they could pretend nothing had happened. "I need it, okay? Do you want me to get fat?"

This led their harried attention to Paul's nakedness, in full view against the bureau. Paul grunted with exasperation, but it was beyond him at the moment to consider the awkwardness of covering himself, so he only crossed his arms, cupping an elbow to prop his cigarette. "What do you want from me?" The small defiance in his stance made him feel terrible again, made his voice wilt into sincerity. "Is this what you've been thinking about?" He examined himself skeptically—his body perhaps hardened by gym work, thinned by fasting, if changed at all since Bernard had last seen it. He ran a hand down his belly to the trimmed strip of caramel-colored hair above his soft penis and prodded for flesh along his hip. Too thin, Kent had said—so his gaze took in a rib or a hip bone, though he'd never much cared for this frontside view, and perhaps for that reason it wasn't Paul's favorite either. In the dream, at least, he'd held still for the blade's efficient alterations the way he might steel himself to have a bad tooth pulled, hopeful of the results. "It's not so much, is it?"

Suddenly this was clear, it seemed, to both of them. Paul's body under lights was like a medical specimen, drained of all mystery. He half wanted to try a backside view, just to see if he could bring back the arrows of lust in Bernard's bleary eyes.

"I want you to leave," Bernard said.

A reasonable answer—Paul had thought of it himself, except that now he felt thoroughly despised and worthless and alone, the world void and nowhere he could go. "That's not fair."

Bernard's jaw stiffened, his gaze on the floor. "And what is fair?

You have no idea."

"I've done what we agreed. You just wanted me to live here. Remember? My own room, my own life." Paul paced, sucking at his cigarette. Bernard was so drunk he'd forget it all tomorrow, including kicking him out and the reason for it, but the thought didn't quell his rising anxiety.

He looked for somewhere to tap his cigarette, chose a magazine. "Look, I feel"—he laughed with sudden giddiness—"really messed up right now. I'm sure that's nothing to you, and I know what we did tonight was shitty, so I don't expect—" Bernard had sunk into a daze of inattention, and Paul stopped. "Bernard?"

Bernard covered his eyes, waved him off. "Just find some clothes. As I recall, you have thousands."

Paul went to the closet and snatched out a pair of snug pants the color of dried blood and made of something both airy and suede-like, slick inside and easy to slip on fast sans underwear. It felt strangely conciliatory to dress for him. "I've never asked you for all this, you know. You buy me things you like. I think it makes you happy."

"You have rather low standards for my happiness." Bernard seemed to choke on the words, while Paul pulled a shirt—liquid black silk with silver buttons, Bernard's favorite—over his shoulders and left it open.

"And you want me to feel like I owe you something. What did you think—that we'd turn into a couple?"

"Yes," Bernard nearly shouted, though he seemed instantly conflicted about his own answer. "Or, I don't know, maybe not that, precisely. But when two people care for each other and live together, love should be simpler than this."

Paul was struck. If anyone else had said such a thing, he might have screamed with hysterics. But coming from Bernard, his great teacher, and the wisdom of fifty-seven years behind it—booze was only a lubricant—it was more than he could take in. He nodded, unable to speak.

"But it's not," Paul said. He shook his head sharply against the long-ago memory of Kent against his back, whispering into the hollow of his neck, *never leave me*, that word *never* astounding, immutable. It had felt, at certain times, that simple and that terrifying.

"You want a child," Paul said. "Maybe a dog. And I want a drink."

The thought was inspiring—this was exactly what he wanted, the answer to every inchoate desire. He'd catch up to Bernard, and maybe the talk of love would come clear. He went out through the living room to the kitchen island that served as the bar, with its built-in forty-bottle wine rack and full array of glassware and pricey liquors. Bending, he uprighted a highball glass and seized from the cabinet a bottle familiar for the bloody drips of wax at its neck. He and Kent used to drink it almost like ritual after a bad fight, the peace treaty begun with a gesture, Kent's, instead of words: two glasses set on the counter, the bottle of bourbon beside them. Standing at the island, he drank, eyes shutting at the familiar taste. Bernard stood by, bear-like and unsteady at the edge of the Italian tile.

"Bernard, please sit down. You don't look well."

Bernard stiffened and stayed put, as if Paul's concern were a challenge or a kind of mockery. "You came to my bed recently. Of your own accord."

A quick wash of sorrow made Paul swallow most of his drink, set down the glass with morbid satisfaction as the liquor hummed into the base of his skull. He missed Bernard terribly.

"That's true," he said. "It was a bad night. I needed you and you were kind enough to let me sleep there. You could have had me that night and you didn't touch me. Why not?"

Bernard blinked. "You, you took me off guard, I suppose. If I'd had some time to…prepare. A little advance warning."

Paul's mouth fell open. He felt gut-punched. "You're kidding me.

Viagra? Is that the time you need?" Arms folded around his stomach, he moved to the dining table and sank into a chair, started laughing.

"You are evil," Bernard said.

"You know, here's what's funny. I actually thought maybe you were trying to be a friend to me. God, I felt so guilty about that night! I never knew how to thank you for just being there, that one time."

He rose abruptly and retrieved the bottle, filled his glass, pouring more than he meant to. His back to Bernard, he drank it down to a reasonable size, his hand shaking. *Stop*, he thought. Before him, the wall of windows hinted equally at the city lights beyond and his own faintly doubled reflection—the table he stood beside, with its boxy, low-slung amber light fixture, his face blurry white, his torso exposed in the unbuttoned black shirt. "I thought maybe things would be different," he said.

A claw hand fell on his shoulder and turned him. "You kissed me. Do you remember that? You kiss like a promise of something, like you kiss someone you love—"

"I do love you—"

"And then you bring that man into my house—"

"But you're taking it wrong."

"Under my nose, you fornicate with him, and it's some kind of game, some kind of punishment. Because you have always resented me for wanting you."

"Yeah, okay." Paul's breath came quickly. He set down his glass. "I resent you for wanting me." Bernard straightened with interest, and Paul backed away, turned about in the center of the kitchen in search of an answer that didn't sound crazy. "I need better from you. You're my teacher. I just want you to tell me if what I'm doing is good, and you—"

He stopped, and Bernard waited, a wry eyebrow raised. "I what? Flattered the poor innocent out of his clothes?"

"Bernard, damn it. I'm not even talking about that. We had sex.

Whatever. Get over it. And yeah, it was my idea, so your flattery, everything you ever said and did for me, it was never about me. It was all about you, your ego. You made me out to be some great talent, the next great thing, because that's who you wanted everyone to think you were fucking." Until he'd said it, he wasn't sure it was true, hadn't known this was what they needed to talk about until here they were in the middle of it.

"That's crazy," Bernard said, his voice unsteady, thoughtful. He closed his eyes with a bit of a wince, as if all of this was just slightly distasteful. "My dear, if our relationship was consensual, and I chose to promote your career, how does this hurt you? I've done everything I know how for you. If I hadn't become ill, I might have done more, I suppose—"

"I don't want that kind of help. God, I just want you to be honest. Help me fix what I'm doing wrong. This is my life, Bernard. I want to know if I can do this or if I'm wasting my time."

"Such an idealist, still." Bernard stepped closer, with the softened expression of overture. "Okay, perhaps I've protected you, *because* you were my student, because you were a sweet young thing from the sticks. But here's the truth, Paul—and you really should have learned it by now. You want to know whether you're good? It doesn't matter. The truth is there is no truth. There's only what you can make someone believe. If I make you believe you're talented, and make other people believe it too, that's what talent *is*."

"What, there's no objective talent?" He managed a scoff of sarcasm, edged to the table for his drink.

"Well, certainly there are broad categories. But among the talented, you, Paul, are only as—no, exactly as talented as I say you are." The anger had fallen from Bernard's voice and he seemed weary and saddened. "If not me, then the next guy who wants to fuck you or make a deal or raise his own stock, and I'll guarantee you it'll be his own piece first. The business is about hype. Every day there are geniuses, more brilliant than you, who are doomed to rot for want of a friend like me."

"I don't believe you." Paul's voice was tight, airless. "I've been listening to you for over a year. You think I don't listen?" He had soaked in every syllable, more than he cared to admit. If anyone was an idealist, it was Bernard, purist of the stage—it was central to Paul's understanding of the man and now of himself, or at least of the artist he wanted to be. How many times had he listened to this man hold forth on the high calling of his art? On the great actors of his generation and before? Paul could see him throned in the calm of the beach condo's sunlit living room on a weekend vacation, declaiming to a rapt audience of three or four of his dearest colleagues—Paul straying close just to listen, then to be welcomed with a warm midsentence smile to slip in and lean against Bernard and be stroked with fond inattention like a little dog while the great man's words reverberated through his body.

The other guests, theater people of Bernard's generation, spoke around Paul and over his head like grown-ups with an indulged child or directed to him now and then a faintly patronizing question, but mostly they limited their notice, men and women alike, to admiring glances, as if he were a prize awarded Bernard for a career of sagacity and artistic prowess. And so what if he was? He'd shared Bernard's bedroom on those trips, all for show, and loved it, honestly—talking until they fell asleep, waking into long lazy mornings of more quiet talk, while the others were up making breakfast and tsking at their closed door with envious amusement. That, the pinpoint balance of perfect contentment. It involved a lie, of course, maybe more than one, but it had felt rich enough to be worth the sacrifice.

Paul held his glass in both hands. "I can't talk about this with you right now. You're just mad at me."

"You go ahead and tell yourself that."

"Even when you pretend to help me, you're just trying to control me. I can't listen to you."

Bernard's voice sharpened. "Then who will you listen to? Who do you have? Mark Westlake?"

"I'm not your pet. I'm not *yours*!" Paul shouted. "I'm not even a person to you. I'm just a thing you made, a show dog you keep for decoration. You never loved me." He choked on a laugh and shook his head. "God, you never loved me."

He drained the glass, heart pounding hard. For a woozy, drunken moment, he was afraid he was talking to Kent, that it was Kent who had never loved him. He gripped the edge of the table, trying to fix on something he could believe in—the table, a solid thing, Bernard and not Kent. "I didn't bring him here tonight because of you." He gazed unsteadily into Bernard's face. "He's got nothing to do with you. I love him." Bernard's jaw twitched, and Paul stepped closer. "And he loves me. His own wife told me so, tonight. Can you believe that? No, I guess not, because you want to pretend I have no life apart from you. Well, *that's* my real life, Bernard. Him. Deal with it."

The fist caught him entirely off guard—in the mouth, not a powerful blow but enough to stun him with pain, send him staggering into the table. He caught himself on a chair-back and cupped his face. Blood on his fingers, and Bernard was hovering over him saying, "Oh, god, baby—"

Paul shoved him back. The bourbon bottle had smacked to its side, the contents glugging unheeded off the edge of the table and onto the tile. "That's it," he said. "You want me to leave, fine. I'm out of here."

"I'm sorry," Bernard hissed, an urgent half-whisper. "Please, I don't want you to leave. You belong here. You just need to see that."

"You're out of control." In Bernard's skittery eyes, he felt the first current of fear. He stepped back into a corner of the kitchen counter, trembling as he prodded his mouth. "You tried to kill me."

Bernard shook his head, stammering, "No, I'd never."

"You put a fucking pillow over my head, Bernard. I should call the cops." He said it softly to himself, like advice. Bernard snatched up his empty glass and flung it into the wall over the sink, where it shattered in a sparkle of sound.

This is how is happens, Paul thought. Next the kitchen knives, and tomorrow we're the front page. "Bernard," he tried. "Let's calm down—" He needed to stop them, say more, but he was aware of a delay between speaking and the sound of it, his faculties muzzy and slow. And Bernard appeared deaf and blind, wailing about ingratitude, groping along the counter as if for more things to break.

"Hopeless," Bernard said, or something like it. It's hopeless. He moved toward Paul with such sudden determined force that Paul dodged backward, his feet skidding in the floor's wash of bourbon. He landed hard against the counter, upright but off balance, and Bernard didn't twitch into apology but continued toward him, each step making escape less simple.

All Paul could think was that he needed to get to the door, let Bernard sober up, find Kent—but Kent might never speak to him again. Even now, he would be curled around Maggie's back, praying for the safety of the sanctified life he had chosen, and it came to Paul that it hardly mattered where his own happiness might lie, whether with Bernard or Kent or with someone unmet in a world he had yet to imagine, but he would find a way to wreck it just as surely as he'd fucked up every sweet safe thing he'd ever been given. If not, he'd be lying in Maggie's place, home in his own bed, even now.

Sometime past three a.m., Maggie crawled up onto the sofa where Kent dozed, the lamp still burning behind his head. She nudged under the crook of his arm until he folded her in, her body buzzing with a sweet exhaustion. "You waiting up for me?"

He shifted into groggy awareness. "How'd it go?"

"Kent, you should have been there. I mean, not literally, but I wish you could have seen it. It was amazing. Everyone says that, but it's just a word until you see it."

Having missed Lila's other births, she'd been determined to be present for this one, thinking it might be her last chance to learn something or at least demystify the process. Truly she had no sentimental interest in sharing her nephew's first breath. But now she didn't know how she felt or how to catch it for Kent in words. So terribly physical, so bloody, her sister exposed and helpless against these assaults from within, unable even to control her bowels—it looked like something that was not supposed to happen. Sadistic, or a mistake of nature, that this was how babies must arrive. They all watched—the midwife, two nurses, John, herself—while a face emerged from the slick, gaped opening in her sister's most private self, uninjured yet covered in gore, like an exceptionally brutal attacker. But this was almost the opposite of violence, bloody murder in reverse, the intruder so innocent it was drawing its first breath of the world's air to scream with while everyone in the room fell into helpless tears of joy.

How to tell Kent, that something so appalling could be beautiful, when this was something fully known and understood in advance by herself and everyone? She made a few muddled attempts that didn't come close before she fell to the usual dry information—the baby's weight: 8 lbs. 6 oz.

"So you want a baby now?" he murmured, his hand in her hair.

"No. Well, I mean, no more than I did before."

"Did you want one before?"

"No, but—it does kind of sharpen the idea, seeing it. You can't help thinking that one day that could be you lying there, you know? It's no fun, but still, you huff and puff and squeeze it out and there's your kid. It's crazy. Anyone could make one. I mean, *we* could make one."

"That's what I've heard."

She lifted her face to gauge his. "Do you want a baby?"

His eyes were half-open, head lolled on the pillow. A slow, wary smile spread in his lips.

"No, don't answer." She clapped a palm to his chest and sat up, pulling her knees up alongside him. "We're not having this discussion tonight, at all. Wrong night. Later, maybe like in three years, we'll have this discussion. Now we're going to bed."

She hauled him up by the hand, sent him toward the bedroom while she went to the bathroom to wash her face and pee and brush her teeth. He took his turn, while she changed into nightclothes. Bed looked more inviting than usual, especially because she had arranged a few hours of morning leave-time so she'd have the delirious luxury of sleeping in. As she slid under the blankets, though, she couldn't help imagining a space in this evening, in their house, for her own baby—where it might sleep, and how her attention might be attuned to its presence; how differently her hours would fall around its needs.

Kent came to bed in his boxers and t-shirt, adorably rumpled and sweet and hopeful for their lives. He saw their marriage as something purposeful that added to the good of the world. If he were having doubts, she thought, a baby could only clarify, simplify, their purpose. But she was no closer to imagining that she wanted one, and to say anything now would make him think she did. She rubbed his arm as he settled on his back beside her. "You got Paul back to his car okay?"

"Yeah." His expression seemed flat, distant.

"He didn't drive you crazy, did he?"

"What do you mean?"

"I don't know. I just got the sense maybe you didn't like him too much." It occurred to her that Kent had a box of old pictures somewhere in which she might have once seen Paul's face. She'd have to look for those, check to see if it was Paul. "I actually thought you'd be against him," she said. "Like, you'd have some story to tell me about his wicked ways when you knew him before."

Kent's brow furrowed, and he looked almost mournful, his gaze up in the ceiling somewhere. "No, he's…he's all right."

"Good." She settled her head on his chest. "He might be fun to have around now and then."

Kent said nothing, only drew her close in a tight embrace and breathed into her hair, and she wondered if he was thinking about the baby concept, wanting to talk about it and holding back for the same reason she did. She felt how they had spoken around the space, talking instead about Paul, bringing him in just a little like a placeholder. Maybe that was what they needed, she thought—some interim substitute. They should consider getting a cat or a dog like other couples did.

At Crush a Sunday tea dance spilled over from the afternoon, with a good DJ flown in from New York and a twenty-five-dollar cover, but it was late and the doorman knew Paul, let him in with a wordless smirk and a two-inch wave of his hand. George was in his customary chair, in the room where the bars were made of lucite lit pale blue from within so that the entire room had a bright aqueous quality like a swimming pool at night. Slipping into a barstool across the room, Paul registered with dread the familiar wounded stare. He wanted to go back in time and do everything better, or at least cross the room and say something to fix it all because if he'd ever needed a man to save him it was now.

Behind the bar, Philip squinched up his face—"Ouch!"—at the sight of Paul's swelling lip and began shaking a dirty martini. Though Paul hadn't spoken to George in two weeks, free and unrequested drinks continued to land wherever he sat, a mysterious oversight not yet corrected. Philip set the glass down like a holy chalice—the rabble at Crush drank their martinis from plastic cups—and poked a spear of olives through the delicate skin of ice at its surface. "Who beat you up, baby?"

He shook his head and didn't answer. "Thanks, Philip." He felt a little spurt of pure love for Philip, who was twenty-six and attractive, a flame-bright and then snuffed glimpse of the life they could have lived together as Philip gave him a pressed, sympathetic smile and moved down the bar. He was already drunker than he'd meant to be, and this lovely thing with its evanescent glaze of ice would be all he needed to knock him into oblivion. Another week of this and he'd turn into Bernard. Just wake up one day years from now and be him.

Around the corner of the bar he spotted a familiar face, chatting languidly with another man, and after a few minutes' strain the name surfaced—Tyler. There, astoundingly, was his last trick, the last dick he'd fully laid eyes on aside from Kent's, and he couldn't calculate the intervening time. Had it been two months ago? Tyler's glance passed over him with no recognition at all.

He finished his drink far too quickly, which plunged him headlong into an intense need to go to George, to just walk over and into his arms. Luckily he was still aware enough to recognize the desire as pathetic, and besides, George was nowhere in sight.

This was what he remembered the next day, and little else: the close-call relief of failing to find George, the panoramic, hard-edged view of Crush's thinning crowd in which George did not appear. Then, jump-cut, he'd fallen into an intense conversation with a somewhat tweaked loan officer from Miami, during which they argued the identities of Warner Brothers cartoon characters until suddenly Paul was on the verge of tears. He was a terrible person, he told the guy, what was his name again? Jerry, like the mouse, right. He told Jerry how he hurt anyone who cared for him and had maybe lost someone he truly loved. He began to hiccup painfully—too many trespasses, too many flaws, black gum on his soul, and now he'd finally done something unforgivable.

They were in the back seat of Jerry's car, Paul's liminal fear at finding himself there obliterated in the ongoing urgent project of convincing Jerry of his bad nature and the awfulness that had happened.

"You're not evil. Someone hurt *you*." Jerry reached to stroke his throbbing lip with a hand that wore a heavy gold band.

"Maybe they should have. Maybe you should. You could be a murderer, you know. Anyone could."

Jerry smiled with dopey assurance. "I'm not a murderer."

But then Paul began to think that this was right, that Jerry was the murderer and he, Paul, was innocent. He'd never meant to do anything wrong, anything hurtful to another soul. He wanted everyone to be happy. Part of him knew he was only exhausted and stupidly drunk and that he needed to sleep, but he was afraid to go home, afraid to face what he'd done to Bernard. *Not died. Will die.* But somewhere in the night he'd become convinced that when he arrived home Bernard's body would be on the floor. He could almost see it, the blood sticky and dark in the wispy fringe of his hair and pooled on the Italian tile—or maybe he only thought he had thought this, later. The next day, trying to remember the night, it seemed to him that he had known this, Bernard dead before he found him that way, had thought *he's dead* before the fact, and *he's all alone, I left him alone again*, while in the back seat of a rented car he let a man named Jerry go down on him. He watched the ringed hand grasping at the front of his shirt, opening and closing there in an infantile way as if seeking something to hold, while he tried to get hard and more or less failed, though Jerry didn't seem to mind, and the night's brown sky became gray and then paler gray.

CHAPTER TEN

Monday afternoon, as Maggie spent an hour at her desk returning calls, she doodled compulsively on the inside of Jamal's file folder: sleeping baby faces, babies swathed in blankets with faces nearly featureless, barely made things. She'd have to tear up the folder and replace it with a new one to avoid someone—Harold—finding it and accusing her of desires she didn't have.

She made a quick call to Lila, who was scheduled to check out of the hospital in an hour. "He's nursing," she reported, her voice brimming with a pleasureful authority, as if she understood the process in rich, layered ways others couldn't hope to. In the background, Maggie could hear the voices of Chloe and Seth, who had been home asleep during the birth but today had begged off school to be at the hospital.

"Is there anything you need?" Maggie asked. "I could stop by later."

Lila said no, nothing, and Maggie knew they'd probably rather have a little peace and family time tonight, without visitors.

And now her child murderer's file was covered in babies. She didn't know what that could mean. A hex, perhaps, to keep any latent procreative desire in check. But she wanted to see it as something beautiful, a sign of hope for Jamal—once a baby himself after all, still a child of God. That would be the key to her case, giving the jury access to the child he had been, once a trial date was finally set. Her present tactic, far less creatively complicated, was to file for change of venue.

Kathy, the receptionist, buzzed at Maggie's intercom. "Do you have a client named Paul Foster?"

She laughed. "No, that one's not a client. Put him through." Her radar began humming though—that he was calling her here, the day after their dinner. She hoped it wasn't just to talk. Stray or not, she couldn't handle one panting at her heels every day. Maybe he'd have a good excuse, had left something at her house.

"Maggie," he said, "I'm sorry." She thought they had a bad connection, his voice was so tense and strange, with a kind of wheeze in the background, and she didn't know what made her go tight with a fear that this was somehow about Kent. Maybe something had gone awry after they'd left the house. Kent had been a sphinx, but she was certain there was something about Paul he wasn't telling her.

"You're the only one I knew to call." He stopped again. "I think I'm in trouble."

He couldn't speak much, couldn't really tell her what was wrong, only beg her to come right away to Atlanta Homicide. She knew her way well—east on Ponce, six floors up in the old Sears building that housed the City Hall annex.

"I'm here for Paul Foster," she said to the desk sergeant. From a small cluster of detectives standing nearby a familiar voice called, "Miss Maggie!" with pointed jocularity—Thornton, a balding blue-eyed brick of a man, the lead detective on Jamal's case.

"What, you're here for *him*? Thought you only did court-appointed. Woulda thought that one"—he jerked a thumb toward a closed door—"would be hiring some fancier counsel, no offense."

"He's just a friend of mine," she said. "As far as I know, he's got no need to hire anyone."

Thornton chuckled, exchanged a look with the two other detectives that made her stomach flip.

"You want to tell me what this is about?"

"Didn't he say? Probably too grief-stricken. Kid's roommate got himself killed last night. *Roommate.*" He made air quotes.

"Or was it his uncle?" said one of the others. They laughed.

Thornton's eyes sparkled at Maggie. "Yeah, uncle, that was his original story. Happened around one or two o'clock this morning, someone bashed the guy's head in. It wasn't your client, though, since he was out dancing at the time. Or, I'm sorry, *is* he your client?" He scratched his chin as if puzzled.

"For now, why don't you assume he is."

"The man's name is Bernard Falk, college professor. Former professor of your client's, as it happens, but of course they're just friends now. And very friendly, since the kid's living there rent-free. But you know about all that, right, being his friend as well?" The irony drained from Thornton's face and he shook his head. "Maggie Schwartzentruber—how could I forget a name like that!" He pulled a steno pad from his pocket and turned a page, fixed an eye on her. "He had dinner with you last night."

"Yes. He did."

"Until when, would you say?"

She almost blurted out the time, as definite as any good witness—she was that certain of his innocence. But she stopped herself. "Has he been charged?"

"No, we're just talking to him." Thornton sucked his front teeth and studied her, as if she had answered a question for him in not answering.

"Look." She dropped her professional front, lowered her voice. "He's a good kid. I know him because he does charity work with me.

He's not violent and he's certainly not a criminal. He didn't do this."

Thornton looked unconvinced, though his sarcasm remained at bay. "What do you know about his relationship with Bernard Falk?"

She had crossed her arms, intending not to answer anything further. But this seemed safe territory. "Not much. I know he lives with him. I know he's been worried about him, because he has cancer, and that they're not sexually involved."

Thornton's narrowed, suspicious eyes prodded her, and she went on. "I didn't know the man, okay, and Paul hasn't told me about him in any detail. But I was with Paul most of the day yesterday, he had dinner with me last night, and all he said to me about Bernard Falk was that he wasn't feeling well. That he was worried about him. If there had been trouble between them, I think I would have picked up on it."

"You must be a good friend, then." He smiled a half smile. "Hey, maybe you were out dancing with him last night and can verify his whereabouts there, too. Maybe you saw him get elbowed on the dance floor, which is how he says his lip got split open."

He watched her closely for a reaction, and she kept her face blank. "May I see him?"

"Of course. Right this way."

The interrogation room—table and chairs, a shut-off video camera aimed from one corner—appeared empty at first. Paul stood pressed into a near corner as if trying to vanish into it, hugging his thin arms. He relaxed when he saw her, stepped toward her, and she met him with a stilling hand on his forearm before he could unfold himself. "Don't worry," she said. She looked straight into his eyes, which were reddened and blank-looking, as if he were drugged—exhausted, she thought. The skin was bruised below a puffiness at one side of his lip, the cut through it a blood-bright line.

"Your friend is here," Thornton sang out behind her. He came in and parked his rear end on the table with a false-friendly presumption that reassured her they'd at least stopped questioning Paul when he'd asked to see her. "And she says you're innocent, and that you probably had a good reason for lying to us and all. But I know you'll want to help us find who did this. Answer a few more questions? Seeing as how it was your good friend, the guy paying your way, who took at least three heavy cracks to the skull with a blunt object. I mean, someone must have been pretty pissed—"

"It wasn't me!" Paul cried, louder than necessary.

She squeezed his arm, turned to Thornton and made shooing motions. "In private, please. Now."

Thornton left with a smile, and Paul groaned as the door shut. "Oh god. Are they listening?"

"No. Sit down, okay? Just relax." She guided him to a chair and he fell into it, dropped his head into his arms.

"I'm sorry. I'm really sorry, Maggie. I didn't know what else to do."

She stroked his back, the fine, light material of his shirt sliding over his vertebrae. "You did the right thing," she said, though she was aware he might have been talking about the crime, not about calling her. She was a little disoriented by the situation—her clients were almost always in handcuffs and formally charged before she ever met them. Almost none of them had the option, as Paul did, of leaving the room. "We're just going to be a little careful, if we can, and try to get out of here without them charging you. Okay? We can leave right now if you want, but it might be better if we talk here. Because we want to help if we can."

He looked at her with slow comprehension and nodded. "Just tell me what to do."

"Okay." She pulled a chair up beside him and laid a hand over his. *Everything's going to be fine*, she almost said—but she didn't know that, didn't know with any certainty that he wasn't about to confess to her. But even then, she thought, there would be a reason. "We'll get this straightened out."

He nodded. "I didn't kill him."

"You went to a club?"

"Yeah. It's called Crush."

"Did you go home after you left my house, or did you go straight out?"

"Home," Paul said, though the answer seemed to require some thought. "I saw him. I don't know when it was, but he was fine—" The word caught in his throat, and he reached for a paper cup of cold coffee that sat on the table before him, held it between his hands without drinking. "Then I came home and he was dead."

"You found him? About what time was that?"

"This morning. Like eight."

"And last night, how long would you say you were home before you went out again?"

He shook his head, lips pressed together. "Maybe an hour. A little longer."

"Okay, so you left my house around eight-thirty, quarter to nine. You went straight home?"

He nodded, his eyes squeezed shut.

"So, maybe it was ten, ten-thirty, when you left again?"

"I guess. I'm sorry. I'm—I can't think straight."

"And all that time you were at the club?"

"Um. I met this guy, Jerry something. I left with him. I was kind of drunk, and it was late, maybe four or five? And then I went and got some breakfast at the Dunk and Dine." He brightened a little, as if this were helpful information.

She nodded encouragement. "Okay, that's good. They're going to care more about one to two a.m., I think. Do you have anyone who can vouch for you being at the club then?"

"Yeah." Paul's gaze darted around the ceiling, lips moving silently in the shape of the times she had given him: *one, two, one, one.* "George Babbish. He's one of the owners of the club."

"Good, good." She let out a breath she didn't know she'd been holding. "That's good, Paul. Did you tell the cops that?"

"No. Maggie, they—they were asking me all these questions, and I could tell they didn't believe me when I told them. And I just got freaked out and quit answering and that's when I called you."

"Yes, sweetie, it's good you did that. That was the right thing. But we'll tell them now, and they'll go find him, and everything will be fine." She grinned with a little thrill of triumph, clapped her hands together. "That's all, see? George Babbish?"

He nodded darkly. "He saw me. He'll say I was there."

"Anyone else? Bartenders, maybe?"

"Um. I don't know exactly." He picked at his fingertips, which were smudged faintly in black.

"Paul." She grabbed his hand. "You let them fingerprint you?" At the same instant she saw a rash inside his wrist, and at the bone above, a neat set of parallel lines scored rawly into the skin. Had they put him in handcuffs?

"Oh. That was earlier, at the condo."

"Did they arrest you at some point?"

He shook his head no. "They said I had to, since I live there. Like, to rule me out."

"Okay, think hard on this. Did they say you had to, or did they ask your permission?"

"Oh, god. I wasn't really thinking. I was a mess. They, uh, did a mouth swab too. I said it was okay. I thought they needed it."

She took a deep breath. "Never mind, it's fine. You were cooperative, and that's what innocent people do, so that's in your favor. How about that cut on your lip? Can this George Babbish or someone else say how you got that?" He blinked at her in a startled way, and she added, "It happened at the club, right?"

"Oh. Yeah, but. I mean, I don't know anyone who can say so, off-hand."

Plenty of other questions buoyed up around this piece of information, starting with Bernard Falk and whether or not they had fought that night. But she held back—keep it simple, she thought—said instead, "It won't matter. An alibi for the time of the murder will be enough."

Paul winced at the word *murder*, squeezed his eyes shut. "God, he's really dead?"

"Yes. I'm so sorry."

"Someone killed him. There was all this blood. Someone bashed his head in." Eyes widened as if he'd just that moment seen the body, as if the news were fresh and he needed to tell her, he nodded with urgency. "Someone did that to him."

"Yes," she whispered.

His face closed down, turned away, and he mulled this over in silence.

"He could have just fell," Paul said. "Like, he slipped. Hit his head?"

"I don't think so."

"I have to go home," he said flatly.

"He's not there."

She took his hand, threaded her fingers between his, while he stared at the table edge, digging parallel lines into the graffiti-pocked wood with a thumbnail. "I can't believe this. I have to talk to him." He giggled once and clamped his lips shut. "This sucks. Because, it's like we were in the middle of this conversation I need to finish. He—"

She waited, but he had fallen silent. His surface was a turmoil, and part of that clouded atmosphere was leading her to sense she wasn't getting the whole story. But under that she could feel the pure, clean ribbon of his grief—it worried her as much as the turmoil. Better to have no feelings, when guilt was in question and the story involved two men. Better to be heartless than to feel too deeply in ways a jury might not care for, might bring assumptions to, let alone cops. Even liberal-minded folks knew passion as an unstable element, fluid, combustible.

"You told them he was your uncle?" she said gently, to draw him back.

"I was nervous. I barely remember saying that. But god, I knew what they'd think, me living there. Was that perjury?"

"No. But they can call it obstruction or just try to use it against you, if you lie about anything. From here on, you're not even going to speak. Not unless I'm in the room. You've been hassled by cops before, right?"

"Yeah." He looked at her askance, as if she were clairvoyant.

"Well, I'm going to tell them that cops make you nervous, and that's the reason you're not going to answer any old question, and they're only to talk to you through me. But for now, we're just going to give them your alibi and hope that's enough to put an end to this. Okay?"

"We can just go?"

"Yeah." She grimaced. "Probably. But don't worry."

Leaving, though, was painless—Thornton and his blue-eyed assumptions gone for the present so that she could give the information to his freckled, red-headed younger partner instead. A hand at Paul's lower back, she ushered his somnambulant steps down the hall, into the elevator and out to her car. He slid into her passenger seat as if hoping to nap there.

"You're tired, huh? How long have you been here?"

"I don't know. Hours. I just want to go home and sleep."

"I'll drop you."

His eyes were closed, head tipped back, and she saw in the sunlight a mark on his throat, a fingerprint bruise along the windpipe. "Paul, what's this?" The question came slowly, her hand slow in touching it, and as she did she shuddered with the memory of the story he'd told her the day before, the rapist who had tried to strangle him, and unbidden she watched her entire case unfurl before her eyes in resplendent awful beauty: another older man with power over Paul, the same attack.

He slapped fingers to his throat with a kind of alarm, but then calmed, waved her off. "That's nothing. This play I'm in—I told you about it. The guy who plays my father gets to strangle me every night."

"Oh." She believed him, his voice so flat and casual, or she believed that this was possible. With some relief, she mentally erased her case. "Listen, you're going to need to stay in contact with me. I need to know where you are at all times, in case the police want to talk to you again. And they probably will, even though your alibi is going to check out, no problem."

He should have been relaxing now, but seemed to grow more tense as she spoke. "Maggie," he said, a low warning note, and when she looked at him she knew that he was suddenly ready to crack, dissolve, spill something terrible. It was as clear as words in his eyes, and bad enough that he was afraid he'd lose her by saying it.

He couldn't be guilty—she wouldn't hear it. Her job brought her terrible truths every day, more and more terrible, more and more hopeless and irredeemable, and she could handle that tide. But this one she didn't want to know.

"What if I—"

"You were out all night," she said, facing him, insisting on each word. "You haven't slept. Things aren't as bad as you think they are. You'll see."

He swallowed and looked away. "I didn't do this."

"I know."

"How?" He cut her a sharp, sideways look. "How do you know?"

It was a good question, and she knew she was in some way lying to him. She couldn't know what had happened. She was just answering, soothing, hoping. She took a breath and examined him now—vulnerable-looking with his bare arms and fidgety hands, ducking a little under the screen of his bangs—for something entirely truthful she could say.

"Paul, I'm just getting to know you. But I don't see any meanness in you. I don't believe you could hurt anybody on purpose."

His eyes softened and he nodded, brought his knuckles to his mouth. "You know that? No one else does." He chewed a nail. "Maybe they're right and I'm a shitty person. Maybe you shouldn't be my friend."

"Don't worry. It's not a choice." She put the car in gear, pulled out onto the road. "Left here?"

"Yeah." He watched her as she drove. "What does that mean, it's not a choice?"

She drew and released a calm breath, a moment's wash of happiness—this was easy to talk about. "Well, I believe people come to me who I'm meant to have in my life. Sometimes those people do bad things, wrong things, like a lot of my clients, but it doesn't make them worthless, or make me any less responsible to them. It's like having a child in a way. You don't choose the child you'll have—it's given to you. But you believe in what you're given." This idea, long-familiar, bloomed into new meaning as she spoke it, her arms still weighted with the shape of her sister's newborn. On some level it had always been true, that her maternal energy was spent in her clients' service, so that the idea of giving birth to her own child was almost redundant. But then Paul made the concept more vivid and concrete, more effortless than it had ever felt to her. She smiled at him as she drove, and he smiled shyly back. She loved this one, didn't have to think about it— had loved him before his case file was even opened.

"Wow." He breathed a laugh, shook his head. "I sort of knew you'd be the one to believe me."

He gave her directions to his place, and she was almost there, distracted by more pressing concerns, before she realized where they were going. "Oh, Paul, you know, maybe I should take you to my house instead. Or do you have friends you can stay with for a while? Going back to your place may not be what you want to do right now."

"It's okay," he said, before the problems seemed to dawn on him as well. "Will the cops still be there?"

"They're probably done. Four or five hours is usually all they need. But it could be a mess. And, I don't know, maybe just not very comfortable for you. Besides which, it's not really your apartment, right? Do you know if you'll be able to stay?"

Wide-eyed, he stared ahead. "I didn't really think about that."

"Okay, never mind. We'll deal with that later. But for tonight, why don't you stay at my house?"

He continued staring for some time as if he didn't hear her. "Oh, I. No. No, I can't. Really," he said, toneless and dazed. He pointed to a building coming up on the right. "Um, this is it."

Across the street was a local news van. Behind it a crew was filming, their camera aimed over the shoulder of a brunette anchor-woman toward the building's door. Paul's startled eyes locked on them as Maggie returned her foot to the accelerator and continued driving slowly by. One of the crew in headphones looked hard at her as she passed—she, if not Paul, almost certainly looked familiar to him.

"*So*," she said brightly, once they were in the next block, "not a good time to go home."

Still, he balked at going to her house. He pulled out a cellphone and began making calls to friends while she drove in no particular direction. He left two messages, then considered and discarded a host of other numbers—all people, apparently, with some connection to the deceased. "God, I have to tell people. Or maybe they've all heard it already. Then what?"

"Paul, I need to get back to my office. I'm going to take you to my house."

"Uh, no, no," he said, and gripped his gut in a spasm. Hunched over himself, he spoke with effortful calm. "I can't do that. I mean, I don't want to be any trouble. Just…I know, drop me at the Starbuck's by my building. I'll walk home as soon as the van is gone."

"No, sweetie, you need to sleep. It's no trouble. I'll have to go back to work for a few hours, but you can just stay at my place and take a nap. Then decide what to do."

He was in a ball now, his feet on the seat and his face in his knees. He nodded without looking at her.

It was four o'clock when Kent pulled his car up to the curb at home, glad to have made it out of work before traffic got too thick. And here was his house in Edgewood on his little square of property, ready for the serious work of spring that he'd been putting off. Gutters. Mend the screens. Pressure wash. Scrape and paint—he and Maggie had talked about trying the house in a bright yellow, with green trim or maybe black like a bee. Once the small stuff was done, they could start thinking seriously about the addition, which might turn into room for a baby, should that come next in their lives. He could see that phantom life, almost, coming to meet him down the front walk—a little girl, for some reason. A dark-haired, dark-eyed girl running through the festival riot of Maggie's spring blooms. Maybe a boy later. It seemed a sweet possibility, fully within grasp.

Last year's enormous orange lilies were soon to open again, straining from the ground around the mailbox toward the sun. Sunlight warmed the fluted azalea blossoms along the walk, deep crimson and white, the last of the pink dogwood petals having fallen onto the stone path. He was momentarily enthralled with his domain, and didn't notice Maggie's car at the curb—he hadn't thought to look for it at this hour, especially when she'd gone in so late that morning. She came down the steps from the house and he blinked up from his reverie in surprise.

"Oh good, you're here!" She breezed down the flagstone path and into his arms and he caught her as she tipped onto her toes, kissed him on the mouth. It was half a beat longer than her usual hello kiss, resounding with an enthusiasm that might have been a product of the exact happiness he felt in that moment, a generalized sunny springtime pleasure of flowers and new babies somewhere in the world—their latest nephew half a day old, his cousin a suggestion in the air.

"I'm not actually here, of course," she said. "Just stopped in. I left you a note inside, but it's easier if I explain. Paul's here. He's taking a nap in the back room, so be really quiet, okay? It's a long and fairly horrible story."

"Paul's here," he repeated, stuck on those words, stuck in his unsurprise. He saw now that the life he'd imagined over the top of this one was too gaudy and bright to be real, with its sun-colored paint and the luminous browns of the children's hair. Here was what he had: the unchanging blue wood, dulled with layers of pollen and soot, the pink-brown petals withering on the walk.

"It's awful, really," she said, and he gathered from her unpunctuated rush what had happened: Bernard murdered, beaten to death, Paul being questioned though not yet charged with anything but sharp enough thank god to call her from homicide to rescue him and now there were *news* vans in front of his building, so.

"Did he do it?" Under his utter numbness, Kent was aware of something funny. It was his voice. He sounded so calm. He sounded mildly horrified and interested in an impersonal way, exactly as he should have sounded if he were able to grasp his role as outsider in this drama. Paul, he thought, would have broken into applause.

"No," she said, baldly dismissive, almost jocular. "No, of course not. He gave an alibi, I'm sure it will check. I mean, come on, does he *look* to you like he'd kill someone? And you know him. Used to, at least."

A ripple of thought crossed her face as she said this, as if she had forgotten that fact until now. He knew her usual case process, could guess that she probably only wondered if he had light to shed on Paul's past. But he couldn't stop the implication from blooming outward until he glimpsed himself as he might end up: a suspect himself, murderer of his lover's lover. His throat closed and he began coughing, involuntarily, but it was enough to distract her with patting and tending him until he could breathe again.

"All right now? I gotta take off." She pinched his elbow. "Don't let him near any sharp objects. Or blunt objects either, I guess. *Kidding*. Seriously, though, try not to wake him. Poor thing hasn't slept since last week. I'll try to be home before seven."

She marched off without looking back, chin up, into her car and gone. So many people to save. And now Paul was one, dumped off in their back room for safekeeping. Kent moved with leaden limbs up to the porch, sat in the wicker chair. Though his anger remained elsewhere, nearby but otherwise engaged, he couldn't get past his foggy sense that this was something to be angry about: a scheme of some kind, Paul's next move. Paul had done this (killed a man? no, no one could be dead, certainly not the man he'd seen flummoxed and ashen in Paul's living room the night before. So, Paul had faked it; yes, somehow fabricated the whole story for Maggie) in order to get back into their house.

But she'd said *police*, and *homicide*. And *news*. So it must be real. The professor was really dead.

Across the street, a neighbor emerged from the side of her gray-green craftsman's cottage that was otherwise a reverse image of Kent's. She wore a broad-brimmed straw hat against the sun's glare, carried a spade and a tray of pansies. Kneeling to work along the flower bed, she turned and waved. He waved back. She nestled three plants into the ground, one after another. She brushed the dirt from her hands and went behind her azalea bushes to uncoil the hose.

A man he'd seen less than twenty-four hours ago had been murdered.

He felt again the watery lucid dark of the condo as he'd walked toward the door, a sort of soft breathing, seething, of emotion from its unseen rooms. The word *rape* in Paul's mouth. *Do you want him to rape me?* Not that, no, and he never would have left Paul so vulnerable once he'd heard the word. Not violence either. But he had wanted something—a reaction, punishment, trouble. He had meant to show Paul how unstable a house could be. But he hadn't thought through the fact that he was leaving the lesson in someone else's hands.

He must have gotten up and moved into the house, because he stood in the doorway of the darkened back room, staring at the spare sofa where Paul lay. Asleep, seemingly, on his side with one arm cradling his face. A dim gold light penetrated tiny cracks in the closed blinds to trace his hand and hair and cheek, his shoulder and hip. In that light, asleep, it was not possible to hate him. It was not even possible, Kent found to his dismay, to be afraid for his own life.

Out of some urge to change this, wipe the sweetness from him, Kent moved to the sofa. He took a firm hold of Paul's arm, lifted him. Paul sat up instantly as if under his own power, eyes open, his breathing heavy like that of someone who had been underwater and dragged to the surface. He made soft chest-level groans of effort to find his bearings. Kent sat beside him. "You're in my house."

It was half help, half accusation. His face sleep-blurred, Paul lifted a defensive hand. "Kent—"

"I'm not going to hit you."

He gripped Paul by the shoulders with a steady, grounding force to bridge him back into reality. Somewhere beneath the grip were rough intentions that failed to reach his hands, his actions of the night before too vivid in his body's memory.

Paul squeezed his eyes shut. "I can explain."

"Maggie told me."

Paul went limp with the release at this neutral information, which Kent saw now for the great kindness that it was. He could have made Paul struggle for the words, left him scrambling to guess and defend against the whole catalogue of Kent's assumptions.

"It wasn't about you," Paul said.

What wasn't? Murder? The ambiguity was sharpened at the tip, like a needle rising through cloth, dragging behind it a thread of fear.

But he meant calling Maggie. "I didn't know anyone else. I needed help."

Paul's eyes were lifted now to the level of Kent's collar. Kent cupped his chin and raised it, passed a thumb over the swollen cut in his lip. Paul inched back from the exam, tucking his chin, and Kent's hand slid around to the side of his head, fingers in his hair, without thought. Was the caress from love, Kent wondered, or did love emanate from the caress? He felt so full for a single burgeoning moment that he had to be careful what he said.

"Did he hit you?"

"I didn't kill him."

He nodded and waited. "But that's from him, isn't it?"

Paul's face sank, eyes closed. "Yes."

"Was that because of me?"

Paul tipped closer without answering, and Kent stroked his hair with the nervous, automatic gesture of holding something back, keeping it still. He didn't want to know this but couldn't stop the fear that was growing, becoming loud now, that in whatever had happened he himself was more implicated than even his paranoia could invent. The question he wasn't ready to ask, that he knew Paul wasn't ready to answer: *If I hadn't come home with you last night, would he still be alive?*

"I hit him."

"What?"

Paul gulped and leaned closer. "I hit him in the head. With a bottle. But I didn't kill him. I know I didn't. It was just once, I think. I was trying to get away."

Kent closed his eyes, put his other hand to Paul's head and braced him there. Paul's voice was soft and cracked. "Kent, I didn't tell Maggie that part."

"Okay," he said. He knew there was a desperate question in this— tell Maggie? don't tell her?—and he didn't know the answer. "Listen. It's good you called her today. She'll take care of it. She's the best." Paul looked dazed, in no position to worry over details or think more clearly than this, a relief to Kent. "Lie down," he said. "Get some sleep."

In a panicky, jerky motion, Paul's hands went around the back of Kent's neck, his panting breath in his face. "Easy," Kent said, and they were kissing. He felt himself give in to it, respond to Paul's brief spasm of need, and then kissed him once more when it had passed, softly, with a closed mouth and ashamed of the rapid thrumming of his heart.

"Lie down now," he said and Paul did. He settled back into the same motionless curl as if sleep were waiting there in his body's position, as close and instant as closing his eyes. Kent sat beside him for some time, one hand resting on his side that expanded and contracted with slow breathing.

Some minutes later, he stood in the kitchen, feeling Paul's sleep in his house. It felt like suspended time, almost welcome, a span of peace before the crisis would inexorably unfold. This was his house still, the same he had intended as the setting for his sundry dreams, altered by nothing more than a few degrees of body heat. His sense of suspension locked him in a trance in the center of the kitchen, distant from all fear except the mild fear of time starting again.

This comes from wanting the wrong things, he told himself. Too much of him had wanted Paul asleep in the house, and now it had come. Another part of him had shaped a dream of murder, and now not Paul but another man was dead. *Crazy. Don't start thinking crazy thoughts.*

But in his household, for now, there was a fragile, undeniable peace. Inside this bungalow in Edgewood, floor and walls and roof, was another house, the one he had made for his life, and it contained the three of them. He hadn't meant to make it this way. But maybe this was how it had been from the moment he fixed his hopes on Maggie while continuing to dream about Paul. Paul had said it, hadn't he?—that he'd been in the house before he arrived in the flesh, and if so it explained the eerie déjà vu normalcy at dinner the night before, the natural sound of Paul's voice lapping over Maggie's as they came in the door.

He went back and sat in his desk chair across the room from where Paul slept. He opened some files on his computer and started transferring text into a new FAQ link for the investment firm, then playing with the fonts and the border, until an hour had passed and he felt Paul's waking in a shift of atmosphere.

"Hey," Kent said.

"Are you ready to kill me yet?" Paul mumbled. He was sitting up but seemed under still, dreaming, with a sleepwalker's empty stare.

"I think I can hold off and wait for the judicial system."

Paul nodded as if this were reasonable. "It's bad, isn't it?" They sat in silence, not quite looking at each other. "I need a favor," Paul said finally. "Take me home? I only came here because Maggie made me, but I need to be there. I need to see it." A rising urgency thinned his voice while his face remained blank. "There are things I need to do, and I can't figure this out or think about anything unless I'm there and see it."

"Okay."

Paul closed his eyes as if soothed by the word. "Just tell Maggie. Say I made you take me."

The light was falling toward evening as they drove to the condo for the second time in twenty-four hours. Paul listened to messages on his cellphone. "Any news?" Kent asked when he'd folded the phone. He shook his head. "Not really." Passing the same buildings, stopping for the same lights at the same intersections, fed some presently inaccessible reserve of Kent's fear and added pounds to the already heavy air inside the car. He tried not to look but could feel Paul's eyes from the passenger seat. They didn't touch, but it felt as if they were more than touching—unpleasantly fused.

They pulled up to the curb a block from the building. Kent said, "Looks okay, maybe. We'll walk up there and see."

Paul stared through the windshield. There was little to note: a few people strolling the sidewalks, the back ends of parallel-parked cars that might or might not have concealed a news van. "You don't have to come with me."

"I will, though."

Paul faced him with a look both intimate and vacant, the look he might give a man who shared his life preserver while they both froze to death in open sea. "I feel weird. I feel nothing."

"I know."

"And you're being so nice to me. I don't get it."

Kent didn't either, but he felt compelled toward the condo in the same way Paul was, to see it. To face what had become of Bernard Falk. "Come on." He got out of the car.

No visible filming happening as they moved up the street, and Kent took a good look around as Paul worked the keypad. "They wouldn't know me anyway, right?" Paul said with a wan smile in the elevator, punching eleven. "At least I hope my picture's not on the wanted poster yet."

In the hallway on eleven, they passed a young man in bike shorts and a tank top carrying a helmet. Mouth open, he almost stopped at the sight of Paul, who said "Hi" and hurried past before the man could make up his mind to speak. Kent quickened his own pace to keep the man from forming too much of an interest in him—who he was, what he was doing there with Paul. But it introduced new worry. Had they passed any neighbors the night before? Had anyone seen him leave? He tried to remember but his brain wasn't working right.

Paul puffed out two quick breaths, like an athlete at a starting line. In one motion, he turned his key and swung open the door. Inside was palpably empty and dormant, like a house returned to at the end of a long trip. But there was a fruity chemical smell that hadn't been there before. The clear gray light of just-past sunset suffused the open room, and through the wall of windows the sky over the city was shot through with strands of pink and orange.

The place looked the same, as far as Kent could tell. He scanned the gleaming hardwoods, the islands of clustered furniture, the rugs. Something unsettled him that he hadn't seen the night before—those floors, the open expanse of light-soaked blond wood under the windows. It was a little like their old apartment in Athens. The place had been Kent's first, a sublet from a friend, too good a deal to pass up but not what he would have chosen: a touch too elegant. Paul, though, had loved it right away, especially that empty floor—theirs had had a pair of wood columns—under tall windows that opened onto downtown like a dance studio. To Kent it had felt like wasted space, not like home until Paul moved in and showed it to him, until he started to see it through Paul's eyes.

"Guess the condo manager had it cleaned," Paul said, reading a piece of paper on the kitchen counter. "And he wants to *see* me." He squared the paper and shoved it into his pocket. In the kitchen area, where the hardwood ceded to a variegated tile of reddish stone, everything shone under the lights like a magazine spread. An answering machine on the counter read 14. Where Paul was staring, the grout between the tiles was white, same as in the rest of the floor.

"I feel like I dreamed it," Paul said. "I feel so weird."

"Yeah." Kent stood beside him and watched the spot as well, as if waiting for something to appear. "That's where he was?"

Paul nodded. "God, there was a lot of blood. I was surprised by that. I thought…I was afraid I hurt him, with the bottle. I was afraid, last night, to come back and see. But somebody else must have." He peered earnestly into Kent's face. "I would remember. You don't forget hurting somebody that much."

"No, I guess not."

"I barely hit him. Do you think I'm crazy? I feel a little nuts."

Kent watched him. "Are you going to be okay here tonight?"

Paul drew a long breath and put on a face of stalwart competence and sanity. "Yeah. I'm good. I've got things to do." He flipped out his cell and waggled it. "Calls to make. Alibis to manufacture. I'm good."

"Paul—"

"It's just about when I got to the club. It's okay."

Kent took a breath. "What about us? I mean, I dropped you off at your car, right? We, I don't know, talked for a while." Saying this, hearing it, made him tighten through the neck and shoulders. "Have you mentioned me yet?"

"No. They haven't asked. But you weren't here." Paul looked

away, one shoulder drawn up to his cheek. "It's okay."

"No one saw me," Kent said, a question turning to statement. "Us. If they did, they wouldn't know who I was."

"Fingerprints," Paul said. The word sounded involuntary, made him blink.

"But they couldn't match them to me." Kent felt he knew this— he'd picked up a lot from listening to Maggie talk about her cases, like the fact that even in ideal circumstances it was very hard to make evidence reveal its source or stick. "I'm not a felon. The prints could be years old."

"Really?" Paul's eyes were solemn with worry.

"I don't think they can know about me unless you tell them," Kent said.

The faint edge of the words made Paul's chin lift. "You think I'm that low?"

"No. But it might get scary from here, you know? A lot worse than today. Seriously, tough questions. You need to be ready for that."

"I can handle them. You'll be fine."

"Paul," he said, remorseful, corrective. He didn't want to be worrying about himself, when Paul's danger was so much more present. But his own couldn't be far behind, and his fate was unavoidably in Paul's hands. If he had to trust anyone he knew to outwit the police, it would be Paul—if he wanted to. If his addiction to risk didn't interfere. And it was a lot of power. Kent looked around the bright kitchen, tried to get his bearings. "Maybe we should say I came up here with you. For a minute, for something. Just in case."

Paul gripped the counter, frozen for several seconds of intense concentration. "No. No one saw us. It will be worse if we say that. They'll have to look at you."

Kent considered this. "Okay. I didn't come here. I left you at your car."

Paul nodded, closed his eyes, knuckles going white. "God, you shouldn't be here now."

His fear on Kent's account was reassuring, as long as it didn't tip into panic. Kent said, "It's okay. I'm just your lawyer's husband. You didn't want to come up here alone."

"Um. Right."

His eyes stayed shut until Kent stepped into the unmarked spot where Bernard's body had lain and Paul flinched, swallowed with distress. Kent felt it too. He put a hand on the nape of Paul's neck. "Will you please not do anything tonight? Just eat something and go to sleep."

Paul's shoulders dropped at the touch. "I can't." He removed Kent's hand, stepped away laughing. "Kent, there are fourteen messages on that machine. I don't even know who knows, or *what* they know, or who I have to call and say what to, and that's all before rehearsal"—he checked his watch—"where I have to be in an hour, basically."

"You're not seriously going to go rehearse some play tonight. How can you?"

Paul's face hardened. "You don't get it. It's important. You don't miss rehearsal. Ever." He spoke with the force of dogma, and the words granted him a steadiness like a crutch—some edict of Bernard's.

"Okay, I know," Kent said. "It's important. But just for tonight. I think this counts as a good excuse. How are you going to concentrate?"

Paul sighed. "Don't worry about it. God, you're making me nervous. I'll get through." He touched Kent's arm briefly, pinched and rubbed Kent's sleeve between his fingers, and walked past. He went out into the open floor of the loft beyond the kitchen's light, toward the circle of living room furniture, and Kent followed.

"Mine now, I guess," Paul said, his appreciative gaze sweeping the room. "For tonight." Though his voice was calm, his words nodded toward the future after time would start again, the very real chance that this was his last night in the condo, his last in any bed in the free world.

"I'd better go," Kent said, prompted by an impulse not to.

"Yeah." Paul faced the windows. "Thanks for, you know. Being here."

Kent went to the door, looked back at Paul standing in silhouette before the windows. The falling light felt wintry, time paused here in its muted shock, and Kent's life was paused along with it, here in a different house where he also belonged, that he had also somehow made.

CHAPTER ELEVEN

P aul felt the door-click of Kent's departure in the pit of his stomach. Still it was hard to feel alone in the condo, any more than he had that morning when Bernard had been on the kitchen tile, open-eyed. Dead eyes were supposed to stare like fish, but Bernard's had been narrowed as if focused on something, almost accusatory though they couldn't find their object. Now, the body and its traces cleaned away, Bernard was even more present in Paul's awareness, as if the man were home as usual but occupied in some noiseless task in another room.

Paul went back to his own bedroom and stood in the door, startled at the unfamiliar order. Too clean. But he had done this himself. At first, in the morning's shock, he hadn't been able to summon a thought more intricate than calling 911 and then kneeling beside Bernard until someone, anyone, arrived to relieve him of the vigil. He'd stayed in the kitchen while the police questioned him, and at one point he'd given them the name of a man in the building, Vernon Dodd, with whom Bernard had been feuding since Vernon had accused him of scratching his car in the parking deck some five years before. Official-looking people scrutinized and photographed and removed Bernard's body and examined Paul's hands and his clothing—clothes they had taken—and perhaps two hours later, while they continued their work in the kitchen, they released Paul to take a shower. It was only then, when he stood damply clean and closed in his room, that he had thought to make the bed—no time to strip the sheets—and cram every loose, suspicious item into a drawer.

That was the reason, he thought, that the room now looked violated and wrong. Even in his rush to straighten and conceal, when he'd been thinking with enough sudden, piercing clarity that he'd used a t-shirt to scrub the headboard and every other surface that Kent might have touched, he had told himself the police would not look back here. They had no reason to.

But they had looked nonetheless. The bed was still made. As far as he could tell, nothing he'd left out was missing or moved. But the cleaning service, called in for the serious work of blood removal, had not extended its work beyond the main rooms, and as he stepped inside he saw a sifting of black soot on the desk and the chair, on the headboard of his bed. Visible within it, despite his efforts, were a few fingerprints the police had raised and lifted and taken. Whose? He studied his own fingertips, held them poised above the dusted whorls.

He pulled open drawers and was relieved to find his profusion of X-rated toys more or less dumped where he'd dumped them. His folded clothes were disarranged, and he was almost certain the laundry in the closet hamper had been upended and returned, so that the oldest pieces were on top. He couldn't name what was missing, but he felt it—something gone.

The idea tugged him back to the kitchen. From under the sink he pulled out the trash can, which was lined with a new, white, empty bag. His one clear thought after calling the paramedics had been to find the bourbon bottle and put it in the trash, nosed in deep under orange rinds and coffee grounds; now the entire bag was gone.

Heavy with resistance but needing to do something, he played the messages on the machine. Almost every call was from a friend of Bernard's. Some pretended now to be Paul's friends by more than association as they addressed him on the machine ("Paul, I'm so sorry, I just heard…"), and there were a few heart-wrenching messages from the blithely ignorant ("Bernard? Did you forget about lunch today?").

Only one call of the fourteen was for Paul alone, the one he was hoping for: "Paul, honey, it's George." *I know*, Paul thought, annoyed in spite of everything that the man identified himself for every call with the same nasal-musical, three-or-four-syllable extension of his name. *Geoooorige*. "I *heard* what happened, it was on the news. You poor baby…" But there was nothing in it, no more revelation than in his earlier, as-yet unanswered message on Paul's voicemail.

Paul had played that first message four times before erasing it. "Hi, Paul, it's George. Uh, honey? The police were here. They were asking a lot of questions, wanting to know if you were here last night. Lord, I didn't know what to tell them! I hope I did the right thing. I hope you're not in some kind of trouble, I can't imagine. I'm worried about you. Please, please call and let me know what's happening, okay? You know I don't hold anything against you. I'd just do anything in the world for you."

Yes, Paul was counting on that. But he didn't know if George would know what was needed without being told, and Paul didn't want to have to tell him, especially didn't want to have to call him and say it on a line being for all he knew tapped or traced. He didn't know if the cops could do that. He'd ask his lawyer if his lawyer weren't Maggie, but with her, he wouldn't risk a question that would lead her to doubt him. George's empty, gushing messages hinted at almost no awareness that he was holding crucial information, but Paul thought it was likely a pretense. He wanted Paul's call. He wanted Paul to need him.

He replayed all the messages, wrote down callers and numbers. The list was daunting. Tristan and Jodi, perhaps Bernard's two closest friends, had left separate messages not so much to offer their assistance as to announce its impending arrival. They would be coming by in the morning, together, "and we'll take care of everything, so you won't need to worry." Beneath their sincere condolences was a clear under-standing of Paul's status as nominal partner only, the partner in Bernard's fantasy life, and they would treat him as bereaved lover out of respect for Bernard's wishes more than for some real loss of Paul's. *Step aside now*, he knew they would say without saying it. *Stand over there and look sad while we handle it.* But Paul would be grateful to have them take charge, return calls, make arrangements; knew they were probably not far from right about him, the narcissistic boy-toy who might as well have been made of feathers and fluff for all the substance he could bring to such a crisis.

There would be a funeral to arrange. This occurred to him for the first time. Bernard's family would come, the way Paul had once or twice pictured it, except that what he had pictured was a doleful wake at the conclusion of long illness, where he himself would cry quietly, accept embraces and nod at kind words and later listen to tipsy, half-lighthearted stories of Bernard's career and his exploits, contributing a few of his own, and feeling under the sadness a kind of wistful pleasure. He'd be able to smile through his grief as he watched Bernard raised in death into his better self, to be fixed there forever like a memorial statue in a noble pose: the Great Man. But that wouldn't happen now.

He decided not to call anyone, to take the damn phone off the hook, and he escaped to rehearsal. Getting through a four-hour rehearsal would be its own challenge, but he could just switch compartments, stay in Silas and his actor self. He wouldn't mention to anyone what had happened.

But one glance at arrival told him that the news had beaten him there. Six actors and the assistant director were huddled tight and urgent downstage right, around Mark, who apparently hadn't heard because he said "Ridiculous!" "*Murdered*," one insisted. "With a baseball bat or something," another hissed, before the door behind Paul banged shut and they all jumped and turned to stare.

The truth was almost as bad as the worst they could imagine and probably even worse than the play Mark Westlake would have written on the topic, and still Paul might have been fine if they had all whistled into the spotlights and pretended nothing was wrong. If Mark hadn't touched him. The day had started with Bernard's corpse for company, then the police, then Maggie, then Kent, and every breath with Kent— even when he was spilling—was an effort of holding back, and with Maggie double the effort, so now when Mark Westlake, a man he didn't even like very much, came to him with puppy eyes and called him baby and held his big arms open, Paul crumpled into hard sobs that almost pitched him to the floor.

Mark led him away. They couldn't get beyond the view of the others, but privacy was a thin commodity in a theater anyway. They'd all know. "Poor lamb, let it out," Mark said, patting his back, and Paul shuddered into sudden control. He didn't want to let it out. He didn't know what *it* was.

"I'm fine," he said, backing away.

The worst was admitting to Mark that he might be a suspect, that for this reason he probably needed an understudy. He was fine, he insisted, for tonight, for every night, he could compartmentalize, he was an actor first, an actor before anything, but just, well, the police might end up with their own ideas. Still, he told Mark, he was doing the play, he was *doing* it, and—he actually said this—even if he were arrested, he could be out on bail for the production, and the run would be over before he ever went to trial.

"See, it's not that bad," he said, which didn't stop Mark from having a little scene of his own, a fit histrionic enough to rival Paul's, and then sending everyone home for the night.

He didn't want to go home. But he didn't want to talk to anyone either—Leah offered to stay with him. "I just want to be alone," he told her, also not true. He drove for an hour through the warm April evening, past his favorite clubs and restaurants, and the way the street-lights and sign lights caught in the eyes and lips of carefree people on the street and shimmered on the brown legs of mini-skirted girls made him dizzy with nostalgia. To be in their company, to have drinks and laugh and think about nothing. The Benz nosed around corners, pow-erful and sleek, his for now, and he flipped the radio station for the sort of song that would say *keep on driving*. Out onto the highway, over the state line, into the next life. But the places he passed were the places he'd been with Bernard, midtown past Piedmont Park in a loose circle around their building, and in the end he went back home.

⌒

Nine o'clock and he was cross-legged on the kitchen floor, his cell-phone in his lap and his knees along the bald contours of Bernard's invisible head, like a wall or a dam. To hold what? He didn't know but felt certain of something seeping, escaping, the failing at this spot. Sit-ting close now seemed at least a kind of recompense for leaving him alone, to die alone, and all the times before.

Every light was on, every lamp, so no trick of shadows could shape a body out of that space, and the stereo blared a little too loud, techno dance music with a lot of bass thrumming up through his butt and into his heart. *How unseemly for grieving*, the neighbors would say, or was that Bernard? He knew he should eat something, but he still tasted Kent's tongue, felt its imprint on his own—evidence of desire however fleeting. It allowed him to imagine Kent with him as a loose wrap of arms from behind, a presence like Bernard's though better company for sure.

Six hours or maybe seven, a long time to be dead alone. He shouldn't have stayed out so long, wasted all that time with Jerry and breakfast. *What, and think about someone besides yourself?* ghost-Kent said in his ear. Kent hated his music too. Kent found his music a "character flaw." Paul told him to go to hell. *Ha ha ha! Go to hell, fucker,* and Kent laughed too and stroked his hair.

He sang a few lines—about being real, being free, like all dance lyrics, as if gay life involved a fixation on one's freedom and one's reality. Maybe losing one meant losing the other. But they couldn't arrest him for something he didn't do. Or didn't mean to.

The cops had said *struck several times,* and he strained for his body's memory, those grand arm gestures Bernard had always insisted on— *make it bigger! Body is emotion, play it to the back row!* Trapped in that kitchen corner, he'd struck first with his hands, but Bernard was too close—it was more like shoving—and Bernard had grabbed his arm as he slid past, wrenching him around, and there was the empty bourbon bottle at his right hand, lying on the table neck out like a stage prop. He picked it up and swung in a single motion, without decision, and he remembered thinking that he didn't have enough power behind it. But he was screaming and blind with rage that the man would take hold of him, force him. He felt the heaviness of the bottle bouncing back from impact and Bernard releasing his arm. One hit, and he was free. He left.

Inside his left elbow now were two round, gray-blue bruises, one of them sliced with a crescent of nail, that no one had noticed yet, no one had asked him about. One blow with the bottle, to get away. And Bernard hadn't fallen, at least not right away, only staggered back. And said something—Paul was almost sure he had cried out, called his name—but Paul didn't look back. He thought, *I hurt him.* That was all.

The recoil of the bottle, though—he could feel it later in the tendons of his hand, and it scared him. Too much. Even in the moment, he'd winced to take it back and half of his fleeing was from not wanting to see. He knew now that it could have been worse than he thought. He saw like a memory Bernard hurling back from it, a tall man with a lot of momentum to fling him toward the floor, head striking the counter's edge and then the tile. That was three. *At least three cracks to the skull…*

Or maybe the soreness in his hand had come from striking more than once, from the raging, blind part of him that had wanted to keep on hitting.

Was the voice he'd heard before he reached the door only wishing? Only now, Bernard calling his name, and not then? He wished the music would shut up. He wanted to rewind their miserable night to when they had been talking and not shouting, having a regular conversation about things that mattered. But all that had truly mattered to Bernard was dead by then, killed by Kent's arrival—not sex, not love, but the tenuous possibility of it, the ideal of a pure, perfect, mutual union that had resided in Paul's unattachment and his presence in the condo. Paul was aware of this dream, understood it dimly as an engine so essential to Bernard's life that its loss might have been what killed him, if Bernard had simply fallen dead to the floor, if there weren't all this other distracting evidence.

He had felt it begin to happen as he led Kent through the door: *we're killing him.* But he hadn't beaten the man to death. He would remember. And he had no meanness in him. Maggie had said so.

His cell rang. George Babbish. He leapt to his feet to turn down the stereo.

"Paul, thank god. Where are you?"

He paced before the windows. "I'm fine. Don't worry about me." Funny, how George compelled him into this role. Even now, in serious trouble, he used reticence to nudge George into imagining ever worse possibilities, as if he were on the lam, in hiding, and it wasn't safe to divulge too much.

"Please tell me you're not in jail at least."

"I'm not in jail. Not yet."

"But they must suspect you. *Promise* me right now that if god forbid they arrest you, you will call me. I'll come and get you right away, post bail, whatever you need."

Paul didn't want to feel so grateful. *No, that won't be necessary,* he wanted to say, but fear was rising in his general vicinity like water, lapping at his chin now, the source of the flood still unchecked, and he said, "Okay."

"But I'm sure that won't happen, because of course you didn't have anything to do with this. I told them if they were looking for some kind of criminal—"

That was it, two empty sentences and the limit of Paul's patience. "George, what did you tell them about what time you saw me at Crush? Exactly, word for word."

"Oh, dear. Well, let's see, I suppose that would be best, wouldn't it? If we told them the same times." He let this hang, and Paul was sure he heard a trace of innuendo, as if he were waiting for Paul to come out and admit he needed George to lie for him.

"I just want to know what you said. This is important, George, please don't make me beg."

George sighed. "I told them I saw you here at eleven or eleven-thirty. Will that do? And that you were on the dance floor dancing your little ass off until at least three."

Paul was silent with shock at the size of that window, the big sweeping lie of it. He wasn't sure about times himself, but it must have been after one o'clock when he had reached the bar stool. He'd been hoping for something equivocal at best, with a little more cushion than he could get from Philip the bartender, but George clearly wanted a bigger part in this play.

"Is that right? You *were* here then, weren't you?"

"Yes."

"Good. I'd certainly hate to be misleading."

"You were definite, about those times?"

"Yes, I think fairly so."

"Okay. All right, I'll be in touch."

"Honey, wait," George said, the irony gone from his voice. "I know you didn't do this. I wouldn't help you if I thought you did. And I can tell how scared and alone you're feeling, wherever you are, and I want you to know you can stay with me, anytime, whenever you need to. Or just call and talk? I don't expect *anything* from you, nothing in return. Just believe that I'm your friend."

Paul nodded, releasing the last of his resistance. "Okay. Thanks, George. Really."

After he'd hung up, Paul stood by the windows. "Okay, okay, okay," he said aloud to his sketchy reflection in the brilliant, every-light-burning mirror of the glass. All of downtown was looking at him, its distant lights half in thrall, expectant like an audience.

⁖

He slept on the sofa, feeling some prohibition from the bedrooms—both of them, for he might have gone to Bernard's as easily as his own. But he wasn't ready to sink so deeply into loss, and his own room was similarly troubled. He turned out the lights and settled into the cushions, the same spot where he'd curled up with his head on Bernard's thigh the night he'd straggled in at five a.m., when he'd dozed a little but had given up before Bernard ever stopped snoring to know he was there. The throw pillow offered a softer, more sunken resting spot than that bone, but was like it enough that, drifting toward sleep, he could feel a version of Bernard awaken to stroke his back with a slow, feathery touch, pleased to find himself with company.

What do you think he wants from me now? Bernard asked with dry amusement, the question for his friends who sat beside him and in the opposite chairs, a quiet gathering like a wake in which they all seemed to consider Paul's sleeping form, his guilt or innocence, and talked about what to do with him. The general tone was friendly enough even if they thought he'd done it, as if he had spilled his food, crayoned the walls, and the mess would simply have to be cleaned up. Then they were gone, and Bernard was gone from the sofa but still there, somewhere else in the room.

Paul woke to a sound, he thought, but now there was only the condo's sourceless humming and the loud silence that follows noise, a bodying silence of presence. Paul shot upright on the sofa, eyes open as if he'd already been awake. His dream had involved the same shadows and arrangement of furniture, and he distrusted that the two were different.

"Bernie?" His heart hammered. He stood up too fast and the room tilted, sent him to his knees like an attack of angry atmosphere. "I didn't." He gripped the arm of the sofa to pull himself up, and slowly the tightness leaked from the room like a bad mood softening. He blinked at the empty condo and cracked a smile, for his own foolishness and for Bernard, wherever he was, who only a year before, upon running out of able students, had taken on the role of King Hamlet's ghost.

"Why, what should be the fear?" he murmured for the room, the skyline lights, then louder, with crisp enunciation, "I do not set my life at a pin's fee! And for my soul, what can you do to that?" He laughed a little, shakily, rubbed his hands through his hair. "Fuck, I forget the rest."

It was 11:15. He found his phone and called Sylvie, who had left four messages since he'd called her from Maggie's car. This time she picked up. "Hey, Syl," he said brightly. "Yeah, um, I was wondering if I could sleep on your sofa. Just for tonight. Kind of freaking out over here."

She said of course, come right away, but when he'd hung up the phone, he was sorry he'd done it. Maybe he could plead exhaustion and go straight to sleep. But she and Eric would want to know everything, and he'd probably spend hours telling the story of last night and today for their morbid enjoyment and pretended sympathy. It struck him, painfully, that they weren't really his friends. They were just people he partied with, deepened one level to include sharing rides and trading stories—what I did last night; you'll never believe what *he* did last night—the kind to keep each other leaning forward in alert fascination and saying things like *no! he did not!* A story with this much weight would fall right through them.

So here he was, seated in Bernard's late-hour, two-bottle corner of the sofa, more alone in the world and already more sorry for himself. Never mind that six other people had within a few hours offered him a place to stay: Mark and Leah at rehearsal, Tristan and Jodi on the machine, George Babbish and Maggie. He was lucky, very lucky, to have so many people ready to take him in and ask nothing of him and at least pretend, for now, to believe he wasn't a monster. Tomorrow he could expect more offers. But he couldn't think of a single friend he'd want to impose on for more than a night.

The short call to Sylvie had hardened the edges of things, enough that the condo now felt fairly normal. Unhaunted at least. He sat on the sofa a minute longer and dreamed the buzzer buzzing, Kent at the door. The only friend he wanted. He laughed at the thought and rose to leave. But if it was stupid, childish, to wish for such a fantastic appearance—Kent like a knight rushing back to share his bed and keep him safe from ghosts—he didn't think it was too extravagant to believe that Kent would at least be lying awake again in his own house and thinking about him.

"It's strange," Maggie said. She stood in the bedroom doorway gesticulating with her toothbrush, her teeth half-brushed. "I mean, how perfect am I for the job, right? Here I am with all this experience. They give him the death penalty heaven forbid and I'm *still* the woman for the job. But it's so different. I can't believe how I'm acting about this. Just because I know him and it's like, he's *mine*. You know? Like he's my kid or something."

"Yeah. I can see that."

They had been talking about this most of the evening, had fallen into it after Kent explained taking Paul home, which prompted her inevitable questions—*how did he seem? what did he say?*—and before he really noticed it, Kent was talking about Paul. He told her that on the previous evening, during the drive back to Paul's car, they had spent some time catching up so that today, tossed into this sudden crisis, they seemed something like old friends. Close enough, at least, that Paul had confided his emotional state and Kent had felt moved to go with him up to the condo. "He seems innocent to me," he told Maggie, which was true in a way, true to Paul's demeanor, and that was all he could tell her about. But in telling her all he could think of that felt safe, Kent had become for her someone with a real interest and a provisional but authentic sympathy for Paul, and now Maggie was talking to him about an open case in a way that client confidentiality almost never allowed her to.

"He's just so adorable and sweet," she grumbled, squinching up her face. He sat in bed in a posture of reading. "I guess that matters. I never thought it would matter to me." She said this walking away, then came back to the threshold again and pointed with her toothbrush. "It's Lila's fault. Having that baby, and now I'm having some kind of hormonal whadayacall. Hysterical pregnancy!"

He laughed, and as she disappeared again toward the bathroom he found he was still laughing, genuinely amused. How could this be

funny? He was sinking deeper into this role he was creating for himself,
and the going was easier if, like a good high-wire artist, he simply
didn't look down. He liked being Paul's old friend, his new one, with a
lesser claim than Maggie's. He was enjoying being Maggie's ally in
this, and he loved her most when she was just this way, vibrant with the
intense forward-thinking vigilance that called to mind cartoon animals.
She was a super-intelligent squirrel, rushing to gather acorns for
winter, hyperactive and fluffy and so bright-eyed cute that he wanted
to pet her, cuter for the fact that she was far too busy with the acorns to
tolerate petting.

In a week, a month, whenever the lies came apart to reveal him, she
would be gone, this life gone with her. He knew this. But however irra-
tionally, he remained hopeful it could happen otherwise, that they
could somehow cross the chasm intact. If crossing required him to keep
his eyes forward, a mental trick, it also required that she know nothing
at all of what lay below, and now he was mainly sorry for having to
withhold it from her. He wanted to start making it up to her, treating
her better.

She returned and sat on the foot of the bed, cross-legged in her
striped pajamas. "I still have this bad feeling. I think I want him to be
innocent so much that I'm pretending it's not obvious that he's guilty.
I mean, the lip thing? What kind of coincidence is that?"

"Yeah. But, wouldn't that maybe be good? I mean, if the guy did
hit him, then that shows it was self-defense. Then it's justifiable."

"Maybe. I'd hope so, but you never know how a jury will see a
thing like that. One little smack doesn't justify deadly force." She
looked toward the ceiling, stroking her throat. "Did you notice the
mark on his neck? Like a fingerprint bruise from being strangled?"

"No." He tried to remember.

"I don't think the cops saw it either. It's not much. It might literally be nothing. I mean it could have been a shadow or a smudge of dirt

or something. But the thing is, *he* knew about it. He gave me this whole story for how he got it, just like the lip."

She was busy in thought, and he tried also to imagine what had happened, to revise his picture of the scene to include Paul in real mortal danger, Bernard's hands at his throat. A day ago, the idea alone might have made him want to go down to the morgue and punch the man in the face, but tonight it seemed he could conjure an image, choreograph the scene, without feeling much beyond an intellectual interest in the puzzle he and Maggie were sorting together. Beneath all this he watched her and waited for a signal that he should tell her what he knew about the fight. The bottle, the lip. He wanted the moment when he could make it appear as the perfect gift, the withheld piece of the puzzle and the exact one she needed. But she was already erasing her mental board, saying, "No, I'm sure it's nothing," a denial that seemed a subliminal message to him in full knowledge of what he held—she didn't actually want it yet.

"But," he said after a pause, "if this man tried to strangle him. That justifies deadly force?"

"Maybe. *If* he did." She gave him a harried grin. "This is such rampant speculation. We shouldn't even be talking about this." She crawled up under the sheets. "It might all break open in the morning. Poor Paul. I hope that alibi is *sol-id*."

He turned off the lamp, scooted in beside her and drew her close, smoothing back her hair, kissing six or seven different parts of her face. He felt grateful for her, and through her Paul was close, almost close enough to kiss in the same act of pressing his lips to her face, but separate as well, like someone asleep in another room. It came to him that he wanted the impossible: to protect them all. In the end he could almost imagine himself resorting to drastic means—kidnapping, fleeing overseas, going underground, anything. But even the most extreme of actions, it seemed, would require choosing between them, protecting one over the other.

"You said the death penalty."

"I did?"

"Like three times. You made glancing reference to it."

"Oh, well. I mean, very unlikely. But it's all about the circumstances. If they come up with a theory of the crime that says this was about money, say. Young thing, wealthy older man. And premeditated, and Paul only got hit because the guy was trying to defend himself from cold-blooded murder." She sighed. "Let's not even think about that."

He pulled her tighter against his body, wanting to cry, wanting her to understand, all of it, everything at once. Her lotioned neck under his mouth, her breast under his hand, Paul—it couldn't be the last time.

"Kent." She laughed. "Okay, but make it quick. I gotta get up early."

"Are you still on the pill?"

She froze. "Uh, yeah!"

"Oh, well, I figured…" He didn't know what he was saying.

She was open-mouth appalled, in a smiling way. "We're not there, are we? I mean, I didn't think we were *there*." She smacked him belatedly on the shoulder.

"No," he said, "of course not." It was the wrong time, the wrong thought strayed into his head like a radio wave from another planet. *But a baby…how could she leave him?*

"That's more like it, mister. You'd better watch it—I've got my eye on you. Still on the pill, indeed! Like I'm having one right now? Five minutes after my sister and in the grip of hysterical pregnancy? Not likely."

"Shh, okay. I'm a moron." He kissed her, rolled on top of her and she was smiling beneath him. When he moved inside her, he felt how they existed together in this protected capsule of space, smaller than the surface of their bed, and outside the membranous walls was a barely perceptible drumming like rain, a battering of hands, the howling of shades demanding to be admitted.

CHAPTER TWELVE

M aggie was up and talking on her cellphone in the kitchen.
Kent had heard it ring and now lay in bed, the morning
light bright in the blinds, straining to hear. "We can't be
there before eleven," she said. "Well, I know. Well, yes, I get that, there's
no need to…voluntarily, yes. I realize. Look, none of this is going anywhere. You do your thing and we'll do ours. Eleven. See you then."

He went to the kitchen, where she was showered and half-suited in
all but jacket and shoes, dialing another call. Standing bent over her
daytimer, she gazed up at him with comic misery. "No one in this world
wants me to eat breakfast."

He leaned to kiss her beside the mouth and since she still wasn't
talking gave her another on the lips. "What do you want? I'm cooking."

"I don't know. Just a bagel." She was distracted. "He-ey," she said,
a long, throaty, flirty greeting into the phone. "Where are you,
sweetie? I need you. Oh, thank goodness. Listen, I need a huge favor.
I have a preliminary hearing scheduled for ten a.m. and I need you to
cover for me. Yes, *today*."

He stood in the door of the refrigerator and held up an egg, walked it along the top of the door until she noticed and laughed. He walked a block of cheddar after it, and she nodded happily. "It's this client of mine, he's about to get arrested for murder any minute, and I have to take him down to homicide this—thanks, thank you, I owe you! Or you don't owe me anymore, how about that? Love you." She was into the daytimer before she clicked off. ¨

"He's being arrested?"

Dialing again, she bit her lower lip. "I think that's going to depend on what he has to say today." She held up a finger. "Paul, hi, it's Maggie. We need to talk about some things, and, let's see...I'm coming to your place and will be there at nine-thirty. So you be there too, or call me and tell me otherwise, okay? Bye."

He didn't like the sound of that, her voice upbeat but brisk, skipping over pleasantries. "What's happening?"

She sighed. "They found a liquor bottle with blood on it."

He cracked eggs into a bowl. "Where?"

"In the trash, at the condo. But it's not the victim's blood. It looks like it's Paul's blood." She sat at the table, face in her hands, then stood abruptly and rummaged in the cabinet under the counter for the frying pan.

"Paul's?"

"His fingerprints are all over it, easily explained since he lives there. But they say they have his print in traces of blood that's not the victim's on the neck of the bottle, and it's upside down—" She demonstrated on the vinegar bottle that sat on the counter, hefting it nose down—"like that, striking position. And there's a bruise on the victim's head that matches the bottle. They'll do a DNA analysis to know for sure it's Paul's blood."

"So that means what?"

"That means..." She leaned back against the counter, and he

reached past her to plop a hunk of butter into the skillet. "They must have fought. Really no way around that. Paul's blood is from the cut on his lip, so that's first. Bernard hits him, then he responds with the bottle. The *good* news—and this might really be—well, maybe it's only relative at this point." She stared ahead, thinking.

He whisked milk into the eggs. "The good news?"

She shook her head doubtfully. "The good news is that the bottle didn't kill him."

"What did?"

"Don't know. They don't have a murder weapon yet." She frowned in thought, moved aside so he could take over at the stove. "He lied. That's not good. He lied to *me*—that's worse. I have to imagine this is just the beginning, if he'd go to these lengths. He's covering more than this." She seemed more and more troubled, almost to the verge of tears. "I mean, otherwise...He should know he can talk to me, right? That I can still help him. If it's self-defense—"

"He's scared," Kent said, before he meant to speak. "He doesn't know what to do."

He'd spoken with too much authority, and now Maggie faced him with arched eyebrows, waiting.

"He told me last night, about the bottle. I wasn't sure I should tell you, or if I should wait and let him do it. But he said all of that. That Bernard was the one who hit him, and Paul hit him with the bottle, to try to get away. And he was freaked out about lying, too. Maggie, I really think that's all there is. I think he told me everything."

She nodded. "That's a little better," she murmured. "I'm glad he at least told you. This is going to be tight, though. That alibi—" She stopped, stricken. "They didn't tell me about the alibi!" She snatched up her phone and was dialing again. He slid the egg mixture hissing into the skillet, with a vague sense of an error too late to correct—he should have left them whole and fried them instead. He would have liked the look of it better. It seemed crucial that he prove himself by offering some kind of effortless beauty on a plate.

"I'm on hold," Maggie grumbled.

He scraped his spatula across the pan's bottom and turned the cooking egg, scraped and turned, felt the error again. He should have made an omelet.

Paul woke from a deep sleep into a profound disorientation, the room cluttered and dense with smells of strange cooking and cigarettes and unwashed clothes. As the kind of actor trained to believe with deep half-deluded conviction that the life staged for him was his own and real, he was sometimes caught in the reverse, especially on waking, his real life a play where he struggled to recall his role. Here, a house-wifely woman—his wife?—in a fuzzy pink robe with sleep-swollen eyes was calling him awake. She brought him coffee in a thick mug. "Not to kick you out, but you really better go. Take a shower if you want."

Sylvie. Sitting beside him, she gave him a droopy-lidded smile, her face all shiny and unguent-smelling and her hair a mess and he thought how pretty she looked this way. He envied Eric for getting to wake up with her in her unpainted and robed state before her voice had cleared, to hang around eating cereal and sharing morning smokes and watching cartoons.

Marry me, he wanted to say, but he couldn't locate the right face-tious tone. Instead he said, "Don't tell anybody at school. I'm going to try to be in class today. I've missed too much already." They had Romantic Poetry together at three p.m. She was frowning at him. "What?"

"I will take notes for you, you know."

"And I'll get dropped with an F." This seemed, at the moment, a disaster, or at least the biggest one he could get his head around and he couldn't even do that—it was just words.

The shower brought him back a little, but not quite enough to face the barrage of obligation at the condo. He arrived within a minute of Jodi and Tristan, who had their own keys and bustled in with energy and purpose. Jodi was in her forties, today in a black caftan that matched her dramatically straight black hair and kohl-rimmed eyes. Tristan was Bernard's age, a shorter man with all his hair, a sweater vest misbuttoned over his paunch, a sweet-tempered man who seemed frail with grief. They kissed him and held him just long enough, about five seconds each, to put him in his place as bereaved partner. They were directing this show, and their first task was to ensure that the mourners were cast as Bernard would have wanted them.

"Have you talked to anyone today?" Tristan asked him, busying himself with bags on the counter. In answering, Paul felt the tightness in his lip, the cut there like a signpost, and realized that Tristan and Jodi had both averted their eyes from it, said nothing. He waited for a blatant question, but they behaved as if all recent events had been explained. Again, he felt he was in the wrong play—in this one, it seemed Bernard had passed away from cancer after all, his friends solemn but prepared. The two of them carried in flowers and made lists; Jodi had spoken to Bernard's sister, who would be arriving that afternoon.

"I have to go to class," Paul said in a sheepish mumble, had to clear his throat midway through and start over. He was unable even to try saying what he meant: that he might have to go to the police station. Tristan said, "We'll be here all day. You do whatever you need to do."

Paul drifted toward cabinets under a gauzy compulsion to help but couldn't remember where they kept the coffee, couldn't manage to look like he lived there and was good for anything. He didn't feel like crying.

He only wanted to yell out for Bernard to tell him where the damn fil-
ters were, and seconds later stupid facts began occurring to him as
noteworthy: *Bernard touched the filter before this one, Bernard was the last
one to lift this lid.* He kept thinking that when Bernard got here he would
take over and things would make sense again.

"Puppet, sit down, let us do," Jodi told him, patting his head and
taking the coffee away. But he suddenly couldn't bear to be in the room.

He went back to his bedroom to change clothes, to replay the message from Maggie, which sounded ominous. More and more he was
sensing how contaminated everything was. If he were thinking clearly,
rationally, he would fire her and call a new lawyer. Until this second, it
hadn't fully sunk in that she was coming here, now, and that there was
no time to plan another meeting place.

His bedroom was still defiled with sooty dust, and he cleaned away
what he could, using the same black t-shirt that he'd tried to remove the
fingerprints with. He sat on the strangely smooth bed, stroked a hand
over the duvet. He'd given up trying to keep track of the evidence,
knew only that the room was dangerously marked somehow, perhaps
invisibly, with Kent's presence. But he could no longer remember what
the police might have found, what it would mean if they did, whether
Maggie might detect these traces as easily, or which of the two would
be worse.

There was a hierarchy and a logic of protection that, under stress,
had begun to warp, to acquire bumps and growths. The cops might
think Kent was involved—this was losing its integrity as a simple concern, its link to the chain of available evidence, until Paul began to feel
it instead as his own suspicion. Deep down, it seemed, he was fighting
to keep from knowing this truth. He made himself whisper its opposite
aloud like a spell to bind him to reality. *Kent did not kill Bernard.* He
added, *I did not kill Bernard.*

Maggie would be here in minutes. He went to his closet and paged through hangers for something to wear: an innocent-looking shirt. The project threatened to crack him up, and rising laughter chopped at his breath. Nothing too expensive, too hip, or too provocative. The gray and white jersey looked right—very boy-next-door, softball-in-the-park. Tight, but in an accidentally over-laundered way, and anyone drawn to look at his body in it would have to feel at least a blush of personal guilt. He put on a loose pair of jeans, sneakers, checked himself in the mirror and added a hemp choker woven with cheap beads and a wooden cross—ha!—that looked like summer camp. His hair was too clean and he finger-combed a little waxy product through it until it fell in limper, more worried strands. But the humor had left him and he now felt only hopeless and sad.

At the same instant he knew—knew before he dug into the drawer where he'd thrown his toys—the handcuffs were gone. He checked three more drawers, under the bed. Nothing. But he could taste the key in his mouth, then hear in his memory the slump and jangle of them sliding in his sleep from the mattress to the floor. They'd fallen, and he'd missed them when he'd straightened the room. Now they were gone. Covered in fingerprints. And it came to him that this, *this*, was what Maggie wanted to talk about.

But no—that couldn't be. Kent had never been fingerprinted, for one. Still, it rattled him deeply, these pieces being gathered, gone from his life and into tagged bags of evidence.

He went back to the living room, where Alek had arrived, another of Tristan and Jodi's crowd, a swarthy Russian and sleazy hedonist. He'd spent one entire beach trip trying to catch Paul in every hidden corner with a *how can I help myself?* innocence of intent, a mostly playful seduction Paul managed to resist, which sprung from ego and hound-dog indiscriminate lust and a complex, quasi-friendly rivalry with Bernard. Perfect. The three of them were seated on the sofas and Alek rose at Paul's entrance, opened his arms, into which Paul walked, surrendered, and though he wanted to sob—they all expected him to—nothing came. He only trembled and lost the ability to speak.

"He's under so much stress," Jodi said, as if summarizing for Alek hours of their intimate conversation.

It was then he understood that they weren't going to ask, weren't going to mention a word about the circumstances of Bernard's death, not now or ever, because they simply couldn't bear to hear and indulge his lies. They were only waiting out this awkward time until the cops arrived to remove him.

Alek ushered him to the sofa. Tristan went to answer the buzzer, came back with a vase full of red roses.

"Red is a little tacky, isn't it?"

Alek was rubbing Paul's shoulders, murmuring sympathy in his ear. He wanted to let Alek lead him away somewhere—Florida, perhaps—out into brilliant neverland sunlight, back to his darkened bedroom while the others were distracted with gathering beach towels and sunscreen.

"Here, baby, you want to read your card?" Tristan, with a stern look, made him lean away from Alek to reach it, adjusting the blocking of the scene. Paul glanced at the roses, a dozen in a glass vase that Tristan set on the coffee table, and knew the sender. The card read, "Be brave—you are safe. Know this is only a token of how much I love you, G." He jammed it in his pocket. Jodi, meanwhile, was answering the buzzer and announced as she returned that Maggie Someone was on her way up.

In his bedroom, she sat in the desk chair, her small hand on the wooden chair-back that he had recently cleaned of black dust, of Kent's fingerprints. He sat on the bed. He'd managed to introduce her to the others as a friend, to say only that he needed to talk to her, and Maggie, with her flippy, unstyled hair and lack of make-up, might have passed for an oddly overdressed friend from school. She at least didn't scream *lawyer* as she came in the door. Now he sat before her, numb with dread, willing himself to concentrate.

She glanced around the room, denuded of much of its clutter but still piled with books and magazines, papers on the desk, photos in frames and stuck into the corners of the mirror—of plays, mostly, of beach weekends and friends' parties. There were two lovely professional candids of Bernard in the throes of instruction taken for the school yearbook, and one snapshot of Paul and Bernard together, their arms around each other, their bodies angled in a way perhaps slightly more intimate than friendship. None of Kent—he had only a few, from years ago and buried deep in closet boxes. But as her glance passed over a wall calendar, it occurred to him—he wasn't sure—that Kent's name was written on it somewhere, not this month but folded back on the previous one. He saw it all now, the room leaping into evidence before her eyes though earlier it had seemed clean.

Her gaze came to rest on a poster that took up most of the wall behind the bed, a *Hamlet* poster in red and black tones whose figure was somewhere between photo and illustration. It was an extreme close-up profile of a face, half swallowed in shadow and angled down; a closer look showed the figure was bent inches from a floor, braced on a one tense forearm, the fingers in the foreground curled around the edge of a crown. But the eye was drawn first to the face, mouth open and eyes closed in a sweaty, disheveled ecstasy that looked more than a little sexual, looked in fact as if the sexual act were in progress outside of the picture's frame.

"That's you," she said.

He nodded, his throat too dry to answer. Her eyes lingered there before settling on his upright form on the bed.

"I'll just say it. I don't think you've been completely honest with me, right?" She watched him with soft eyes, and he searched for traces of restrained fury, something that would come lashing out once he'd been lured into ease. She sighed at his silence. "The police have enough to prove that you and Bernard fought that night. They know you hit him with a bottle. Why don't you tell me about that part of it?"

He opened his mouth, shut it again, pressed his damp palms to his thighs. He was innocent, sitting before the person whose belief in his innocence mattered more to him than anyone else's—more than Bernard's friends, more than the police. But before her, he couldn't believe it himself. He was mute, stuck searching for the tricks and props and expressions of innocence while all around him the room glowed with the iridescent trace evidence of Kent's presence.

"Kent told me," she said, very gently, as if reading the fear directly from his mind. "I mean, he didn't have to, because the police had basically told me already." She tilted her head, dark eyes luminous with curiosity, sympathy, nothing else that he could detect. "It's okay, Paul. I admit it's not the news I wanted to hear, and I completely understand why you're freaked out right now. But we'll work with it. Whatever happened—"

His eyes filled, blurred. "I'm sorry, Maggie. Please don't hate me. I don't think..." She rose and came to sit beside him on the bed, put her arm around his shoulders. "I didn't mean it to happen like that. I can't stand it if you hate me."

"I don't hate you," she said. "Sweetie, I'm not going to hate you, whatever happened. We'll sort it out."

He nodded, pushed at his eyes, sure now that she must be talking about Bernard. She said, "They know it was you who hit him with the bottle, and it left a little mark, but that was *not* what killed him. They don't have the murder weapon yet, and that's—well, that's good or bad, I guess, but they can't say at this point that they know you killed him."

Paul blinked. "What do you mean? What did kill him?"

"Well, something else. Something narrower than a bottle, like a re-bar or a cane."

"He didn't…hit his head on the counter?"

"No." She smiled crookedly in confusion, almost laughed then at the aghast look on his face, his hands pressed to his chest. "You really thought you might have killed him? No. No, he was struck very deliberately, three times."

"Oh my god. Oh. Okay." He was light-headed with relief, then stronger. Of course this was right. The confusion of the awful scenes he'd imagined, the lies, the appearance and what everyone else would think whirled away like chaff and left him with a new truth. He shrugged, shook his head in wonder. "I didn't do it."

She asked him about the bottle and he told her, tried now to remember everything he could about it. He showed her the pair of fingerprints inside his elbow where Bernard had grabbed him. Bernard smashing a glass, Bernard hitting him. "It wasn't like I hit him back," he said. "I only hit him because he grabbed me and it scared me. He had this crazy look in his eye, and I really thought he might kill me or something. He's usually not like that."

"Did he make that mark on your throat, Paul?"

He froze, caught in her deep gaze. He could feel that she wanted him to say yes, her mouth open in anticipation—she was almost nodding for him. He touched his throat and felt Kent's fingers there, more evidence to shove aside, bury in drawers if he could. "Yes," he said, the sound so faint and indefinite he added, "I think. It's hard to remember."

"That would make sense," she said softly, seeming tugged by some other thought. "What were you fighting about?"

"It was a big mess. Complicated. Me and him, we weren't in a relationship at all, but I guess he wanted us to be. If you ask some of his friends, they might tell you I was his lover. I used to be. But most people know it was just for show, me living here." This didn't answer the question—she was still waiting, nodding. "He was jealous, I guess. He didn't like it that I went out, hooked up with other guys."

"You did that a lot?"

He nodded, then wanted to take it back.

"So what was different this night?"

"I don't know." But he *had* to know—he could see it in her keen expectancy. This was the one thing that he could not be unclear about. No one would believe Bernard had been the one to start the fight without a solid, convincing story. He stalled. "A lot of things. It had been building for a while. He really wanted us to be together. But—"

"But?"

"He found out. That I was involved with someone." Because he'd been holding it back so hard, and it was the truth, the rest spilled out with a kind of relief. "Bernard, he didn't actually care so much if I hooked up. It was this thing with one guy, who was more, like, serious."

Once he'd heard it aloud, it didn't seem so wrong after all. No reason to name the man, and he could think of half a dozen reasons to refuse if anyone even cared to ask. Maggie's eyes brightened with the answer—this was what she wanted. "Just that night, he found out?"

"Yeah. I think he really knew it before then, but it kind of came out. I mean, I told him." Speaking this emboldened him—his freedom rested on this, and an unforeseen pleasure was that she, of all people, had to hear it. She had to sit there and listen. "I told him I was in love with someone else. That we were in love."

"And Bernard got angry," Maggie nudged.

"Very." He laughed, startled with memory. "He actually—I was taking a nap, before I went out, and he came in and tried to smother me with a pillow. Seriously. And then we just, I don't know, started arguing about stuff like it didn't even happen. I think it was so extreme that I kind of blocked it, you know?" She was nodding with fascination, and he felt encouraged. "Then we went to the kitchen, and started talking about these halfway normal things like my acting, and then I told him about being in love with this other guy, which is when he hit me. And that's when I kind of realized about the pillow, and I said hey, you tried to kill me and I'm not staying here, and then he got scary."

"And you hit him with the bottle."

"Yeah, because he had hold of my arm, and I panicked. I just wanted to get away, and I did. He let go of me."

"Then what, Paul?"

"Then I left. That's it. That's everything. I went to the club like I said."

"Okay." Maggie stood up from the bed, began pacing the room slowly, and he felt for the first time, the inner, knowing glow of a good performance. She was his again. "We're going down to homicide this morning and the police are going to ask you about all of that. You just tell them the truth, okay? I'll be right there, and I'll let you know whether to answer something. You have an alibi for the time of the murder—that checked out. But I should tell you, that may not mean a whole lot with the circumstantial evidence since you were the one who was here and you fought with him, and you lied about it. We could go with self-defense, but that would mean that you *did* inflict those three blows to the head. You came back, maybe."

That she was leading him to this late confession seemed another sign of her confidence, even as she watched him narrowly, but he was calm and sure now. "No. I hit him in self-defense, once, that's all."

"They're not going to find *any* evidence later that you did?"

"No."

"Okay, that means someone else did it. No forced entry, nothing stolen. Can you think of anyone who would do this?"

"There's a jerk in the building he fought with all the time. I told the police."

She nodded, returned to the bed. "Good. They'll be checking that. Anyone else?"

He shook his head, but he was trying to picture it, Bernard opening the door, some person stepping inside, swinging something narrower than a bottle, and *tire iron* popped into his head. But no. No, no, no, Kent did not kill Bernard. He knew this wasn't possible, wasn't a rational thing to think.

He drifted into a stupor, and Maggie fixed him with a severe look. "Paul, you need to hear this. Possibly the only thing that's going to keep you from being arrested today is some proof that it wasn't you or some other lead. Even if what they have on you right now won't hold up at trial, that doesn't mean it's not enough for an arrest."

"But I didn't do it. They can't say I did because there's no evidence." His voice rose to a high, sharp pitch.

"Don't panic. Just think. *Anyone* who might have had a reason to do this."

"There's no one," he said, too quickly. "Just that guy, Vernon Dodd, on the fourth floor. He could have done it."

She glanced away, troubled at his delivery. "You said Bernard was angry because you're involved with somebody. Maybe the police should talk to that person."

"No." He leapt to his feet, dizzy at the rush. "God, it wasn't him. He's never been here. He doesn't even know where I live, he doesn't know Bernard exists."

He gripped the desk chair for balance while she peered up at him sternly from the bed. "They will ask about him, Paul. They'll need to know why you fought with the victim."

"Well, I won't tell them," he said, his voice strident, beyond his control. "I won't give his name. I won't. They can ask me all fucking day. They can't have him." She was standing now, palms out, calming, hushing—but she had no idea what she was asking.

"I'll say I did it," he said, an inspiration that quelled his panic. It hardened for him into near fact as he spoke it, steadied him. "I did it. I killed him in self-defense."

He swallowed as this sunk in, a replacement truth—he would do this, he would do anything—and though it scared him, he glimpsed the elegant shimmer of the aftermath. Now Kent would see, have to see, how stunningly wrong he had been in judging him, for what could be more selfless than this love? Or maybe Kent would never know, maybe Paul would go to prison without the truth ever coming to light, and this didn't cancel but only deepened its beauty. Let his life be a lovers' tragedy, *Romeo and Juliet* and not *Hamlet*, the prince who never fully loved anyone.

"I did it," he whispered, but Maggie's hands were on his shoulders and she was saying shh, no need for that. No need. He was overreacting.

"You won't have to tell them who he is," she said, soothing. "That's your choice. Just don't answer. But Paul, this is the main thing: do not let them scare you into lying again. You *cannot* lie anymore."

There wasn't an ounce of doubt in her eyes. She hadn't believed his sudden confession for a second, but now he could see from her settled look, her concerned and pensive silence, that she had shifted at least some of her suspicion to this lover.

CHAPTER THIRTEEN

With a little time to spare before they were expected at homicide, Maggie took Paul to a coffee shop known for outrageous desserts. Her idea had involved something layered in berries, frosted in fantastic peaks and shaved Belgian chocolate, but when she took in his glassy eyes and jittery fingers on the counter's edge where he stood unable to order, unable to want anything, she decided he needed simple nourishment more than indulgence. She chose for him: a banana, a carrot muffin, and coffee. They sat at a small metal table by the street window.

"How do you feel?"

"Okay." He pulled the muffin apart, ate a chunk of it. "Really. I feel better now." Though he'd lost the vitality she'd grown accustomed to while working with him at the store, he did at least seem peaceful in the white glare of the new day. "It's just something to get through," he said with a shrug. "A formality, right?"

She nodded, nearly a lie. "You'll tell them exactly what happened," she said. "Everything that you told me. If they come at you with a question out of left field, look at me before you answer. If it's outside of what we've already talked about, I'll probably shut it down."

He nodded, ate more of the muffin, then the banana, while she went on laying out for him what would happen when they got to homicide. He sipped his coffee and rested the side of his head in one hand, the fingers playing in the ends of his hair. His irises were lit pale with morning light, and his shy, intimate glances from the table to her face made something stir in her gut. Watching him, she found herself curious, on a purely personal level, about the man he said he loved— who he was, whether he in fact loved Paul in return as Paul believed. What would it feel like, she wondered, to be that man, sitting across the table from Paul in a quiet moment, to be loved by Paul? Whoever he was, maybe he'd felt it enough to kill for.

"Would you be praying if you were me?" he asked, thumbing the rim of his coffee cup.

"Not a fair question. I pray all the time."

"See, how could I ever catch up to that?" He smiled dreamily, briefly, with a visible sadness that compelled her to speak where she otherwise wouldn't have.

"Paul, do you want to pray? We can if you want."

He shook his head. "No use, I guess. I'm going to hell anyway." He said it airily. "And not just…Maggie, I've done so many things to hurt people. I bet you have other clients like that. You know, they're creeps, and they didn't do the one crime but they did twelve others they never got caught for, so what's the difference?"

She watched him. "You were raised in a church that emphasized sin."

"Yes."

"I think differently. As a Mennonite, as a lawyer. Crime, punishment—that's how the prosecution thinks. I'm more interested in human beings and causes of behavior, the potential for change, accountability, redemption. And there's a kind of parallel there to my beliefs about God. If what you want is a relationship with God, if *that's* what you're thinking about, Paul, it doesn't really matter what you did or didn't do. It's a process, for everyone. For me, it's something I'm always working on."

He smiled a little at the table. "Like Magdalena. We're all sinners?" Face lowered still, he lifted his eyes, fixed her with a crafty look. "Except you. I bet you don't ever really sin at all, do you?"

It may have been the dark slice through his lip, less swollen now, that gave him a slightly dangerous air. If not for that look, the trace of a purr in his tone, she would have answered lightly. *Of course I do.* But he meant something by it and she didn't answer, until not answering became an answer of some kind—she wasn't sure what.

With a barely-there smile, he sweetened into himself again. "I'm sorry, I don't mean to be weird." He shook his head, looked away. "I'm just a little nervous."

"Don't be." She laid her hand over his, and he bowed his head toward their joined hands. She gave him a little time in that posture before saying, "We should go."

꙳

In spite of everything, she hadn't been prepared for another surprise. By the time she was sitting beside Paul for the interview, Thornton and his partner across the table and the video camera's red eye trained on Paul, she'd convinced herself that his freedom rested only on these two men believing his story as she had, and that this would be the problem of the morning—getting them to accept what would otherwise, in any other case, have been a somewhat implausible story of innocence.

Otherwise. Later she saw that she had created in herself a groundless belief that this case was special. And it wasn't that he had tricked her again, lied to her again. It was her own mistake now. She had invested too much in her idea of who he was, so that her fiction of him became more crucial to her than knowing the truth. She had done the same with Kent, she knew, in her transitory fear that he'd been cheating on her. Though she now believed he had not strayed, she remained aware on some level that her belief came from a choice to believe. And perhaps she had acquired the habit, since from the first minute of Paul's call to her office, she had felt herself looking a little away.

This time the overlooked detail was something that she knew with more than intuition, because Paul had given it to her: that other man. But she had tucked it away into a slot for possible leads, tagged it with an understanding that set its priority: Paul was afraid the man might be involved. It hadn't occurred to her that Paul might actually know it. What had he said about the smothering pillow—blocked it? Maybe she'd done the same.

"I must have blocked it"—he said it again for the detectives, when they asked about the fight, how the violence had begun and how it escalated. They asked him about the location of each struggle, the impetus for each swing, the exact position of their bodies, and she thought he came off every bit as credible as he had for her. He still couldn't say with any precision what time he had left the condo, though he'd given it more thought, he said, and decided it may have been a little later, perhaps eleven.

"But let's go back to that pillow," Thornton said. "If you were taking a nap, and this was before the fight started, what made him attack you?"

Paul tipped his head. "I don't know. Jealousy, I guess."

Thornton's eyes narrowed in a confusion that looked feigned. "But it was *later* that you told him about the other man. When he hit you in the kitchen. Right?"

Paul didn't waver. "No, that's when I said I was in love with the guy. I had already told him we were involved. Weeks ago."

"Sexually involved. Having intercourse."

"Fucking, sure. Among other things. Would you like the list?" His skin, so translucently smooth, and the fine bones of his face made him appear oddly pure despite the frank talk, as if sex were only these words that passed through him without leaving a mark. If innocence and truth had a look, it was Paul's.

"Was anyone else at the condo that night besides you and the victim?"

Paul blinked, a half-beat of a pause, and his settled gaze deepened. "No."

"Are you very sure about that? I think maybe your boyfriend was there that night. I think *that* may have been what started the fight."

Paul had become rock-still in the chair and didn't answer, didn't turn to Maggie for assistance, and even his eyes in their sockets were unmoving, as if he had simply turned off, his consciousness gone from the room.

The quiet partner chimed in. "He was there, wasn't he? Your boyfriend?"

"No," Paul said, the word uninflected. But Maggie knew then. Somewhere between his shutting down and the round, cool syllable that followed, it came to her that the detectives had the story. And she hadn't even thought to ask him the question.

Thornton smiled, complacent, as if all the evidence were in hand. "We know there was someone else there with you. What we're wondering now is whether you're concealing a witness, an accomplice, or the real killer."

Paul set his hands flat on the table and leaned forward, arms tense, voice throttled into control. "The only one besides me who was there that night is whoever it was who killed Bernard."

With Paul's shift forward, he was close enough that Thornton, directly across the table, could take hold of his hand, one thumb settled into the meat of his palm, and turn it over. "That's a fresh mark." His voice quickened with a growl of pleasure. "That's from Sunday night, and it was made with these." He reached into the accordion folder beside him and slid onto the table a plastic bag containing a set of steel handcuffs.

Paul jerked his hand away, not before Maggie had a clear look at the marks on the bone of his inner wrist, a neat set of parallel lines burned raw enough that now there was darker scabbing over what she had seen the day before. Seen and promptly forgotten.

"You were having some fun in the bedroom that night, maybe? But you obviously weren't alone, and you weren't with the victim. You were with the person whose fingerprints are all over those cuffs."

Paul folded his hands against his body without leaning away, and didn't break his gaze from Thornton's. "No, I wasn't," he said. But there was effort, a hint of tremor, in his voice. Still he didn't look at her. "There was no one there."

She was afraid he would panic next, and she strained to think of a graceful way to call the whole line of questioning irrelevant or blather some empty analysis of the case thus far, simply to cut the tension, give him time. But she was temporarily stuck, and Paul found the ground first. "I'm sure you guys enjoyed concocting that little fantasy," he said. "And I don't want to spoil it for you or anything, but if you really want to know, *this*"—he erected the wrist for them, the hand a fist—"didn't happen at the condo, and it didn't happen that night. I took the cuffs out with me the night before. This happened in a completely different place, on Sunday morning."

"Oh, yeah?" Thornton ground his teeth. "You go out a lot, don't you?"

Paul folded his arms again, his shoulders dropped inward, head tipped, a slight, overall softening like warmed butter in a pan. It was as if he were watching himself, Maggie thought, had noted the defiant fist reminiscent of protest riots and adjusted his attitude and posture for better effect.

"I guess that's one of the reasons Bernard was mad at me."

"So where were you then? Your boyfriend's place?"

Paul gave an impatient sigh, rolled his eyes to the ceiling. "Look, the thing is, I don't actually have a boyfriend. That's just a story I told Bernard." All three of them widened their eyes in surprise, waiting. He bit a nail, casual, impassive. "I know, I know *now*, I shouldn't have. But he was so controlling. I was just trying to make him back off. Show him he didn't own me." He blinked wet eyes. "I'm sorry I did it, okay? It was a bad decision."

"A story." Thornton rose to pace, to take this in. Maggie mentally scrolled back over everything Paul had said in this room and it was true—he'd never said the man existed outside of a story told to the victim. But of course he existed. She knew it from the force of his reaction in the bedroom, knew he was lying now despite her counsel.

Thornton rubbed his chin. "So whose place were you at, with the handcuffs? He doesn't exist either, I suppose?"

"That's my private life," Paul said mildly. "Where was I last night? Where was I a week ago? It has no connection to this." He was drinking in the detective's face with an intensity of expression—not desire but something like it, open and inviting, that neutralized any offense in his words.

Thornton smirked. "We'll need a name so we can verify that story."

"No," Maggie said, speaking up for the first time, "he's exactly right. Whatever your theories, the marks on his wrist are not evidence of anything."

She waited for a rejoinder, was sure they would have it and whip it out onto the table in victory—some other proof that the owner of the cuffs' prints had been at the condo. But the detectives glanced at each other and moved on, to the time question again, and his movements after leaving the condo—what had he been wearing? what car had he taken?—and after arriving at the club. What had he done at every minute and who had he seen? Paul responded with patience, repeating several answers. The questions, she thought, had become dull with procedural routine and overly plentiful, belaboring such fine points that she felt a weight being lifted as the minutes passed.

At the end of three hours, miraculously, they said Paul was free to go. For now. Keep him where we can find him.

⟫⟨

As they drove away from homicide, having addressed in a rudimentary way how the day had gone and where the case stood—leaving aside, for now, his reckless lies and the questions they raised—Paul asked to be dropped at the university.

"Why?" she asked.

"I have class." He looked at her askance: this was self-evident, had already been discussed. When they had left the condo together, he'd announced to the people gathered there that he was "going out, to class and stuff." The bulky backpack he'd hoisted over his shoulder as proof now sat at his feet.

"Class? Really?"

"Yeah." His voice rose at the end like a question. He seemed at the edge of a delusion, unable to imagine why she'd find this strange.

"Are you sure? You think that's necessary today?"

"Yeah." He nibbled his thumbnail. He looked twelve, a boy who didn't want to miss a quiz in social studies. But he sighed and said, "I should. And it's better than dealing with those people back at the condo."

She pulled into a sandwich shop to get them some lunch. Really she should have ordered to go, taken it back to her office where other cases were waiting, but she wanted a little more time with him. Something in his manner, this regressive-looking quiet after the potent, adult assertiveness of the interview, troubled her.

Once they were in a plastic booth with sandwiches and chips and drinks, her restless concern had added the handcuffs into the mix. Their mere existence was disturbing, and it was more than the sense, grown now to near conviction, that he was covering for a man who may have killed Bernard Falk.

"Paul, I don't know whether they believed that story or not. As long as they buy it and it doesn't get you into deeper trouble, we let it stand. But that wasn't a good idea. I understand you love this person, you're trying to protect him, but you tell one lie and you're a liar. You get that? It calls every honest answer into question."

He looked at the table. "*If* he exists, and I'm not saying he does, I had to lie. It's complicated. But for other reasons, not because he's involved in what happened to Bernard."

"This hypothetical person."

He didn't flinch at her tone. "You have to trust me. It's nothing at all about that."

"What about the handcuffs? Was that the truth?"

"Yeah." He bit into his sandwich.

"They're yours?"

He raised his eyes to hers, chewed and swallowed. Seconds passed, and his gaze didn't move but seemed to open, taking her in, tasting her, something near the leer of the morning, the look he had given the detective, an *I know you* of the subconscious.

"You don't like that about me," he said. "You wish they weren't mine. Does it bother you, that I would own them? Use them for pleasure?"

"No."

"Don't worry, I'm not secretly a big S & M freak or anything. I just have them." He blinked more benignly. "Does it make me less innocent?"

"No," she said, though he wasn't entirely off the mark. "It's not that."

The corner of his mouth quirked. He seemed to be enjoying this, though something like guilt swept the pleasure away in the next instant, made him look down with the wide-eyed blankness of the boy trying to get to school. The effect was almost that of deeper innocence, like a kid pretending to sexual experience he didn't have at all. She knew Paul had it, plenty of it, but the handcuffs had called to mind again his first experience—rape—his dismissal of it as a crime. Later he'd been involved with his professor, now with a man who could be identified only by that mark on Paul's wrist, as brutal as the one to his face. It was little to go on, a thin, pale picture of his life, but it made her wonder if he had a full grasp of what consensual sex was.

"What?" he asked, under her scrutiny.

"I don't want to pry, Paul. And maybe I'm completely off base here. But is someone hurting you?"

His mouth fell open, and he paused a little too long. "No."

She was ready to drop it, but something close to fear in his eyes wouldn't let her. "You can tell me, if there is. I won't tell anyone. I know how it can be sometimes—" She struggled for words, to read his eyes. "If you love someone, you can get into a pattern of letting them hurt you, letting that amount to love. You even want to protect that person, maybe."

"No one is hurting me." He smiled but looked pained, as troubled as her. "I promise, Maggie, it's not like that. It's just for fun. A game, you know?"

"Okay." She bit into her sandwich.

It was true, the handcuffs sickened her, and for this she felt a touch of rebuke—maybe her fear was only prudishness, or simple inexperience. Maybe the majority of people in the world were as casual as Paul about bondage in bed. But knowing he was concealing this man, she couldn't stop from imagining more than the obvious. An effort to picture the scene brought with it a fierce urgency to be there, to step between them, unlock the cuffs before—what? Because the mark on his wrist, she realized now, was not from being restrained. It was from struggle against it. And Bernard Falk, perhaps not jealous at all, no one's attacker, only trying to intervene.

⬩

"This case is making me crazy," Maggie ranted over the phone. Kent was in a cubicle, doing essentially nothing, edgy and waiting because she'd said she would call. After reporting the lack of an arrest, a few of the day's highlights, she tumbled into the afternoon and her showdown with the head of her law firm. "The worst part is that I don't know if Howie's going to give me the time I need for it. I had to pass off *another* case to poor Brad today, which did not make Howie happy, since without charges filed this one's not supposed to be a priority. But I can feel it already—this case could get very big, and very complicated, and it needs all my energy. Or half my energy, and Jamal gets the other. Meanwhile, I'm wondering if I'm too close to this one to see it as clearly as a different lawyer would. You know?"

"No," he said, "slow down."

"He's still lying to me," she admitted with reluctance. "And I think he's got a good reason for it, but he's forcing me into all this crazy supposition. I can't *stop*. I just want to find a way to help him, and he's *so* not helping me."

"What's he lying about?"

"This is top secret. Your ears only, okay? I know he's innocent. I'm absolutely convinced now. But I think he knows who did it, and he's covering. He's involved with somebody. In love, I guess. And I'm positive, almost completely positive, this man was at the condo that night. The cops suspect it, but they can't prove it. They have someone's fingerprints on a pair of, well, handcuffs—don't ask—for which Paul fed them a pretty good story, quick too, but I could tell. I could just tell. The guy was there. There's more but I shouldn't go into it."

Kent's head was buzzing. He set the receiver on his thigh to try to get his bearings, returned it to his ear. "Wait. You're saying you think this other guy is the actual killer."

"I'm almost sure. The way Paul's acting. What I can't tell yet is if *he* knows, or if he just suspects. He seems authentically in the dark about how it happened. But either way, he's not letting me anywhere near this guy."

"So the cops—they don't know who the man is?"

"No." Her tossed-off tone was comforting, as if their knowing were an impossibility. "Paul told them there *was* no man, but I doubt they believed him."

"Is that who they're after now? This guy?"

"I don't know. As of today, I'd say Paul's still the prime suspect. They don't have anything on the other guy, at least not that I know about. And they might never feel like looking too hard in that area as long as Paul looks good for it. Which he still does, I hate to say."

"Are you going to tell them? I mean, about what you think."

"*No* way, uh-uh. Not my job. That's someone else's job. I'm going to sit back and hope they can't scrape up enough to bring charges on my client, period. If they arrest him, then we'll see."

"See what?"

"Well, I'm not letting him go to trial on something someone else did! Especially when—" She stopped, sighed. "I don't know, but I think this guy might be a real lowlife piece of scum."

He could hear the resistance in her voice to every word, but still it shocked him. In child molesters, serial rapists, killers who tortured their victims, she found a teaspoon of humanity to fix her love on, to redeem from the unfeeling system. "I know, I know," she conceded, though he'd said nothing. "I never use those words. I don't think this way. This is not me! It's just different when it's your—which is half of why this whole thing is so crazy, because Paul is *not* my child, or my brother, or my second cousin. And besides, all of this is now based on a very thin theory of how it *might* have happened, and I'm already way ahead of myself."

"How did it?" he stammered. "Might it?"

"Oh, you shouldn't indulge me. And I shouldn't indulge myself. There's too much that doesn't quite fit anyway, so I'm probably very wrong."

"Probably," he muttered. It was him—*he* was this man who lived in her mind, skewered there, not only in legal danger but at the mercy of her thoughts. Even not knowing, he was certain he could never do anything as reprehensible as whatever he was doing right now in her mind.

"We'll just hope I am," she said, "because if the guy's not a scuzz, and he really loves Paul as Paul seems to believe, then maybe he'll come forward and turn himself in. Anyway. How is your day?"

When he'd hung up, he went straight down the hall to the john, which was mercifully empty. A powerful afternoon sunlight flooding the window's clouded glass lent a softness to the urinals and sinks and angled-open doors of the stalls, a clean corporate restroom that nevertheless reeked faintly of old piss and ammonia and something less repellent, harder to locate, a blunted, denser smell like loamy earth and vanilla. Often it was Paul he thought he could smell in restrooms, when he was alone and unrushed, Paul he wanted to find conjured out of dusky light and the drip of water, and even now he suffered a moment's delusion, sex so urgent and simple it could erase the rest of his life like a drug, deliver him to the bliss of oblivion.

In the mirror, from a little distance, he looked like himself in an open-collared blue shirt, the contours of his face the same he'd shaved that morning in the bathroom mirror at home. But it wasn't him. Weeks ago, he'd set things right, or thought he had, yet some part of him had continued to degenerate through whatever unstoppable process he'd set in motion and that no longer required his participation, that had moved beyond him like infection out into the world. Lies upon lies doubled back, warped and distorted, to lead Maggie astray in her work, to conjure monsters.

And all day Paul had been adding lies—to protect him, it seemed. But this seed had taken root in his wife's mind, and maybe it had been Paul's planting, to turn her against him.

He took out his cell and dialed. The outgoing message on Paul's voicemail—"Sorry I'm away. Leave a message"—had a lazy, intimate rhythm, soft but distinct, as he would speak to someone standing closer than normal. Not even his name. A smile curled in the voice, as audible now as it had been in the past months when Kent had felt it was directed to him alone—an arousing voice, laden with the promise of sex, or infuriating when it mocked him. But it was always the same sound. The message had been recorded maybe a year ago, the Paul who spoke it innocent of all the days that had followed. Kent almost hung up. But the beep came and he began to speak.

"Paul." He looked around the men's room, agonizing in its emptiness. "I need to see you, really need to see you, right now. This is a mess. Maggie thinks, god, crazy things about me and I don't even know what they are, like that I'm the one—or not *me*, but you know—and worse than that, something really awful, and I need you to tell me what's going on." He took a breath, thinking *you sound like a lunatic*. "Just call me as soon as you get this."

He clicked off with a frustrated jab, tucked the phone away. Maybe he should begin with himself. Tell the truth. He knew he wasn't thinking clearly, needed Paul to tell him why this was a bad idea, but to have even this tenuous plan made him feel better, cleansed and good. He faced the mirror, considered his reflection. He wanted to be himself again. But the situation was delicate, and he couldn't guess how it might crumble, from what touch.

When Paul returned the call, twenty minutes later, he was back at his desk and had lost contact with everything but the need to see him.

"God, Paul—"

"Kent, shut up and listen"—Paul's voice was like a whip snap, almost angry—"because this is the last time we're going to talk. The police are looking for you. You cannot call me again, ever—they can trace that. I can't call you either. I'm at a payphone right now, but they could be watching me. Maybe the second I leave they'll come figure what number I just called. Do you understand?"

"I need to see you," Kent said. "Right now. We need to talk."

"We're talking. And for like a minute, okay? It's too dangerous."

"No, I'll meet you somewhere. Where are you?"

"Are you listening to me?" he hissed, and there was a series of clicks on the line. *God, he's right*, Kent thought, *they're tracing the call*. "I'm doing everything I can, I promise," Paul went on, with distinct shift in pitch—he was crying. "I don't think they can find you if you stay put. But they think I'm involved with either a witness or the murderer, and that means they're probably following me right now."

His voice was a choked rush, and Kent made hushing sounds into the phone, suddenly aware of the office around him, the open cubicles and unknown numbers of ears just beyond. "Hold on," he said, and made himself walk casually, the phone to his ear, across the floor and into the stairwell. Inside that echo chamber, his own voice entered his ears louder than he liked. "Okay. Paul, let's try to be calm. Are you on the street or what?"

"I'm in the student union. It's safe, I think. No one can hear me where I am, and I can see everything. There are just students around. A cop would stand out."

"Okay, good." Maybe he was only a sucker for tears, but he found it touching, soothing, that Paul sniffled into the phone. It seemed like a devotion he could trust. The more scared Paul sounded, the calmer Kent felt. *This is the last time we're going to talk*—that was loyalty in the extreme, if only words. "Paul, stay there, okay. I really need to see you."

"No, forget it. I'm leaving as soon as I hang up."

Kent started at a trot down the stairwell, though he didn't fully believe Paul was going anywhere. Then he knew this, that Paul would be compelled to wait if there was even a chance he was coming, and knowing this quickened rather than slowed his pace. It granted him a strange assurance, rare in his recent life—the sense that he was headed in the right direction.

"Look, it's not as dangerous as you think," he said. "You watch too much TV." The casual humor of his own voice helped shrink the situation to a size he could handle. "It's perfectly fine for us to talk. I'm your fucking lawyer's husband. You're a friend of the family."

More breathy sounds on the line, but it was laughter this time, the lilt sliding into the softer ease of his voice. "Kent, please don't. I don't know if I can stand seeing you. I'm trying to keep it together here, you know?"

"I know." He paused in a glare of sunlight beside his car. "Believe me, everything's going to be okay." He drove in a giddy awareness that he might be losing his mind, but his plan made a kind of sense that comforted him.

In the center of the student union's broad, open floor, at the far edges of which sat clusters of stuffed chairs and potted plants and reading students and chatting groups of students, Paul stood alone. He stayed locked in place as Kent approached, a two-handed grip on the backpack over his shoulder—stilled like a rabbit that was ready to break and run in any direction. The tips of his ears and his cheeks and his throat were tinged pink, but his face was washed and empty. Too scared, it seemed, to fully meet Kent's eyes or say hello, he allowed Kent to lead him to an empty bench along one wall. They sat a generous two feet apart.

"Don't smile," Paul said, looking a little green and resentful of Kent's calm. "God, this is such a bad idea."

"You've got to relax."

In his own voice he heard Paul's, speaking in the kitchen of the Edgewood house with Maggie just beyond a wall. *You've got to relax.* The memory swept Kent up into some higher angle of perspective, where the distance from that night to this moment all but disappeared, could be crossed on the slipstream of those few words. And farther back, months, years, Paul's voice and those words. From above, the future was only another slide away, a letting go and a breathless rush, not the desperate agony of decision that it felt like to live through a minute.

"I can't," Paul said. "I'm the one stuck right now trying to keep *us* out of prison. Keep that in mind."

"Okay. You're right."

Paul looked out somewhere in the middle distance of polished floor. "You didn't kill him, did you?"

The question was so quiet and flat that it took Kent a few seconds to grasp what was being asked, that Paul could have imagined such a thing. "No. Jesus, Paul—".

"I didn't think so. But then, I thought. It was possible maybe. It's been a crazy day."

"What did you tell Maggie?"

"Not that." Paul gave him a doubtful glance, as if this suggestion were clearer evidence of insanity than his own. He shrugged. "It's just what she thinks. I mean, how could she not? If she weren't...who she is, or you weren't who you are, I wouldn't be hiding so much. This would be a very different situation."

"She's got it in her head that the man you're involved with is some kind of reptile."

Paul rubbed a wrist, and after a few seconds Kent realized Paul was showing him the red wound there. "The handcuffs. Your prints. I mean, *his* prints. She thinks I'm being abused or something. I told her she was wrong, but why would she listen to me about that?" He cocked an eyebrow, smiled a little. "How fucked up is this? Here's something else funny." He stroked a finger along his throat, where the bruise had become bluer and more definite. "I told her Bernard did that one."

Didn't he? he almost asked, almost reached out to touch the mark. But in the act of restraining himself, he remembered stopping the car, his own grip on Paul's throat. It jarred him. If murder had crossed his mind when Paul had been in the house, he had felt in the car neither an urge to kill him nor even a desire to inflict pain. He'd wanted to get Paul's attention, nothing more.

"God, Paul. Am I—I'm not what she thinks."

"No," Paul said, with enough insistent eye contact that there was pain in the prohibition of touch. From his lingering higher perspective, the past remained in view, all that expanse of time when he'd been free to touch and hadn't, when he could have kissed Paul gently on the throat and had let the chance pass. Even in the car that night, he could have—could have turned time, slipped them all into a new present.

"You were justified. You were right. I came into your house." Paul sighed. "I started this, Kent."

"Did you?"

He didn't want to feel this way anymore. He couldn't stand for Maggie to go on imagining him as some monster, both knowing and not knowing, as something alongside of what he was but was not.

"Paul, I think I need to tell her."

"Tell her what?"

"Everything."

Paul stared. "I knew it," he said. "You've lost your mind."

"No, I think maybe this—"

"Kent, you are not allowed to have a breakdown right now. You had *all* that time before now to flip out. Now is not the time. That's my lawyer you're talking about, remember?"

"Yeah, I know. But—" Paul was right, the reasonable one for once. Or had he always been? "She needs to know, doesn't she? I mean, it's not fair. To make her do this. And she needs to understand just to defend you. Or, us." But he saw that clearing himself, at least from the worst of her malign thoughts, meant endangering Paul's chances by alienating her. He wanted a way not to explain it to her, confess, but to pass understanding in some cellular form like a transfusion, so that she'd simply have it. So that she might adjust, turn away from this lead and go on.

"It's not fair," Paul agreed. "But we're stuck here for now."

"She told me, Paul, she said if I were a decent human being I'd turn myself in."

"Not you. Him. *He* would turn himself in. You didn't do it."

"Right," he said, though the logic of it felt frayed, incapable of supporting much weight. It upset the serenity of his plan.

"You're not that man she has in her head."

"Right." Of course, right, and he felt mildly grateful for Paul beside him, keeping things straight. "First things first," he said, though his own precise meaning eluded him. He took a long breath and released it. "I mean, let's go get some groceries. I'll cook us something at the house."

Paul grinned, too surprised to restrain it. He dipped his eyes and shook his head in condescension. "Honey, I'm sorry, but you really have gone crazy."

"No, this is an entirely rational plan." He was wistfully reluctant to admit this—crazy might not be so bad. "If anyone's watching, this is our reason for being together. I'm here to get you for dinner."

Paul took that in, rose with him as if accepting a dare. They left through the union's glass doors, drove from the college, stopped at the store, wandered together through the produce section picking out tomatoes and zucchinis and yellow peppers, Paul playing along amiably as if waiting for the catch—if it was a contest, he wouldn't be the one to blink first. Kent didn't know himself what the catch was, let alone when to reveal it, so he paid for two sacks of groceries and they returned to the car and drove to the house in Edgewood.

In the kitchen, Kent made a call to Maggie and filled her in—Paul was coming over for dinner. Okay? Great. The tilapia thing, you know, with the stewed vegetables. Under control. He hung up and pulled out a cutting board and sliced vegetables, tossed them together into a pan and set it aside. Paul stood and watched, turning over the paper-wrapped fish fillets on the counter. "I'm not actually staying for dinner, you know."

"You're not?"

"I have rehearsal at seven. By the time Maggie gets home, I'll have to go."

Kent checked his watch. Paul leaned against the counter, fiddling with his scabbed lip.

"I'll fix you something else."

"I just ate." He smiled a little. "Don't worry, Dad."

Kent didn't return the smile, only watched him a moment. "You didn't sleep much, did you?"

Wary, obviously unwilling to take the question as the simple thing it seemed, Paul didn't answer. Sincerity now was a dangerous thing, potentially overwhelming. He seemed about to back away as Kent approached and drew him into his arms, then he gave in, relaxed. He laid his face on Kent's shoulder. They held each other in the center of the kitchen. Paul's slim torso was a hot thing against him, so much emotion bolted down tight and contained in his skin, enclosed in Kent's arms, and Paul's arms were around him, loosely, maybe feeling something similar in him. It was very quiet, the clock ticking audibly on the wall. Paul's breath on his neck was slow and even. The house didn't fall down around them. Nothing happened. And if Maggie were to appear in the doorway, what would compel them to break apart, retreat to their opposite corners?

He took Paul's hand and led him to the bedroom, flicked on the light over the bed, which had been made smooth. The pillows, his and Maggie's, were tucked neatly under the quilt and the quilted throw pillows perched above. Just inside the door, Paul stopped, only his eyes moving, darting around the room as Kent lay down, patted the space beside him. Paul stared, then, unlocking himself by degrees, moved as directed. He eased himself halfway down, stepped back to remove his shoes. When he finally lay on the bed, he seemed to hover, as if intending to leave no impression in the smooth arrangement of the quilt.

"It's okay," Kent said. Paul's body was folded into the mirror image of his. He searched Kent's face, waiting for more instruction. *Trust me*, Kent didn't say, touched that even after the disaster of their night at the condo, it didn't need saying.

"What are we doing?" Paul asked.

"Just go to sleep."

Kent watched him until his eyes closed, then he closed his own. He knew Paul's were open again almost instantly, staring with worry, so he shifted closer, dropped an arm over Paul's side. His hand rested lightly at the small of Paul's back, less a command to stay than a promise that it was safe to. In a few minutes, Paul relaxed under his arm and later he was asleep. Kent dozed as well but mostly he was awake. He watched Paul sleep and waited for Maggie to come.

CHAPTER FOURTEEN

The overhead light was off when Paul opened his eyes, alone on the bed. *Their* bed. No sound from the house behind him. In the striped twilight from the blinds he could see Kent's dresser in the shadows and his own hand before his face, resting on the quilt. Earlier, he'd noticed the quilt's pattern, circles of blue and green on white, little scraps of gold—the one called double wedding ring. His grandmother had once shown him a quilt in that pattern, at a flea market when he was ten. Every newlywed couple should have one like it, she'd said, and one day she would like to make one for him. He remembered his fascination with the pattern, his amusement at the wrongness of the name—it wasn't double rings but dozens of them, so many rows of interlocking rings that at first he hadn't been able to see them, could see instead only the horizontal and vertical ripples like repeated infinity signs made by their multiplicity of joinings.

Barely moving his finger, he traced a few stitches. He was meant to have this, and here it was, his for the moment. He could hardly believe Kent had offered it freely, had chosen to lie beside him, a hand on him like a claim. But it was only for the moment, like everything Kent had ever been able to imagine for them. Today, now, and probably tomorrow, but no promises. He was a guest, and it felt like a cruelty that the resting place offered was so comfortable he didn't want to move.

"He's sleeping," Kent had said minutes before, outside the open door at his back, and the words lingered with him.

Soon he could hear their voices in the kitchen. Mostly Maggie, with a strained note of concern. Then Kent, brief questions. He caught infrequent words, Maggie saying "he" and then "he" with a negative cast— *he's not, he won't.* If he could have picked out a few more that might pass for a confrontation, he would have lain still and listened, but already the fantasy was skewing, dissolving.

He made himself get up and go into the kitchen. Kent's back was to him, Maggie so engrossed in a low stream of speech that she didn't see him right away. "Rice Street Jail is not some podunk holding cell with a sheriff sitting outside the door. He can't stay there—"

She startled a little, seeing him, then closed her mouth. Kent jerked in turning, and they both stood looking at him.

"Jail?" He rubbed his eyes.

They didn't break into laughter, explain what he had misunderstood, as he half expected. Sleep still protected him with a thinning cottony haze, and he'd had just enough time in the house to begin to feel that safe. Maggie stepped forward. Kent stayed where he was. "Hey," she greeted him, with a forced cheerful note. "Come sit down."

He sat where she guided him. It felt like his chair now, his place at the table. Maggie sat beside him and began to speak in a low, serious voice. Yes, she said, unfortunately, he was going to jail. Tomorrow, he would be going to jail, for a very short time, maybe only one night, and Maggie would drive him there and drop him off. It was like going on a trip, she seemed to say, a necessary trip, which they would make less tiresome by planning certain elements of departure and arrival but would unavoidably involve a brief stay in a lousy hotel.

But I didn't do it. Saying this again would not be the magic key to freedom it should be or at least seemed to be in his head. He sat blinking in the brightness of the kitchen and listened.

The cops don't have a case, she said. Not much of a case. The bad thing that had happened was that his alibi had come under doubt. The police had talked to Stephen, the bouncer at the club door that night, who could say with some precision when Paul had arrived. Though George Babbish still insisted on his own version of times, the story had been embellished to involve his sneaking Paul in through a backroom private office, and, basically, the police no longer believed him. Basically, the police were pissed. They didn't like being lied to, and they didn't like conspiracies to lie. They wanted hard evidence now—a witness, the murder weapon—and they believed Paul had at the least something to give, that an arrest would convince him to give it.

Luckily Thornton seemed to like Maggie, and whatever his belief about the case itself, he didn't seem to consider Paul a public threat. He had agreed to let her bring him in the next day—none of that messy handcuffing-in-the-street. They could even wait until afternoon. Also, she was hopeful that she could talk Thornton into recommending bond to the DA, which would mean a lot, which otherwise they might not get at all. If all went well, Paul might have a hearing within twenty-four hours and be out the next day, as soon as he could post bail.

And by the way, Paul had not been meant to hear what she'd said to Kent before, about the Rice Street Jail, where, yes, he would be staying, briefly, and which really wasn't such an awful place. It was clean. Only one other person to share a cell with. True, he would be on the sixth or seventh floor, where they kept men with the more serious charges, like murder. And sometimes there were fights, but these could be avoided—just keep your head down, keep to yourself, don't challenge anyone but don't look too meek either...

Kent had moved back into a corner of the kitchen while Maggie spoke. Paul couldn't help looking in his direction, because some voice in his head was saying *Run away*. He needed a signal. But Kent's face was expressionless. Paul might as well have been alone in the room with Maggie, who was so caught up in her worry and her effort to pretend she wasn't worried that she hardly seemed aware of Kent's presence. Her eyes shone with love all the while she spoke, and Paul couldn't help loving her back for this, though he remembered intending to hate her, once.

"It's okay," he told her. "I can do it."

"Sure." She smiled uncertainly, chaffed his forearm that lay on the table.

"Really." He leaned closer, with a soft, steady look that removed Kent from his eye line. "I can handle it. You don't have to worry." The assurance made her brow crease with more visible concern. "It'll be good for me. The part I'm playing right now is a guy who just got out of prison, so I'll use it."

His calm felt like more than a show for her benefit. He was suffused with something like relief, and he straightened in the chair, palms pressed flat together and arrow-like before him. "Bernard's dead," he said. Kent drew back into range, near the opposite end of the table. "I mean—I'm *not* innocent. I didn't kill him, but I still sort of feel like I did. And he's gone, he's dead. It can't be the worst thing for me to go to jail."

He glanced at Kent—too briefly to identify the heat of emotion that was visible again in his eyes, but he was glad for it, he'd take it, whatever it was. He turned back to Maggie. "They're wasting their time on me, though. I don't have anything else to give them."

When he checked his watch, said he needed to go to rehearsal, no one objected or called him crazy. Kent offered to drive him. Maggie would meet him at the condo the next day, two o'clock, which would give him time to make whatever arrangements he needed. In the meantime, she'd work on securing a bond recommendation.

Paul was too preoccupied to be aware of the drive, to think *what now?* though he was mildly surprised when Kent pulled into the theater's parking lot, their stated destination, and up into a tree-shadowed corner past the building's entrance. His face was tense in profile, the engine running. Paul thought maybe he was meant to open the door and leave without another word spoken between them. But Kent was only gathering something.

"I'm sorry, Paul. Really. I feel like this is my fault."

"Why?"

Kent turned off the engine. He pressed his lips, shook his head. "Maggie, you know, she's really—she's too involved. She's blowing everything out of proportion. She has a thing about you. You know that, right? It can't be that bad." He was trying to convince both of them, apparently. He was quiet for some time. "Maybe we should go somewhere."

The words were so feathery they might have been a question. Paul smiled. "Like where? Mexico?"

Kent didn't smile or register the notion. "I don't want that night at the condo to be—" He stopped. "I don't want to be that person to you. And Bernard...I just feel bad about everything. You were saying before, how you feel like you killed him. I feel like I did too." He seemed puzzled, struggling to understand as much as explain. "I hurt him. And I left you there to hit him with a bottle. Such a fucking mess."

Paul sighed. "You feel guilty about Maggie. That's all."

"I guess. And you." The back of his hand brushed over Paul's, dropped near enough as if by accident that their fingers were touching.

Paul nearly winced, held himself in check. "I have to go. Someone will see us."

"So? What if someone did?" Kent's voice strained to sound casual, almost flip. "Maggie saw us. On the bed."

"She did?" Paul's heart pounded. "Did she—?"

Kent shook his head. "She was too busy worrying about you. About the arrest. I should be jealous, I guess." He cracked a faint smile and Paul smiled with him, but Kent's had already fallen away and he returned to brooding. "What should I do? Should I turn myself in?"

"You didn't do anything."

"But I was there. I could say we left together, that he was alive. It would explain a lot, explain why you lied."

"Then Maggie would know. Then you'd be a suspect."

"Right. But then, I don't know, maybe they wouldn't arrest you."

Paul's throat constricted. "God, Kent." He hadn't even been looking for it and here it was, love, of the kind Paul hadn't felt since their old life together, when love hadn't quite counted until it demonstrated its purity through a clean divorce from reason. *Run away*, his head said again, and maybe they were parked at the edge of a possibility, a few careful sentences away from driving off into another life.

He hooked a pinkie through Kent's and studied his face in the shadows of the car, tried to memorize it, for he had the sense that he would later be looking back on this as the one time in Kent's married life that he'd possessed him almost completely.

"You're not doing anything crazy like that, okay?" He felt Kent acquiesce as he spoke, expecting to be talked out of it. "You're very sweet, but I'm tougher than you think."

Frowning, Kent nodded. He shifted his body squarely ahead, releasing Paul to go.

"I love you," Paul said, matter-of-factly, knowing Kent wouldn't say it back. He wanted to say something else—not goodbye, but something like *remember. Remember this later, how you feel right now.*

He squeezed Kent's finger and loosed himself. "Guess I'll see you later."

⤜

Paul thought he'd understood what was happening. But when he said it to Mark, to explain why he couldn't make the next night's rehearsal, it became real. "I'm being arrested," he said, the echo of it reverberating in his skull. *I'm being arrested.*

Once Mark felt reassured he'd be returned to the free world soon enough for the play's purposes, he pursed his lips, studied Paul with a crafty expression. "Well, Silas. How life imitates art, hmm? This might not be so bad for publicity."

Paul pondered that backstage as he put on Silas's skin: Silas the killer, probable killer, who may in fact have been innocent though what could that matter when he had no soul, who in the scene they were about to rehearse would plead with his gullible brother to believe he'd been wrongfully accused, falsely imprisoned, and in the next would be poised to seduce the brother's young wife.

But he had not killed Bernard. He was being arrested for what someone else had done. He tried to throttle his growing fear and think who. Vernon Dodd. George Babbish. Bernard's various rivals: Alek, Mark, others. Maybe a student with a grudge—there were plenty of those. The names accumulated, making him feel a little speedy, half-elated, though for each one he could argue against as easily as for. He needed paper. Meanwhile some other sentient portion of his head, timed to the beat of the play, caught his cue to stride on stage and speak as Silas.

As he exited, the power of Silas like a current through his body, crackling out his fingertips, he understood more fully what Mark had meant. Who would have bothered to see this play before one of its unknown leads was arrested for murder? Perhaps if he and Mark fed his arrest to the media in connection with the play, they would get press for both. And if his case helped the play, maybe the play would help his case. He could give interviews, explain his innocence, captivate his audience and exonerate himself before the world. They would love him and they would fill the theater to the walls.

He peered out at where Mark sat six rows back in the darkened house, scowling over his glasses at the actors onstage. Mark Westlake had never half-filled a theater in his life, or so Bernard had once said. Bernard had claimed he could charge twice per ticket and sell more seats to a college production of students reading from cracker boxes than Mark could sell to his own "professional" version of *Cats*.

So maybe Mark had killed Bernard. Crazy, sure, but what if Bernard had said something, or even been meddling somehow with the play, once he knew Paul had been cast? And murdering Bernard would in itself lead to an extraordinary box-office boost, wild popularity for the play, thereby proving Bernard wrong on the very grounds of their hostilities.

Ten minutes until his next entrance, and he could tell the news of his arrest had been whispered around the wings. He was getting those glances from the others, though they kept clear. Leah, exiting the stage, approached him with worried eyes. "I need paper," he whispered, mimed writing, before she could ask him if it was true. Caught in his urgency, she turned wordlessly to help him look. His backpack was out in the house. Prop lists tacked to the walls could not be moved, playscripts lying discarded on chairs had no unprinted space, and he felt he needed a lot of space, because what was forming in his head was not a list but a play called *My Innocence*.

He found a stub of pencil, and then Leah was beside him, smiling in triumph, two clean sheets of notebook paper in her hand. He kissed her forehead, held his cheek there before he sent her out to meet her husband on stage, shrilling "Devon, where have you been?" as she went. He watched the scene, the paper to his lips—enough paper for the beginning of something if he could remember anymore what it was. He knew he could one day write a play better than the one he watched, but for now he thought it would be enough to perform well in this one. To have that chance. They were talking about him again, his guilt or innocence, the danger he may have harbored like a secret power. He, Silas.

⤳

Bernard had a sister named Deirdre who was a restaurant critic in Charleston, a buxom woman with a gray pageboy, warm eyes, and a ready laugh. Paul had met her twice before, once when she came down for *Hamlet*—to see this *wonder boy* her brother had been raving about, she confided to Paul—and once again in the fall, when Paul's status had altered significantly but Bernard had obscured for her the standard-issue story, as he did for no one else Paul could think of. ("You remember my brilliant student, Paul. He's staying with me for a while.") Paul had been invited along for several of their outings, during which he and Bernard had their customary joined and knowing exchanges—Paul, you would know that. Weren't we there in July? Didn't I say that just the other day?—but without the endearments and the touching that otherwise marked public appearances together.

"Oh, she knows," Bernard had said afterward, an impatient sweeping assessment that seemed to include his sexuality along with Paul's supposed position in his life. "And she doesn't like it, not that you'd ever guess. Dee is charming, amusing company, especially when she doesn't care for you. She simply pretends you're the person she'd rather you be. It's her neat way of rearranging the world to her liking."

Runs in the family, Paul thought, liking her perhaps a little more for her vexing of Bernard, who had also accused her of lacking real warmth under all that charm. She seemed to take an intense, personal interest in Paul's talent and prospects, as if she had spent a good deal of her free time pondering them, and on her second visit she accosted Paul fondly about his *career* and graduate schools and what the next step would be on the golden path that fate had surely laid out for him. Like his grandmother, she was effusively maternal in ways that obliterated his guard.

She had been in town since the previous day, Paul knew, had stayed the night in a hotel. Several hours before his scheduled arrest, she arrived at the condo flanked by Tristan and Jodi and trailed by two grown daughters—leggy, athletic, diffident girls around Paul's age—an entourage that seemed to insulate her from Paul's approach. He'd expected to be sought out, embraced without hesitation. He didn't know that he'd been waiting for her, craving her arrival and the comforting pillow of her breasts, until she set him back with a cool nod of greeting.

When he went to help the girls with drinks, he found the refrigerator had been stocked with foreign juices and the girls knew where the glassware was. So they had already gathered here without him. The girls were somber, funereal, though he didn't think they'd ever been close to Bernard—Bernard had once called the pair "a little thick"—and they eyed Paul in silence and kept clear. He asked simple, polite questions and they looked at each other before answering.

When he returned to the living room with his portion of the drinks, after the girls, all the chairs had been taken. The conversation hushed, and glances slid from him to lower places or each other's eyes. He leaned against the side of Tristan's chair—and it seemed, in fact, Tristan's, the sofa Deirdre's and her daughters', himself an unwelcome visitor.

"Deirdre," he said, "I'm so sorry about Bernard." His voice wobbled with the lack of breath behind it.

"Yes," she said flatly.

In the awkward silence that followed, he understood that these people had been talking about him, perhaps in this very room the day before, and had come to an agreement. He set down his glass and stood. "Have you talked to the police?"

"The police have been here, yes." Deirdre blinked mournfully, as if this had been done to upset her. "Asking a lot of questions." There was a weighty pause on the last word.

"About me, I guess."

"Paul." Tristan stood, reached for his arm. "Why don't we go talk?"

He drew back from Tristan with a cornered alarm. "You think I did it. You all do." He looked from Tristan to each of the others, caught the round, staring eyes of one of the nieces. "*You* think it. You don't even know me."

"Mama," she said, her face pulled to a grimace as if Paul were coming at her with a knife. Deirdre put a hand on the girl's arm and they all looked up at him openmouthed. The rush of adrenaline made his limbs feel like iron. Tristan was coming at him hesitantly with both arms open as if to catch a loose horse, maybe wrestle him to the ground, and Paul blocked him with a rigid forearm. Tristan stepped back.

His breath came fast, and he stood straight, calmed himself. "I didn't kill him." He looked straight at Deirdre, demanding her response. "I didn't do it."

She watched him with a hard wariness. "We'll let the police determine that."

"Oh," Jodi moaned, "oh this is not good."

"You don't know anything." His voice was back now, behind it the diaphragm power Bernard had taught him. "Look at all of you. You accuse me, like you know anything about my life, or Bernard's. Sure, you cared about him, I guess, but you didn't know him. You didn't live with him." His voice broke, and he lost what he was trying to say. Tristan's tentative arm came around his back, hooked over his shoulder. "What do you know about anything?"

Deirdre raised her chin. "We know you hit him in the head with a bottle on the night he died."

He snapped back, "Do you know why?"

She only stared at him in silence, and he saw then that he couldn't explain. He was guilty of this, and in a gathering of mourners it was enough to be guilty of.

Tristan had withdrawn his arm. "Let's not do this," he said, to everyone. "We don't know what happened."

"No, I would like to know," Deirdre said, blinking at Paul. "Go ahead, explain."

Paul shook his head uselessly, folded his arms. Tears started to rise in his voice, though his eyes remained dry. "I wish I hadn't hit him. I wish that wasn't the last time—the last minute we had together. He meant a lot to me. I never got to tell him I was sorry for, well, other things too, besides that." He took a breath. "You don't want to hear that he was violent, but he was, recently. He was depressed. He was scared about the cancer. He could be hard to live with. And I was the one who was here with him, not any of you."

Deirdre looked at Jodi, who said with a shrug, "Yeah. He was depressed. Erratic, probably."

"We had a fight," Paul said hopelessly, needing the bare word to explain more than it could. "That's all. I wish it wasn't that way." He closed his eyes, surrendering to the inevitable—he might as well say it. "I wish they weren't arresting me today, but they are. So that should make everyone happy."

He turned away and shook loose of Tristan, who followed him anyway back to his room and closed them in. "Please go." Paul crawled onto his still-made bed. The room reeked of day-old roses. "You don't need to pretend to be my friend. I get it, okay? I'm leaving. I just need to—" He sat up, looked around the room that contained everything he owned, though the furniture was Bernard's and half of everything else bought by him. "Some of this stuff is mine, okay, so don't let that witch carry it off to South Carolina or sell it or whatever she plans to do." He got up and began to snatch his pictures out of the mirror frame.

"Paul, don't think too harshly of her." Tristan looked helpless, arms at his sides, unable to find a sentence he could speak with conviction. "She doesn't know you the way we do, and we, Jodi and me, we know you wouldn't have done this."

"Do you?"

"Oh, Paul." He began to cry. "This is so hard. I can't bear for you to feel this way, alone, everyone against you. It's so awful."

"But it's true." He dropped his handful of pictures on the desk. Tristan cried quietly, filling Paul with a contempt that was calming, empowering.

"When is the funeral?"

"Tomorrow. Two o'clock." Tristan wiped at his eyes.

"Great. Maybe there will be a miracle and I'll be out of jail by then." His tone made Tristan blink despite the tears. "Or maybe you could make it a day later, so I can be there."

Before Tristan could work up a response, there was a light tapping at the door, and Jodi came in. "I talked to her, Paul. She's emotional, we're all"—she glanced grimly at Tristan, who struggled to dab his eyes dry—"emotional. And we all, I think, need to step back and reconsider. We've been jumping to conclusions, and we have no right to. We're sorry."

Paul crossed his arms, met her eyes with a softened, neutral look. "Somebody else did it."

She took a breath, nodded hesitantly.

"I don't know who. I don't know if the police care about that, or if anyone cares. But while I'm in jail, maybe you could at least think about it."

She lowered her eyes, nodded again. She had been crying as well.

"If you want to come join us in the living room, you'd be welcome to, I think." She gathered Tristan, and when they had left him, he felt sorry to have imagined he knew so easily what they were going through, that his own pain was worse. Considering how guilty he must look, they had been kind.

He picked up the stack of pictures, sat cross-legged on the bed and glanced idly over each shot. Maybe it was one of these people. Maybe someone in the next room. He rubbed his hands over his face and reached into his back pocket, withdrew a stiff square of paper. The card from George. He'd only skimmed it before, now read more slowly. "Be brave—you are safe. Know this is only a token of how much I love you, G."

This, a token. This being a dozen roses. This being an alibi. But what if *safe* meant not safe from arrest, from suspicion, but safe from Bernard? Even then, it might only be a tacky reference, a backhanded celebration of Bernard's demise. And George was surely too meek for murder—the idea of him engaging so physically with anyone was almost laughable. It was the "how much I love you" that kept Paul pondering.

He whisked the card across the edge of his hand, considering the putrid roses already dropping petals to the desk. Of course he'd sent roses. If nothing else, he knew Paul tolerated men he didn't love in order to live comfortably. Soon Paul would ask him for bail money, and asking would require pliancy, and from there what grounds would he have, homeless, to refuse George's house, to make any other claims about who he was?

From the next room, Tristan's sad, querulous voice rose into the range of hearing and fell again. In an hour he'd be free of them. Free, funny. Compared to the bunk he'd be sleeping in tonight, George's hospitality was hard to dread.

The photos had spilled from his lap to a scattering on the bed, and he picked up a black-and-white candid of Bernard. It was a three-quarter head and torso shot, eyes fierce and locked on some student target off the side of the frame, an arm outstretched with stiff, upcurled fingers that might have palmed an invisible skull. The dark of his brow, the light of his eyes. It was mesmerizing, his full power of years past sparking and visible. Paul knew the picture well, as he knew the life it was drawn from, one of any hundred instants during Bernard's classes or his direction of a play when Paul had scrutinized the man with as much love and intricate attention as this camera lens. His mouth was open, speaking some instruction, and right now Paul wanted nothing so much as to hear what was being said. He was almost sure it was meant for him.

CHAPTER FIFTEEN

W hen Paul's mug shot came on the TV screen the night of his arrest, Maggie wasn't terribly surprised. Still she let out a cry and cringed into Kent's shoulder.

"Shh," he said, leaning forward and turning up the volume on the remote. Paul, drained by stark lighting, covered the screen, then was reduced to a corner of it.

"Sources say Foster, a former student of the victim, had been living with the fifty-seven-year-old man since last September, and that the two began a sexual relationship while teacher and student. Charges have not yet been filed in the case."

That was all. No pause for perky rejoinder—the anchor moved on to the next story. Maggie breathed again, shook her head. "I knew it. I knew they'd pick this one out of the pile. You know why? Because look at him!" She gestured at the screen though his mug shot had been replaced by a DUI graphic. "He's *blond* and young and cute, and they managed to dig up a juicy story out of ancient history that's not even applicable." Kent rose abruptly and vanished into the kitchen. "Hey, where you going?"

Silence. She heard the refrigerator open. "I'm getting a beer. You want one?"

"Sure, I guess."

She went into the kitchen, sidled up to the counter where he stood opening bottles. "This is a whole different case now. If I were going to say he did it, I could feed all this into self-defense and get him acquitted on sympathy, easy. But if we're saying he *didn't* do it, people are likely to buy the more interesting story, the lurid one about jealousy or money or revenge or whatever." She swallowed from the beer he handed her.

"So do you change the story?"

"No," she said with a sigh, too distracted to consider it deeply. "God, I hope he's okay. I wish I could go see him right now."

"Why don't we?"

"We?"

"Sure."

"I just dropped him off like four hours ago." She pursed her lips, eyeing him as he sipped his beer like an evasion. "Besides, visiting hours are over," she said, a stress on *visiting* that came out faintly sarcastic. After all, she could see him now as his lawyer if she chose to, if she had a reason.

But she didn't go, and all the next morning she was busy running from the DA to the presiding judge to secure a bond order in time for his first appearance hearing, scheduled for three o'clock. She did not see Paul at all until he was led into the low-ceilinged complaint room. He caught her eye with a sideways look, enough glint in it for provisional relief. Taking his place at her shoulder before the magistrate, he lifted his bound wrists to show her. "Handcuffs," he whispered, as the docket number was read, and gave a little sexualized grunt of mimed struggle. She shushed him, suppressing a grin.

The magistrate waved through the DA's charges, and she couldn't complain there either: one count of malice murder, one count of felony murder, and one count of aggravated assault. Bail set at one hundred thousand.

She visited another client and then hung around a little longer, checking the parking lot now and then for reporters, until Paul made bail. His cuffs were removed, his few possessions returned to him. As he was signing himself out he motioned her to the desk—she assumed to ask about the paperwork—but he hooked a hand around the back of her neck and whispered into her ear, "Get me out of here." His cheek was against hers, and she was conscious of his fingers on her neck and the rasp of invisible stubble, his breath in the tiny hairs of her earlobe. "Say I have to go with you. Just take me."

His bail had been posted by George Babbish, the short, bearded man who stood against the wall in the waiting area, staring at them with doomed eyes. The man with the alibi. The man with ten thousand dollars at the ready to whip out and pay to a bail bondsman for Paul's release. From interviewing Babbish earlier, she had formed an impression of him as warm and generous, if twitchy, full of an over-anxious fatherly concern that had led him to lie for Paul and to ask her many questions about the case and Paul's chances. She hadn't wondered if this were the lover Paul protected until he'd shown up for today's hearing and seemed distinctly uncomfortable to see her, nodded in greeting, and in the waiting area kept a room's length away from her.

She leaned beside Paul while he signed another form. He muttered, "That guy gives me the creeps."

Minutes later, Paul was embracing the man with every appearance of easy affection, pressing his hand, thanking him for the rescue. Babbish's face flushed a deep, unhealthy red, and his response was choked and difficult. "Of course, it's the least, it's nothing." He stood apart then, his glance turning again and again toward the exit. Surely this was not Paul's lover, though his agitation seemed somehow sexual, the guilty shame of a man caught paying for a hooker.

Maybe it was only her. Though she didn't remember it well, she was almost certain that a few nights earlier she'd had a sex dream about Paul. When his mouth was at her ear, she'd felt it again in a flash—not a present desire but a memory of it. The giggly excitement of being naked with him—maybe him, she wasn't sure—and an effort to say no, it was wrong, she was married. Yet she'd wanted it in a way that she almost never *wanted* sex, with immediate craving. Her yes and the act had been sweaty and quick but extremely erotic, left her with a feeling like her memories of junior year in high school when she'd first let a boy touch her breast in her bedroom, her parents downstairs. In the dream, as then, she'd felt distinctly that what she was doing couldn't be that wrong.

Undeniably she was fascinated by Paul. In love, perhaps—but only in a way she would freely admit to her husband. If the dream were about anything, it was more likely to be about the case and its mysteries, which were redolent of sex, her desire more for a knowledge of Paul's hidden life. The yes and the no of it, for she both wanted and didn't want to know.

Since the dream, her mind kept touching on three images. One, Paul's face: the clarified light in his skin and eyes like paintings of Renaissance angels while he spoke casually of base sexual acts. Another, the *Hamlet* poster on his wall: Paul at four times life size and caught in a position that alluded to sex, suggested it, but maybe only to her. It was perhaps no more than an accident of candid shooting of some scene of the play, Paul as Hamlet and unaware of the photographer.

And third, her husband and Paul on the bed together. The scene at a glance had been so odd, just at the edge of wrong, that a narrative had instantly tried to impose itself without her effort. That Paul was stressed, exhausted, in need of comfort. His back was to the door, a long, narrow body in a tight shirt and loose jeans, barefoot on the still-smooth quilt, facing Kent. They weren't exactly cuddled up together—there seemed to be a good body's width of space between them—but Kent's hand, the ringless one, rested on Paul's back just above the curve of his hip. Neither hurried nor hesitating, Kent sat up at her arrival, his half-lidded eyes unstartled. Standing, he smiled at her with one side of his mouth and rubbed his tousled hair, just as he would have if caught napping alone, and joined her outside the room.

"He's sleeping," he said, before she had found the question to ask.

"O-kay," she said, with a tone she didn't intend, a *whatever you say, but that's a little, I don't know,* weird. *Isn't it?*

Kent had begun talking about dinner, and with Paul's arrest then imminent there was no time, no room, to think any more about it. It simply passed from her awareness, forgotten, and had come back only today as she waited for his release, a tickling oddness that echoed this paradox of Paul, sex and innocence. For nothing had been happening, not as if she'd caught them in bed—they were simply *on* the bed.

And now George Babbish, whose interest could only be sexual and who had made a ten-thousand-dollar purchase, yet Paul shied away at George's murmured offer of a ride home, said, "Um, I think we need to—" and looked to her for the end of the sentence.

"Yes, we have work to do."

"So I'll see you later, okay?" Paul finished, a warm, apologetic tilt to his head as he squeezed George's hand.

George looked as if he wanted to swallow Paul whole and might not release him. "Will you need a place to stay? You know I have the room."

"I think I'm okay. I'll call you. Thanks again for everything." He spoke over his shoulder, nudging Maggie ahead of him toward the doors.

She caught his rolled eyes and tortured expression as they walked away, but stayed quiet until they had passed through several sets of pneumatic doors. "What was that?" She still felt his earlier touch on her neck, his body against hers, couldn't help wondering if escape from George Babbish really required that much contact.

"It's looking like an obligation," he said darkly, but she didn't follow. "Put it this way. I have bad luck with men." He gave her a sweet, close-lipped smile. "Unlike you."

"Unlike me," she repeated.

To chase those thoughts down with a question, even a silly one— *you want my husband, don't you?*—seemed to risk calling something into being that didn't exist at all. Couldn't. But she was aware, too, of the time Kent and Paul had now spent together, almost all of it out of her presence. Her glimpse of them on the bed was one of the few times she'd seen them interact, and Paul had been asleep. She wished she could see how they behaved toward each other when she wasn't around.

They were nearing the external doors and she stopped him while she went ahead to check the parking lot. Sure enough, a news camera waited between pillars of the sheltered walkway, one and maybe more. She returned to Paul, pulling a jacket from her bag and wishing she had dragged Harold along from the office for extra muscle.

"We'll have to make a run for it. Put this over your head."

Paul blinked in a stunned way at the wrinkled jacket she'd put in his hands, an old navy windbreaker of Kent's. He folded it over his arm and stroked it slowly as if it were a nervous pet, looking toward the doors. "It's okay. I'm fine. I want to talk."

"Paul. You can't talk."

He was already walking ahead of her and through the doors. The cameras, two of them, taken off guard, staggered forward, led by two microphoned reporters, and Paul halted. She missed the incoherent questions that lapped over one another, but when she reached Paul's side, he was answering.

"I'm innocent of this crime. Bernard Falk was a very dear friend—" The sudden tug as she caught his arm and propelled him forward brought from him a gasp of choked emotion. He turned to the reporters as she pressed him along toward the car, his voice free of anger and sounding only sad, calm, deeply sincere. "I'm not afraid to face you or anyone. I wouldn't do anything like this, ever. That's not the kind of person I am."

There was a microphone near Maggie's face and she spoke into it to keep what little control she could of the scene. "This was a groundless arrest. There's no evidence against my client."

They were shouting for Paul, demanding to know if he'd had a sexual relationship with the victim. One arm around his waist, she held him nearly pinned to her passenger side door while she worked the lock. Paul turned and faced the cameras. "That was a long time ago. I was very young, it was wrong. He knew that. I forgave him." *Him?* she thought. His eyes were velvety with compassion, and all around him was a sudden intensity of stillness and silence, the recording equipment drinking him in. "He made a mistake, but he was a good man. He was a wonderful person, a wonderful teacher. We had gotten to be friends recently." Emotion stopped the words in his throat.

She pushed him into the car, and only then did the shouted questions resume. "That's all. We're done," she said, though he leaned forward at her shoulder, trying to hear a question. But he submitted without resistance, and she shut the door on him, pushed past them to her own side.

"Well, then!" she exclaimed, aghast as they drove away. Paul was breathing as if he'd run a mile to reach the car. "That was"—she shook her head—"quite a performance."

"Did I screw up? I wanted them to know."

"I don't know, Paul. You made it sound like a child molestation case."

Still clutching the jacket, he brought it to his face and breathed into it, staring out at the road. Maybe it wasn't bad. In the glimpse her memory had stored, he appeared nearly Christ-like, damp-eyed and beneficent with his understanding of the weakness of others. Footage like that could be picked up by the national news, for no better reason than a boy's appealing face, and that could be good or bad.

"Don't worry about it. We'll see how it plays. But next time you're going to get in front of a camera, why don't we talk about it first."

"Sorry."

She glanced from the road to his face. Reaching to stroke aside a strand of blond from his eyes, she considered his appearance after a night in jail. Eyes clear, lips and cheeks touched with extra color from the adrenaline. "Didn't even need to primp for that, did you?"

He snapped down the visor mirror and glared into it, threw it back up with a scowl, as if beyond words for the ugliness of himself. "God, do you have a cigarette? No, of course you don't smoke."

She drove around a few blocks to make sure the cameras weren't pursuing them. It was nearly happy hour, so she circled back to the Mexican place just around the corner from the jail and parked, led him inside. They found a seat in the restaurant's dim, sparsely populated front room. "I'm getting in the habit of craving a margarita every time I come to jail," she said. "Seems like the right response, you know?"

Paul agreed but was listless and quiet, staring at the table's checkerboard oilcloth. It worried her that he didn't seem relieved at freedom or able to locate the spirit of the post-jail drink. She ordered two margaritas anyway, on the rocks.

"What happens now?" he asked.

"Now we wait for the grand jury to convene and decide if there's enough evidence for trial. That won't happen until the DA's office thinks it has enough for a case against you. Right now they don't. But there will be more questioning, more pressure on you to talk. Charging you is to show they're serious."

"Can I leave town?"

"You want to leave?"

He shrugged. "I don't know. I kind of want to go home for a while. But I have this play to do. And I don't know that I want to tell my dad about all this anyway. Can you imagine?"

She closed her gaping mouth. "Paul, you haven't told him yet?" He shook his head. "Honey, if he lives in Greene County, that's not far. I think he knows. This hit the news last night. And tonight, well, you saw to that."

He pressed a hand over his eyes for several seconds, withdrew it with a sigh. "Yeah. Right. Well, that's done, isn't it?"

"Better if you could have told him. But—not that we're going to trial, but if we do, you'll want him there." He looked skeptical and resistant as she spoke. "Paul, the more family you can gather around you, the better. For your own well-being and for the case too. A jury will notice if your family is there to support you or not."

"So I should round them up and convince them to fake it?"

She frowned at his smirk. "I'm sure your family loves you more than you imagine."

The waiter set glasses before them. Paul stabbed his ice with his straw. "Magdalena"—his voice was stern and precise, annoyed with her or pretending to be—"what makes you think you know these things?"

"Well, they know you, I assume. So just a guess, but I don't think it's possible for them not to love you."

He shook his head with a quizzical look, indulgent now of her absurd delusion, and she glimpsed again the dream of his bare body lowering to press against hers, the sly, boyish grin. She reached for her salt-rimmed glass.

Paul's eyes turned blankly toward the window. "I guess they buried

Bernard today. Those people, his family, they don't understand—he would be so pissed that I wasn't there. I was supposed to stand there and feel bad about everything, you know? Regret all my failures of affection." He smiled into his glass. "But this he would have liked. I guess I can drink for him now, if nothing else. Cheers." He tapped her glass with his, raised the rim to his mouth and downed several gulps, chased salt with his tongue.

"Paul."

"I keep feeling like he's still alive. And there's something I'm supposed to do right now, like meet him somewhere, and he's mad at me for not doing it."

She could think of nothing to say that would help, that didn't sound empty. "Do you want to go see where he's buried? We can go right now if you want." He considered a moment and nodded.

She let him finish his drink, and they drove to the cemetery on the north side of town, where the azaleas were shriveled and brown on the bushes, the hydrangeas in bloom like balls of blue popcorn. The breeze ruffled the tree branches and drew pollen into golden ribbons along the fresh-laid asphalt of the path. Leaving the path, they crossed the lawn to a treeless spot amidst the other graves, distinguished only by its heap of raw red earth.

Paul sat in the grass beside the grave while she hung back, reading the names on nearby stones. Between Paul and the erupted ground, a history, a communing like prayer over what they both—the dead older man and the living young one—knew and what she could not. However the news might seek to distort, it was hard to imagine any scenario in which sex had not somehow led to this death. Bernard Falk had been intemperate in his desire, a teacher who had bedded a student. He was also the one, she felt certain, who had designed Hamlet as erotic, even wantonly sexual, had in fact posed the picture to match his desire. But Paul loved him.

At Paul's glance of invitation, she moved to sit beside him, knees folded to the side in her narrow skirt. "The play I'm in opens next week," he said, facing the dirt. "It's so like him to find a way to get out of seeing it."

She smiled at that, but he was struggling not to cry. He slid up close and laid his head on her shoulder. The sun's slanted beam in her eyes may have caused the heat and flush in her face. She put her arm around him. Because no words came to her, she pressed a kiss to his damp hairline. He was salty like the tequila. He turned his face and kissed her neck, a soft, searching brush of lips that lingered enough to suggest a possibility, not much, only an unhardened question in her mind of what he was thinking and doing and what would follow. But almost from the moment of contact, he choked into a sob.

"It's okay," she said. He pressed his eyes to her shirt at the shoulder and then pulled away, drew up his knees and wrapped them in his arms; she kept her hand on his back until the contact was innocent again.

"Lately all we did was fight," Paul said, brushing his eyes. "But he was all the family I had, or felt like it sometimes. I can't believe he left me. And he's under all that dirt, just dead. He's never coming back."

A red-tailed hawk wheeled through the late-afternoon sky. Its shadow crossed the mounded dirt, passed beyond them toward the far trees. She rubbed his back. She wanted to promise him he wasn't alone, to ask where his lover was. And he had a real family somewhere. But she recalled that he had told no one about his rape. Without her own family and her faith, she didn't know how she would have survived her own; but Paul had felt he had no one to tell.

"I have an idea," she said. "Something you might like."

She took his hand and helped him up, put him back in the car. "Remember my sister, Lila? The pregnant one?" she said as they drove back downtown, against the thick of traffic coming the opposite way. "She had the baby. A boy, born Sunday night. Actually it was early

Monday morning, 2:31 a.m."

Paul absorbed this in silence. "I was at the club," he said eventually. "Bernard was dead already. Or dying."

Before Maggie had fully considered what she was doing, they were on the front porch of Lila's house admiring the hydrangeas. Cemetery pollen from their clothes would drift into her sister's garden, breed a new strain of flowers. Would what grew be stronger for that brush with death? The Yoders had heard all about Paul's recent adventures, and they had seemed willing to accept that he was innocent as she accepted it, by faith alone. Still, a little piece of her recoiled now in doubt, the frantic, irrational kind inspired almost exclusively by fear for the safety of children she loved.

There seemed little question of going inside, disturbing the family. As if by previous arrangement, they took seats on the porch furniture. Chloe insisted on being the one to fetch the baby. As Lila handed them iced tea from a tray, Chloe emerged with the baby dressed in a clean, white onesy. Maggie stood to say hello, coo over him and remark on how much he'd grown in the day since she'd seen him.

Chloe settled in the chair closest to Paul, the soundless, staring baby propped in her lap. Enthusiasm stretched her face from eyebrows to chin, though she kept her lips over her braces. Her hair was loose and freshly brushed. "Isn't he great? Do you want to hold him?"

Paul flinched, sat back in his chair. "No, that's okay."

Undisturbed by rejection, Chloe held the baby's arms balanced on her palms, danced them to a song she hummed. Paul leaned forward again, studying the baby.

"Excuse me." He stood abruptly. "Do you mind if I use your bathroom?"

"Not at all." Lila opened the door and directed him, took her seat again and met Maggie's inquisitive glance. "What?"

"Nothing."

"All right then." The three of them regarded each other and their surroundings in silence, as if the porch with its hanging plants and tin art flowers and slow-turning ceiling fans were a gallery exhibit.

"So where's Seth?" Maggie asked.

"He's at a friend's."

They were quiet again, until Chloe sang under her breath to the baby, "*Murderer in the bathroom.*"

"None of that," Lila said sharply, stifling a smile. "Not even in jest."

Paul returned, took his seat in a position of hunched discomfort, arms tight to his body. He looked straight at Maggie with something desperate in his eyes. "I had to wash my hands. I shouldn't be here at all." He turned to Lila, confessional. "I've got jail all over me."

"Don't be silly," Lila said, with impressive lack of hesitation. "You're fine."

"I'm not going to touch him or anything." Paul's voice was fragile and so painfully earnest that all three women crumpled a perceptible degree in response, and Chloe let out an *oh* of sympathy that made her clamp her mouth shut. She brought her face down to the baby's ear, said brightly, "Look at that baby!" as if the exclamation had been for him.

Paul's mouth parted, his cheeks red. He cleared his throat, and his voice shook a little though he'd dried it out flat as an old husk. "I mean, I know how you get nervous with a new baby. And I'm not good with babies. He's really cute though. Luke, right? Is that his name?"

Lila smiled her bounteous-hearted madonna smile. "Yes."

"Paul's had a rough day or two," Maggie said. "I thought seeing the baby might cheer him up a little."

"Of course. Babies are good for that."

Chloe, uncharacteristically quiet, played with the baby's feet. Luke blew bubbles from his red lips, let out his first sound of the visit, a loud and articulate "Gah." Chloe grinned, flashing a bit of metal, interpreted for Paul. "He likes you."

Paul smiled, shyly embarrassed as if given a compliment. Lila turned to Maggie with an *aw, sweet* look. Chloe began to chatter about the baby, how good he was, how smart he was, what he already liked and didn't like, and Paul leaned toward her with rapt attention, hands still restrained with prophylactic care around his elbows. For no good reason, Maggie recalled an article she'd read just that morning about dogs, which had argued they were not furry bundles of unconditional love but social parasites, intricately evolved to manipulate their human hosts with feigned emotions.

But why feigned? she had wondered. Why couldn't an animal's real feeling serve the same purpose?

She touched the side of her neck absently, where she could still feel that graveside kiss. He'd been seeking comfort, it seemed, simple contact. But *comfort* was a slippery term, the need easily contrived. And she had allowed it, a kiss a shade beyond innocent. It seemed now some door had been left open. That he had not crossed beyond was no sign the door had closed.

⁓

The instant she was home, Kent asked her about Paul. He'd been at his weight bench in the back room and trailed her to the bedroom wiping sweat from his bare chest with a t-shirt. While she changed her clothes, she reported that Paul seemed to have survived jail without a problem. She mentioned the incident with the news cameras. There was much more she was prepared to say: that Paul was depressed about Bernard, grieving and lonely, in need of a substitute family, that she had taken him to the cemetery and then the Yoders in an effort to answer his needs. Her ideas, she thought, had been good ones, met with some success, for Paul seemed restored and grateful, almost cheerful as she sent him off to his evening rehearsal. On the Yoders' porch, she'd indulged a vision of Paul befriending Chloe, joining in the family's late-night card games, an adopted member of their larger, collective household as she herself had been with the Yoders when she'd first arrived in town alone. Everyone needed a family, and her own had always been rich in love and generous toward those in need, taking in outsiders with little question.

But she didn't say any of this. She looked her husband in the face. "You care about him a lot, don't you?"

"What do you mean?"

She felt her mouth start to stretch toward humor. It would have been easy to make a joke, turn it to nothing. But she was feeling distanced from Kent, closer to Paul after their strange day, its moments of skin contact bent toward the erotic. She felt *possessive,* if there was a word at all for this deeply curved blade of emotion rising from the premise that Paul himself, perhaps even more than her husband's care and attention, rightly belonged to her.

"You're worried about him getting hurt," she clarified simply.

"Not *worried.* I mean, yeah, a little. I'm just wondering."

She could see he was struggling to dodge an accusation he couldn't quite identify. She had no intention of accusing him, only testing something. She was thinking about her dog theory, some offshoot of the child phenomenon that she and Kent had already discussed. If she'd fallen in love with this stray boy, and Chloe and even Lila had fallen, with that collective relaxation of boundaries that begins to make a little provisional place for him in case he chooses to stay, that says *yes,* as long as he proves healthy and gentle with children and current on his shots, *sure, why not, we'll keep him,* then why couldn't Kent fall as easily? But she already knew of at least two small flaws in her notion. One, her own love had along the way slipped past simple feelings for dogs and children. And two, Paul had sex with men, a fact that reversed the implications of whatever similar emotion she and Kent might have felt for him. However eroticized, hers was permissible; however inno- cent, his was in question.

"Admit it." She smiled, playfully, though she had to force it. "You have some kind of a thing."

"A thing?"

"A thing about him. You're all—" She made a vague hand gesture.

"All what?"

"Worried!" She was relieved that he laughed a little, quizzical and confused. Part of her, she realized, actually wanted him to say yes, to confess some inordinate fondness on par with her own, something they could laugh about and normalize together. Paul needed them. She wanted him around, wanted Kent to want it. But she was suddenly nervous about pushing him.

"You like him," she said, stalled. She might have suspected then that she was only berating herself, accusing him to avoid being accused, but for the one thing that wouldn't go away. It was burned into her mind: the two of them on the bed, Kent's hand fitted to the dip of Paul's waist where he was impossibly slim, elegantly curved. From behind, he could have been a girl. Their child, their dog, could have curled up with Kent in that pose and it would have been nothing but sweet and appro- priate, would have sent her running for the camera. And though she wanted Paul to somehow fit that picture as easily, he simply wouldn't. The picture remained wrong.

"I like him," Kent said. "So, he's…?"

"He's fine," she said, relenting. Kent watched her guardedly still, and she had to rinse the remaining innuendo from her voice. "Really, I'm glad you like him. He might end up needing to stay with us for a while."

Now Kent reacted, head drawn back as if she'd swung at him. "Oh yeah?"

"Well, it's not something we've talked about. I'm just thinking ahead for him a little." He could stay in Bernard's condo—she had explained that the sister couldn't evict him without sixty days' notice. But Paul, she thought, would not insist on his legal rights if he felt unwelcome there.

"There's a guy planning to take him in, I think," she said. "This creepy guy who paid his bail, and Paul's kind of scared of him. I just want to make sure he has other options."

"Yeah, but." Kent chewed his lower lip, looked around as if for an objection. "We don't have a whole lot of room."

"We've got plenty of room!" His resistance surprised her. If they didn't have room for a short-term guest, where did he think a baby was going to fit? "I'm sure it wouldn't be for long. Besides, we're not there yet." She narrowed her eyes, studying him. "You don't like the idea."

"I don't know. Sharing the house. It just seems—" He didn't finish, but she could see it in his eyes, was certain the word he didn't say was *dangerous*.

⌒

Less than an hour before rehearsal, Paul returned home to find the condo greatly changed. Half the furniture was missing. Deirdre had selected the antiques and expensive pieces, left the sofas and the discount store stuff and auction house bargains behind. The TV and DVD, the stereo system and computer, gone—it was the missing TV that made him let out a curse, since he'd been hoping to catch the news. Every knickknack was gone, valuable or not, the walls denuded of art, desolate-looking in the evening light. They hadn't touched Paul's room.

In Bernard's room, the bed was gone. The enormous lacquered bureaus were still in place—Paul couldn't imagine how Bernard had gotten them in there to begin with—but their drawers were emptied.

Only trash remained: hangers on the closet floor, an ugly blue candle on the bureau, a bottle of single malt scotch on the carpet near the doorway, open and on its side but not empty. Looking at the savaged room, the wrongness of it, Paul began to hyperventilate. He sat on the floor and cradled the scotch. The smell nearly turned his stomach, and he knew instantly Bernard had been drinking this the night he died, maybe sitting where Paul sat now to swallow it down, his back to the door. But he had not been looking at the bedlessness of the room, as Paul was—a life just gone, a life partly his own.

Gone. Bernard was under dirt and blue sky while his family set about coldly dividing and selling what remained. Paul doubted they even knew that the enormous abstract triptych that had hung over the fireplace—red, gold, and black oils set with glittery broken glass— and most of the smaller paintings as well, had been done by Bernard's dead lover.

He took a fast shower, tried to scrub off as much jail as he could in time for rehearsal. He'd stopped at the condo only to shower and pick up his car. *His car*, however, was a concept he hadn't thought about in a while—it nearly surprised him, made him flush with anger, that the Benz was gone from its space in the garage. The Cobra too, Bernard's only child: a hot little 427 Cobra roadster that lived under a sheet and had touched the street only once in the past year, to seduce Paul. He'd never been allowed to drive it, but he wanted to kick himself now for not thinking to take it, to hide it somewhere and say Bernard had sold it.

He considered his own car wryly—a twelve-year-old putty-colored Dodge, banged and rusted, semi-reliable, the car he was born to and was lucky at that to have. He didn't like himself much for thinking of George at that moment, who could with some careful effort be trained to make life easy for very little reward. To banish the thought, he conjured a picture of himself looking competent and self-reliant and damn near cute in a coffee shop apron, taking orders for lattes from hot guys. He could do that. He was almost ready to graduate. Maybe when school was over, he'd be able to work enough hours to support himself and still keep the rigorous schedule an acting life demanded. It was the argument Bernard had used to talk him into moving in in the first place—let me support you, I have money and room, you need the time—and Paul had been gullible enough or vain enough to believe his career was Bernard's first concern, worthy in itself of any generosity.

The car smelled of mildew, cranked reluctantly on the third attempt. After today's pricey rescue, he owed George at least a call.

At Paul's arrival, Mark cried out, "There's our jailbird, thank god!" The others gathered on the stage broke into applause. Paul, once he'd braced against his urge to hide behind a curtain, was obliged to take a few bows.

"In character still, I trust?" Mark said.

"Of course," he replied smoothly, though the character he was in had not benefited in the least from a night in jail.

Maybe if he'd had more time there, found some equilibrium, he might have located Silas. But for that brief stay, he could think of nothing but survival, one minute and the next. It had meant closing himself off from Silas, from himself, from terror as much as he could. He focused on doing as he was told. When he was sitting on his cot he thought about sitting. He exchanged a few words with his cell mate, a quiet guy his age who held him in disdain if he thought of him at all, and Paul hadn't even asked his name but the brief exchange cost him all the energy he could scrape together. Nothing bad had happened, though he was so distanced from himself that if it had, he might not have felt it or remembered it later.

The character he was now in was the same old Silas he'd set aside, the one whose prison had been brutal in the same colorful, painless way a dream was brutal. Candyland, he would say, no big deal. Same tough smirk.

Maybe it should have bothered him, that breath of suspicion that his acting was inauthentic. But Silas wasn't him, no matter Bernard's theories about becoming the character—and who knew, anyway, if Bernard himself had ever believed a word of that bunk. What mattered was not whether he was real but whether the others bought it. And they did—actors themselves, they believed him.

In his heartbreak of a car, he drove from rehearsal to George's house, a restored Victorian in a gentrified in-town neighborhood, white with green trim, sweet multicolored inner rooms with stylish, comfortable furnishings. *Home*, he told himself experimentally, parked at the curb. He had spent an idle morning or two when George was away pretending it was his. And he'd pretended so for Kent, had perched in proprietary fashion on its concrete steps, now pale in the moonlight, the day Kent had given him the cat. That picture alone kept him from driving away. He wished for a cigarette, wished Sylvie were there to hand him one. Finally he made himself dial George's number—George in the house a few yards away.

"I need to stay at the condo tonight," he said. He hadn't known for sure he would say it, but as soon as he heard George's voice, he knew he couldn't bear to see him. Embracing him at the jail had been like speaking to his cell mate, arduous and terrifying. "There are some things I need to do."

"All right. Whatever you think best."

Paul had been ready for a fight, but even George's agreeableness grated, made him nervous. It almost seemed as if George had changed his mind, didn't want him there at all. He continued to sit for a time after they'd hung up.

He drove away, past the turn for the condo, and ended up at Kent's house. It was nearly midnight, all their lights out. He sat in his parked car. By moonlight the blue shingles of the house were the blue of everything. With lingering attention he gazed at the house's shadowed contours, the windows with their ironwork, the sag in the rain gutter, the silvery dogwood leaves that fluttered along the chimney.

☙

Some asshole had been calling all morning. It couldn't be his father, whom he'd spoken to the night before and calmed with half-truths—*it's nothing, a technicality, I'm not worried, it will go away soon, no reason you should come*—that his father had gratefully believed. He had hoped to sleep well in his own bed, since he'd been awake of necessity all the night before, but his sleep had remained fitful and haunted until near sunrise. By then he'd fallen deep enough to ignore the repeated ringing from the outer room.

Half past noon he was awake, seeking breakfast in the kitchen and relieved to find the everyday dishes and flatware still in the cabinets, though the china cabinet and dining table were gone. He wore only his underwear and hoped Deirdre would walk in. Four messages on the machine, which he didn't care to listen to. He poured cereal into a bowl but the milk had gone sour, so he ate it dry with his fingers. The phone rang again and he let the machine get it, let Bernard speak from the grave for the fifth time that day and say *Paul and I,* which it pleased him to say though no one ever called that number for Paul.

"This is Mr. Leavitt again, trying to get in touch with Paul Foster..."

Paul picked up with a sigh. Mr. Leavitt introduced himself as the attorney for Deirdre Millstone and her family. "I understand that you've been living on the premises, and Ms. Millstone is willing to accommodate you for a few more days until you can make other arrangements—"

"Sixty days," Paul said. He felt Silas flicker in him, come awake. He'd take what was his. "I get sixty days' notice."

"All right, then you should consider yourself on notice. I'll send it in writing." The man's voice was disarmingly gentle, almost apologetic. "In the meantime, the remaining furnishings will be collected, including the ones in the bedroom you're using, and the condo will be put on the market. By next week, you should start expecting realtors in and out at any time of day."

The voice cowed him a little, deep and masculine, seemingly kind. He remembered, from somewhere in the previous night's dream, walking into a room where Bernard lay on a sofa. "Hi," Bernard had said, warm, mellifluous, the word expressive of the long and trying day they had both had, and Paul said "hi," simple as that, and lay down in his arms.

"The unit has been surveyed, so you'll be responsible for any damage to the premises or remaining furnishings from this point forward. Ms. Millstone will pay the utilities necessary for showing the place but other services will be disconnected shortly…"

Paul scooped a handful of cereal and chewed it. He would have liked to find some way to fight back, to at least make himself bothersome to Deirdre, but in reality he knew he wouldn't stay any longer than he had to. Already it made the skin around his eyes warm, just to know that this complete stranger with the pleasant voice wanted him to leave.

"Also, I need to make it clear that you should not assume yourself the owner of any property at this point. The codicil would obviously be void if you are convicted of any charges related to the murder, and that includes civil charges that may follow the resolution of the criminal case. In the event you are found innocent of all charges, the family intends to contest the will regardless, so don't—"

Paul forced down a mouthful of cereal. "What?"

"It's a sensitive matter, I know, but the family seems to feel you've exerted some undue influence over the deceased. Also there is a discrepancy between earlier and later versions—"

"What property?"

"There's only one property in question." At Paul's silence, he said, "Didn't you know about the condo in Florida? He left it to you."

CHAPTER SIXTEEN

Paul lit the blue candle from Bernard's dresser, set it on the floor before the bank of windows in what had been the living room but now, devoid of furniture, was only blank, unroomed space. It was Saturday night, all the lights out, and the single flame-glow touched almost nothing but the polished wood floor, a span of glass, and Paul. It cast his reflection onto the windows while adding little to the blue-gray half-light of the electric urban night outside.

Eric and Sylvie were out there tonight, had each called separately and begged him to come. Eric's best friend from high school was visiting, and they were splurging on drugs, taking him around the clubs. They wanted Paul to fill out the group, stay the night too—share beds, sleep on the floor, whatever. They wanted, though they didn't say it, to see what adventure would shape itself around Paul now that he was nearly famous and his story was being passed through the clubs from mouth to mouth, often with passionate opinions attached, and people might be inclined to treat him like a celebrity. It would be fun, they insisted, and he needed a night out, needed to get high and drunk, to dance and forget—never mind that forgetting was not something he'd be permitted tonight in a club.

They wanted him to be himself, and he didn't think he could do it. He felt as if he'd aged twenty years in the past week. Fun didn't sound fun anymore, attention held no appeal. Even the suggestion of drugs made him recall the boy who'd been booked into jail ahead of him for having two hits of X in his pocket.

He'd been in tech rehearsal all afternoon, and now the condo floor felt like a stage, the start of some Act II after all the furnishings had been spirited away during intermission to signal how far the hero had fallen. Before the movers had returned for the final load, he'd stashed a reserve of supplies in his closet—a few dishes, forks and spoons, two boxes of macaroni, the corkscrew, and several bottles of Bernard's good wine. As it turned out, though, they'd left him the whole liquor cabinet and the food in the pantry. Once again, they had left his bedroom alone.

The candle was the only thing he'd been able to secret away that had anything close to sentimental value, but even this had no meaning to him. Come To Me stamped on cheap glass—it didn't look like something Bernard would own. Lit in the empty room, though, it felt powerful, holy, and he thought of Kent. The absence shaped by the condo's emptiness seemed more Kent's than Bernard's now.

Fear of the police was the only thing that kept him from calling, cajoling Kent into coming over to share his spartan outpost warmed with wine and candlelight. The police had been oddly quiet since his release, undemanding of his company, which made him imagine they were staked out in unmarked cars outside. He ticked over a mental list of men, those he'd hooked up with, or could, and had found interesting for one reason or another before the season of Kent. But the only number he wanted to dial was Maggie's.

She was quilting. "Really?" he said. "You're joking. That's actually what Mennonites do for fun on a Saturday night?"

She laughed. "Seems so. I'm at my sister's church. We've all been working on one big quilt for a relief sale and we're trying to get it done tonight. I've done nothing, so now it's my turn."

"What kind of quilt?"

"Fancy one. It's all covered in tomatoes and vines."

"I want to quilt," he said suddenly. "Can I help?" It seemed the perfect droll answer when Eric and Sylvie asked how he'd spent the evening without them: quilting. The piecing is the hard part, his grandmother had said. The stitching is easy.

"You could, sweetie. But we're almost through. Besides, you're not that hard up on a Saturday night, are you?"

"I'm trying to stay out of trouble, I guess. But it's strange being alone over here. I'm just sitting on the naked floor, drinking a really excellent pinot grigio out of a dixie cup. I won't keep you. I just called to talk about some things." This was not the truth, though he had some legal concerns he could call up if pressed. "It can wait."

She said nonsense, she'd drop by on her way home. "In the meantime, why don't you call Kent? He's not doing anything."

Just like that. He had to remind himself that he could not do it just because Maggie said so. *Get him and bring him over with you*—but it would sound unreasonable, too interested. He was hungry for Kent, a glimpse would do, and the prospect of the three of them gathered in the condo appealed to him. But having Maggie alone held its own strange potential. He didn't know yet what to do with her interest in him, but he felt drawn to feel out the shape of it.

He was surprised by her clothes when she arrived: clogs and a short, flared skirt, a striped tailored shirt, a knit cap with an enormous sunflower on the front. She looked younger and brighter than herself, like a girl he could have tossed into his car with Eric and Sylvie to go dancing. "Look how cute you are, you fashion plate." He kissed her on the cheek, a little reflexive smack the way he greeted Sylvie and his gay friends, never Maggie until now. He took her by the hands and held them out to admire her, twirl her around. "I had no idea you had such great clothes."

"It's my other life," she said, grinning under the attention. "Sometimes I do the vintage thing when I work at the store, but usually not all-out like this."

He kept hold of one hand to lead her inside. "You should dress that way more often. Wear that to court for my murder trial. The jury will love you."

"Oh, right! *If* we go to trial, I think you're stuck with the bad suit." She stepped away from him, looking around the empty condo, which in darkness was dazzling in its desolation, nothing but electric view. "Wow," she said. "Did they cut off your power too?"

"No. I'm just experimenting, I guess. I wanted to see what it would be like."

The floor gleamed like water under moonlight. He led her to the spot near the windows where he'd left the wine, and they sat on the floor. "You like red?"

"What happened to the white?"

"It went to a better place." He smiled, aware that he was being Bernard in Bernard's absence—a kind of tribute, he told himself. He poured some of the French red into a novelty glass shaped like a snowman. "It took you an hour to get here. What else am I doing?"

"I see I get the fancy glassware."

"That's for company." He'd found it in a cabinet, one of many trashy items that had emerged from the rubble not taken. He'd never seen these things. Maybe they had been Bernard's, but Paul thought it more likely they'd been left behind by the boy before him, John Brady, or the one before that, whoever he was.

She sipped and took in the view. "Well, still nothing." They'd talked by phone twice already that day, three times the day before, so that she could tell him essentially this.

He frowned into his wine. "I was thinking. Are they going to decide I killed him for that condo in Florida?"

"No," she said, the word drawn out as if the idea were ridiculous, then she paused. "Well, I hope not. Gosh, that would be bad."

He sighed. "I really didn't know he was leaving me anything. It's still so weird. I don't know why he'd do that. And then not tell me about it." He'd been wondering since the day before if he'd really known Bernard at all. Maybe he'd been secretly into snowman glasses and tacky hoodoo candles too, a whole underground life. Maybe when Paul went out, Bernard didn't languish on the sofa but hopped into the Cobra and roared out somewhere to live it.

"We won't worry about that now. It may not come up." Her admiring gaze traced the edges of the towering windows. "If he'd left you this place too, and a hunk of money to go with it, then we might be in trouble."

"And his cars. Wouldn't that be nice? I'd be set." He leaned back on his hands, brushing her shoulder with his. "I wouldn't mind keeping this view a little longer."

"Views down in Florida are pretty nice, I hear."

"Yeah, but what am I going to do down there? It's nowhere near a city. No life, just beach."

She was smiling, her eyes downcast. "It's where you go to get away from life, I guess."

"Yeah, but that's for people who have a life to get away from."

He could feel the warning speed of his heartbeat—they were skirting dangerous territory. It was where he intended to go, in a way, but by a different route than Florida. The conversation had shifted with his brush of her shoulder, turned slower and softer, their eyes meeting often as they sipped wine. He tugged, carefully, and she followed. They now faced each other rather than the view.

"You have a life," she said. "Though I confess I don't know that much about it."

"Sure you do. You're looking at it, for the moment at least." He tipped his cup in toast to the empty room.

"And I don't believe that for a second."

Lines of Silas's were flooding into his head, making him duck and smile into his lap—they were edging that close to the script. *I'm the blank page you scribble your fantasies on while your husband reads beside you in bed.* He said, "The play I'm in is reminding me a lot of my life right now. You'll have to come see it."

Her eyes were incredibly large and dark, glowing with candlelight, her eyebrows heavy. He noticed a shadow of mustache on her upper lip.

"Is there a murder in it?"

He thought about it. "In a way."

"Did you do it?"

His chest tightened, almost to an ache. "No. It's me. I mean, I'm dead at the end." She tipped her flower-topped head, looked genuinely saddened. "Don't worry," he said. "That's not the part I was thinking of."

"Good."

Something in the tone of the solitary word, the way she was looking at him, crossed a line—he felt it too—made her suck in a breath, look away, begin talking of the case again. In three months of wearing away at Kent, even winning extravagant concessions now and then, Paul still wasn't sure he would do anything in the end other than go back to his wife. But Maggie was a quantity less defined. For one, she hardly ever talked about Kent. She didn't seem to know him in the proprietary way of wives or feel the deep attachment of two lives joined into one. She was the pious one, the one who, despite all her acceptance of sin as the natural state of mankind, would never consider cheating. Yet the flaw that mattered was in her.

She was telling him things he already knew about her last talk with Thornton, just talking, and he drew her back at her next pause. "What about you? Are you happy with your life?"

"Very happy."

"You like being married?"

She nodded.

"Of course," he said. "Every girl wants to be married, right?"

An answer stopped in her mouth, she smiled uncomfortably. He kept talking, his voice languid and quiet. "Marriage is strange to me. And interesting. My dad remarried when I was around twelve, but it still feels like a foreign concept. Before that, it was like my dad and I were together, like *we* were kind of married, only it was given to us as a state of nature. We didn't choose it."

There was a pang in the memory, which turned easily like a sphere revolving into a memory of Kent, and for a flash, a second, he hated Maggie again. He went on in the same quiet voice. "Marriage seems to me like this big dance hall, all the girls lined up on one side and the boys on the other, and you look across and say, 'that one. That's the one I'll attach myself to forever.' It's so arbitrary for most people. How can you find your soulmate that way?"

She considered this, tilted her head. "But it can't be that different for gay men. You have to look and choose."

"Oh, sure. But that's sex, really. You meet, make connections, you move on. Most guys I know don't think about attaching themselves to someone forever, so when people do find their soulmates, it's really pure and honest. Love is supposed to be something you fall into, like falling, an accident. How can you really fall if that's what you're trying to do?"

"That's interesting," she said, thoughtful.

Older than him by ten years, and so unjaded. He could guess that whatever version of Kent appeared in her dreams, whether he held roses or not, had never come at her with a razor blade. He poured her more wine, and she stopped him with a hand over her glass. "That's plenty. I have to drive home."

"Stay for a little while. I'll stop talking nonsense."

"I don't think it's nonsense."

He watched her watching him in the blue candle's glow, on their stage. Silas had slipped back into the wings, too brutal for this scene, and instead he imagined himself in Kent's body, seeing what Kent saw as he gazed at his wife. She was beautiful, and he loved her, didn't understand her, wanted to protect her. He needed her strength but maybe not as much now as her weakness, her understanding that most people were far weaker than she wished them to be.

At her forehead, an inch of hair poked out from under the hat's rim, and he reached to lift a little piece of it and smooth it back, letting the touch linger there. If he kissed her she'd blink awake, withdraw. His fingertips slipped lower and stopped beside her ear, so feather-light it was barely contact, until her questioning look became direct. But still she didn't move. It was enough permission, and he leaned and kissed her lightly on the mouth, a brush like moth wings, and he saw her eyes close just before. He sat back and looked at her, her eyes round and blinking though she remained still.

"What was that?"

He smiled a little, a charming half-smile he aimed somewhere between sheepish and amused.

"You're gay," she said, as if reminding him.

"Yes, I am."

"And I'm married."

He conceded this.

"So then—"

He shrugged. "Don't you ever feel like stepping out of your life sometimes? Just to see?"

"No." Her voice was soft, her forehead creased with distress. "No, I never think about that."

"Or just doing what you feel?" He cracked his neck, leaned back on a hand. "I feel like if God gives me an impulse, I should at least consider it."

She smiled slowly. "You're a believer now."

"I was always a believer."

Suddenly they were back in this flirty, intimate conversation, all discomfort gone, as if nothing at all had happened or maybe everything had, and they were speaking like a couple lying in bed after sex. She hadn't moved from her spot, hadn't backed away. But a few minutes later, she was exclaiming over the lateness of the hour, gathering herself to go, and would not be talked into staying to finish the wine.

⁊⌒

Bill Friesen, a member of Lila's church, had been married only two years when a car accident left his wife a quadriplegic. This was the only thing that Kent knew about him, other than the fact that he made his living as a social worker, and was a handy amateur plumber, and that he had cared devotedly for his crippled wife for the past fifteen years. And would continue to do so, Kent supposed, into the future, forever. He had met Bill briefly once before, one of a crowd of Mennonites at work on the purple house in Cabbagetown, and they had not really talked. Now he and Kent were alone in the house, Bill having chased down the house's last stubborn leak and cornered it under the kitchen sink.

He was a wiry, long-haired man in his forties, a happy man by all signs. He was happy to put in an hour of work in the time he could find between one kind of work and another, happy to locate new problems, happy to discover he'd left his wrench in the truck and had to go back for it, happy to slice his thumb on a rusted bolt. "Good thing I've had my tetanus," Bill said, rubbing the thumb on his coveralls. Kent had opened every window in the house that morning, and Bill grinned and said, "Smell that breeze. That's something."

"Yeah, sure is," Kent said, though what he really wanted to say was *How's your wife?* How much did you have to love someone to stay in such a situation, for any reason other than guilt? Marriage, he realized, in itself wasn't commitment at all, could come apart without effort when faced with a real question. Commitment was this choice Bill had made after the accident, nothing else. Was it the strength of the man or the strength of the love? He wanted to know, but he and Bill didn't have the common ground to talk about anything other than pipes, the peccadilloes of house repair, and the weather.

"The women have finished the painting, I see," Bill said, though his head was under the sink. "It's good to have someone moving in. Helps motivate us all. That sense of working toward a purpose."

Kent, whose own work was more or less complete, went outside and sat on the front steps, which he and two of the Mennonite men had rebuilt with new pine boards. The white paint was now dry and shining. He sat long enough to feel the sun begin to bake his forearms with summer's first unmistakable heat. But there was a breeze too, and this might have brought the chill he felt as Paul's car nosed onto the gravel and stopped.

That car—he hadn't seen that ugly thing in years, hadn't imagined Paul with or without it, but there it was, glossless but still running, windows down to emit thin music, and then Paul stepped out of it into the hazy lemonade of sunlight. It was the car that made his arrival seem so casual, made Kent imagine he could remember a time when everything about Paul had been simple.

Maggie had asked him to meet Paul here. In the space of a day, she'd abandoned her notion of Paul living with them, relieving him of the need to seek arguments against it or wonder if he even wanted to argue. Wonder if he wanted, more than anything, to sink into that fate.

Paul stopped before him, in the leaf shadows of the yard where the steps ended. He wore a tank top that melted against the length of his torso and left a strip of belly skin above the frayed, low-slung edge of army pants. He parked his fingers in his front pockets so that his shoulders, thinner in their bareness, hunched a little. Kent met his gaze, too long. They hadn't seen each other since the night before he went to jail, and the silence lasted until there was no longer a way to speak. Kent looked down at the grass, and then Paul stepped back to appraise the house with a private smile.

"Can't say I ever pictured myself in a purple house."

Don't get too comfortable, Kent wanted to say. He wasn't sure why he was suddenly angry at Paul, angry at being here on his behalf. He'd lain awake the night Paul was in jail, dreaming up one bloody scenario after another until he was sure Paul would be dead by morning, and even once the ordeal was over he'd not quite believed Maggie's report of his survival and had ached to see him, just to confirm it.

"There's a plumber inside."

Paul arched an eyebrow as if this were salacious code. "And what does that mean?"

Kent stood, gave him a flat stare. "That means there's a guy inside fixing leaky pipes." He opened the screen door and Paul came up close beside him.

"That means behave?"

"Exactly."

Paul tipped his face within an inch of kissing as he passed, but inside the house he kept apart, hands in his pockets, quiet as a stranger. Kent led him through the front rooms, which had been recently scrubbed and painted by a small army of church members, furnished with second-hand tables, chairs, lamps, an old pull-out sofa in the living room. He pointed at the fireplace, said in stern monotone, "Don't ever try to use that," and Paul said nothing smart in return about it being nearly May and since when had he ever done anything remotely like build a fire? Kent had to turn to make sure he'd heard, and he had, for there were Paul's eyes full of meek attention.

The look annoyed him, though he didn't know what he would have preferred. He flipped the rotary dial on the little TV. "There's no cable, but you can pick up a few of the networks on this."

He led him into the kitchen, introduced Bill. "Only one burner on the stove works," Kent said, but Paul was chatting with Bill, who was seated on the floor before the sink, Paul saying, "It's just for a little while. I'm sure there are people who'll need it more than me."

"We welcome you," Bill said. "We hope you'll stay as long as you need to."

"Thanks. It's really nice of you."

"And if other folks come along, well, there's four bedrooms, counting that little extra space this guy here converted, and two baths. So lots can fit. And you're doing us a favor too, just to be here looking after things."

"I'll show you your room," Kent said. Paul lingered, talking to Bill, and Kent stood outside the door, staring at the far wall like a military escort.

He turned away as soon as Paul moved, led him to the end of the hall, where bedrooms opened on either side. In the last room the walls had been painted a bluish lavender. There was a desk, a dresser, a night table, white curtains the Mennonites had sewn and hung from the two windows the day before, a white spread on the bed. On the bedside table, someone had set a slender vase of wild-looking flowers. The open windows admitted the voices of school children down the street and a breeze that sent the gauzy curtains undulating. "Is this okay?"

"It's fine. It's nice." He was staring at the bed, a full-size topped with a close pair of pillows. The bang of pipes was audible from down the hall.

"We'll try to put in an air conditioner before it gets too warm."

Paul went to the window. The curtain spread itself back over his nose and cheek, then lifted and folded him in like the embrace of a wing. "It's strange to be on the ground," he said, turning within the curtain, his face shrouded. He stepped forward and the curtain slid over his face and released him. He went to the closet, glanced inside, back to the other window. Even when he was quiet like this, his notice seemingly elsewhere, every breath, every footfall and tilt of eyelash and chin, the passage of his tongue over his teeth and his manifold thoughts were all visibly mapped around Kent's space in the room and dependent on it, waiting for him, calling to him, responding.

Paul sat on the bed. "Did you do all this for me?"

No was the honest answer—he hadn't. But he had spent his Sunday scraping paint from the sealed window frames, fitting new screens, and repairing the locks so that when Paul arrived the windows could be open to this weather, this breeze.

"I did a lot of the work on the house. You living here was Maggie's idea." But Paul knew that. Kent's eyes narrowed with suspicion. "Or yours. What did you say to her?"

"Nothing."

Kent swallowed a bitter taste, shook his head, marking the kitchen noises. "She wanted you to move in with us, Paul. She changed her mind."

Paul's eyebrows lifted, innocent, curious. "So...you wanted me to move into your house? Is that what you're saying?"

"No. No." He wasn't sure what he was accusing Paul of, if anything, other than having private conversations with his wife. He'd been worried about what would happen when Paul figured out he could ask Maggie for anything and get it, that to a Mennonite a request from anyone was next thing to a command from God. But in that case, Paul was right: he'd be moving in with them instead of into this house.

Paul sighed. "Then can we not do this thing where you're pissed off at me about nothing?" He rose and approached, his voice softening to a murmur. "Tell me what you want and I'll do it."

He stood before Kent with a tender expression, as if to say that anything was possible, doable, and Kent studied his face. He searched it for some clue to the power in the arrangement of these features, a thing that made Paul different from Maggie. If it were Paul crippled, for instance, would Kent be more likely to stay? He didn't know, couldn't tell if there was a difference, but he felt how it might be the wrong question. If Kent were the one stuck in the wheelchair—that was the question, and he knew both answers without thinking. Maggie would stay with him forever. Paul wouldn't wait around for goodbye.

But it wasn't what he asked of Paul, eternal love. Together, they had never quizzed the future, never needed to know such things. He stood pondering all this long enough that Paul made a smiling grab for his zipper and Kent pushed him back, not roughly. But what he started to say tasted like bile and he clamped his mouth, turned away sharply and went out into the hall, Paul following.

"Bathroom," he said, continuing the tour with a terse wave toward its door.

"That does it for me," Bill said when they reached the kitchen. "My number's on the counter there, Paul, if you have any trouble with the plumbing." Paul thanked him, trailed him to the back door.

"Again, welcome. Hope the place is good to you."

Kent heard the truck starting in the yard as Paul shut the door, turned to face him. "What a nice guy. What nice folks."

"You should be thankful."

"I am. Seriously, I feel guilty already. I'll pay rent when I can." Paul reached up to stroke the handle of a cabinet door.

"They won't take your money. They're good people." His voice strained and caught a little.

Paul gave him a level look. "So am I. So are you."

"I don't like this." He shook his head, waved off Paul's response. He went back out to the front porch and sat on the step. Paul came out and leaned against the railing post, waiting.

The argument against Paul living here that had been forming loosely in his head scattered, drifted, left him nothing to grab hold of. He said, "This is where I found that kitten I gave you." This, it seemed now, was the reason for his anger, though it came out flat—just as well, since it was a stupid thing to be angry about. But it stayed in his mouth like grit he couldn't spit out, that Paul had tossed away his gift, a thing of breath and blood, that it had meant nothing to him. And it made more sense to be angry about a cat than about being abandoned in his speculative wheelchair as blithely as he'd been left three years before on a Georgia day in May.

Paul sat beside him at a neutral distance. "I didn't give it away." Arms upturned over his knees, he glanced to meet Kent's scrutiny. "It got sick."

"Got sick."

Paul picked at the skin around his thumbnail. "It had leukemia." Before Kent could form a sentence, Paul said, "I know. I was mad at you." He chuckled sadly. "I spent about twelve hundred dollars of Bernard's money at the vet. And you know, he didn't say a word about it either. Anyway, it didn't matter. They couldn't do anything."

Paul's quiet manner, stripped of artifice, made Kent regret his suspicions, and next wonder if he'd been under more than one misconception, had failed in larger ways to see Paul clearly. The cat, Bernard. Too much death, besides a murder charge hanging over his head, and he wasn't running anywhere, persisted in school and his play, sat on the steps of the strange house he'd been driven to and looked calmer than Kent.

"You should have told me," Kent said—stopped himself, tried

again. "I'm sorry. About the cat. I shouldn't have even given it to you. It wasn't fair."

"I'm not sorry you did." Hunched over his knees, Paul rubbed at his fingers, looking out at the horizon where the sky was brushed with feathery, fan-shaped clouds. "Hey, um, there's a thing I need you to show me. In the bedroom."

Kent hadn't felt it until then, how much he wanted Paul. He shook his head against it. "I don't think so."

"I really miss you."

Tough shit, he wanted to say, but his stomach clenched with responsive feeling. "Yeah." Even for that syllable, his voice shook, and he could no longer remember the reason he'd come out here, to the bright world of the porch, the whole house empty behind them. He got up without a word, and Paul followed him inside.

⌒

On opening night there was no room in Paul's thoughts to worry about who was there and who was not. The house was nearly full, ticket sales spiking in response to the arrest and its rumors, just as Mark had hoped. Still it was surprising how quickly the city—or maybe it was only the gay city—had learned his name. He knew most of them had come out of curiosity, but somewhere in the crowd there would surely be a few who could appreciate the play for whatever it was, might notice the lead for some indefinable quality of his look or ability that meant he was going somewhere. Reviewers were out there, maybe others who mattered and could help.

Kent and Maggie were there. He'd tried not to see where, and then tried to forget, but the spot was burned into his brain, about ten rows back on the left aisle. Together, dressed up like a date, Kent guiding Maggie with a hand on her back as they moved into their seats. He had no time to wish he could inhabit their separate thoughts as they sat side by side, maybe even holding hands, but facing ahead. Waiting for him.

Eric and Sylvie were somewhere in the crowd, with a gaggle of mutual friends—he'd seen them come in, and had seen an astonishing number of acquaintances from theater and school and bars, people who would never have come to see him before infamy made their tenuous connection to him interesting. Even Eric might have blown it off in earlier days. George, he was sure, was out there as well, since his roses had arrived backstage. *Ever yours*, the card read—not even an initial.

It was during the second act, as he was in Silas and preparing to speak, that he noticed who was not there. In such a weighted moment in his performance, there should have been no audience at all to worry about and certainly no individuals there or not there to snag him away from Silas and back to himself. But he did notice, and was knocked into a void from which he had to deliver three lines by rote, no more than a mimic of the sound scored on his memory after so many nights of repetition, before he could find Silas again and re-enter the dream of him.

And again, as he lay on his back, stage left, while the others continued speaking about him, when he was dead and he no longer mattered. Fresh from his father's grip at his throat and their shared problem of getting him to the floor and dead without actual injury, he was granted his first true freedom of the evening to think about the performance and to wonder next, he couldn't help it, what Bernard would think and to what excessive pitch he would tune his enthusiasm. At the close of *Hamlet* he'd waited this way, his back to the hard stage floor until his corpse would be borne aloft by four boys into the wings, and before the curtain had fallen he would run to the shadowed alcove where Bernard waited in the death's-head guise of his father's ghost, and the ghost would bend to kiss him, answer enough, and then say it anyway. *You were beautiful.*

No one would carry him from the stage tonight, and backstage no lover dressed as his lost father would be waiting to answer his question. Once he'd hated the answer, too easy, too constant, then hated the one who gave it, but now he thought he would gladly relinquish other dreams—his own father, his future fame—just to have Bernard waiting in that alcove. It made no difference that he had arrived at this night by his own power with his stomach calm and his wrists free of rash, or that the affirmation might have meant nothing more than *I want you*, but he needed it anyway, might never stop needing it.

A full three minutes he played dead, while the last act eased into its cruel denouement. By degrees, Silas was forgotten. His father and mother, his brother and his brother's wife, shaken by the violence and this loss, wailed and gnashed for the first minute of his death, and in the second made a plan for what they would tell the police, and in the third, composed, began to speak of their lives without him as if his body were not in plain view.

Dead but not dead, his body under bright lights on the kitchen floor. Had Bernard been so sentient, heard those voices? Did he have to think, lying there, how to breathe without motion, how to soothe the itch he couldn't scratch? Did he take some little pleasure in the knowledge that Paul would be the one to find him, or regret that he would never see this night or ever again see Paul on stage? Luckily, the tyranny of Stanislavski did not extend to the unwalking dead—the corpse need not be infused with its own emotional life, though in rehearsals he'd played at coming back to life horror-flick style, grabbing the first ankle that came near. His only task now was stillness. But it meant Silas was gone, Paul alone for three minutes with Bernard, who would not speak.

The lights went down. Applause, a few hoots and shouts within it. He was already on his feet, soundless, and gone.

CHAPTER SEVENTEEN

At the last minute, Chloe Yoder changed her mind about what she wanted to do for her fifteenth birthday. It fell on a Thursday, and Paul's play had been extended for an extra week, and it seemed like fate, God's will even, that she should get to see it again. Because she didn't know how to ask for what she really wanted, which was to go alone, she asked her parents to get a sitter for the boys and see it with her. Even in the company of parents, dinner and a show sounded appealingly grown up.

The Saturday before, on the original closing night, Paul had comped tickets for the whole family. But her father decided to stay home with the baby, and Seth as well, who was seven and too young for "adult" plays, so Chloe had gone with her mother. "Adult" was Paul's word for it, when Lila had quizzed him about its content, and he included Chloe as if she were an adult herself, saying with a smirk of an aside to her, "I mean, it's not porn or anything." To Lila he said, "I'd call it R-rated, but it's art, so that balances out to about PG, right? Like naked pictures in museums."

"Are you going to be naked in it?" Chloe asked.

"No!" Paul grinned at her. "Listen to you!"

She pursed her mouth, brushed the tip of her braid against her chin. "Well, actors have to be naked sometimes, you know. Have you ever done a naked play?" She was glad when her mother interjected a "Chloe!" to shut her up—who knew what she might have said next?

It had taken her a while to find her tongue with Paul, to treat him with the usual dry, cheeky humor that was her manner with the world. When she'd first met him, in the back room of Ten Thousand Villages, it had come easily, and he'd fallen in love with her boldness, called her "cute thing." But since then she'd thought about him too much, lost her rhythm.

She couldn't have said what had captivated her so completely in the play, since seeing Paul on stage was almost the opposite of what she'd hoped for. At first she had to concentrate to see that it was Paul at all, for Silas Kingsbury—besides having greasy brown hair and visible stubble—was slouching and slow, rough-voiced, alarming in the way of certain quiet dogs. He was tattooed, regally bored, scratched himself. He was not, by any stretch, a romantic lead, though he participated in what romance the play offered, a spiteful pursuit not far from rape. Every time he approached another character, Chloe cringed as the characters cringed, expecting sudden, extreme violence. Everyone but his mother was subjected to Silas's aggressive feints, his derisive laughter. That this person moved about in Paul's slight body only made him more dangerous, a small package wired to blow.

Yet Silas became beautiful at times. He told rambling, self-justifying stories about his rotten childhood and the years after, stories he seemed to believe so deeply that they wounded him still. He shielded his sensitive nature with a continual bluff of violence. She wasn't sure that she was supposed to cry in the end or even like the play as much as she did, since Paul had warned them reluctantly that it wasn't very good. But something about it electrified her and made her at the same time want to be alone, in bed with the covers over her head where she could dream her way back into it.

And was it Paul she thought about? She still wanted to be near him, when her aunt Maggie brought him around for dinner and card games, but it was mainly to marvel that, despite the brotherly resemblance, he was not Silas. She didn't care to hear him talk about the play. It embarrassed her to reconcile the two of them, to have Paul lay bare the mechanics of the process by which he became the other. And yet, she doubted the play could have affected her the way it did with someone else in the role, someone she didn't fancy she was having a secret affair with—so secret not even the two of them knew about it. The Paul of her dreams was a third person, also named Paul but sometimes named Silas, as like Paul and as unlike him as Silas was. All this didn't confuse her in the least, though it was beyond speaking. "I don't have a crush on him!" her mother forced her to insist on several occasions, and this was not a lie. "He's gay, you know," she would add sometimes, true also, of Paul the person. It all made her want to be alone in the dark. It made her want to see the play again.

Her parents agreed to this. The second time, though, she found it impossible to see past the performance and into the play, and instead she was able to observe his transformation. Paul and not-Paul. It seemed a formidable talent, and she was envious of others around her who were experiencing the play for the first time, being drawn into the dream as she had been. At the end, when the lights went down and allowed Paul to change himself unseen from the corpse of Silas Kingsbury to something more like his own living, smiling self, when he returned after all the others had bowed to take his own solitary bow on a wave of applause, and gesture gallantly to the director, and step back to join hands with the two women he'd so recently injured and bow again deeply at the waist, all of them together in infectious jubilation, and exit the stage still holding hands as if after so much strife a pure and abiding love had been resurrected from the ashes or simply created from nothing, Chloe Yoder, fifteen, drew a long breath, as if she could breathe in the whole stage and hold it inside her.

On the way home, she informed her parents she was going to be an actress.

"The hardest part you have to do in your head," Paul told her. "Nobody helps you. If your character's angry, you can't just 'act angry'—you have to get into the character's circumstances and *feel* it. You have to imagine everything about the person you're playing, until you know them better than you know yourself. It's confusing some-times. You can forget who you are."

It wasn't hard for Chloe to make Paul her mentor in the ways of the stage. Not only was he living in the house her church had helped restore, in the room with the white baseboards she had painted herself, but he had become delicately webbed to every member of her family, one thin thread to each of them too tenuous to acknowledge. He was not yet enough of a relation to come to her house except in Maggie's company, but it seemed now that Maggie and Kent came around more often for dinner and cards, usually bringing Paul when they did. He washed the dishes with Chloe, played video games with Seth, went with her father to inspect the new greenhouse he was building in the yard. He held the baby now, and though he remained shy about asking, he clearly wanted to, as he wanted private time with each of them. And always he wanted to play Dutch Blitz, with whichever three would join him.

Somewhere along the way, they all seemed to have forgotten that

Paul was still charged with murder, that only a few weeks before he'd been in jail. Even during the play's run, when he came to Sunday dinner with Silas's barbed-wire prison tattoos still banded around his upper arms, the family only admired their realism and complimented his performance in a role so utterly unlike himself. Chloe still from time to time allowed the word *murderer* into her head, for the thrill of it, but it seemed now worse than rudeness—it would be cruel—to speak it aloud or mention the situation at all.

"A vonderful goot game!" Dutch Blitz called itself, on the box decorated with the same marching Dutch boy and girl that marked the cards, and Paul read the motto aloud as usual. From the four packs of cards emblazoned with plows, pumps, buckets, and buggies, he selected his own pack with a sense of ceremony—the plows tonight—like a talisman against the terrors of city life. The game had surprised him with its rapid simultaneous play, especially when Maggie, Lila, and Chloe were all at the table, hands flying to the numerous Dutch piles at the center, cards slapping, Chloe out of her chair for better reach, a threshing machine in which the fourth person hardly stood a chance of escaping without finger wounds, let alone playing a card successfully.

"I thought Mennonites were pacifists!" Paul had said the first time, taken aback.

"That's all a lie," Kent said. "They're vicious, remorseless people."

Maggie smiled. "This is our outlet."

If Kent and Paul were both at the table, the play slowed considerably, became less dangerous, the two women making idle talk while the men were silent with concentration. Paul managed to Blitz now and then, which made him happy. He improved slowly and didn't seem to mind losing in the end by the embarrassing extremes that marked outsiders. "If your score is a positive number, you're doing great," they assured him, tallying their own scores in the hundreds. Just to sit at the table, to be deemed worthy of real play at the family level, seemed to satisfy him, and he wanted it over and over.

Fli-fli-flip fli-fli-flip went Maggie's cards, audible in the next room. The women and Paul were playing, while Kent leaned against the counter behind Paul sipping a beer. No one at the table had the leisure to eat or drink. "That's a tactic," Kent said, not a whisper but low and channeled at Paul. "She doesn't need to flip that loud, she's just trying to intimidate you. Tune her out."

Chloe, who could monitor everyone's cards simultaneously, had her eye on Paul's blue four that he didn't see to play, but knew her mother was probably watching it as well. Kent stepped up behind Paul and tapped the four. "Oh, shit," Paul said, and played it. "Oops, I mean—" Chloe and Lila pounced with their fives before Paul had let go. "Mine," Chloe cried, and her mother withdrew the card, slapped down another, and Paul said "Crap, I mean, stop!" because a minor jam had been unknotted with his play and cards now flew to the blue stack and to others, Paul missing three plays in a row, and Maggie shouted "Blitz!" just as Chloe was about to play her last card. Already on her feet, she stomped three times, smacked the table. "Dookie!"

Maggie smiled sweetly at Paul, who cringed behind his hand. "It's okay. We all curse in this game."

"Dookie?" Kent asked Chloe.

"Yes, you see, some of us have self-control."

"Oh, whatever!" Paul laughed.

For the rest of the night, Kent watched the game from behind Paul, offering what assistance he could. Chloe kept waiting for Paul to be annoyed by it, for Kent to get bored and wander from the room. Soon they were "they," the men, the outsiders, a kind of team united against Mennonite domination.

"They are of the world," Maggie said serenely, midplay. "We of the true faith have nothing to fear. The devil keeps them too distracted to pose a real threat."

Though Chloe knew she was joking, that Paul wouldn't take offense despite seeming to want so badly to be one of them, a line was being drawn and she had a momentary urge to shift her allegiance. Be of the world with them. Or was it their adult maleness she wanted to be near, that secret life, promise of future love? Maggie's teasing only prompted Paul to ask more questions about the church and their lives, as if he were conducting a study, preparing a role. And he didn't seem to mind being relegated to outsider if it aligned him with Kent, where his eyes often rested, the same silky caressing gaze he gave all of them in turn except, for Kent, a little longer and more. Chloe wondered if Maggie saw it. If Kent did.

Two nights later, Chloe rode her bike over to Maggie and Kent's for more Dutch Blitz. Kent was out fixing a crash in someone's network, and Maggie and Paul could have played, but Maggie said it was "more fun with three." Chloe hoped the real reason she'd been called was that Paul had requested her presence. He'd taken to kissing her cheek and calling her "Gorgeous," "Darlin'," playing with her hair, asking how she managed to keep the boys off her. Their alliance consisted of a dry repartee in little asides that the others did not share in, and this served her well enough for romance.

But maybe he needed the others as audience. Tonight, after kissing her hello, he seemed distracted and quiet. They played around the kitchen table, the game calmer with only three. Several hands in, as Paul dealt his cards into their stacks, he said, "I'm graduating." They looked up, and he glanced back and forth between them. "From college."

They congratulated him, while he pressed a hand over his mouth as if to stop himself from smiling or perhaps, too late, from blurting this out. "We'll have a party!" Chloe said, turning hopefully to Maggie.

Maggie smiled at Paul without catching her excitement. "Didn't you know?"

He shook his head. "I thought I might have another class to go, but it turns out I'm done. I have to apply for official graduation, or whatever, so the diploma won't come until later. But then that's that, I guess. Time to start my life."

"Do you know what you'll do?"

Chloe cried, "He will act, of course! He'll be a brilliant star of stage and screen."

"Yeah, right." Paul turned to Maggie with a resigned look Chloe recognized, the understanding that passed between adults. "I should have changed my major. Then I'd have another year at least. I asked my advisor what I'm supposed to do with a degree in theater, and he said basically I should get myself a nice job in data entry like everyone else."

"You'll find something you want to do."

Paul nodded, played a card into the center to start the game. Chloe wanted to ask why he was worried, when he had everything she could only wish for—talent, knowledge, skill, his whole spotlit red carpet of a future stretched ahead of him.

After an hour of cards they drifted to the living room. Paul found the photo albums, and Chloe and Maggie sat on either side to narrate while he moved lingeringly from page to page, beginning with the childhood pictures of Chloe's great grandparents, the unsmiling elders in traditional clothes hitching a horse to a buggy, plowing behind a mule, some of which the family had acquired in later years from the outsiders who had taken them. No detail bored him, nothing induced him to turn faster. Chloe had been teasing him lately about wanting to convert. He'd even gone to church with Maggie once.

It grew late, and Chloe lay down on the couch, fell asleep to Maggie and Paul's low voices over the albums on the love seat, back and forth in a soft accord. It was an intimate sound and she dreamed the two of them, Paul and her aunt, were moving to a farm together and buying a mule, taking Chloe with them.

"Wake up, sleeping beauty." Kent was leaning over her. "Come on, sweetheart, it's late. I'll give you a ride home."

Only Kent and Paul were in the room now, murmuring together at a little distance while Chloe put on her shoes. Outside, the night was warm, the full moon looked like a wedding cookie rolled in powdered sugar, and she felt dreamy and alert at the same time. She sat in the back seat, Paul up front and Kent driving, and she was infused with the excited sense that the car could turn at any minute and take her down an unfamiliar road into secret adventure. She felt chosen, lucky to be in their company, these beautiful men who called her sweet names from fairy tales about love. But she had only a few blocks to ask them everything she needed to know.

She touched Paul's shoulder. "What's your dream?"

He blinked at her with sleepy ease, his head nestled against the seat. "Still looking for one."

"Fame, money, or love. Pick one."

He looked at Kent, a smile playing in his lips. "Fame."

Urgent to be part of it, she said, "You *will* be famous, you know. Kent, tell him he's a brilliant star and he needs to go to Hollywood or whatever actors do and not be a stupid file clerk. Don't you think?"

"Think what?"

"That he should be serious about acting. Tell him how good he is."

Paul started laughing, low in his throat. Kent chuckled too, said, "He's very good. He knows he is," and gave Paul another soft glance that made him stop laughing.

"Now you." She touched Kent's shoulder. "Pick."

He looked out at the road. "Love, I guess."

"You already have love." Married people, she thought, were like ball players safe at home plate when it came to love—there was only the one goal, one marker of its achievement, no degrees of more or less.

"True. Maybe there should be other choices." He glanced back at her. "Less selfish ones, huh? Which do you pick, missy?"

"Me—I want all of them."

They both laughed. Paul said, "Oh, *all*. If I'd known that was an option." Kent teased her, "Since when do you want money?"

"I'll use it to feed the poor. And buy presents for my family."

Too quickly, the car reached her house. Too late now to suggest they drop Paul first, which would have given her five more minutes with them. They said goodnight, and the car waited while she climbed the steps and fit her key into the lock. When she turned to wave, they were both looking up at her through the windshield, adoringly, she thought, as if they meant to keep her in sight until the last second. But Paul's face turned away to Kent, settled there, and she wished some piece of her could have stayed hidden in the car as they drove off into the night.

⫸

Without trying, Kent began to rise earlier in the morning, waking with his wife's alarm to start breakfast, then shower while the bathroom was still damp and thick with her steam. They dressed together, with a shared sense of hurry or leisure, sat for a hot breakfast at the table when there was time or stood at the counter with toast he buttered for her, juice he poured, when there was not. He left the house when she did, turned the lock behind them, kissed her at her car.

He drove from Edgewood to Cabbagetown and parked a street away, walked to the purple house and let himself in with his key. From there he reversed his movements, undressing, carefully folding his clothes over a chair, easing into the bedroom and back into bed. Paul didn't always wake up, his sentient body adjusting and resettling, and Kent was grateful on those mornings to simply go back to sleep with Paul close. Sometimes Paul was awake when he arrived, waiting to pounce, and sometimes they woke into sex after an hour of sleep, and once or twice sleep was so sweet that they forgot sex altogether.

The first time he'd gone to the purple house was an impulse, a compulsion, Paul's first morning after moving in. He hadn't told Paul he was coming, only appeared at his bedside, and Paul bolted up out of a dream breathless and frozen.

"I'm sorry," Paul had said, unable to stop shaking—while Kent tried to say no, he was sorry, he hadn't meant to scare him. "I'm kind of nervous here by myself. I've never lived alone before."

"Never?" Kent knew this, he supposed, or could have figured it out, but still it amazed him. He'd created an idea of Paul as the tough, self-reliant one, out there braving the world without him.

He never contradicted Paul in this, but he meant to, in a way, as the mornings became habit. *You don't live alone.* Kent now had two houses, both keys in plain view on his key ring.

Paul said, "We were married back then, in our old life, you and me. You just didn't know what to call it."

"Neither did you."

Kent recalled then something he had forgotten, a turning point in their former lives, one gray, misty morning late in the fall. Paul barefoot in the living room, wrapped neck to ankles in the blue comforter from the bed. Kent said, "I'm the one who had the dream. Remember? And you got all freaked out about it."

"What dream?"

"I dreamed you were pregnant." It sounded silly as soon as he said it, but his memory of it was serious, the way dreams feel. "Not showing or anything, no belly bulge. You were just sitting on our sofa, in the dream, and you told me. With this little cat-that-ate-the-canary smile, and all bright-eyed. Very serene, very happy."

Paul blinked from the pillow beside him. "I don't remember that."

"Well, there was a scene when I told you. You got really upset, until I felt bad for having the dream at all. But I couldn't make you understand that it wasn't sad or—" He could feel Paul tensing even now under his hands. "You took it literally, I guess. But it wasn't about babies. I didn't want a baby. I tried to tell you."

The corner of Paul's mouth quirked, his gaze calm and direct. "You always thought I'd turn into a girl, if you waited long enough."

"No," Kent laughed. "No."

"You did, Kent. Some part of you did. You were half out of your mind back then." Paul wasn't going to react, but the shield was coming up in his eyes.

"You're wrong," Kent said. "You weren't a girl in the dream. You were you. And it wasn't a baby we were going to have, it was something else, something totally new and beautiful. It felt right. But I couldn't explain it to you. You fixated on the baby thing."

"God, can you imagine me with a baby?" It was a defensive, joking comment—intentionally misconstruing him again, Kent thought. But still, it could only lead them both to the same image: whenever they visited the Yoders, Lila handed the baby straight to Paul, and he would keep it entertained for as long as they would let him.

"We could adopt," Paul said, with a smile that was gone before it appeared.

"I don't want a baby."

"Right. I mean, no. I mean, never mind." He giggled. "I was kidding."

There were other mornings as dangerous, rife with allusions to impossible futures or their former life. They echoed playful dialogues of the past, or wrestled as they once had, marveling over the effects they could produce in each other's bodies, Kent's wild heartbeats, the traceable patterns of flushes in Paul's skin. One morning Paul cut Kent's hair. It was something Paul had done for him in the past, one of those oddly painful things Kent had continued to miss after he was gone.

But there was contentment in these morning visits, neither one desiring more or less. When Paul asked to play Dutch Blitz, it was plain he wanted not to see more of Kent but to see Maggie and the Yoders, this tacit family they secretly shared, and with them as well he seemed to have reached a limit of closeness, wanting no more than the measure he had established. When the subject of Maggie came up between them, as it often did, Paul insisted with offhanded equanimity that she came first, the marriage was first, as if these mornings bore no resemblance to another marriage but were only a thing mutually agreeable on the side, bounded within careful limits.

At the same time, something had clearly shifted. Kent didn't ask whether Paul was seeing other men. He knew he wasn't. And Kent had lost the urge to fight his situation. He rose from Maggie's bed and returned to Paul's, rose again and went to work, returned home to his wife. He was happy and he forgot, with perhaps a degree of willful intention, that there was any reason not to be. From time to time, in a lull of quiet with Paul, he would say, "I have to do something about this. I have to decide," but he didn't mean it, and Paul barely seemed to hear, didn't argue one way or the other. "Why?" Paul said, if he said anything at all, but it wasn't a question.

In the Yoders' backyard, Paul walked along the flower beds with Lila, squatting on his heels to stroke a leaf, ask a question. Ribs smoked on the grill, John Yoder with the basting brush and tongs. Maggie held the baby, talking to Kent, and when Paul wandered up to them Kent draped an arm across his shoulders, the same friendly, thoughtless way he would have if it had been Chloe or Seth who had appeared beside him.

Paul finished college, took a job at a neighborhood café, made forty dollars in tips his first day and felt like a rich man. He developed an affection for the purple house and for his time alone there. He checked out books about gardening and began planting little shrubs and flowers in the yard. One of the church members brought him an old hammock, which he strung up in the sideyard, and afterward he could be found there on his free afternoons, reading fat nineteenth-century novels in dappled shade.

It began to seem like a life, time passing into time that might continue with little to disturb it. But it had been only three weeks since he had moved into the purple house, only four since Bernard had been put in the ground. It was no more than the usual amount of time it took for a grand jury to convene.

☙

In the blue room, on the white-sheeted bed, the blankets were kicked aside and whorled about Kent's bare flank. He lay on his back, Paul with his knees planted on either side where the soft belly flesh tempted him to flex his thighs as if he were on a horse—only a nudge, enough to make Kent tense in apprehension of the vise grip he might have achieved at a whim. Paul laughed, and Kent said, "Watch it," grinning, took hold of Paul's hips.

Paul went on laughing, softly to himself, arched backward far enough to brace his hands on Kent's thighs. He faced the ceiling, and Kent disappeared. It was like being alone on a carnival ride, but under his own power. Only a moment, and he swung forward again, to bring back Kent's face. To kiss him next, because if anything was better than locking eyes while their bodies were joined it was kissing that way. Kent's soft eyes sought his from deep in the pillow, exactly as he knew he'd find them, unguarded and at ease in the oblivion they had created.

Except that someone had passed by the window. Through the parted sheers, the form outside had been milky and then vivid in color, and Paul had caught it in his peripheral vision as his gaze slipped from the ceiling, even as he was returning to the safe home of Kent's eyes, the mouth he still wanted to kiss, even knowing. He sucked a breath, twisted to the window, and though nothing was there he knew what he'd seen.

"Maggie," he said.

Kent was upright in a second. "Maggie? She saw us?"

Paul thought back. "She saw me, maybe, if anything. She didn't see you. I don't think she could have."

Kent scrambled to the window, shucking the condom into the trash, and peered along the outer wall toward the front of the house. "Are you sure it was her? What's she doing here?"

"You think I know?" Their eyes darted around the room, came to rest on each other as they heard faint knocking at the front door, the front door opening, Maggie's voice calling for Paul. A questioning sound, no detectable anger.

The bedroom door stood open, but the front door was at the other end of the house. Paul's hands went blindly to Kent's shoulders, and he made his voice firm, slow, very quiet. "Everything's fine. Don't move. I'll go talk to her." He grabbed up his black robe and lashed it around himself.

"She didn't see me?"

"No. I promise."

He gathered himself in a long breath as he slipped out, shut the door behind him. Teeth gritted into a smile, he went up the hall to where daylight and Maggie peeked around the open front door—she was still half-outside on the porch. "Sorry," she said in cringing apology and he said it at the same time, in the same tone. He told her to come in, and they struggled together with which of them should be more embarrassed. She had seen—but what? Her expression was troubled in an ambiguous way that could have meant anything, and he spoke quickly to take the blame, fill the void.

"Listen, I know maybe I shouldn't have brought anyone here—" He gestured toward his room.

"No," she said, distracted, "no, nonsense."

"But he's someone I know. I wouldn't bring some random stranger here."

She found her balance then, on the firm ground of his story, touched his arm. "Paul, it's your house. You can have people over."

"Well, still."

"I'm really sorry." She sighed, shoulders dropping, her hands open and helpless. "I didn't mean to—you know. But I needed to see you right away. I was knocking. I guess you didn't hear."

In his fear, his rush to allay any suspicion she might have, it hadn't occurred to him that she would have come for a reason. He stepped back, touched the wall. "Oh. It's happening."

"The police want to talk to you. I don't know what about." She stepped toward him, and his instinct was to step back, to turn and run. He made himself stand still, and she reached out slowly to stroke his arm through the silk sleeve of the robe, a gift from Bernard. She touched in the same lingering way Bernard might have. "Just some items to identify, they said. Don't be afraid. It might be nothing. It could be good news."

"Really?"

"Let's not speculate." She was talking to herself as much as to him, repeating her recent mantra, but he'd heard enough of her thinking out loud on this topic to know her hopes: because the police had been quiet when they should have been questioning him, they might be busy pursuing another lead. Of course, they might have been merely delayed, or ready to go before the grand jury without further effort. There was no way to know what was happening, she cautioned. It doesn't help us, so let's not speculate.

"You get dressed and we'll go down there, okay?"

He glanced back down the hall. "Give me, like, half an hour? I'll meet you there. I just need to—" He held a hand toward the room: *get rid of that guy you don't know.*

"I understand."

They looked shiftily at each other, each struggling with another apology but the embarrassment seemed to balance on the scales, while bigger problems loomed. Her eyes went to her watch. "Okay, homicide, ten-thirty. I'll call and let them know."

She left, and Paul waited at the front window until her car vanished down the road. Thank god Kent had kept the habit of parking elsewhere—it wouldn't have surprised him to look out and see the gray sedan in the yard, now that they had grown so comfortable. What worried him more was that he looked for it. That however unlikely, some part of him knew it could be possible for Maggie to walk by Kent's car and to speak to Paul the way she just had, refusing to acknowledge the obvious.

Light-headed, knees wobbly, he went back to the bedroom. Kent was dressed, sitting on the bed with his back to the door. "She's gone," Paul said. He sat on the bed, slipped his hand absently into Kent's. They faced the window. "She didn't see you."

⌒

Kent was gone when Paul got out of the shower—just as well, though he was lonely now and nervous. He glared at himself in the black-spotted mirror over the dresser, rubbed hard at his hair with the towel. Maybe a quick call to Sylvie, for grounding—but that might be less than helpful. She had recently worn out the thrill of Paul's celebrity status and gone through a radical change of heart. How could they dream of going out, having fun, when Paul might be facing life in prison? With tearful histrionics, she recounted long dreams involving death row, and Paul and Eric had learned to let her talk or risk an explosion at their insensitivity.

The funny thing was that he'd grown so used to her mooning that he'd stopped granting it any credence, as if not only the crazy death-penalty notion but the murder charge itself were her fanciful inventions. He laughed now, remembering her tirades, laughed harder that he could imagine calling her for comfort, until he started to hyperventilate and had to press his face into the towel. "Okay," he said, "okay," and got dressed.

He called his manager at the café, explained to the answering machine why he had no time to find a sub for his shift that started within the hour. He'd be in trouble for that, and Kent had made him late for his lunch shift once already that week. But he had no time to worry about his job.

No time, either, to worry about Kent. Maggie was another matter—he'd be with her again in minutes. He trusted her, knew she would protect him as his lawyer if not his friend. But he imagined how a suppressed understanding could surface with violence, in the midst of a police interrogation, make her react in some way she couldn't control.

She was leaning against her car as he pulled into the lot, a tall paper cup of coffee in her hand and another waiting on the hood. She said nothing, handed him the cup. They didn't speak until they were in the elevator, alone, and the silence began to feel punishing.

"I'm scared," Paul said, without meaning to, a plea for mercy, pity, whatever she could spare. She looked up at him with dark, solemn eyes and said nothing.

His fear of what was in her head made him doubly unprepared for what happened next. As soon as they entered the sixth-floor homicide unit, they were ambushed, separated. "We need to borrow him for just a minute," Thornton said to Maggie in a chummy way. "Alone. Don't worry, he's not going to be asked any questions without you."

Maggie blinked in sarcastic surprise. "I think not. Whatever you've got planned, I'm going to be there."

"Not this time, counselor." Thornton smiled, calm and confident, and sounded so incontrovertible that Paul's heart began to thud in his ears. They were led toward the now-familiar door of the interrogation room and then they were taken in different directions. Maggie could watch—he understood this much. Whatever was happening, she would be able to watch it from behind the glass, and one of the cops removed the still-full coffee from Paul's hands, and he felt a dreamy certainty as he was guided alone into the room that he had arrived for his execution.

In the room was George Babbish. Paul stopped, his mind swept clean and blank. George stood wringing his hands, his eyes full of the same naked pleading Paul had felt in his own throat with Maggie minutes before.

"Alone you said!" George snapped, as if chastising a dog on the floor, and only then Paul realized that Thornton and the younger detective had come into the room behind him.

Thornton spoke quietly. "This is as good as it gets. We can't have anyone getting hurt, you know."

George was red-faced, explosive-looking, though he stood very still. His voice rasped. "Why would I hurt him? I've explained to you."

"George?" Paul's voice came out similarly strange, and George looked so fretful and weepy in response that Paul took a step closer.

"Don't worry," George whispered. "I'll fix everything. You won't be hurt."

Like burning he felt Maggie's eyes through the window. George snarled again at the floor, "I won't give you anything unless I can see him alone first. It's all I ask. One minute alone."

The detectives balked, but glanced at each other as if weighing the options. Paul said, "It's okay. Let me talk to him." He understood that this was his choice to make, that he'd become cloaked in a provisional innocence and had this task to complete, this meeting.

Thornton finally agreed to leave George handcuffed to the table, and this was done, George seated in a chair. "Don't watch or listen," George shouted after the departing men. "I don't want anyone behind that glass, you hear me?"

Paul felt cold as soon as they were alone, George's eyes gazing up at him with more than the usual love, generous and unconditional. "Sit down, Paul. You look so uncomfortable there."

He fumbled for a chair and drew it up to the table, its corner between them. George laid his free hand on the table and caressed the wood with his fingertips. "You look good."

It had been weeks since they'd seen each other or had any contact, but there was no complaint in George's tone, only relief, as if his deprivation had been someone else's fault, not Paul's. George looked down at his fingers. "This is harder than I thought. I started to write you a letter, but I needed to see you, just once. I couldn't bear not seeing you. Do you know what I mean?"

"Yes," Paul said.

George didn't raise his eyes, his voice soft and halting. "The police will explain it to you. I'm afraid to say it. I don't want you to hate me when you shouldn't. When I am sacrificing my life for yours. That's how much I love you." He looked up. "And that's it, that's all you need to remember when this is over, that I was the one who saved you."

Paul couldn't speak, couldn't ask whether George had murdered Bernard or only concocted some new lie to distract the police. George's face was bland as a potato, wrinkled and weary about the eyes, and he remembered the night at Crush when this same man had seemed like a savior, and being saved had seemed worth wanting, at least for an evening's entertainment. He remembered the song that had been playing, *that's what takes me higher,* and how his desire had vanished before he had turned his face, stepped away toward the door and his friends, the next club, the next song.

"Tell me you love me," George said. "Say it just once. Even if you don't mean it, say it, because you will mean it later when you understand what I've done for you."

He heard only Bernard, *what I've done for you. It will come upon you, it will knock you over,* Bernard nursing his dark wine and unsung life. "I'm sorry," Paul said, to George because he couldn't say love. To Bernard. "I'm sorry."

"Don't cry. It's okay now." George let out a great sigh, smiling, as if Paul had said what he was meant to. He nodded. "I'm ready now."

Someone came in and Paul, hardly aware of what was happening, was taken from the room. He was led into another room and into a small gathering of people who all faced one direction. One of them was Maggie, and she took his arm, drew him up beside her and away from the others. They were all quiet, watching a show in progress through the window. It was the room he had just been in. George was in the chair, and the two detectives hovered over him, their voices low. Maggie drew a tissue from her bag to blot his face. He stared into the room, a brightly lit, unshaded window into some other life.

"It's almost over," she said, a murmur at his shoulder.

"He did it? Really?"

"It looks that way."

"He's confessing now?"

"Yes, I think so."

"Why?" Paul felt woolly with confusion. He strained to hear what the detectives were saying, but they were too quiet, and one of them blocked his view of George's face. *To save me?* he wanted to ask, but couldn't find the words. "I mean, why now?"

Maggie didn't answer for half a minute. Perhaps she was only listening to the interrogation, but something slipped in Paul during her silence, divided, so that George and the detectives became as insubstantial as the floor beneath him and the only firm reality was Maggie looking through the window. "Because he got caught," she said.

Voice shut in his throat, he couldn't ask how. She said, "They've found some blood in his car. They started looking at him after one of

his bartenders came forward, talking about how crazy he was. Philip
something? He said he saw you come in that night. Said George saw the
cut on your lip and left, within minutes. That was it, I guess."

He touched his lip, long healed and without a scar. "He just went
and killed Bernard. For that?" Though he saw dimly how the pieces fit,
there was nothing in this news he could believe. He'd been unprepared
to accept that any man, any person he could see and touch, would ever
be found to have real blood on his hands. Somehow he had expected it
to remain his own crime forever, unpunished but unstolen.

"He's crazy, Paul. Don't start blaming yourself." Maggie's hand
was on the base of his neck, her hip against his thigh. He looked down
at the dark curve of her eyelashes, her eye aimed at the window ahead
that might as well have been the other window, and he felt horrid and
shameful and small.

"I don't know how it could have happened that way," he whispered. "I didn't want anybody to get hurt." But she shushed him and
leaned toward the glass, because George had begun to speak.

CHAPTER EIGHTEEN

"I t's over." She kept saying it, at fifteen-minute intervals through their remaining hours at homicide, and she held Paul's hand and squeezed it. "It's over."

But there was another hour of questioning. The interrogation had turned friendly, apologetic in an offhanded way, and if Paul was due more recompense for his trouble he didn't seem to notice. He was asked only about his relationship with George Babbish, when it had begun and ended, how George had behaved at different times, and Paul answered in a voice that was definite but soft. His eyes didn't fully focus. As the detectives drew him into recounting his memories—his glimpse of George at the bar the night of the murder, their phone calls in its aftermath, the roses—his jaw might tighten, or he would seem tearful, but he didn't cry, didn't rant or hurl blame. From time to time he cast a dejected-dog look at Maggie, as if asking if they could leave now, if it was over yet. "It's over," she assured him. But it didn't feel true.

When released, they were slow to leave, slow in their steps down the hall and out the doors. At the parking lot, cars whizzing past out on

Ponce, the bright glare of sun overhead, Paul stopped under the covered walkway at the curb. He sat on a bench, and she sat beside him and after a moment held his hand again.

"You're such a good friend to me," he said. He pulled her hand into his lap, not looking at her. "What would I have done without you? I want you to know—" He stopped, at a loss. "I don't know. There's nothing I can say."

"You don't have to thank me. I didn't do that much."

They sat awhile in silence. She said, "We'll still see each other. A lot. Of course."

He nodded. "I hope so." He glanced at her and away, his forehead screwed into a frown. "I'll pay you, when I can. And rent for the house, I'll pay that too."

"There's nothing to pay, Paul."

His look remained clouded, and he pressed each of her fingers in turn as if counting them. "Okay. But if there's anything you want me to do, I'll do it."

She surmised that he was afraid to get up from the bench, get into his car, face his life. It was a common thing in parolees, and Paul had come close enough to that fate. There was the condo in Florida, the probate situation that she thought she could help him with—more easily now that his name was cleared. But imagining what he might do next, today, this week, far into the future, led her to wonder about the man who might play a role. If there was such a man, he was not the murderer after all. He must have been the one who had been in the house that morning, in Paul's room.

"Who was that you were with this morning?" she asked. She hadn't meant to say it aloud, and she turned her face sharply away as if maybe someone else had said it. Paul didn't answer, and she hadn't known what she was afraid of, what had shipwrecked them here, until his silence shaped it. Her hand was sweating in his.

After a minute, Paul cleared his throat. "I told you about him. He's that one."

"Your lover?"

He nodded. "I don't know if that's the word. It's complicated."

She could have asked when she'd get to meet him, could have told Paul to bring him along to dinner one night at the Yoders—maybe a celebration dinner for today's surprise victory—but she sensed the inexplicable inappropriateness of such a meeting. As often as she had tried to imagine this man, the closest she had come was imagining herself in his place, in a man's body she couldn't picture from the outside. What he looked like, who he was, remained a blank, which was all she'd seen of him through the window, a gap that it seemed could not be filled now in a normal way. But she understood, at the same time, that Paul would answer whatever question she asked.

She stood from the bench. "Listen, I need to do some things. I'll check in with you later, okay? Are you going home?"

Driving away from homicide, Paul forgot where he lived, drove up Ponce past Boulevard, which was the turn to Cabbagetown, and on up to Peachtree and the Fox Theater, where he turned, unthinking, right. By the time he noticed his direction, he was near enough to his old building that he turned onto its street. As George must have done, close to one-thirty that Monday morning. Above him the bright glass rose skyward, the eleventh floor indistinguishable. From farther off, at night, George might have watched through the lit windows. And there may have been other times, too, when George had parked out here, prior to the final night, when he'd known where to go as if the building were his own.

Paul didn't stop to look. The whole building seemed a bombed-out shell to him now, empty and dead. He only slowed and moved past, put it behind him.

Back on Ponce, the smell from the Krispy Kreme slipped through his windows and drew him into the lot. Minutes later he was headed home with a flat dozen box on the passenger seat and a carton of milk. It was warm outside and he wanted the heat, didn't even unlock the door of the purple house but sat in the sun on the porch steps and worked his way steadily through the donuts and milk. He'd forgotten how insubstantial donuts were, how they melted into sugar and grease and were gone in three bites.

Once or twice he'd made fun of George for locking The Club through his steering wheel every time he parked. He remembered seeing George's hands on it, bolting it into place with automatic motions, no matter how safe the lot, how long he'd be gone. Even Bernard's precious cars were not so protected. But maybe, Paul thought now, they should have been. Better if Bernard had been more careful altogether. What sort of man tossed his Benz keys to a reckless boy and said go, however far, wherever you like?

That night George had left his car unguarded. It would have taken only a handful of minutes, perhaps, once he'd slipped through the street door as some resident went out—no miracle required from so large a building, full of people like Paul who lived nocturnal lives. Aside from the coded entry, the building wasn't well guarded—no desk to pass, no code for the elevator. Or it might have taken longer, because he told the police he had gone to talk, with a steel bar in his hand. And Bernard had opened the door.

From Paul's split lip to Bernard's broken-open skull. What was gained? He'd had no choice, George told the police, over and over, but to protect Paul. Defending a life—justifiable homicide. Paul was relieved the police were scoffing at the excuse, that they seemed confident of a charge of first-degree murder. Not likely to be a trial at all, they'd told him. The confession would stand, a lawyer would convince him to plead out, no need for Paul to testify in court. Though he'd felt guilty in the past for George's misconception, he also knew he had never lied about Bernard, had in fact told George repeatedly he was wrong. But George had been fierce in his belief. He had wanted to believe, just as he wanted to believe himself a knight, duty-bound to slay a beast for his beloved. But he was not a knight, only a man too weak, once the daylight revealed the deed for what it was, to take responsibility for it. He'd had the courage to kill a man on Paul's behalf but not to protect him, when he truly needed it, from the real-world consequences.

There were two donuts left in the glaze-slicked box. He felt ill. He went inside and lay on his bed, where the blankets were still tossed from sleep and sex, his head in the hollow of the pillow shaped by Kent's head.

A while later, he found his phone, brought it back to the island of the bed. He thought it was to call Kent but instead he called his father. He wanted to tell someone about what George had done. To talk until it made sense, until George alone was responsible and it was not Paul, Paul's place in Bernard's life, that had killed him. No matter how he turned the events in his head, he could not obscure that simple fact. He wanted a man's voice that would promise him he was innocent.

His father traveled a three-county area as an insurance adjuster, and now that he'd finally gotten a cellphone, he was always reachable. He picked up and Paul said, "Hi, Dad. Are you busy?"

"A little. What's going on?"

Paul pictured him out on some muddy farm at the edge of Greene County, the farmer nearby and waiting for an estimate—*cow struck by lightning*, perhaps, their old dinner-table joke for a typical day's work—while his father took the call. He wouldn't have the leisure to hear about George, about Paul's lingering, terrible guilt, and Paul was relieved. He'd been dreaming to imagine he'd ever be able to talk to his father that way.

He sat against the headboard. "I wanted to let you know that everything's fine. They arrested someone else, and he confessed and everything, so I'm off the hook."

"Oh. Oh, Paul. Oh." It shouldn't have been so surprising that his father struggled for words, even sounded tearful—but anything other than stoic, reticent pleasantness in any situation was so unlike him that Paul teared up listening. "Son, that's a relief."

Once they had hung up, his father would have to say something to the farmer to explain the call, the emotion of it. "My son," he'd say. "He's been in a terrible situation but he's fine now. He's going to be all right."

Maggie ended up at home for a late lunch. From the kitchen, she called into her office, got her boss on the phone. "You will not believe—" she began, and reported the outcome of Paul's case, each phrase punctuated for humorous effect. Her head felt hollow, and part of her listened, detached, to the raucous sound of her own voice speaking the story. She told him she'd be in later that afternoon, but he assured her there was nothing pressing. She could take her time, take the day if she liked, and celebrate.

Without thinking, she made herself a peanut butter sandwich, something she hadn't done since she was a teenager, and stood at the counter chewing it slowly. Paul's name in her head. His body as she had seen it through the window of the purple house, a cream-colored inverted question mark bare from his bent knees to the curve of his behind and up the length of his torso to his shoulders, a shape without visible parts that only alluded to the obscene, like those abstract carvings in the store. His face turning to the window—but she hadn't seen that, had looked away, she was sure, before he turned. Of the other man, she'd seen so little that she wasn't sure how she'd known there was a man there at all. It had been clear to her that Paul was having sex, but for a partner her memory offered only blank space.

And it offered Paul's face, turning toward the glass, which she hadn't seen at all. His expression was all wrong for the circumstances. He appeared utterly calm. He looked sleepy, his smile a little sly, his whole being exuding warmth and a bed-ruffled intimacy. His eyes were full of love.

Nonsense. She was confused, because he'd looked at her that way before, late evenings when they were alone or nearly so, sitting close and talking in murmurs. A similar look, at least. She was certain that he hadn't looked that way through the window, that her glimpse through glass and screen had been hazy at best, no more than a shape she could not have sworn under oath was even Paul's. But she knew where to go now.

Carrying the remains of her sandwich on a plate, she went to the back room where Kent's old boxes remained unpacked, lining the wall. She slid some out from the wall, lifted others down, uncovered one she recognized—one she'd packed herself and marked with a star in bold red ink. Inside, on top, was a plaque, his name engraved on blue metal fixed to wood, that he'd won in a high school talent competition for performing an original song on guitar. *That's adorable*, she had said when she'd found it, way in the back of a closet. *We have to hang it on the wall in the new house. Please?* He laughed when she brought it to him and said no, no way in hell.

Reluctantly she had returned to packing. This was in his last apartment, over in Midtown, *their* apartment after they were married, but so briefly that her spartan possessions had stayed, for the most part, boxed and compressed while his, preceding her by a year, sprawled. Through his twenties he'd moved from one place to another never throwing anything away, so his sports equipment and outdated electronics and piles of clothing unworn in five years and keepsake trash-or-treasure bulged from closets, filled the spaces under furniture, accumulated in corners. She remembered packing this one box from the hall closet, full of items she deemed too precious to discard, and she'd packed slowly, lingering over what she found, making him a time capsule.

Under the plaque was a shoebox full of photos. She'd found them stored this way, loose in the shoebox in the back of the closet, and remembered thinking *I have to get that boy a photo album*, but she'd forgotten about it once they moved. A box of photos—she might have tucked it straight away into her larger box, if she'd been in a hurry, but she had time, and Kent was busy packing in another room, so she stole the chance to look through the random images of his life before her. The top one was of his parents, posed at a waterfall. Then his sister and her children in a green yard. Mixed in with the family photos, as if the stack had been shuffled like cards, were shots of strangers in their teens and twenties, friends of his she didn't know. She knew no one from his Athens life—more than ten years of it, college and after—and she hadn't imagined at the time, when she'd first seen these photos, that she never would, that these people were permanently lost in his past.

It came over her again, as she sat on the spare sofa in the window light and looked for the second time through the vaguely familiar shots, that he mentioned the names of old friends but never saw any of them or spoke to them on the phone—not even a card at Christmas. *I don't do cards*, he'd told her once, in a moaning, boyish way when she asked for addresses to add to her list. *Never mind my friends. No one worth the effort, really.*

There were pictures of fraternity formals, stamped with the event's name and date—she remembered the first time scanning these for Kent, so cute in his youth, then for the taffeta- or silk-draped girl on his arm, pretty girls she felt an immediate dislike for, especially when they opened their red mouths to the camera, laughing. But at least they were not Kristin—Kent had once told her he'd gotten rid of those. There were pictures of muddy, shirtless touch-football games, outdoor parties, the usual grinning people with their arms around each other. Shots of his old band playing in a bar, a series of these in the same bad light. A family reunion, cousins and grandparents, and now she was in known territory, for these people she'd either met or she recognized from other pictures she'd been shown. She knew his whole family, she realized now, but not a single one of the happy, youthful, fun-looking friends from before her time.

Toward the bottom, she found what she was looking for, tossed amid the rest: Paul. There were two shots of him, and only two, fewer than of many other strangers in the box. His hair was shorter. He looked like a young boy, though he was probably eighteen. He was alone in both shots, seated in a dim room, wrapped to the neck in a blue blanket. In one he was brooding, or maybe only sleepy and unaware, his eyes away from the camera, hair bent and tossed, his chin nestling on his knuckles where he held the blanket together. In the other, he looked at the camera with a smile coming on, only a hint, eyes partly lidded but something in them nevertheless so open, so knowing and tender and scolding, so free of barriers, that when she'd first seen it, she had stopped her flipping perusal to draw it closer to her face. *Who's that?* she'd thought, filling the strange gap that opened in Kent's life with *cousin?* because he had no brothers and at the time she hadn't known his cousins by sight. *Must be a cousin,* she'd thought. Because the blanket and the mussed hair looked like a sleepover, and the boy was young, and his eyes loved too openly to be a friend. His eyes spoke it, looked past the camera and into the eyes of the one who held it.

Even now, looking at what was clearly Paul, she clung to the notion of cousin for longer than she should have. Then she thought, *Well, they knew each other.* The pictures were innocent enough, and only two among so many, and surely there were any number of reasons for people to sleep at each other's houses. But Paul's expression in the second shot had a smoky luridness to it, his cheeks flushed, something freshly ravaged about him. The blanket had slipped from his neck to reveal the smallest wedge of skin along the plane of a shoulder, enough to suggest he was shirtless underneath, if not naked.

She searched her mind for something more logical. A beach trip, maybe. Kent had mentioned someone with a beach house around Hilton Head, where he and his friends—frat brothers, the guys in his band—had spent occasional weekends, piling in whomever they could fit. Maybe Paul had gone along once. When she looked at the picture again, it was innocuous, snapped out of playfulness some morning before breakfast, by anyone, Paul's look only sleepy and a little annoyed.

Except that she had known it for strange when she'd first seen it. The boy in the blanket had made such an impression on her mind that when he had appeared in the store, several years older, she'd been struck by his resemblance to someone she'd once known or was supposed to know, the cousin she'd taken him for. Even then she'd known him, with a little frisson of recognition. She'd known, too, on a level deeper than consciousness that for her husband to lie on the bed with Paul, with that hand on his hip, was no moment's charity but a piece of something, of meaning, clicking into place.

She took the two photos with her empty plate back to the kitchen. She poured herself some apple juice and sipped it, holding the pictures before her, evidence of nothing. She had understanding for which she had no evidence. She had understanding that made no sense, none— she laughed aloud—because Kent wasn't gay. Sure, it happened all the time, to other women—she'd known more than one—but those were other men and anyway hadn't surprised her much. She didn't think herself that stupid, that blind, capable of such an error.

But more bits of their lives, hers and Kent's, were snapping into place, flying faster than she could control. And the most damning piece of evidence, she saw, was the one she'd had from the beginning. This good-hearted, loyal, likeable, easy-tempered man had kept no friends from his life before her.

She set the photos on the counter and picked up her phone, though she didn't know who to call or to say what. Lila was the one, before Kent, before Paul. Lila had seen Paul and Kent together, and besides, surely harbored all sorts of complex opinions about Kent she would never voice unless cornered. *Maybe*, Maggie could hear her say. Or, *it kind of makes sense.* Or, *well, I was wondering when you'd notice.* More likely, though, she would ask patient, half-dismissive questions until Maggie's every suspicion was reduced to the dust it was. She'd send Maggie home laughing at her own foolishness, freed of any burden to confront Kent at all.

But already she was arguing in her head with Lila, who didn't have the whole story. She left the house, and the sun struck her with a pleasant heat. She was driving and didn't know where she was going— no court today, no office if she didn't want to go. Jamal's file would miss her. Jamal—his court date still floated in the distant future, uncal- endared, because the hulking machinery of justice was slowest to gather force and motion when it meant to kill a man. She had an uncanny feeling now that she would never see that court date, and was suffused with the guilty relief of not having to think about him any- more, as if she were preparing to quit her job. She would start a new life, and someone else would deal with his mess.

An hour had passed, and Paul had not called Kent. He'd called Sylvie as an alternate, but again talked only briefly, found himself unable to achieve the ecstatic tone she expected for his news or to form a coherent thought. He arranged to meet her and Eric later for a drink and hung up. He felt unaccountably sad, with a misty dread that made him stand at the front window with his forehead to the glass. Then Maggie's car pulled into the yard. She sat in the driver's seat watching the door.

He slipped out onto the porch, barefoot, leaned a shoulder to the post beside the top step. She was still sitting in her car, engine off. Finally she got out, climbed the steps with a grim smile. "I want to talk to you. Let's go in, it's too hot out here."

He led her inside and they sat on the sofa. "I found these in some old boxes of Kent's," she said, her voice neutral. She placed a pair of photos in his hand.

Paul drew a breath, looked. He looked a long time, turning from one to the other, expressionless. He knew he should feign surprise, laugh, widen his eyes with interest, but it was clear enough why she'd gone looking, why she was here. Even if she knew nothing at all, she knew. And he dimly grasped that somewhere between the elevator ride to the sixth floor of City Hall East and the ride back down, he might have reached the limit of his capacity to lie to her.

"That's me," he said. "I don't remember where." He tried to hand them back to her. She didn't take them, and he let his hand drop to his thigh, nervous under her scrutiny. "In a box?"

"Why does he have them?"

"I don't know. Honestly, I don't." He drew a knee to his chest and faced her. "Why do you think?"

"I don't know what to think, Paul. I think Kent is lying to me. That there's something going on behind my back." She fought to control the breaking of her voice, turned away from him. "Maybe I don't want to know this."

He waited in perfect stillness, beginning to see his error. *Lie*, a voice told him. Lie now, and quick, and make it good, because he didn't owe her honesty. He owed her only what she wanted, and maybe what she truly wanted was the same thing he did, an extension of the unknowing bliss that had kept them all happy together until now.

But he was too slow to decide. She was speaking again. "Maybe it's not even behind my back. I think it's just happening and I'm letting it. The two of you—I don't know, maybe I'm crazy. Maybe I'm wrong." She met his eyes. "You can tell me if I'm wrong."

You're wrong, so easy, and it stuck in his throat. He reached for her arm and she was up before he could touch her, on the other side of the room, a hand on the mantel to brace herself. "Oh, God," she said, "I don't believe this. I don't believe this."

"Maggie." He stood, and she turned to him, her face open as if hopeful that he'd deny it now.

He looked at the floor. "You should talk to Kent."

"You did this to me. How could you do this?"

"I didn't do this to you. It wasn't about you." He stepped closer, straining for a way to speak to her that wouldn't hurt Kent. "I wish I could explain. He loves you."

Sudden anger lit her eyes. "No, Paul, skip the bullshit. Just tell me what happened. Everything. From the beginning."

He winced at her tone, the flint in her jaw. "You should talk to him."

"I will, but right now I'm talking to you. This morning, you said anything I wanted. This is what I want, Paul. I want to know."

He nodded. Maybe, he thought, by telling her the truth he could spare Kent the hardest part. It was all the loyalty he could see room to offer.

"He's wanted to tell you," he said. "For a while. He hates this. He just didn't want to hurt you. We tried to stop." Already he was lying, worming in that *we* when he himself had wanted nothing more than Kent without end.

"When did it start?"

He hesitated, as if he could choose now. To be the friend who came into her house, seduced her husband. Or the friend who was a lie all along.

"January."

Her mouth fell open, wordless. When she could speak, her request was calm. "Can I have some water?"

He went to the kitchen for a glass, filled it, and when he returned she was sitting on the sofa. She was stunned past anger now, since he'd begun to speak, and the easing of her posture granted him permission to sit beside her. "You're surprised," he said softly, handing her the glass.

"No." Her eyes had gone half-vacant, her voice dull enough to sound casual. "I knew. I mean, I had a feeling. Something. Not this."

"Not me."

She shook her head slowly. "January?"

"We didn't mean it to happen. We ran into each other, by accident. It was one minute, you know? We lost control, and we never got it back."

"All this time."

"Off and on."

"This morning."

He hesitated. "Yes."

She blinked. "So he's gay. My husband is gay, that's what you're saying."

"No." He touched her arm, drew the hand back. Her eyes were on his now, wounded and questioning. "It's not that. That's what makes this so complicated. Part of it. He's very attracted to you, to…women. He's not running around after guys, like that. It's just—" He had wanted this to be the easy part, the one piece of good news, but he could see now that by comparison, a gay husband might be welcome, a simpler transgression, and more forgivable.

"Just you," she finished, her voice croaking in her throat. She sipped the water. "How do you know that? You can't know his whole life, any more than I do."

"I guess I don't. But we have history."

"Athens. Those pictures."

"I really don't remember those. But if that's all you found, maybe he burned the others. It was crazy that we ever got together. I don't think either one of us knew how it happened. But we were obsessed with each other, for a while, and it ended kind of abruptly. And I don't know why I'm saying all this except I want to explain how it happened again, this time. He loves you and he's so, so faithful to that, I know. But this other thing—I guess it was still burning out."

She said, "But—" and stopped herself, blinking, processing. "Oh. God."

"What?"

She looked at him in disbelief. "You're the one. You're Kristin."

He stiffened with surprise—or maybe it was only the sound of the name that still sent a little current through him, equal parts pleasure and pain. He was Kristin. He swallowed hard. "That's what he told his parents. That he lived with a girl named Kristin."

She was quiet for a time, shaking her head. Trying to connect the two, he thought, or resisting it, the same dual reaction he went through himself, with nausea the likely result. Her voice dropped lower, became firm. "And in January. How did it start?"

He made himself answer, quietly and fully. He told her about the library, the beach, and after their return to the city, where and how often they had met, and how many times Kent had tried to end it. He bent it a little, making Kent less involved than might have been the case.

"In my house?" she asked.

"No, never."

"That night on the bed. I saw you."

"Nothing happened then. But he meant for you to see that, I think. He was trying to tell you."

Listening, questioning, she grew steadier. She was a lawyer interrogating a criminal. By the time she remembered how she knew him, she already had more than she needed.

"So you came to the store. That was no accident."

"I wanted to see you. What you were like. I didn't mean to stay."

She looked away, and he leaned toward her, trying to turn her face back. "I'm not sorry I did. That part. I never lied to you about our—" He couldn't say *friendship,* it was too presumptuous. But he felt the loss keenly. "I really liked being with you. It was one little lie, in the beginning, and the rest was real. That part, us. And I guess you're going to hate me now. I guess you should." He laughed, painful and abrupt. She glowered into the room before her as if she hadn't heard him.

"Do you believe me?" His voice strained to a higher pitch, and his fear that she would hate him, not just who he was now but the memory of him, made lies spill from his mouth. "I never wanted to hurt you, I tried to stop, I tried to tell you." He caught his breath. "Do you believe I was your friend?"

She glanced his way, eyes vague, as if vexed to find him still beside her. "What does that matter? Do I believe. Your performance, you mean? This isn't an acting class." She said it softly, with a gentle scolding.

"Okay," he said. "More. Give me more."

"More what?"

"Anything. Talk to me. Call me names, scream at me. Whatever you want."

She shook her head, distracted. "Not now." She was quiet a full minute—thinking about Kent, he supposed, and what she would say to him. *Call Kent,* he told himself. God, the second she leaves.

"Can I ask you something?" she said, not looking at him.

"Anything."

"Am I just stupid? Not to know this? Because I always thought I had a sense about people. That I was a good judge of character. I've always trusted that." Though her eyes were not damp, her voice had taken on a mournful note. He remembered her rape then, how little trust she must have.

"You're not stupid—"

"Find the good, don't trust," she muttered, to herself it seemed— a mantra or warning she must have used in facing handcuffed men. "And you." She cut him a look. "I loved you. What does that say about me?"

Love surprised him, and then it didn't, and he felt oddly grateful that she would offer it that way, even as she was taking it back. He sucked a breath at the sting. "Maggie—"

She turned to him with a hard, searching gaze, as if he might be ready to give her the answer she wanted, but he had nothing. "Please," he said. "Understand."

"Okay. What? What should I understand?"

"I love him." He meant it as last-chance excuse, apology, the only way to justify himself. His face crumpled and he struggled to stay calm. "I can't help that. There was nothing I could do. And you. All I wanted was to keep it this way, the three of us—"

Maggie was openmouthed, astonished. Before she could find words she stood, waved a dismissive hand at him and headed for the door. "Enough of this."

He followed. "Don't go yet. This doesn't have to be the terrible thing you think it is." He took hold of the edge of the open door, blocking her. They were nearly in waltz position.

"Are you crazy?" She asked it like a real question, her voice sad and gentle.

"Maybe. I don't know. Stay for a minute."

"The three of us." She looked up into his face, blinking. "Why did you kiss me that night?"

He had no answer, could think of none, but he was desperate to keep her there long enough to reason her out of hating him, to talk all of them back from this wreck. He said, "I'll tell you if you stay. Please, just a minute."

She considered this and shook her head. "I don't want to know that bad."

She pulled the door from his hand with steady determination, was out on the porch, and he called after her, "Because you wanted me to!"

He had blurted it without intention, without a thought formed to back it up, but he would finesse an explanation if she would only turn and look at him with the outrage or derision it deserved. But she didn't turn; she hunched her shoulders and hurried toward her car, as if the words were birds diving after her.

He was down the steps fast, at her back. "You wanted it." Spotting that weakness turned him predator, but when he was close enough to see she was blushing fiercely, ducking to hide it, he softened. "Maggie, it's okay. I only wanted to let you in a little, in with us, so you wouldn't be so, I don't know. Excluded. And you wanted to come. It's not a bad thing. It doesn't have to be."

"Stop it, Paul." She was half in the car, wrestling the door from him.

"You're not perfect either."

"I know that." Her cheeks looked burned. She raised her eyes. "Just let me go, okay? I need to think."

"Can we talk later?"

He held the door, kept her there, until she said yes. Then he stepped back as she jerked the car onto the street, stood watching until it was gone. He ran back inside to his phone. The urgency kept him from stalling long enough to be afraid, and until Kent's voice reached

him through the receiver he felt little more than the clattering high of
adrenaline. But the sound of Kent's voice was its own loss, rushing
through him. *I will lose this.* "Kent," he said, and he couldn't speak
more than that name, over and over.

"What, Paul? What was it? What happened? Maggie's not
returning my calls."

Kent didn't know yet, and there was sweet concern in his voice,
even love. Maybe he'd forgotten Maggie at the window. Maybe he'd
thought of nothing since that morning but Paul's fate with the police.

"Can you come over?"

"You're at home?"

"Please, Kent. I need to see you."

Silence, and his voice became firm. "Tell me."

⌒

A car behind Maggie honked, making her move through the inter-
section where she had come to rest. Not a thought in her head, yet her
car was dragging her like a dog toward Lila's house. At the next cross
street she forced the wheel away from Lila's and toward her own.

It was nearly five, so Kent would be home soon, sooner once he'd
talked to Paul—or possibly, for the same reason, later. She couldn't
guess which, and it seemed to her now as if she knew nothing about her
husband, the circuits of his mind or the habits of his character. All she
knew for sure was that Paul would tell him, that he would arrive when
he did knowing how much she knew, and though a small, thorn-like
part of her wanted to confront him by ambush, hear him lie, she was
relieved that she wouldn't have to suffer through that charade.

At the McKutcheon-Schwartzentruber house, the living room was
saturated in diffuse golden light from the west-facing windows. Always
her favorite time of day, the time when she most liked this house,

though she couldn't look at the sofa without seeing Paul on it—hardly more than a week before, his cheek resting on one bent arm along the back cushions, the same light in his hair and his eyelashes. Her angel, her demon—whatever he was, he'd been hers, not Kent's. Safe on a technicality, but radiant with the formless need that had doubled and tripled since he'd first shown it to her in the store, that was now boundless enough that he shouldn't have been there with Kent gone. He was barely able to locate an excuse for stopping by.

She could feel it on her skin, that need of his. Often she'd thought about how a man would answer, since he would want a man. But she did her imagining from a distance, tucked herself into the sofa's opposite end, turned away when he fixed her with looks that lasted too long, rose to fuss with irrelevant objects when he slid closer. There was too much of him to handle alone. Barely twenty minutes and she was on the phone to Chloe, asking her to come over for Dutch Blitz.

It wasn't that he was dangerous, a sexual predator like his character in the play. A large part of his appeal lay in the fact that he was the opposite of that man. Inert, almost, in his desire for her. It was she who was dangerous, or could be, if she chose. Oddly, now, it felt as if Kent were less her husband than some part of her, less restrained, wily enough to slip through a hole in the fence and take what she wanted.

She sat on the empty sofa, which faced obliquely the kitchen door, and considered the quiet of their house. *Our house.* Somehow she and Kent had come to inhabit its rooms, having arranged its furniture so as to obscure a fault in plain view. A normal room, a normal-looking house, and suddenly her problem with vision seemed a product of the arrangement of furniture. Which one of them had decided on this angle for the sofa, the rug there, the TV in the corner? What was hers about this? Almost all of the furniture itself, the wall hangings, the piano, she had brought into the marriage from her life before. She must have been the one to arrange them too, but she couldn't remember.

Without a plan, she began to move things, an end table against the wall, a chair beside the fireplace, and she was dragging the sofa around to face the door when Kent came through it.

"What do you think?" she asked him. She'd broken a sweat and was fanning herself with her blouse. The arrangement had an unformed promise to it—adjustments were needed. She moved a table into place at the sofa's arm. Kent watched her in silence, then stepped forward into the room and sat in the newly angled armchair, hands pressed between his thighs like a nervous guest.

"Will you sit down?" he said. She examined the furniture critically before she complied, sat on the sofa facing him. The sun had passed from its blinding angle, and in the new light, a clear, pale, less transformative shade, Kent looked sorrier than she had ever seen him. They had, it seemed to her now, never had a fight, let alone a crisis powerful enough to call up this deep, melting sadness in his eyes.

She was oddly aware of her body, her erect posture, hands folded tight on her lap, what he would see as he looked at her. In her newly skewed environment she must have appeared to him assertive, territorial, as if the house were hers to do with as she pleased. But she didn't mean it that way. It was only that she'd rather do almost anything than confront him. She was too shocked, too hurt to be angry yet. She wasn't guarded against feeling sorry for him, which she was, almost as soon as she looked into his face.

"What he told you," Kent said, his voice hoarse, the start of some sentence he was unable to finish. She waited, but he fell to helpless silence.

"Yes," she said, more answer than question. "It's true, then."

"I wanted to tell you. So many times, but I couldn't. I couldn't hurt you."

Though her throat was dry, she felt oddly calm, tired. "Tell me what? That you were cheating on me? Or that you're gay?"

"I'm not gay. I know how it looks. But I'm not. And cheating on you—Maggie, I'm so sorry about this. I am. But it never felt like cheating on you." She made a disgusted, inarticulate sound that he spoke over. "I swear, Mags, I still feel like I would never *do* that to you. I'm not trying to minimize this. I'm just saying I don't really understand it either. But I love you."

"You're going to have to do better than that."

"I know. I will." He sighed miserably. "I'll try."

She was feeling strangely comforted by his demeanor and his struggling words, his reassurances of love. She believed him, at least, enough to question him. "How can you say you love me and"—she couldn't say it—"be with him? For months. What do you do with him anyway?"

"I don't know," he said, an answer to her first question that ignored the last. He stammered toward more explanation that she didn't fully hear, because her questions had started projectors in her mind, and memories, swift and piled upon each other, that she hadn't been clear-headed enough to recall before now. What came to her was that here, sitting across from her, was the very man Paul had talked about, the man he had protected through the murder investigation and swore loved him.

Her jaw fell in a shock that stopped his faltering efforts, and she regarded him narrowly. "Are you in love with him?"

He went rigid, then crimson. "No," he said—too unsteady, too late.

And all his concern over Paul's case. She saw the past six weeks of Paul in their lives in a rapid reel, like a familiar film shot from a slightly altered angle. It had been the startling nature of the transgression, perhaps—Paul's gender—coupled with her own disturbing feelings that had kept her caught there until now, thinking one thing: sex. However traumatic and extreme, it was something she could at least approach in questions. An act. A sin, a definable crime. Maybe even something—

though she wasn't aware she'd thought so far ahead—they could overcome.

But this was an angle she hadn't considered. "You love me"—she lifted and dropped her shoulders, looked around bewildered—"and you love him. You *love* him."

"No." He ducked, eyes squeezed shut.

"God, Kent."

He drew a breath and trained a fierce, determined gaze on her face. "I don't love him. I love you. All that, with him, that was"—he looked away with a sweeping dismissive gesture of his hand—"a mistake. A big mistake."

She shook her head, almost laughing. "You wish it was, you mean." She stood. "I don't understand this, Kent. I don't know if there's anything *to* understand. But if we're going to sit here and have this conversation at all, you've got to at least be honest with me."

Red-eyed, he nodded with the quick, jerky motions of a child. He seemed unable to speak now—unwilling to lie, incapable of saying to her face what was plainly true. *God*, she thought. She couldn't find her anger.

"To think we could have had a child," she said, her voice laden with more contempt than she expected. He winced as if she'd slapped him. "I'm sorry," she said, feeling on the verge of tears herself. She passed a hand over her face, walked behind the sofa. "Maybe it's not your fault."

"It is." He leaned toward her, his expression earnest. "This'll sound stupid, but I never wanted anything but to be worthy of you. And I'm weak. I failed."

"Maybe you wanted the wrong thing," she said. She had a sudden stark, almost gleeful awareness that they had committed so little to this life—a childless year and a half—that it wouldn't be terribly hard to pick up her marker and set it at some other go, begin again.

"I want what I have with you." He seemed steadier, calm and quiet. "This is the truth, Maggie, the only way I know how to say it. You need to know this. That there's nothing about you, our life together, nothing I didn't want. You're everything"—he stopped, voice caught. "You're perfect."

There it was, the very echo of Paul's words in opposite. "I am not perfect," she said, with a growling undertone as if he'd accused her of something out of spite. She aimed an index finger. "This is about you, not me. I don't want to hear about me, and what you think about me, these crazy ideas you have, Kent, about who I am. I want to talk about you."

He blinked, taken aback. "Okay."

He waited for a question, but she felt at a loss, stuck between trying to picture what might have gone on between them and trying not to. What did she want to know? Paul. Only what that felt like.

"Was it worth it?" she asked softly, scornfully.

CHAPTER NINETEEN

Kent's car was at the curb, pulled up tight behind Maggie's in a way that rankled Paul, as if cars could hold hands and whisper. A house and a half away, he sat in his own parked car, windows down to catch any sound. He judged himself invisible from the house, since he could see of it only one windowless front corner, stiffly skirted with hydrangea. The puffy blooms, going to brown, had recently matched the blue of the paint that flaked up from the shingles. A creeping, greenish tint like algae bled from under the wood.

He was surprised by the silence. The house, he thought, should be shuddering with screams, cracking apart, sending tremors out to the street. If Kent were to come running out, Paul would be waiting to carry him away and make amends. Why didn't he come? How could they talk for so long? He wished he could be inside with them, no matter what punishment they would hurl his way—the more the better, if they'd only allow him to be there.

Hurt at being unneeded, ignored, he was twisting the ignition to drive away—toward a drink, he thought, a celebration, and he knew where—when he was stopped by a disastrous, unexpected sound.

Almost at his ear, a bright, familiar shout of greeting. "Hey!" He jumped, banged his knees on the steering wheel, his elbow on the door. Laughing down at him through the driver's side window, straddling her bike, was Chloe. Her hair was in braids, her t-shirt damp at the throat. "Scare ya?"

"Fucking Jesus," he hissed, which sent her into a peal of horrified giggles. He clutched his chest. "God, Chloe. Oh my god."

"What are *you doing* out here?" Were she calling out to someone two blocks away, her wry, merry, accusing voice could not have been any louder in his ears, and he shushed her with frantic motions. He had to stop himself from dragging her down from the bike, a hand clapped over her mouth. Round-eyed at his reaction, she covered her mouth herself, then said in a stage whisper, "Oh, drama! What's going on?"

No time to think, he waved her into the car. She leaned her bike against the rear door and scurried around on tiptoe, tumbled into the seat beside him with her closemouthed grin and glittering eyes, rubbing her hands together in anticipation. "Tell me, tell me."

"Shh." He laid a hand over hers, lowered them, held them in both of his, which were shaking. He didn't know what to say to make her not there.

"Listen, if you're going to visit them, now is probably not a great time," he said. Her expression plummeted into concern, and he rushed to reassure her. "No, it's fine, everything's fine. It's nothing awful. It's not even anything bad. I promise."

God, what was he saying? He couldn't bear for her to know this, ever, to ever think anything bad about him. But how could he stop her from knowing? His crime was against her too, against her whole family, all of them.

"I wasn't going to stop. I was just riding by. I saw your car." Her voice was hesitant, bright and dark by turns, as worried as if she herself had done something wrong. She was a beautiful girl, in every way. Damp and freckled, the downy lip over her braces, sleepy eyes almost nothing like Maggie's except in being brown. Without thinking, in a fit of sadness, he reached to touch her cheek, stroke it with the backs of his fingers. She blinked at him in wonder.

"Chloe," he said, smiling, helpless, and she smiled back. "Sister girl, you know how beautiful you are, right?"

She chewed her lips, pleased and distressed at once. He looked down at their clasped hands. "Do something for me, okay? Pretend you didn't see me today. Go on with your ride and just forget all this."

"Why are you out here?" Her expression was grave.

"It's nothing. I was just leaving." Finally he had found the poise and tone to make everything casual, no matter what she'd just seen. He squeezed her hand in a chummy way, slumped against the seat. "You just startled me. I didn't mean to make a big production."

She looked uncertainly toward the house. "You promise everything's fine?"

"Of course."

She studied his face with a half-comic show of skepticism, but he wasn't worried now. She would trust him because he asked it. Under the spell of first love, she would turn whatever he said to gospel. And though looking at him brought out the woman in her eyes, the woman she would be, she was barely fifteen—a child, and for all her boldness a soft, protected one. No one had ever told her about Maggie's rape. They wouldn't tell her this either. She never had to know.

"Aren't you going to ask about the audition?" she said, coquettish.

Alice in Wonderland, a summer children's production at the community playhouse. He'd forgotten. "Yes—oh, honey, how'd it go?"

She lifted her chin, flipped back a braid. "Too mature. They want a younger Alice. But I'm going back tomorrow to try out for the Queen of Hearts."

"They'd be crazy not to give it to you."

When he sent her peddling on her way, she was happy again and oblivious of all trouble, though it was hard, watching her go, to feel at ease, or to hate himself any less. She was out of sight before it occurred to him that he'd forgotten to tell her the good news. He wasn't a murderer anymore.

꙲

Crush, open 24/7, was not a place to go for happy hour. Almost no one crossed its threshold before eleven p.m., and its daytime clientele, when there was such, tended toward ragged bands of tina queens from the previous night who had forgotten to stop dancing. At least this was what Paul had always imagined to be the case, from some of Eric's stories and those of others, whose drug exploits of the night before were often the highlight of casual or pre-trick conversation. *Oh, my god, I was dancing until four in the afternoon!* Today the techno music played to an empty floor, but the place was so cavernous, multi-floored, lousy with rooms, that he found at least a few people around every corner, shooting pool or drinking at the upstairs bar—the only bar open—a pair of guys laughing uproariously on a far sofa.

He had come hoping to find Philip, to thank him for his life and hear the news and have a drink with him before he went to meet Sylvie and Eric, who had insisted on the patio bar down the street where Eric was pursuing a waiter. But Philip wasn't working. Some new guy Paul didn't know was behind the bar, a nervously aloof young thing who must not have been advised that his job was to shake a martini at Paul's approach. Paul ordered his usual without comment, asked after Philip's whereabouts—the kid knew nothing—but before he'd poured Paul's drink, a small buzzing circle of tight-shirted Crush employees, then more curious folk, had formed around his stool.

What did he know about Babbish? They began volleying rumors: the man had been hauled out in handcuffs, beaten half to death, no, he bit a cop's ear off, was charged with capital murder—you know, the death penalty? No, it was drug-related, tax-related, plainclothes cops sitting on the club for months, federal agents, the mob's involved, and I don't know about that, but I hear this place is going up for sale at police auction and we're all out of a job.

It came to Paul like the jabber of a foreign language, punctuated with the gestures of sculpted arms and whiffs of expensive, subtle cologne. Not long ago, he might have liked nothing better than to sit at the center of this attractive attention and deliver his news.

"I really don't know much," he said. "I was hoping you guys would know."

"But he was arrested, right? For murder? He's the one who went after your sugar daddy, who they thought *you* killed, that's what I heard."

"Mm-hmm, I heard that."

"That's kind of hot, I say. Romantic and shit."

"Not that you want to get romantic with that."

"I'm just saying."

"What's tragic is what about us? Where will we go when Crush is gone?"

"He's only part-owner, you know," Paul said. "Whatever happened, I'm sure the club will be fine."

He tipped the new bartender without paying for his drink and left the half-full glass on the bar. Down at Joe's patio he ordered another martini, sitting at a wrought-iron table in leafy shade, alone, and watched the sun slip down behind his old building until it seemed to be burning dead-on through the glass on the eleventh floor. Nighthawks wheeled in the deepening blue overhead, slender as boomerangs, while the busy road past the porch rail fell into shadow, headlights came on. He felt unpleasantly light, disconnected from everything. He was grateful for the murmur of the waiter bringing his stemmed glass, the glances of strangers at other tables on the mostly-full patio, proving he wasn't invisible. By the time Eric and Sylvie walked up from the street, he'd had as much as he could stand of solitude.

And he felt entitled to the scene they made in their corner, Sylvie squealing while Eric lifted him off the ground, swung him around, released him so that Sylvie could have her turn to cling for a hopping, ecstatic full minute like a crazed fan. No one at the surrounding tables could avoid looking at them. When he finally peeled her off, she was crying, as he knew she would be. "Okay, baby," he said, laughing, "deep breaths. You'll wreck your mascara."

She pressed her eyes. "You could have died. Electric chair—that's all I'm going to say." She patted his chest and, to his surprise, released the breath she might have been hoarding for a final epic fit.

They sat at the table. Eric said, "She's been a frigging banshee all day. You're so lucky you missed it."

"I'm done now. I'm just happy it's all over." Sylvie opened a menu with glacial calm, then, remembering herself, turned back to Paul with a grin and rubbed his arm. He suspected she was truly a little disappointed it was all over, their lives less interesting now.

"So the wife knows," Eric prompted, on to the next drama.

Paul spun the remaining gin in his glass. "The wife knows." He told them about his recent drive by the house, and he included Chloe's surprise visit because it made a good story, and making it a story served to buffer it. Eric listened with his eye on the overly tanned waiter working the higher level of the porch. Their own waiter, who might have been the twin of the other—they had identical haircuts—brought cosmopolitans for Eric and Sylvie. Paul ordered another martini.

"Now," he said, "I need to figure out whether to call. I just want to leave a message on his cell, you know? But he's dumb enough about phones to pick up, and that's the last thing I need, to be all *hello, it's me* in the middle of whatever's going on over there."

"Then don't call," Sylvie said. "He can figure out to call you."

But there was something essentially helpless about Kent in this regard that made Paul imagine Shakespearean tragedies of missed connections, Kent finding the purple house empty at the wrong moment and throwing himself off a bridge.

"So this is good," Sylvie said. "The wife will kick him out, right? Then he's yours."

Yes, maybe, seemed logical. But Paul was unable to feel this as good news. "He'll hate me," he said, hoping it wasn't true. "He'll blame me for telling her, first of all, which I kind of did. Besides"—he didn't fully know this until he was saying it—"I don't really want them to break up."

Sylvie goggled her eyes at him. He screwed his face into a frown. "I guess I don't. It's weird, but I like them. They're kind of a good couple. Me and Kent, we're totally dysfunctional—"

"You said everything is so great between you two!"

"I know, that's the thing. It has been, lately. It's because he's married, I think. How twisted is that?" He laughed, finished his drink as the next arrived.

"Ah, the competition." Sylvie's look was both scolding and admiring. "You're not interested unless there's a challenge."

"Maybe it used to be that way. But I think it's different now. It's like, the three of us are a great couple."

"Now that's twisted."

"Like *us*," Eric enthused with a glass raised in toast. "Hey, I know how we should celebrate your freedom. Let's us three go down to that condo of yours in Florida! I want to see this place."

"It's not mine yet," Paul said. He didn't explain, didn't want to think, how he needed Maggie's help to get it. How he needed Maggie for more than that, for everything he wanted. Because somehow it would be up to her, though he couldn't picture any reaction, any outcome that would return him to the Eden that had been the bed with Kent that morning, much less bring back her own sweet company or the family that had begun to seem his.

He humored them instead with beach trip plans, trying to catch the tycoon spirit of his freedom and new wealth of property. The life without Kent. But it wasn't enough to distract him. Finally he turned away furtively to his phone, got Kent's voicemail—to less relief than he'd expected—and left a quick, shame-ridden message. "I'm out having a drink," he said. Worried it sound too light-hearted, he added, "Many drinks. Call me as soon as you can. Please. I need to see you."

Eric and Sylvie's second cosmos arrived and were such a lovely pink in the summer evening light that he ordered one for himself. Sylvie raised a toast to his victory—his salvation, she added—and he downed the dregs of his martini. It hit him like a wave of night ocean, an undertow tug of fear. He saw a flicker of vivid premonition: driving home in the dark, wasted, wrecking his car. A hospital bed, beep of machines, Maggie and Kent at his bedside for a tearful reunion.

"I'm so sorry," Maggie would say to him, before he was ever made to feel the first heat of her anger and his own remorse. "I didn't understand how little it all mattered."

"I shouldn't be drinking like this," he said to Sylvie. "Don't let me drink too much, promise."

***

After the message on his cellphone, Kent wasn't surprised when Paul answered his own phone with boozy cheer, crowd noises and a thump of mechanized drums backing his voice. He had the hiccups too.

Two hours before, with Maggie, Kent had started on the bourbon him-self, though he hadn't felt it much and now was only tired and a little dazed, sober enough to be annoyed by the state Paul had gotten himself into.

It was nearly midnight. "I'll be right there," Paul said, then remembered to ask where there was.

"Your place," Kent said. Under a hazy, waning moon, he sat on the purple house's lightless front porch. He supposed he could have let himself in, but it didn't seem right. He was an outcast.

Twice he had made her laugh. He remembered that now. Once in the middle of crying, she'd laughed, her nose red and her face wet, and the sound against all logic had warmed his heart. They had talked for seven hours, while Maggie slid from one emotion to another, and if she had yelled at him, broken down in tears, those were only peaks spiking between long troughs of calmer moods. "I'm starving," she'd con-fessed at one point, and it was as if she had said, "Let's forget all this, go back to the comfortable routine of our life." He followed her to the kitchen where she pulled out apples, bagels, cream cheese, and while listing his crimes she had sliced him a bagel. She'd sat cross-legged in the bedroom chair while he packed a duffel bag, and still she was talking. He had talked far more, though—his throat felt raw with it—had been pressed to answer question after question, all she could think of, in painful detail. Seven hours, as if she did not really want him to leave. But he moved only at her direction, so she must have.

Paul's car pulled into the yard, headlights doused. He tripped get-ting out. Kent sat still enough on the shadowed steps to be invisible as Paul approached out of the dark. "You think that's smart, driving that way?"

Unstartled, Paul reached for the rail, squint-eyed and smiling. "I'm totally fine. Why're you sitting out here?" He dropped down next to him with a thud, close, his boozy breath coming short and quick.

Kent rubbed his hands over his face. "You must really miss jail. Not even a day past this mess and you're ready to get yourself locked up again."

"Kent, what happened? Why are you here?"

"I don't know." After a time, Paul aquiver and silent, he said, "I guess because she told me to come here."

"She did?" Paul sounded sober now. "Why?"

To test this life? To decide what he wanted? Something like that—irrelevant, it seemed, when the choice was out of his hands. He felt thick with exhaustion. "I don't know that I want to talk about it."

"Are you mad at me?"

"A little. Less than I was. Honestly, I'm too tired to be mad, or much of anything else."

Paul's hands slipped around his arm. "Let's go in and have a drink."

"A drink," he said, derisive, but then it sounded good. "Yeah, all right." It was the moon watching them that made him remember, as he turned toward the house, the night Paul swam out drunk into the seething gulf, the terrible, reckless abandon of it, and somewhere behind it the desire that had driven them to that beach in the first place, which he could hardly remember now.

In the kitchen, Paul held up a bottle of Maker's Mark for display. "This brings back old times, huh? Except it's Bernard's."

"How about water for you," Kent said.

Paul reached into a cabinet, set two glasses on the counter. He stared at them as if getting his bearings, then took Kent's collar in his fist. It was a hard, desperate kiss, and Kent stood still under the assault until Paul got frustrated and quit.

As if nothing had happened, he uncapped the bourbon and sloshed it into the two glasses. Kent took one glass and set it down past the sink, caught Paul's wrist in the act of lifting the other. The wrist went rigid. Kent pried the glass from his fingers and emptied it into the sink, while

Paul struggled and shouted. Kent set the empty glass down, pinned both Paul's wrists in one hand and slapped him hard across the face. His every movement, in contrast to Paul's, was steady and deliberate, but as soon as he felt the impact in his hand, saw Paul stunned before him, he didn't remember meaning to, couldn't believe what he'd done.

In the past he had let Paul strike him more times than he could count and never hit him back. Or maybe he had, but rarely—to calm him down, or for far better reasons than whatever drove him tonight. Paul licked his lips and swallowed, didn't flare as he should have. Of course he didn't, because he took this as punishment, assumed it was deserved. He dropped Paul's wrists, took him softly by the shoulders. "I'm sorry. God, no, I'm not mad. Don't." Don't what? Maybe he was talking to himself. All night a fist had sat coiled inside him, urgent to slam some wall, some thing, and he was lucky an open hand had sufficed.

He passed a hand over Paul's hair. Paul tipped his forehead to Kent's shirt, mumbling sorrys. "It's my fault," Kent said. "All of it." Knowing Paul wouldn't argue now—all the fight was out of him—he turned and filled the empty glass with water from the sink.

Passive, one side of his face blushing pink, Paul waited for his water. "I killed Bernard for hitting me like that," he said.

"You didn't kill Bernard." A hand on the back of his neck, Kent steered him in to the sofa.

"Tell me what happened. What she said."

Kent had left his drink in the kitchen but he didn't want it now. "She said a lot of things."

"She was mad?"

"Yeah."

"Did she kick you out?"

"Not exactly. I think we more or less agreed I would leave. For a little while. She's very confused—about the sexuality thing, for one. Which is understandable."

"Does she blame me?"

"I doubt she's thinking about you."

"She hates me." Paul sighed miserably, laid his head on the sofa's back. His eyes were bloodshot and bleary. "She came to me and asked. She knew, but I could have denied it. I could have tried. Maybe she wanted me to. Maybe she would have believed it."

Kent had been thinking the same thing, knowing it was pointless to reimagine it. "Maybe. But it was going to give somewhere."

"What are you going to do?"

"Wait, I guess."

"Here?"

"I guess."

"Because she told you to come here?"

Kent was silent, cocooned in his exhaustion. Paul said, "What do you want? If it was up to you."

"It's not up to me."

Paul gave him a wobbly look of disgust, as if for that response, but then lurched to his feet and staggered down the hall to the bathroom. After a while Kent heard the toilet flush, the water running.

"Better?" he asked, when Paul came back.

Paul sat delicately. "Yeah, mostly."

"Let's put you to bed, huh?"

"I'm not that drunk." He remained immobile, a residue of tooth-paste edging his lip. "Do you still want me?"

"Not at the moment."

"Be serious. Do you love me?"

The question found nowhere to land, his mind a blank field, as if Paul had asked him the chemical formula for sand. For months he'd refused to ask himself this, to allow himself even to think the word, so that denying it to Maggie hours earlier had felt almost like honesty. But she had corrected him, and he accepted what she said, though the question now seemed to have nothing to do with anything. "Yes," he said, his voice uninflected.

Paul brooded. "It doesn't have to be up to her, you know. It can be up to you."

"How?"

"Choose me."

Another non sequitur, it seemed, until he thought about it and saw Paul was right, in a way. If Paul were his choice. So the crisis was not, as it had seemed to him, that he lacked any control over his fate. It was worse: granted total control, he wouldn't know what to make happen. He couldn't picture a life with Paul, couldn't picture returning to Maggie on her terms, without him—if she would give him terms at all. He was only waiting for her to open the second option so that he might find another balance in a perfect state of indecision.

"Is that what you want?" Kent asked. And this, he knew, was half the reason it was impossible to imagine. He had no certainty Paul was capable of it. "Well?"

"Maybe," Paul said. He settled his gaze on Kent's. "It's something to think about, isn't it?"

"I guess." Kent shook his head, uncertain of anything. Paul had a talent for appearing sober, for contributing meaningful bursts of rhetoric and making sincere-sounding promises he was too drunk to remember the next day.

"We should go to bed," Kent said. "Talk later." But he didn't move. He meant for Paul to go to bed. He himself felt stalled in a grainy, wakeful consciousness, an intimation that he wouldn't be sleeping tonight. Paul's eyes closed after a while, fluttered open, and he stretched out over Kent's lap, settling his head heavily on Kent's thigh. Kent allowed it, though there was something disheartening in the resulting glimpse of domesticity between them. He tried imagining a fire burning in the hearth, but that wasn't the problem—the house was already too warm.

"I think she'll forgive me," he said softly. "That's the thing about Maggie. With her you just know from the beginning you're forgiven." True as this might be, though, he could find no comfort in it, and with Paul passed out in an insensible sprawl across his lap he felt worse than alone, despicable if not despised, emptied of any quality worthy of her love.

He had been so happily married. He couldn't stop thinking this—how natural the state of marriage seemed, how his own soul more than anyone's he knew had been a thing born for commitment.

⟿

Seven hours had slid from Maggie's life, washed through it, and now her house was her house. Only a few things were missing—Kent and what he had put in a duffel bag—but nothing new had arrived in their place. No understanding. Even his absence was a provisional thing, her own request, and she could call him back as easily, tell him where to stand and in what pose, this man of hers. Or he might think of the one thing to tell her that would explain it all and come back on his own. She didn't want him back, though. She was numb, wanted nothing but to understand.

His bourbon glass was in the sink. She took it out and held it, smelled what little remained, walked with it unthinking into the bathroom, where less than an hour before he'd put the seat down for her. He was generally considerate about it now—they had once had a discussion or two on the topic—but tonight it seemed a cruel kindness, a purposeful erasure of himself and returning of the house to her.

But it seemed pointless to be here without him, in this life without him. She strolled into their bedroom, straightened the rumpled quilt with a smile at the foolishness of doing so. Then laughed once, aloud.

She didn't belong in this life, any more than he did. But he had made her believe in it.

On this bed, he had made her believe. He granted her faith that she could be a whole woman, a whole answer to a man's desire, and emerge from it still herself, unhurt. Her mind paged back over figures they had made on the mattress, sounds that had come from him, looking for the thing missing. It had always felt so good to her, complete.

"It's just different," he'd said of Paul, squirming, when she pressed. He wouldn't say *better*, wouldn't supply a quality to the difference between them, except to heap Paul with sincere-sounding negatives—how poorly they were matched, how disinclined to meet the other's needs, how little Kent was even attracted and how often repulsed by a male body. In bed, he implied, their congress was a narrow, troubled thing. Far from perfect. But—and this he would not say—it drew him, powerfully enough to make him spit on all he claimed to want.

Oral sex, perhaps—though it struck her as ridiculous to imagine a man's needs might be so simple and debased, when the usual sort of intercourse seemed to her adequate to the same ends. She'd always stopped him when his mouth moved too low on her body, as it had more than once and often enough to make her consider offering to do it for him. But she was nervous. Probably she had never made the offer clear. And he had never asked her for it, this thing she wasn't at all sure she would know how to do, except that when she pictured Paul in her place it was all she could see. It turned her anger to a blade against Paul, honed on the stone of her remembered love for him—that semblance of warmth he could cast with a careless glance. All along, what she had believed her own private bond with a husband had belonged to this person. But even if her marriage had never been anything more than the lovely, brittle convolutions of Kent's tortured deception, still she found she wanted to break something of Paul's, take it away, felt then in the

burning of her eyes and face that she was crying again and so disconnected from herself that for a moment she couldn't remember her name.

Because this wasn't her. Men couldn't do this to her. She had been
through worse. It came to her that in all the hours of this wretched day
she had not prayed. She pulled herself onto the bed, sat at its center.
Hands over her eyes, she drew and released a long breath, and she
opened herself to God. *Show me what do, Lord,* and the glow that filled
her and calmed her showed it in an instant. She remembered herself,
felt the power in loosening her limbs, disengaging—a secret known to
few, that nothing stronger lay in human reach than pacifism. She would
not do battle with her enemies. She would not resist. She would turn the
other cheek and offer more, and let God sort the casualties, and when
it was done she would rise and go on.

But the glow faded as quickly. She was weary of this stance and
had, literally in this case, nothing left that she could think of to offer.
I'm tired, Lord, she prayed, tired of men and their shit, their brute
taking, their lies and lack of love, and the voice came back to her
without pause like an echo. *But you will get through.*

And next, more surprising—and she knew this from knowing
them, from loving them still, whether she chose it or not. *They are more
unhappy than you.*

⌘

Paul spun through fitful, drunken dreams—the kind that felt real
and relentlessly urgent, and Maggie was in them all. At one point she
appeared at the door of the purple house and commanded Paul and
Kent to have sex while she watched. "I need to see it," she said,
sounding reasonable and resolved. "I need to make peace with this. I
need to understand." Paul was perversely overjoyed at the prospect,
shaking with performance anxiety, because her tone and posture told

him that if they played their parts well enough to please her, she might join them. What he would be at a loss to accommodate in life was in the dream a chance at salvation.

In another room, the mood darkened. She and Kent were in their wedding clothes, arms around each other, Kent's face burning with anger and Maggie's cool. "You did this," Kent told him, speaking as one with her. "You wrecked everything. But we can fix it." They planned to kill him, it seemed, a cleansing act to which he was half resigned. He felt drugged and at their mercy, hints of a cauldron bubbling nearby, while they discussed in dryly sinister tones how to do the deed.

He was immobilized on some floor, maybe dead already or dying, and Kent bent over him, coldly amused. "Hit him hard," he said, but the blow didn't follow. "God knows. Martinis, is my guess."

A hospital room with sighing machines. Paul had wrecked his car after all, was hurt enough to make them come. Kent said, "Gets reckless when he's upset. For attention. I don't know." They murmured together in strange, brief phrases cushioned by long silences, their voices mournful and calm. "No," Kent kept saying, a gentle corrective to Maggie's murmured complaints, "no, it's not like that. You have to believe me." Between them, in his hospital bed, Paul mimed unconsciousness, struggling to conceal his glee—he must be dying. Now she couldn't hate him.

Kent said, "I don't think he ever thought about how it would hurt you. And he's afraid of what will happen now. Afraid I'll leave him, I guess."

"Will you?" Maggie asked, distinctly.

Long silence, and Kent's lamenting voice. "How can I know that?"

"Don't look at me. I'm not the one with the answer."

In every shift of the dream, Maggie was really there, the three of them in their tense-limbed triangle, and Paul's spinning brain searched for the thing he needed to do, the one thing that would mend it all.

The word "sex" bumped him into a higher level of consciousness—the sofa's arm under his head where the denim warmth of Kent's
thigh had been. Without opening his eyes, he could feel his back to the
room. Kent's voice acquired an undreamed reality. "It's about sex and
it isn't. He pretends that's all he wants. Sometimes I do too. It's hard,
you know, for both of us to see what else there is. A blind spot, I guess."

"Do you think that will change?" Maggie's voice prickled the hairs
on his neck. She was really there, in the house. Was it night? How did
she get there? How could she? He didn't dare move.

"He's changed." Earlier, Kent's voice had pulsed out through
Paul's blood, closer and deeper than his own voice could ever sound.
But Kent had moved, and his gruff whisper was now far away. "It's
funny, I always thought he was the problem, but now I think it's just
me. I'm everyone's biggest problem."

Maggie's voice, scratchy and harsh. "Can you be happy with him?"

Paul was vividly awake, listening hard, but no answer came. Was
he nodding? Shaking his head?

"I'm happy with you," Kent said. Then, "I'm happy with both of
you."

It was surreal, the way they were talking, with a muted equanimity
as though nothing were wrong, as if above all else they were taking care
not to wake him. Their words were slow, with frequent gaps of silence
in which he had earlier drifted in and out of a dream state but now
stayed awake, waiting.

"You know," Maggie said, "I've spent so much time thinking about
the three of us together in some way, that I feel like I invented this. Like
I made it happen. I know that sounds crazy."

He felt they were both looking at him—Kent from the other end of
the sofa, Maggie from somewhere out in the room. Kent said, "Is it
strange?"

"It should be. I don't know why, but it's less strange than a woman would be. Or a stranger."

Restless, unsure of his wish to be with them, Paul turned in his sim-
ulated sleep, settled again with a hand before his face. A spear of pain
struck his head as he moved.

After a lull of silence, Kent murmured, "He's awake."

"How can you tell?"

"Just can."

The proprietary tone of this was too pleasurable to argue with, and
even Maggie's question had felt layered with meaning, a careful probe
into their mystery. He cracked his eyes open, sat up even more slowly
than he meant to under the ache of his head. He groaned, hands over
his face, fingertips gouging his skull. "What time is it?"

"Around four," Kent said. "Hungover already?"

"Mmm. Hi, Maggie."

"Hi, Paul."

He ruffled his fingers through his hair, achieved a squint. Maggie,
in the plush chair beside the sofa, wore sweatpants and an oversized t-
shirt, ripped at the neck, that looked like sleepwear. One leg bent into
the chair, she was puffy and tired-looking—it hurt him in a way he
wasn't prepared for.

He drew his knees up. "You're here."

She shrugged, sighed—he couldn't imagine words more expressive. For maybe an hour, she must have been in that chair, her voice
slipping in and out of his dreams. Quietly, seated, she and Kent had
talked, on top of the seven hours before, and she was still here, still
calm, able to look at him and speak his name. He wanted to cry with
relief.

Maggie's red eyes shifted away. "I don't want to hate anybody."

He didn't know whether to answer. After a moment, he said, "I
don't want you to."

She met his eyes, her gaze as mild and level as her voice. "I came to see what you're doing with my husband. In this house I gave you. You don't mind, do you?"

Rigid, he restrained himself from glancing at Kent, unmoving in the sofa's corner. "No. Nothing. I mean—" He stopped, swallowed.

"I tried sleeping," she said. "But it was all a little much for me. I thought it'd be better to face it now. See it. I figured at this point I've got nothing to lose. Maybe something to gain. I don't know."

He nodded. "I'm glad you came."

"I'm wondering if you have what you want, Paul. I hope you knew what you wanted when you came after it."

Without Kent beside him, he might have cried out *No, I didn't, I don't*. But how could he say, given the chance to go back, he wouldn't do again exactly what he had done? In honesty, all he wanted now was for her not to be hurt by it, for her to smile and say please continue, let's all continue.

"I don't believe in monsters," she said. "No one is bad by nature. But it takes reminding, sometimes. I guess I came to see something I can't possibly see, that you two can't tell me either, which is"—she squinted, head shaking, looking for words—"what it's like when you're alone together. Whether you're laughing at me, or happy now, or what."

Reflexively, he said, "We're not laughing at you." He glanced at Kent, who was slumped in the sofa's corner. More firmly, because however late the hour, however drunk or half-asleep, he knew it was true—a look at Kent confirmed it—he added, "We're not happy."

Kent gave him a soft, pained glance, and Paul, meeting it, felt soothed in a small way, that they could agree without words on this one thing. He looked from Kent to Maggie, stricken by how much he loved them both and how miserable he'd made them. "I don't know what to do," he said. "Maggie, I don't know if I wrecked your marriage, or he did, or if you're supposed to be together. If you'd be happier if I never came along. I don't know."

Kent pressed his lips together, his brow bunched. Paul spoke for him. "He doesn't know either."

Maggie was silent, head tipped, looking off somewhere to the right of Kent. Paul watched her awhile in that inattentive study. She had forgotten, he was sure, about her own flirtation with him. He said, "I'm just glad you're here."

"Why?"

"It's good to see you. To talk. Maybe we can"—*be friends*, he couldn't say. "Talk. You know?"

"I guess that would be good." Maggie sighed, blinked at the room, and her expression lightened into something that looked like a willingness to be amused by the sheer ridiculousness of the situation. Paul still couldn't believe she was here. He searched for some way to nudge this scene a degree or two warmer, make the three of them friends like he and Eric and Sylvie, equal and platonic all around, friends who might reasonably decide to throw a spontaneous slumber party and stay up all night.

"I can make us some coffee," Kent said, as if sharing the notion.

Maggie regarded Kent with a gentle, noncommittal look. The long silences between them were controlled by her, a slow absorption of her new surroundings.

"Yes," Paul said, to Maggie, "we should have coffee." He gave her a cheeky, squint-eyed grin. "Irish coffee."

Kent snorted, smiled, but offered no comment.

Maggie's smile was only perfunctory. "I think I'll go. Believe it or not, I do actually have to be at work in a few hours."

Kent rose when she did. "I'll walk you out."

Paul stood suddenly, afraid she would be gone before he could think of what to do to keep her. "Maggie?"

She looked at him with her glazed calm. Before he knew what he was doing he stepped toward her, embraced her. She remained as she was, not stiff, not responsive, and he released her, kissed her cheek, as he would in saying goodnight to any casual guest. She met his eyes then, her expression unchanged. "I love you," he said.

Instantly his eyes were wet and so were hers. Or he thought so—she turned away before he could be sure. Kent escorted her outside, and then Paul was closed on the wrong side of the door. No peephole. He leaned against it, afraid to watch out the window, and tried to glean by clairvoyance what was happening through the wood. Already lifting away like a vapor from the room was some ghost of happiness for the three of them, something they might have arranged by shares, that at some point in the night and probably while he was passed out had been close enough to touch, embrace, name, but they had missed it, and it seemed certain now that they would never find it again.

⟿

The bed was too small for two, Kent said, though the size had never bothered them before nor kept them from mornings of comfortably tangled sleep. Kent said he'd sleep on the sofa. Paul was too tired to argue, too disheartened by this defection to suggest they pull out the sleeper and share it. In his own bed, he sank into dreamless, alcohol-infused slumber and woke even more tired, more hungover, and for the first morning in a long time, alone.

Out in the living room, Kent slept on. Paul squirmed up beside him, nudged him over until he made room and folded him in. After a minute, he felt Kent's breathing in his hair, then his hand there. Paul lifted his face into the cup of Kent's stubbly neck and kissed it.

"How're you feeling?" Kent murmured.

It was close—something akin to the way they should have been, the world to themselves.

"Crappy."

"I'll bet."

"Was Maggie really here last night?" He knew she had been—his memory wasn't as fuzzy as that—but it felt like a thing he should have hallucinated.

"She was."

"I don't get it. Why would she do that?"

Kent sighed. "She's really very remarkable. Isn't she?"

CHAPTER TWENTY

In June, from the eighth-floor balcony, the beach seemed hardly the same place it had been in winter. Crowds moved over the hot glare of sand, children in noisy hoards running between the water and towels topped by tanned, gleaming parents or red-tinged, doughy ones; children in water wings squabbled over rafts, splashed out to where their parents stood waist-high in the gentle surf. The lisp of waves, the cries of gulls: the same sounds heard in winter but drowsy with the sun's heat, softened and distant. The gulf water that in January had been light-reflective and opaque as metal was now jewel-toned and translucent, and from his balcony post, Paul reported large fish and sea turtles, their silhouettes passing not far beyond the human heads that sprinkled the water close to shore. Once an enormous manta ray, six or eight feet across, flew along just under the surface.

Almost three weeks had passed since he'd been cleared of murder charges. It was their second full day at the condo, and Paul stood out at the railing in late-morning light, his red trunks wet. Mildly offended by the onslaught of families—*breeders*, he sneered—he took quick, solitary dips, returned to the balcony to view the scene like a prince surveying his realm.

Kent watched him from the sofa, where he lay in a stuporous lethargy he couldn't shake. *Depressed*, Paul said, but Kent didn't agree. It was only that he didn't know why he was here and didn't feel like doing anything. Paul, on the other hand, seemed to him an unreasonable blur of energy. The pebblestone wall that edged the balcony was already half-covered in the shells and sand dollars he had found, each displayed first for Kent's approval. If he spotted porpoises cresting near shore, he'd bolt by Kent, out the door to the elevator, return wet and smirking, shaking his head. He was buttering toast, talking breathlessly. He was digging through closets and drawers, hauling out old board games, puzzle boxes, ten-year-old magazines, plunking them down before Kent.

"My sofa," Paul said, hands on hips, with a satisfied twitch of his nose. My TV, my coffee table, my balcony, my bed, my other bed— each item filled him with an awe that was only half-joking, compelled his spoken claim. "This is my mug," he said, lifting the cold remains of Kent's coffee from the table beside him. "Can you feature that? Can you fathom?"

"Yes. You own things."

"Damn straight." He knelt and set the mug back down like a piece of art, fingertips at its edges, adjusting. His breathing was faintly quickened and shallow, through his mouth, in the way that had become the norm for him since they had arrived, as if he were often running, or as if whatever his eyes fell on was a little too much to take in.

Sitting on the carpet, he slid up against the sofa, fragrant with marine water, his hair dried to spikes. "Are you ever going to get up from there?"

"You need your sofa for something?"

His head touched Kent's bent knee. "Let's go for a walk. I want to see how far the beach goes."

"My guess is pretty far."

"But let's see. I want to find a beach with no one else on it. There has to be one out there, if we walk far enough, don't you think? An undiscovered spot?"

No, Kent thought, but he said, "Okay."

They didn't move. This was the way Kent had been in the weeks since Maggie had sent him away, not opposed to action, but failing to rise when the moment came. In bed the same. So far, Paul was choosing not to make an issue of either.

"I tried to make her come down, you know," Paul said. "I really tried."

"I know you did."

"I told her we both wanted her to be here. That we could each have our own room, and I don't know, boil up a mess of shrimp, have cocktails on the verandah. A vacation. I think she almost—well, I think she thought about it." He smiled crookedly against Kent's knee. "Can you imagine, if she'd said yes?"

Kent smiled a little and said nothing. Paul's ready blush and sly eyes suggested he was imagining much more than Kent was, as if they might somehow all wind up naked in a bed together. Odd that it was Paul nursing the fascination—Paul who had always been fond of women but had never, even for show, lost a minute of his life to contemplating sex with one. Kent himself, in his most unfettered fantasy, could picture nothing more unified than his own freedom of movement between adjoining bedrooms. The wall between them simply did not come down.

Paul shook his head, the blush faded. "It's silly, I guess. The three of us. Besides, she's never going to forgive me."

"I wouldn't put it past her. She got you this place."

Maggie had stepped up to handle the business of the probate

hearing with perfect poise, even a measure of warmth. It had taken less than a day—so simple that it had upset Paul deeply at the time. He had hoped his innocence might bring Deirdre's forgiveness, that she might somehow fold him into the family as an honorary member. Didn't Bernard's naming him in the will make him a kind of family, or at least someone who should be acknowledged? But he received a brief, formal letter letting him know that his legal innocence only made his role in what had happened more painful to her, and in the end she had decided it was better to give up contesting the will than to have to think about him anymore.

On top of that rejection, Paul's time with Maggie had been shortened. He had hoped to use a drawn-out legal battle to smooth things, win her back, but later, going over the day's proceedings minute by minute for Kent, he could say only that she'd been cordial to him.

The week before, Paul had met her over coffee to sign the final papers on the condo, and it was then, somewhat desperately, that he had broached the trip to the beach, the three of them. He had tried alternate combinations as well. She and Paul could go alone. She and Kent could go alone. She could go all by herself, or bring Lila's family, leave Paul and Kent out of it. Even that was more than she would agree to think about.

"Maybe she'll show up today," Paul said.

"What, she's going to drive down and find us?"

"She has the address. She has copies of all the papers on the place. So she'll hop in the car and come."

Kent smiled, indulgent. "All right, dreamer. What happens next?"

We live happily ever after, Paul didn't say. He picked a piece of lint from the sofa cushion. "Then we see."

He went back to the balcony. Kent picked up a book from the stack that Paul had deposited on the coffee table—all plays or anthologies Bernard had stashed down here; the one in his hands was Aeschylus. Ancient Greek, appealingly removed from his own life. But the opening lines were about a woman's heart, "in which a man's will nurses hope," and then, a few lines later, music, the cure for heartsickness. Paul had talked him into bringing his guitar down ("Why don't you play anymore? You used to play every second, through dinner, having a conversation, always with the frigging guitar."), not that Paul himself cared for it much. He could sit for a song and a half and he was done. Still, he recognized that Kent wasn't quite himself without a guitar in his hands. Kent thought about getting up to find it, but continued reading instead—the play was vaguely familiar. He was pretty sure that Agamemnon was going to die, and that the woman whose heart held all the promise of the early lines was going to be the one who killed him.

An hour later, and not far into the play—he kept losing his place—he made himself get up from the sofa. Paul was no longer on the balcony, but the day beyond was sun-soaked and bright, a breezy, glittery invitation. He scanned the figures below for Paul's red trunks.

But he was back in the condo, cross-legged on the kitchen floor, digging though cabinets. Kent leaned at the counter and watched him. He had covered the tile with blenders and bowls and cookbooks and pots and pans. He looked up mournfully, an egg whisk in one hand, a spiral-bound, plastic-coated guide to seashells open over his knee.

"I don't know what he wants me to do with all this."

"You taking inventory?"

"Seriously. What? What am I supposed to do? It must mean something."

⌇

Eventually, Kent said "Stop." It wasn't going to happen and they both knew it. Paul slid off to one side, crawled up toward the pillows and lay on his belly, propped on an elbow. He sighed lightly, raking his hair—trying, Kent knew, to be unaffected by this recurring failure. But it had been too many nights, too long.

"You're tired of me," he said, so casually it was almost cold. "It's over."

"Paul."

"You can tell me, you know. It's not like you're my whole life. I can find someone else."

"Don't be mean to me. This is not a voluntary thing."

Paul pressed the top of his head into Kent's shoulder. "Sorry. Kent." He shook his head. "Fuck."

"I'm sorry too." He tucked his hands behind his head and watched the water shadows ripple over the dark of the ceiling.

Paul leaned to kiss a bicep, rested his cheek there, his expression flipped like a card—an actor's trick, perhaps—from stony to mild. "I don't mind it so much anyway. It reminds me of being here with Bernard. He couldn't get it up either, no offense. It was really kind of nice, just lying here."

"Right here, huh?" He hadn't thought of Bernard in this bed when they'd been here the first time, but it shouldn't have been a surprise. It was the nicest room. He watched Paul's face. "You miss him?"

Paul studied the mattress, quiet for a while. "You know, when I think about him now, I mostly think about this bed. I think it was the only time he wasn't lying to me." He set a hand on Kent's chest, pensive, as if looking for Bernard in him, and Kent felt emanate from the touch a premonition of his own late middle age, the hair on his chest gone gray—whose hand would it be then, fingering the texture, combing it to swirls?

Paul turned onto his back. "Yeah, I miss him. Especially when I have to think about auditions or moving to New York or what I'm supposed to do next with this whole acting thing. Whatever it is."

Moving to New York was not something Paul had mentioned

before. Kent decided to ignore it. "What did he want you to do?"

"Who knows. He'd throw out ideas now and then, but he was hard to take seriously when he was chasing after me, which was most of the time. He'd say anything." He smiled and closed his eyes, body straight and palms flat. "I'm hoping this mattress will tell me."

Kent shifted onto his side and set a palm to the mattress as well, listening, feeling for vibrations and watching Paul's closed eyes, the inches between them.

He slept awhile, woke some hours later. Paul was not beside him. He listened to the condo—nothing but faint surf sounds that seemed to come from the hallway rather than the beachside window. It was a little after midnight. He got up and went to the living room, found the door to the balcony standing open. The night was balmy and deep blue, the sky cloudless, the moon casting brightly from somewhere out of view. He went to the rail and looked first—why?—straight down, in case Paul had jumped eight floors, then out to the shimmer of water, scanning for a figure that might be Paul's. Far off, out on the beach or maybe on another balcony, some invisible sexless person was laughing in a way that made him lonely and nostalgic, the feeling not unpleasant.

The smell of smoke made him turn, catch the tip of Paul's cigarette glowing in the shadows of the balcony's opposite corner. It surprised him, since he'd been sure without quite looking that Paul wasn't there. That he had gone—maybe that was it. That he would have simply disappeared into the night.

He moved to sit in the chair beside Paul. The proximity was comforting, though they didn't speak. They watched the gulf through the rails and Paul smoked.

"It's a nice little piece of the world," Kent said.

"I think I'm going to sell it."

The idea was a jolt. Kent had never imagined selling as an option. It seemed disrespectful, like returning a gift. Or unlucky, to spurn the

deeper purposes of fate. Also, without wanting to be here or consciously thinking the thought, he had begun to attach himself to the
condo and its expansive view, absorb it as at least partly his own. It was
the place he had arrived at and would remain, indefinitely, adrift, not
altogether unhappy. Now he felt startled awake in reality.

"Sell it? Why?"

"Money," Paul said. "A lot of money, I'd guess."

He smoked and let that sit, finally turned to meet Kent's questioning eyes. "I'm trying to figure out what he'd want me to do. I don't
know why he'd want me here, on some beach. I think he left it to me
because it was what he had, you know? Because he couldn't leave me
what I need. And I think I need a teacher." He drew a long breath of
air, released it. "I think I'm going to take the money and go to New
York. To school."

"Why New York?"

"The good schools are there. I have some contacts there who can
help, friends of Bernard's. Hollywood—that's bullshit, at least to start.
I want to do theater. I want to be someone he would respect."

Kent was at a loss. It sounded so right that it scared him, a little
flutter of the panic that hadn't come when he imagined Paul had vanished into the night.

Paul watched him. "I want you to come with me."

"New York?"

Paul's voice carried a wistful, minor-key note that didn't belong,
like apology or regret. "Yes. New York. We'll find an apartment, I'm
sure something tiny. You can get a job. Or not. Dust off that guitar, play
in clubs. Do whatever you want. I'll have money enough to get us by
for a while. Years, maybe." He turned back to the gulf, drawing on the
cigarette. "They say everyone should live in New York at least once in
their lives."

New York. He tried to imagine it. He had been once, in college, a trip of less than a week, the city expensive, overwhelming, thrilling. He had envied the people who lived there without ever forming a desire to join them.

He said, "That's where I always thought you went. When you left me."

"I did. But I didn't stay that time."

"You didn't come back either. You didn't call, nothing." His thoughts began to crystallize around this unanswered, unasked question from the past. Maybe it was only a way of avoiding Paul's unasked question, his floated offer, but it seemed more than relevant.

Paul said, "I know. I thought it would be better that way."   .

"How could that be better?"

"It was hard." Paul flinched a little in his seat, drew up a knee. "I thought you wanted me to go. I never knew I hurt you that much. You never told me."

"You didn't give me a chance, did you? God, you disappeared." His voice had grown loud, raw, and he clamped his mouth into silence.

After a moment, Paul said quietly, "I don't think you remember how it was. You were not happy." Kent began to object, but Paul continued over the top of him. "You were a fucking basket case, Kent, kind of like you've been lately, only much worse, and I know you loved me, but it was killing you. And you didn't have the willpower, the strength, whatever, to do anything about it. So I did. I did that for you."

"Oh, that is such crap."

"Deep down, it was what you wanted. It was what you were always waiting for." He sighed. "Even then, you were thinking about Maggie. I mean, you had this woman in your head you were going to marry one day, whenever your real life began. You were just killing time with me."

Kent gritted his teeth. "I loved you. I never stopped thinking about you, even—"

"You never started thinking about me, Kent. All that time we were together, you never imagined a real life with me, a future. Not forever. It wasn't in you."

He seethed to refute that. The intensity of his feelings seemed more than ample evidence, but before he could find the words it came to him that Paul was right. He had always known this, always hidden it from himself as much as Paul. He'd told himself more than once they were too in love to worry about petty notions like the future, when in truth he had fully expected a thing that intemperate to burn itself out, sooner or later, to burn away every trace of itself and usher him, cleansed and new, into a different life, a normal life, one that waited for him always on the other side.

"I loved you," he said again, helpless.

"I know. I'm really sorry."

"You could have called. Explained."

"You would have just made me come back. You, I don't know, would've begged me. Or not, but I'd hear your voice and I'd fold. You don't think I wanted to? How many times did we do that?"

Right, Kent thought, though he didn't want to know this. He wanted to go on nursing his pain, to have that one resentment to hold against Paul and justify leaving him, if that's what it came to, though he couldn't picture leaving him, or going to New York, or anything, any future other than the passive continuation of this present, measured out minute by minute in the deep breathing of the waves like someone beside him asleep.

"You shouldn't sell this place," Kent said, after a long silence. "Not altogether. You might regret it later. You could rent it out or something, pay for school that way."

"Yeah?" Paul sounded more amused than interested.

"Or, I know. Most of these places down here are time-shares. Do that. You know, you sell it to people in blocks of time, a month here, a few weeks there. You can keep a couple weeks for yourself if you want.

Once a year, you've got that little piece of time that's yours. Then you'll have the place later if you want it."

Paul chuckled, cut him a sardonic look. "That's handy. What an idea."

"Seriously. Think about it. What?" he said, because Paul was laughing uncontrollably, arms folded over his stomach. "What's so funny?"

"Oh, nothing." He stifled himself, pushed tears from his eyes. "It's all just kind of overwhelming, I guess. Real estate, who knew? This balcony, this chair, this railing. What I own is a little cell in a giant building full of other people. And it's valuable because of *that*." He held out his hands, palms up, to the view. "What part of that beach is mine? You and Maggie, you own a plot of land you can map, with a house at the center of it. But there's no square of sand or cupful of water that's mine. If there were, it would have no value. It needs all the rest, everyone's little pieces of it put together."

"So you share it. Mine's really the same, you know—my little piece of land is in Atlanta, rather than, say, in the middle of a cornfield in Iowa."

"Hmm." Paul's cigarette glowed.

"If you want, you can say that it's all yours, everything you can see from this spot. No one else has this exact view."

"That's nice. Even the stars. Look, mine comes with actual, visible stars! Unlike, say, yours. How often do you get to see a thing like that?"

"Rarely. In New York, never."

⌒

Sunday, the day they should have been headed back for Atlanta, but they were out on the beach at midday. They had brought down the cooler and the same blanket they had used before, a spread the size of a

bed. Kent lay on his back getting a tan, which felt like a useful enter-
prise, healthful, restorative. Paul lay beside him for brief spells between
swimming and finding other amusements to draw him away. Kent
spotted him standing at the water's edge talking to a dark-haired boy,
early twenties, with a smooth, brown body—athletic, bigger than Paul
but not by much. His waist tapered into blue trunks, the long muscles
of his back dipped at the spine. A good-looking guy, Kent supposed,
though between the two it was still Paul his eye was drawn to, Paul who
was clearly flirting. He laughed at something the other boy said, and his
open grin, the way his chin popped up and fell against the bright water-
light behind him, made Kent's heart catch.

Paul returned, dusted sand from his butt and reached for the sun-
block. "Do I look burned to you?"

"You look utterly white next to that guy."

Paul lifted the sunglasses from his nose and squinted appraisingly
at Kent's torso. "I don't tan, but you'll be there soon. If we stay another
week."

"What's his name?"

"Anthony."

Kent repeated the name mockingly and was ignored. "Goes to
Duke. Down here with his family." Paul sat and spread lotion over the
back of his neck, down between his shoulder blades, didn't ask for
assistance.

"Your own age. That's new."

"Jealous?"

Grinning and smug, Paul stretched out on his belly, and Kent
watched him. "That doesn't cover it."

"Really." Paul's expression softened with interest. "What covers it?"

"I can't explain."

I'm happy for you, he might have said—happy to see Paul interested
in someone who might be an appropriate partner. Except that he wasn't

at all happy. He still wanted that person to be himself, but maybe in another life, a parallel one. He wanted to be that brown-skinned boy at the shore, to be ten years younger and certain of who he was and meeting Paul now, for the first time—to be, most of all, someone other than himself, with a chance to be the person Paul deserved.

Paul settled his head on his crossed arms. "You want to have him over for a three-way, right? I can go see if he's into it."

Kent sat up. "We should really head back today, you know?"

"To what?" Paul's eyes were closed, his voice dreamy.

"I need to be at work tomorrow, for one. Don't you have a job yourself?"

"Screw my job, screw yours. We're kicking loose and going to New York." At Kent's silence, Paul sighed and sat up, studied his face. "You think she's going to take you back?" It was barely a question.

"We might try some counseling. She sounds like she'd do that."

Paul snorted in disgust. "You think what you two have is worth going through all that?"

"We're still married, you know."

"Yeah, you're married, you've been *married*, but what the fuck do you *want*? We can have a life together, me and you. You don't even want to try?"

"I don't know, Paul."

Paul rolled his eyes, a flush coming into his cheeks. "You love her. Fine. Hell, I love her too. But even *you* can't feel the same way about both of us. There's got to be a difference."

"Of course."

"So who do you love more? It's that simple."

He met Paul's eyes gravely—love still such a tricky, shifty word between them. "It's not that simple. Not even close. There are other things to consider. Like, here's one—Maggie and I are supposed to get the Yoder kids, if John and Lila die together in a plane crash or something. They even drew up papers. That's a reason. I'm supposed to be there, in case. Sometimes I can't see how anything could be more important than that. It's almost like having my own kids."

He wasn't prepared for Paul to flinch as if burned, turn away blinking. "Okay, I guess."

"I—I didn't say that to hurt you."

Paul wouldn't look at him. "No, I get it. You're totally right. I'd pick them too if I were you. You know I would."

"Paul." Kent had sensed this injustice before, now written plainly in Paul's face—that Kent could have a family if he chose, while Paul could not, when maybe a family was all Paul really wanted.

Love, Kent remembered, the original question, now forgotten. "You want to put it on the scales? Okay, then I love you more."

"Shut up," Paul said, soft and a little choked. Seconds afterward, he heard it. He turned back slowly and stared, solemn and watchful. Kent held his eyes for as long as it took; a pack of shrieking children ran past the blanket, and neither one moved. Finally Paul nodded. "But it doesn't matter, does it."

"It matters—" Kent stopped himself. *And that's why I have to end it.* He still didn't believe it, didn't know if this was what he wanted or meant to do. But Paul knew it, said it for him.

"Your turn to leave me for my own good?"

"You'll find someone better." It was the best he could do. Looking at Paul now, the intensity of trust in his eyes, the wariness in them only of being left, all Kent could think was that he couldn't bear for anyone to hurt him, above all himself.

Paul glanced wistfully toward the water, though Anthony was long gone and there were only the children jumping over waves. "There's no one perfect like you think. You're about as close as I've seen."

"You're young. You'll see more."

⚓

They decided to stay until dark, drive back under the moon, avoid the heat. Paul had perked up when he remembered the red royal shrimp and that Bernard had told him where to find the beachside shack that served them. So they'd eat dinner and get on the road for home. A little scorched, they went back inside for a few hours of the afternoon. Paul took a shower and went off to find the condo manager, intending to ask about time-share potential and local real estate agents who might handle things for him. Kent, alone in the living room, picked up his guitar.

His mind was empty of intention, but "Angel From Montgomery" was the one that came to him first. He missed Maggie, and he played without singing, imagining it in her voice. It was her song if she had one, or their song, and the last one he had sung with her, but it occurred to him that he had never written a song for his wife. He had meant to. But it hadn't happened, maybe never would. He had, on the other hand, never meant to write a song for Paul, but there were more than a dozen of them. They were anguished and bleeding, or drifting and lost, with lyrics blurred enough that nobody else had to know, though people who'd known him well in his old life usually did. They'd trade glances, mouth Paul's name. Even people who didn't know the context could pick those songs out from his oeuvre, lay them end to end in a series like a nearly coherent narrative, because whatever the tempo or tone they were of a piece. They were forged out of pain. They were his best work.

He kept playing "Angel," over and over, the spare, simple chords, as if something would come of it. Paul had been gone half an hour, and before Kent had really thought what he was doing, he had left the guitar and was dialing his home number. "Hello," Maggie said. He couldn't believe she was there, as if she had stepped into the room with him, as if speaking were forgiveness.

"Mags, it's me."

He heard her breathing, shifting the phone. "Hi."

"How are you doing?"

"Well enough. Are you at the beach?"

"We're coming back tonight." *We*—why did he say we? But she knew. Better to be casual, he thought. "Paul's taking care of some things before we go. He's thinking of selling it or turning it into a time-share. He's moving to New York. He wants to go back to school, graduate school, I guess, in acting."

"Oh yeah?" she said, neutral.

"We're ending it. For good. I wanted you to know."

"Okay."

What did he expect from her? "Is there a chance for us to fix things? I miss you. I miss us. I want to try again."

"I don't know why," she said, and he bit his mouth to keep from answering, listing the hundred reasons. He sensed she wasn't done. "I don't know why people are together at all anymore."

"You don't mean that. You know."

"My job keeps me really busy, Kent, too busy for me to have a life like other people. I'm just not that way." God, he thought, it was the speech she'd given the guys she'd slept with before him, the ones she'd gotten rid of without ceremony. He was the one she had allowed in, and he'd taken something from her.

"Don't, Maggie. Listen. You matter to me. We're married."

"Yeah." She sounded impatient.

"Just say you'll talk to me."

"Yes, Kent. I'll talk to you."

"Counseling. We can do that."

"Yes."

But he didn't know how hopeful to be. She had to say yes—it was the Mennonite in her. And he didn't know how much to want his marriage restored. He wanted only to stop hurting her, to have her again as his friend. He wanted the same thing from her that Paul wanted, it seemed, though sharing that desire did nothing to help their chances.

⁊ͣ

As the sun began to descend, they walked along the beach in swim trunks. Paul's were wet from frequent dips, but he could not induce Kent to join him and always returned to shore to continue the walk beside him. They were going to keep walking, Paul said, until they found the undiscovered cove he was certain must exist. "If we don't find it," he said, "we're staying another day."

But it was clear they would never find it. There were people everywhere, passing them along the shore, or camped on the sand before their own buildings—condos, high-rise hotels, a house now and then. On every plot of land above the tide line and sea oats and dunes, another building, and spilling from it, people.

"You used to talk nonstop about sailboats," Paul said. "Whatever happened to sailing away into the sunset?"

"Reality, I guess."

"Fuck reality. I'll buy you a boat."

Kent smiled. "No, you won't. You're going to school on that money."

The water, bubbling warm over their feet, was a silvery pale blue in the troughs and out toward the horizon, an unreal color, the sky above going pink. He told Paul about his call to Maggie, how bad he felt about it, how hopeless it seemed. But his voice was placid, and it was hard to feel despair when the water was warm, sliding over his ankles and shins soft and continuous as breath, and the beach, however populated, kept stretching on and on before them.

"You can still come to New York with me," Paul said. He was sincere, Kent knew, but equally certain of rejection. He had been from the first offering.

"I sort of wish I could come," Kent said. "It might be nice."

Wading at a deeper level, Paul kicked a spray of water at him. "You suffer from a limit of imagination. I could cure you of that, you know. I have ways."

"Too late. I think it's terminal."

"Bullshit," Paul sang in falsetto, a silly, almost joyful note.

"Maybe if we had never ended it in the first place. If we were still in that life."

We're still in that life. He wanted Paul to say it, whether it was true or not, or worth saying anymore. But Paul had come to a halt behind him.

Out in the silvered surf, some little distance past the breaking waves, porpoises were cresting. Five or six of them, their bodies the precise color and gloss of the water, looping at the surface in slow arcs. They were barely moving—feeding, probably.

Paul held out a hand to him, waved him forward. "Come on," he whispered. And he was in the water before Kent could blink, swimming out.

Kent didn't think. All weekend, he hadn't been in the gulf higher than his thighs, but the water was as warm as he knew it would be, salty in his mouth, and he was close behind Paul, already well out beyond a bottom he could touch, then lifting himself through the sharp peak of a wave. They were in the waves still when he looked around again, the water rougher than it appeared from shore and the porpoises not in sight. Paul was enough of an ocean virgin to imagine he'd catch one, and Kent hadn't done the work of talking him out of it, had let him spend two days racing like a terrier from the balcony to the beach in pursuit. Now they were past the breaking waves and Kent recalled the undertow—the warning signs, he was certain, posted along the beach farther back.

Paul stopped in the water, turned to face him. He started to smile, to say something, surprised to see Kent had followed after all. *You came*, he might have said. *You're here.* But in that moment a porpoise crested, close. They both jerked in fright, stared as it sank again—an enormous thing, far bigger than they could have imagined it, a creature loose and mobile and with them.

In one stroke, he was at Paul's side. They treaded water, turned nearly back to back with vigilance. Over the tearing, sibilant hiss of the waves nearby, he could hear Paul's breathing and his own.

"Where is it?" Paul whispered.

"I don't know."

Paul laughed, at nothing, and Kent caught the giggles too, a panicky, giddy thrill. Why wasn't he more scared? There was no undertow that he could feel. The water rolled with them, lifting and settling, deep, powerful swells of boundless water but gentle as well. Like a giant hand buoying them up, playing with them.

"Was it like this, when you swam out that night in the middle of winter without me?"

"Nothing like this."

Looking toward the horizon, Paul made a sudden, spastic motion. "Fuck, it's under us."

"What?" Then Kent felt it too, felt it slide along his foot, slick and warm. A nudging, wanting thing. He sucked in a long breath, certain he was going under, that he would somehow be seized and taken into its medium and spirited away. But still he wasn't afraid, not exactly.

Beside him, Paul's eyes were wide. The porpoise, or one of them, crested, but farther off this time, then another, and a third far out into the water, well beyond range. They were leaving. Then they were gone.

"Wow," Paul said.

"Look." Kent touched his shoulder, pointed. They were so far out, bobbing in open water, that the shore seemed to curve around them, a whole landscape in view whenever the water boosted them. Far down at the edge of vision was the pink stucco building that held Paul's cell, his tiny piece of the world for now. "Look how far we are."

Paul grinned. "I was thinking how close."

"You want to keep going?"

"Where, out to sea?"

"Yeah, why not?" Kent laughed, as Paul did. But he felt exhilarated by the porpoise's touch, as if it had granted them the power not to drown in trying it.

"Told you I'd cure you," Paul said, a murmur almost lost to the waves, a look like a kiss. He tipped his head back in the rocking water and gazed into the sky, as calm as Kent had ever seen him, and so at one with the world he'd found that he might have been speaking to himself. "I'm ready to go."

ACKNOWLEDGMENTS

I'd like to thank the many kind people who helped with the research for this book, in particular Paul Kehir at the Metro Conflict Defender for welcoming me into his offices and to Jan Willy Hankins and Susan Wardell for contributing their time and expertise. Becky Kurtz, Paul Kvinta, and the folks at the Atlanta Mennonite Church provided much essential assistance. I'd also like to thank my many friends who were helpful in reading portions of the manuscript, especially the irreplaceable Lauren Cobb, as well as Ed Hohlbein, Buck Butler, Andrew Beierle, Peter McDade, and Beth Gylys. I'm indebted to my agent, Mitchell Waters, for his generosity and good faith. And deep gratitude to everyone at MacAdam/Cage for responding to this book with such enthusiasm, especially my editor, Kate Nitze, for her indispensable wisdom and support.

Special thanks to the MacDowell Colony and to Yaddo, where some of the work on this book was completed, and to Georgia State University for supporting grants. Grateful acknowledgment is made to *The Kenyon Review*, in which a portion of the novel in altered form first appeared.